JULIETTE AND THE BILLIONAIRE BOSS

by

SERENITY WOODS

Copyright © 2024 Serenity Woods

All Rights Reserved

This book is a work of fiction. The names, characters, places, and incidents are products of the writer's imagination or have been used fictitiously. Any resemblance to persons, living or dead, actual events, locales or organizations is coincidental.

ISBN: 9798324835422

CONTENTS

Chapter One 1
Chapter Two 11
Chapter Three 20
Chapter Four 28
Chapter Five 38
Chapter Six 47
Chapter Seven 58
Chapter Eight 68
Chapter Nine 77
Chapter Ten 86
Chapter Eleven 96
Chapter Twelve 106
Chapter Thirteen 113
Chapter Fourteen 122
Chapter Fifteen 134
Chapter Sixteen 144
Chapter Seventeen 156
Chapter Eighteen 165
Chapter Nineteen 173
Chapter Twenty 183
Chapter Twenty-One 193
Chapter Twenty-Two 202
Chapter Twenty-Three 211
Chapter Twenty-Four 221
Chapter Twenty-Five 231
Chapter Twenty-Six 240
Chapter Twenty-Seven 252
Chapter Twenty-Eight 261
Chapter Twenty-Nine 271
Chapter Thirty 280
Chapter Thirty-One 288
Epilogue 297
Newsletter 302
About the Author 303

Chapter One

Juliette

"You okay?" Henry asks me. "You're very quiet today."

The two of us are sitting next to each other in the boardroom of Kia Kaha, the company where we work, waiting for the other members of the senior management team. Through the glass walls we can see people drinking coffee, turning on computers, and opening mail at their desks, the usual morning routine carried out in offices all over the country.

It's the twenty-first of December, early summer in New Zealand, and we've opened the sliding doors onto the terrace. I can hear ducks squabbling in the river and kids playing on the opposite bank. The aroma of apple and cinnamon muffins wafts in from the café down the street.

Despite the pleasant atmosphere, Henry's comment makes my stomach flip with anxiety. Sliding down in my seat, I pick up the Rubik's Cube from the table in front of me and begin turning the sides to mix up the colored squares.

"I had an argument with Cam this morning," I admit.

Henry frowns. "How bad was it?"

"Pretty bad."

"What was it about?"

For a moment, I don't answer. The Rubik's Cube is now a jumble of colors, and I slide it across the table to him. Automatically, he begins to turn the sides, rearranging the faces into their proper order.

I watch him for a moment. He's a big guy—six-four and huge—and he has large hands, but they move deftly, his fingers flicking the sides around with ease. We've been doing this—me mixing the cube up, him solving the puzzle—ever since the day we first met six years ago, when I spotted the cube in front of him on the table in the bar.

SERENITY WOODS

While Alex told me about Kia Kaha, and they all tried to convince me to join, I mixed up the cube, and Henry solved it, over and over again.

It always fascinates me how quickly he can finish it. His record is seventeen seconds—I actually timed him. He says he'll break the world record one day. I believe he can do it. He's the most determined man in the world when he puts his mind to something.

His dark hair falls forward across his forehead as he concentrates. His gaze is fixed on the cube, but as I stay silent, he glances across at me. He has light-brown skin and dark hair, but blue eyes. I know his Dad was Māori, but I don't know whether he had blue eyes too. I've never asked, because he died when Henry was twelve, and Henry doesn't like to talk about him. His Mum's mother is Māori too, but her father is Pakeha or white, so maybe his blue eyes are from him? I'd like to know.

I have a huge crush on him. Always have had. But I don't know if he feels the same about me. When we met, he'd just proposed to Shaz, and I'd already met Cam, so we've never discussed our feelings for one another. We're good friends, though. He texts me all the time—always has done, with memes and jokes or links to songs throughout the day. On my desk he often leaves a message on a Post-it Note—nothing romantic, just a quote from a book or a movie to make me laugh—or a mini chocolate bar, or an iced coffee.

Sometimes, when he thinks I'm not watching, I catch him looking at me, and I swear there's desire in his eyes, a heat that suggests he's wondering what I look like naked, but you never know, do you? I've never mentioned it, and neither has he.

The only time I've had any hint of how he feels was at our friend Tyson's wedding. He and his new wife, Gaby, were in the process of cutting the cake when an earthquake hit. After the tremors died away, James—who was Tyson's best man—gave a speech saying it was a sign to appreciate the loved ones in our lives, and he told everyone to turn to the person nearest them and show them how you feel about them. Even though I'd gone to the wedding with Cam, I was standing next to Henry at the time, and he turned to me, slid a hand to the nape of my neck, and kissed me. It was only a brief kiss, no tongues, and neither of us has ever mentioned it again. I've convinced myself it was born out of the heightened emotions we were all experiencing after the earthquake, but sometimes, when he looks at me as if he's thinking about what I taste like, I wonder whether there was more to it than that.

I sigh. "Cam wants to move to Australia."

His hands stop moving, and he stares at me. "What?"

"He hates his job. He wants to get a new one, and he says there are more opportunities over there."

Henry studies me for a moment, then he looks back at the cube in his hands. "He's probably right."

"Yeah."

"So… are you moving?"

"That's partly what we were arguing about. I don't want to go. My life is here. My job, my friends. But he's unhappy. And relationships are about compromise, right?"

"That hasn't been my experience." His voice is a tad flat.

Of course, he broke up with his wife because she wanted children, and he can't have them. She didn't compromise and say she'd have IVF or a donor or adopt; she went off with someone else. "I'm sorry," I say quietly.

He huffs a sigh. "It's not your fault. Shaz called yesterday to tell me she's pregnant."

My jaw drops. "Oh, Henry."

"I'm pleased for her. It's what she wanted, and she's happy now."

"Maybe, but even so… I am sorry."

I'd talk about it more, but he shrugs, finishes the Rubik's Cube, puts it on the table, and changes the subject. "So you're thinking about going with Cam?"

I scratch at a mark on my trousers. "I was. But he was mean to me this morning, and now I just want to tell him to go fuck himself." My bottom lip quivers, which kind of detracts from the strong, independent image I was trying to project.

Henry's gaze hardens. "Mean to you? He didn't…"

"No," I say hastily, "he wasn't physical. He would never do that. It's just… he can be cruel, sometimes. Whoever said words can never hurt you clearly had no idea what they were talking about."

Henry looks baffled. I'm sure he doesn't understand what Cam could possibly have said that would have upset me so much. I don't want to tell him the truth—that we were arguing about sex, again.

"I don't understand," Henry says. "How can he be cruel to you, of all people?"

"You mean because I'm his girlfriend?"

"Because you're you." His eyes look very blue in the morning sunshine.

"I dunno," I say, "I'm nowhere near perfect."

"You are to me. If you were my girl, I'd treat you like a queen."

I blink, taken aback by the compliment. He's never said anything like that before.

He doesn't look away; he just holds my gaze. The sudden heat in his eyes makes me blush from my toes to the roots of my hair.

"Henry!" I scold, my heart hammering.

He looks amused. "I'm just saying. You deserve more." He glances at the door as it opens. "Morning."

I tear my gaze away from him as the other members of the senior management team—Alex, James, and Tyson—come in carrying laptops and all talking at once, Alex's puppy, Zelda, running around their feet.

"Um, morning," I say, flustered. Out of the corner of my eye I see Henry give a short laugh before he pushes the Rubik's Cube over to me.

While they get coffee and take their seats, I begin to mix up the colors, using the time to gather my wits. It strikes me then, for the first time in six years, that maybe the cube is more than just a puzzle. That actually, Henry and I communicate through it. It's a private message we can send in front of everyone, like Morse code. A simple signal that we're thinking about the other. An unspoken love letter.

Without looking at him, I pass the cube back. He picks it up and begins to turn the sides, his fingers moving over the surfaces where mine have just been, almost like a caress.

*

I don't get to speak to him alone again that morning, and soon the memory of his words fades like smoke as I deal with the events of the day. Work is busy, as usual. Kia Kaha makes specialized medical equipment with the aim of helping people with restricted movement to gain back some of their mobility. I'm the head physio, and after the meeting I have three morning appointments and two afternoon ones, as well as a team meeting with all the other physios. After that I have a Zoom call with a company in Australia at five p.m. for an hour, discussing a new robotic knee brace I helped to invent.

During my time at Kia Kaha, encouraged by the guys who are so innovative and smart, I've become more and more interested in orthotics, which is a medical specialty focusing on the design and application of orthoses, also known as braces or calipers. I'd love to study the discipline, and the guys have always supported me with any career development, but there's no course available in New Zealand at the moment.

I didn't tell Henry, but I've been looking at a university in Melbourne that offers a Masters of Clinical Prosthetics and Orthotics. Cam would prefer to go to Sydney, but I'm hoping I could persuade him to switch cities as a compromise.

Leaving Kia Kaha would be a wrench. I love all the guys, and they all form essential parts of the company. Alex is the spine, with his vision and his work ethic that keeps us all moving forward; James is the face of the firm, and his business acumen has made the company so successful financially; Tyson, with his courage and determination in learning to walk again after his accident has been our inspiration and our driving force for what we do; and then, of course, there's Henry.

Henry is the soul of Kia Kaha. It was he who liaised with the local *kaitiaki* or Māori guardians who advocate for elements of nature when we designed the office in order to make it as beautiful and sustainable as possible. Every time I walk into the lobby and see the carved, light wood, the river stones, and the native plants, it makes me think of him. Henry has a deep spirituality that rings through every part of this building, and I would miss it—him—immensely if I were to leave.

But Cam's my partner, and I want him to be happy. So maybe moving to Melbourne would be a compromise. He gets to go to Australia, and I get to continue with my passion. Win win, right?

With this in mind, after the Zoom call finishes, I ask to speak to the head of the company alone, as I know she trained in Melbourne. Once the others have left the call, I bring up the topic of the university and ask her opinion of the orthotics course, and we chat for a while about it. By the time I end the call, I'm buzzing with enthusiasm. It sounds perfect, and she said she'd be happy to provide a reference for me if I were to apply to study there. Excited, I'm about to write up my notes when I get a text from Cam. Startled, I realize it's the fourth he's sent in the past forty minutes.

SERENITY WOODS

Where the fuck are you?

I look at the time. It's nearly ten past six. We're meeting at the Pioneer, a local bar, at 6:45 p.m. for a Christmas trivia quiz, and I still have to get ready, but we live minutes away from the bar, so we've plenty of time yet.

I text back, *Keep your knickers on, I won't be long. We've got plenty of time.*

Immediately, he sends another message. *I told Mum we'd call in at five thirty so I could see Alan and Pete. Now we don't have time.*

Alan and Pete are his brothers. Alan lives in Sydney, and Pete lives in the UK, but they both arrived in New Zealand with their wives today and are spending Christmas here.

I text: *I thought we were going to see the two of them together tomorrow morning.*

He replies: *I haven't seen Pete for two years. I wanted to call in today.*

I grit my teeth. I'm in no rush to see either of his brothers. They're racist and sexist, and their wives don't have a brain between them—all they're concerned about is the color of their nails and whether their hair has enough blonde streaks.

Yeah, I know that sounds bitchy, but I'm in that kind of mood.

Me: *Why didn't you tell me?*

Him: *I did!*

Me: *At five p.m.! I was working! I didn't see your text.*

Him: *JUST COME HOME WILL YOU?*

Me: *Stop yelling, I'm on my way.*

Mumbling under my breath, I close my laptop, pick up my purse, and head out.

Anxious and stressed, I drive through the busy traffic. I haven't spoken to Cam since our argument this morning. I texted him at lunch to ask how his day was going, but he didn't text back, so I know he's still angry with me. It seems to be his default setting at the moment, and I'm beginning to feel nervous at the thought of going home.

But I have no option, and five minutes later I park in the car park beneath our apartment block and take the elevator up. Cam's an accountant, and my job at Kia Kaha pays very well, so although we're nowhere close to having the kind of money the guys I work with have, we're relatively affluent, and it's a decent area and a good-sized apartment.

I let myself in, close the door behind me, and walk through to the living room. Cam's sitting at the dining table working on his laptop, but he stands as I go in.

"Get stuck in traffic?" he asks sarcastically.

I toss my keys onto the table and walk through to the kitchen to get myself a bottle of water from the fridge. "I'm sorry I missed your texts, but I was on a Zoom call. Look, why don't you go over to Pete's now, and I'll go to the bar on my own?"

"And leave you alone with Henry?" he says sarcastically. "I don't think so."

I flush. "I don't know how many times I have to tell you that there's nothing between me and Henry." He's insinuated that I like Henry several times. The heat intensifies in my face as I think about the Rubik's Cube. We never do it in front of Cam, so I guess it does mean something. But apart from at Tyson's wedding, we've never kissed, never touched inappropriately, and never discussed our feelings for each other.

I'm nowhere near perfect.

You are to me. If you were my girl, I'd treat you like a queen.

Cam looks at my red cheeks. "Yeah," he says. "Right."

I glare at him. "I'm going to get ready." I march off.

I strip off my business suit and have a very brief shower, towel myself dry, then come back out into the bedroom. I'm startled to find Cam leaning against the door jamb, hands in his pockets, watching me. He's already changed out of his suit, and he's wearing a white shirt with his jeans.

A little unnerved, I put on a fresh bra and knickers, then pull on a petticoat and do up the drawstring. I slip my feet into a pair of high heeled sandals, don my new coral-colored blouse, then take out the sari of the same color and start wrapping it around my waist. My father is Indian, and I often wear a sari for social occasions.

"Can't you just wear jeans tonight?" Cam asks impatiently.

I tuck the silk fabric into the waist of the petticoat, drape the end over my shoulder, then start pleating the remainder of the fabric, conscious of Cam watching.

He wants me to argue with him. To tell him I'll wear what the fuck I want, and to insist he's not going to speak to me like that. I know if I do, it'll please him, and his eyes will light up the way they always do when I'm being aggressive. Maybe it would even lead to us going to bed.

But I can't bring myself to do it. I don't want to. Not tonight.

Unbidden, I think of Henry, and the way his gaze always softens when he sees me in a sari. The way he's so quiet, and supportive of me at work, but when I'm cheeky to him, he gives me a look that suggests if I was his, he'd bend me over the table and fuck me until I saw stars.

Ah, I can't think about it or I'm going to cry.

I finish pleating the fabric and secure it with a big safety pin, then look over at Cam. He's six-one, with dark-blond hair, and he looks handsome tonight in his shirt and jeans. I just wish he was looking at me with love rather than irritation.

We've been together nearly seven years now. Our relationship started well but it has gradually deteriorated, and I'm tired of the brittle atmosphere. I think about my conversation with the company director on the Zoom call. Mentioning it would be an olive branch. A sign that I want him to be happy, and I'm prepared to negotiate.

I take a deep breath and say, "I'm a bit late because I was talking to someone this evening about a Masters in Orthotics that's available in Melbourne. And I was wondering what you thought about maybe moving there instead, as a kind of compromise?"

His eyes narrow. "I don't want to go to Melbourne," he states. "I want to move to Sydney."

He waits for me to argue with him, and I have no doubt that if I did, if I employed the tactics I know he responds to, I could make him do what I want. But I want a proper discussion, with no power play, no dynamics. Just a conversation, as equals. Why can't he see that?

He walks out.

I look back at my reflection and swallow hard as tears sting my eyes. I swallow hard and lift my chin. I'm not going to cry. He's being snotty because of our argument this morning. Maybe later, when he's calmed down, we'll be able to talk about it again.

After I finish pinning the fabric, I visit the bathroom to touch up my makeup. I don't have enough time to redo my hair, so I leave it pinned up, but I add kohl to my eyes, some glittery eyeshadow, and a new bindi, peeling off an orange sticker surrounded by tiny gold stones from a special pack and placing it carefully between my eyebrows. I slick on some lip gloss, and then I'm ready.

I go back into the living room and collect my purse. "Ready?"

He grabs his keys and heads to the door.

"Aren't you going to say I look nice?" Even to my ears, my voice sounds pathetic, and I bite my bottom lip, trying not to wince.

He stops, though, his hand on the door handle, and turns to look at me as I walk up to him. "You always look stunning," he says gruffly.

I hesitate, wanting to put things right. "Cam, about last night…"

His expression darkens. "Don't," he says. And he opens the door and goes out.

*

We walk around the block to the bar in silence. He doesn't offer to hold my hand, and I don't take his.

It's a beautiful evening. The sun is low in the sky, bathing the city in a beautiful pinky-orange light. The streets are busy, the bars and restaurants full of people out having Christmas parties. Most of the shops have spray-snow reindeer or presents on their windows, and fairy lights blink around storefronts and in the trees.

I'm struggling to feel the Christmas spirit, though, and I suspect Cam is, too. It's going to be a poor festive season if we can't figure out this problem between us. And I don't mean him wanting to move to Sydney. At the core of our relationship is an issue that's like a crack spreading through the foundations. Cam is a damaged man, and although I've given him all the love in the world—as much as I have inside me—I'm beginning to think it's not enough to mend whatever's broken inside him. I've spent years trying to make him better, and all it's doing is draining me and making me unhappy.

I love him, and I don't want to abandon what I've spent years building. But I've tried so hard to be the kind of girl he needs, and for the first time it occurs to me that maybe I'm not that person. I'm just not strong enough, not good enough for him.

The thought hits me hard, and almost takes my breath away. My eyes sting again, and I have to be careful not to let the tears fall, not wanting to smudge my makeup.

It's Christmas, a time to celebrate the birth of things, not the end. It can't all be over. Can it?

We're heading toward the bar when he pulls out his phone and reads a text. "Pete and Alan want me to go over," he says.

"When?"

"At ten."

My heart sinks. "I was hoping to have an early night."

SERENITY WOODS

"You can do what you like," he says. "I don't give a shit." He pulls open the door to the bar and steps back to let me pass.

I clench my jaw to stop my bottom lip trembling, and walk past him. It would be too easy to let him spoil the evening. But I've been looking forward to this, and I want to see my friends. So screw him. I'm going to have a great evening, and he can go fuck himself.

Chapter Two

Henry

I'm the first to arrive at the Pioneer, so I grab myself a beer, pick up a newspaper that someone's left on the bar, borrow a pencil from the bartender, and lean on one of the standing tables to do a crossword while I wait for everyone to arrive.

After only a few minutes, I glance up and see a group of young women at the bar watching me as they talk behind their hands, giggling as they see I've noticed them. They're in their early twenties, dressed to the nines, and all gorgeous. I smile politely and look back at my crossword.

Thirty seconds later, Alex comes in, no doubt eager to meet Missie Macbeth. He gets himself a drink, then stands next to me and blows out a breath.

I give him an amused look. He's never nervous. "So you are human," I comment.

"I feel as if I've eaten a hive of bees," he replies, rubbing his stomach.

I chuckle. "She'll be here, don't worry. It's going to be a great evening." I smile at Gaby and Tyson as they approach. "Evening, you two."

"Hey, Henry." Gaby kisses me on the cheek.

Tyson slaps me on the back. "You know you're being eyed up by four twenty-somethings over by the bar?"

"They're just looking for someone to reach the bottle of tequila on the top shelf."

He grins. "Want me to talk to them for you?"

"What are you, twelve? No, I'm fine, thanks."

"But there are four of them. Imagine the fun you could have."

"I'm an old man now, Tice. I'd have a coronary before the first one got her underwear off."

He snorts, and Gaby's eyes twinkle. "Oh, I don't think Henry's interested in those bright young things. He has his sights fixed on a rose by another name, don't you, sweetie?" She glances over at the door, and I follow her gaze to see Juliette coming into the bar.

Tall, slim, and naturally elegant, Juliette Kumar is wearing a sari tonight. The silk is the color of the setting sun outside, which compliments her light-brown skin, making her look young, healthy, and beautiful. The sequins sewn along the edge of the material reflect the twinkling fairy lights. She draws the gaze of every guy in the bar as she walks across to join us, and I'm not surprised. She looks fucking amazing.

Gaby bumps my shoulder with hers. I ignore it and say, "Hey," as Juliette approaches.

"Hey." She gives us both a bright smile. There's something fake about it, though, and her eyes don't meet mine. Behind her, Cam walks up and nods curtly.

"What do you want to drink?" he asks her.

"Chardonnay, please."

"James has set up a company tab," I tell him.

"I think I can afford to buy my girlfriend a glass of wine," he snaps, and he walks off to the bar.

"Ouch," I say, amused.

Juliette blushes. "Sorry," she mumbles.

"Don't apologize for him," Gaby says. "He's a knob. You okay?"

She nods and clears her throat, then leans on the table and looks upside down at the crossword I'm doing. "How's it going?"

"About three quarters done."

"Come on then, give us a clue."

I look at the list. "Spheroidal dilated parts at the end of an anatomical structure. Five letters, beginning with B, ending with S."

"Boobs," Gaby says, and Juliette giggles.

"Bulbs," she corrects, and I grin and pencil it in.

"So why's Cam got the grumps on?" Gaby asks her.

Juliette's smile fades. She shrugs. "He wanted to call in and see his brother before we came to the party, but I was late leaving work, so we didn't get time."

"I thought your last appointment finished at five today," I say.

"It did. I had a Zoom call with a few of the staff at Artemis about the robotic knee brace, and then I had a chat to Gillian. It took longer than I thought."

Gillian Taylor is an expert in orthotics, and I know it's an area that Juliette would like to get more involved in. They're based in Melbourne. Did Juliette talk to her about a job? Ah, shit. She really is thinking about moving to Australia.

She's looking down at the crossword at the moment, and the gold eyeshadow on her lids glitters in the fairy lights. Then she looks up at me. The bindis she usually wears are simple flat discs, but the one between her brows tonight is coral-colored with tiny gold stones, drawing attention to the gold flecks in her brown eyes. The look in them is full of misery and pain. She's terribly unhappy, and I bet I know why. Ah, Juliette… why are you still with that fucking arsehole?

I let my gaze linger on the glittering bindi, fighting the urge to lean forward and kiss it. She's always worn one from the moment I first met her in the university bar. Me, Alex, James, Tyson, and Damon, who now lives in Wellington, all studied computer engineering at university together. In our final year, Tyson was involved in a horrific car accident that left him in a wheelchair. The rest of us decided we were going to help him walk again, and we began to work on an exoskeleton that would help support him while he regained his mobility. The one thing missing was a physio who would help us with the medical side of things, someone to carry out the exercises. That problem was solved when, during a rugby match, Alex injured his hamstring and met Juliette. Impressed by her work, and liking her sense of humor and enthusiasm, he invited her to join us in the bar that evening to talk about what we were doing at Kia Kaha.

When she walked in, she was dressed much the same as all the other women in the bar, in tight jeans and a tee, but the blue bindi between her brows marked her as different right from the beginning. Over time, I learned that her father is a doctor originally from New Delhi who moved to New Zealand over twenty years ago, and that her maternal grandmother is Māori and her maternal grandfather is English. Juliette is a combination of these different cultures, all of which are very important to her. She has a Māori tattoo on her right arm, a rose of England on her left, and she wears a bindi between her brows as a symbol of her spirituality. I asked her once if she was a Hindu like her father, and she said she had faith, but not religion, which I thought was a great answer.

I've known her for six years, one month, and five days. And I've been in love with her for approximately six years, one month, and… yeah, five days. Not that I've ever told anyone, least of all her. When she came to the bar, Juliette was already dating Cam, and, to top that, we met the day after I proposed to Shaz. I loved my girlfriend and so I stayed with her, and went ahead and married her, and did my best by her, but sometimes I wonder whether my marriage would have had a different outcome if Juliette hadn't been around.

I kinda hoped that when my divorce came through, she might finally ditch her wanker of a boyfriend, but even though they've had their ups and downs, she's stuck by him. I'd never make a move on a woman who was taken, so here I am, still single, still in love, and still fantasizing that one day she'll come to her senses and realize she's picked the wrong guy.

I don't know how Gaby has guessed how I feel about Juliette, because I've never discussed it with her, but hopefully she'll keep it to herself. The last thing I need is Alex finding out. He disapproves of relationships in the workplace, and he'll blow a gasket if he discovers I have feelings for her.

Cam comes back now and passes Juliette the glass of wine.

"Thank you," she says. "Are you going to—"

He turns away from her, rudely cutting off her question. Her face reddens, and her eyes shine.

Fucking bastard.

Gaby exchanges a glance with her, then says she's going to check what table we're at, and gestures with her head for Juliette to go with her. She puts an arm around Juliette as they walk away, murmuring to her, so I know she's trying to console her.

Cam looks down at my crossword. "Go on then, give me a clue."

"Standing right in front of me," I say, without looking at the paper. "Four letters. Begins with a C. Ends in T."

Alex is in the process of having a mouthful of beer, and he coughs into his glass. Tyson stifles a laugh.

Cam's eyes flare, and he stiffens. "Fuck you," he says, with feeling.

I straighten, holding his gaze. At six-four, I'm a good three or four inches taller than him, and probably at least thirty pounds heavier, because he's a skinny fucker.

"You want to say that again?" I demand.

"Oh look," Alex says with heavy sarcasm, "here's Aroha. Hey."

Gaby's best friend, Aroha, approaches us, and we all say hello, transformed back into gentlemen by her presence. I'm still bristling, furious at the way he's treating Juliette, but Alex frowns at me, and I lean on the table again and return my gaze to the crossword.

"Everything all right?" Juliette asks me as she and Gaby return, obviously picking up on something.

I glance up at Cam, who's still glaring at me. "Fine." I return to the crossword.

I don't say anything else, concentrating on finishing the clues. Missie finally arrives just as I fill in the last one, and I return the pencil to the bartender, then pick up my beer and follow the others over to our table. I'm not really in the mood for this tonight, but it's too late to back out now.

I take the last seat on the bench, trying not to crush Aroha, who's sitting between me and James, and find myself opposite Cam. Great. Now I have to spend the evening being glared at. I decide to ignore him completely, as I'm sure that will wind him up more than if I glare back at him.

Gaby and Tyson pull up two chairs at the end of the table, one of the waiters delivers a bowl of mulled wine, someone else hands out paper and pencils for the quiz, and then the MC begins his introduction.

From the start, there's an awkward atmosphere around the table. It's obvious to me that Juliette and Cam must have had words before they came out, and something's also going on with James and his girlfriend Cassie, because she pulls out her phone and spends the whole of the first half of the quiz flicking through TikTok and not saying a word.

But the rest of us soldier on with the quiz, and as the alcohol continues to flow, we start to relax. Missie has managed to distract Alex, which is a relief, and Gaby and Tyson are on good form. Those of us who aren't really into the mulled wine switch to whisky, and James orders doubles, so after a couple of drinks I'm feeling nicely mellow. Cam's glares have intensified, though, probably because I'm ignoring him, and that amuses me. Everything would be perfect if it wasn't for the fact that Juliette is quiet and obviously struggling this evening.

At the half-time break, the simmering tension finally comes to a head. James murmurs something to Cassie, who then announces loudly, "Fuck off." She picks up her purse and phone. "I want to get up, please."

"Cass…" James pleads.

"Now," she snaps.

I stand, Aroha scoots along, and James follows. Cassie gets to her feet and, without saying goodbye, heads for the exit. James puts his hands on his hips for a moment, then, without looking at us, follows her out.

"Are they coming back, do you think?" Gaby asks.

I shrug, and after Aroha has slid along the seat, sit down again.

We talk quietly amongst ourselves for a few minutes, and then James comes back into the bar.

"Stay where you are," he tells us as we go to get up, and he climbs over the back of the bench and slides into the corner beside Aroha.

"All right?" Alex asks.

"Hunky dory." He finishes off his whisky, then blows out a long breath. "We broke up."

"James!" Juliette exclaims. "Oh my God, I'm so sorry."

"Are you okay?" Aroha asks.

He nods. "It's been coming for a while. Sorry, I didn't mean to bring the mood down. Would you rather I go?"

"Absolutely not," Alex states. "Time to drown your sorrows. Consolation whisky, anyone?"

I nod, and so do Tyson and Aroha.

"Cam?" Alex asks.

He's checking his phone, and he shakes his head. "No, thanks, I've got to shoot off soon."

Juliette stares at him. "You're kidding?"

"I'm going to see Pete and Alan," he says.

"You promised you'd stay till ten," she whispers.

At that, he glances across the table in my direction, then looks back at her and raises an eyebrow. Clearly horrified, she blushes scarlet. What the hell's that about?

"Maybe we should have another bowl of mulled wine, what do you think?" Missie says brightly to the girls.

"Sounds great," Gaby says.

Juliette is looking at Cam with a hurt expression. She murmurs to him, and he says something that makes her inhale and her eyes flare. I bristle again, hating the fact that he has this power to hurt her so badly.

"Probably best if I go now," Cam says, getting to his feet. "See ya." He strides off without a backward glance.

"Cam!" Juliette calls after him, but he doesn't look back. She watches him go, then turns back to the table and lifts her chin. "I'm not going after him," she blurts out. Then she looks at me, and her eyes fill with tears.

I want to get up, pull her into my arms, and promise her that I'm going to kiss her until she forgets that bastard ever existed. But I can't, so instead I push my glass over to her. She looks at the last half-inch of whisky in it, then knocks it back in one go.

"Euw!" She pulls a face. "I hate whisky." She puts the glass down, then covers her face with her hands. "Oh God. What have I done?"

"You haven't done anything," Missie states firmly. "You're staying with your friends for the evening, that's all. I'm sure he'll calm down after a few hours."

Juliette mumbles something under her breath. I think it was, "No, he won't." Finally, she lifts her gaze to me.

I don't know why Cam looked at me earlier, or why she blushed in response. It suggested they'd argued about me—why would that be?

I give her a small smile. I can't deny that I'm glad he left. I just hope she doesn't go after him.

"Well, this is turning out to be quite the evening," Tyson states. He looks at Gaby. "You want a divorce now or do you want to wait until the end of the day?"

Juliette snorts and James gives him the finger, which makes the rest of us laugh.

The waiter comes back with the whiskies and a fresh bowl of mulled wine.

"Are you staying?" Gaby asks Juliette.

"Yeah," she says. "Fuck it." She ladles the wine into her glass. "I'm going to get drunk and enjoy myself with my friends."

"Glad to hear it," Gaby says cheerfully. "To friendship." They clink glasses, and everyone else joins in. Then there's no more time to talk as the MC starts the next round of the quiz.

Now that Cassie and Cam have departed, the mood around the table improves vastly. We order some platters of food and mince pies to follow, and the waiter is kept busy bringing more mulled wine and whisky to the table.

In between rounds, we chat and tell jokes, and I watch Juliette start to unravel. It's like everything about her is turned up to eleven; her eyes are too bright, her laugh too high. She's in seven kinds of pain, but she's determined to ignore the fact that her relationship is crumbling around her ears.

When the quiz finishes and we collect our prize for coming second—a box of chocolates—the music starts. We all continue to chat for a few songs, but then Justin Bieber's *Mistletoe* starts up.

"Everyone up," Alex states, and we all groan. "I want to dance and I'm not making Missie climb over everyone—up!"

We all slide along the benches and get to our feet. Tyson leads Gaby onto the dance floor, and Alex heads off with Missie.

Juliette watches them go, then looks at me. Jesus, she's so fucking beautiful. I know she belongs to someone else, but he's not here, and she's unhappy, and all I can think is that I want to make her feel better. So I offer her my hand.

I half expect her to decline and say it's time she left. But her lips curve up, just a little. And then she slides her hand into mine.

My heart soars. I lead her away, onto the dance floor, turn to face her and slide my right hand onto her waist. Then we begin to move.

Out of the corner of my eye, I see James and Aroha also take to the floor a few feet away, but I don't look at them, giving them their privacy. There's magic in the air tonight, the whisper of promise, like rustling presents beneath a Christmas tree, and I'm not interested in anything except the woman in my arms.

For a long while, we don't say anything. Juliette's left hand rests on my shoulder, and we move slowly together. To an onlooker I'm sure we must look like strangers, with our pose formal, and a good six inches between us.

But I can barely breathe. I know she wears Shalimar perfume because she loves the story behind it—that Jacques Guerlain decided to pay homage to the way that Mughal Emperor Shah Jahan built the Taj Mahal to honor his beloved wife after her death—and the fresh, sensual scent brings goosebumps out all over my skin.

My fingers curl around hers, and I have to fight not to brush her skin with my thumb. She keeps her gaze fixed on my throat, so I have plenty of time to study her shiny brown hair in its neat twist, her smooth, flawless skin, her long dark lashes.

We dance for ages, and gradually, her stiff spine begins to relax, and she moves closer to me. We speed up for a while with Mariah Carey's *All I Want For Christmas is You*, and I spin her around and make her laugh, but when Judy Garland starts singing *Have Yourself a Merry Little Christmas*, we move closer together again. Juliette lets out a little sigh, then finally closes the distance between us and rests her cheek on my shoulder.

I wish it was romantic, but I can feel how melancholy she is, how sad. Wanting to hold her, I slide my arm around her waist and pull her against me, and we move slowly to the music. I press my lips on the top of her hair in a gentle kiss, and I know she feels it because she sighs.

"I'm sorry," I murmur, not sure why she and Cam were arguing about me, but hating the fact that I might be the source of her misery.

She lifts her head and moves back from me a little. Her eyes glisten as she looks up at me.

"You always make me feel better," she says.

I look into her big brown eyes. "That's what I'm here for."

She swallows hard, fighting against tears. Ah, she's so unhappy. It's breaking my heart.

"Why don't you talk to me?" I ask. "I'm your friend, right? Tell me what's bothering you."

She glances around. "Not here. I don't want to bawl my eyes out in public."

"You want to go somewhere else?"

She hesitates, then nods, so I take her hand and lead her off the dance floor, and together we head for the exit, out into the balmy night.

Chapter Three

Juliette

We go out of the bar, and I pause on the pavement, looking up and down the street. It's busy everywhere. All the restaurants and bars are bursting at the seams, oozing music and laughter. To our left, a fight breaks out in front of one of the noisier pubs, and people start gathering around, cheering. In the distance, the first sirens begin to wail.

I feel miserable and a mess, close to breaking down, and I don't know where to go. I don't want to be around people, but I don't want to go home, either.

"Come on." Henry leads me away to the right, resting his hand in the middle of my back, guiding me through the crowd. I let him steer me, then stop at the end of the pavement, not sure where we're going.

We cross the street and continue down a side road toward the Avon, then turn toward the Cedar Hotel. It's one of the small, boutique hotels that he stays at from time to time when he doesn't want to drive to his house out at Sumner Beach. I think he's staying here tonight.

"It has a great bar," he says. "Hopefully it'll be quiet there."

If it were any other guy, I might feel nervous that he'd taken me back to his hotel without asking, but Henry is the definition of a gentleman, and I've known him a long time. We're often alone together—at the office, or in the car on the way to meetings, and he's never once acted inappropriately. I think it's one reason why I find Cam's insinuation that there's something between us so upsetting.

He leads me through the front door and into the lobby, then stops, surprised. It's bustling with people—it looks as if a coach load of visitors has turned up. The queue for reception is about twenty people deep. We walk along to the bar and find it packed, with all the tables and chairs occupied.

"Shit," he says. "That's Christmas for you."

My ears ring with all the voices and music, and I feel overwhelmed by everyone's energy. I can't face the thought of battling our way to the bar, or going back out into the busy, noisy streets. "I just want to get inebriated in silence," I say miserably. "Is that too much to ask?"

"You want me to order you an Uber?"

I shake my head. "I don't want to go home." My throat tightens, and I swallow hard.

"You don't have to do anything you don't want to do." His blue eyes study me. "Look, we're friends, right? And you need somewhere to stay. I'd get you a room, but I'd imagine they're fully booked now. I'm in a studio apartment. How about we go there, order some booze up, we'll get trashed together safely and you can cry until all your mascara has run, and when you've had enough, you can pass out on the bed, and I'll take the sofa?"

My eyes water, and I rub my nose. "Are you sure?"

"Of course. I'd only be watching *Die Hard* on my own anyway. Come on. Fuck everyone else."

I nod, my spirits lifting a little at the thought of escaping with him. "Yeah, fuck everyone else."

We go across the lobby to the elevators, and we ride up with some of the visitors. We stand in the corner, not touching, not speaking, but I can feel his concerned gaze on me. I think Henry sees himself as the father of Kia Kaha. He's the oldest of the guys, if only by a few months, and he's the one who always organizes a designated driver or transport home when we go out, who insists any women don't walk home alone, who makes sure nobody's feeling left out in a group, and who—more than any of us—is inclusive and supportive no matter of the person's age, gender, color, or sexuality. I love all the guys at the company, but I feel safest with him.

Not that I think of him as a father figure. I'm acutely conscious of how gorgeous he looks tonight. He's wearing black jeans and a burgundy-colored Henley that clings to his muscular torso and bulging biceps. The undone top button reveals his Adam's apple and the hollow at the base of his throat. His dark hair is shaved at the nape of his neck, with a fade that leads to a longer section that tends to flop over his forehead at the end of the day. He has a five o'clock shadow across his cheek and jaw. He's so big all over—big shoulders, big hands, big... feet.

I wonder if any other part of his body is larger than usual?

Juliette! That's so inappropriate. I turn my gaze away, embarrassed by my thoughts, and rub my forehead. I hate Cam for making me feel guilty when I haven't done anything. I like Henry; he's my friend. He's a good guy. He's kind and supportive, and I know without having to ask that he'd never make a move on a girl who was in a relationship. I hate that Cam turned what we have into something cheap and tawdry.

I blink as the elevator stops and the doors open, and Henry gestures for me to precede him out into the corridor. It's quieter here, and we walk all the way to the end, where he unlocks the door and opens it to reveal the apartment. I go in, looking around. It's large and stylish, the walls white, with Art Deco furnishings—all geometric shapes, florals, animals, and sunrays. There's an open-plan living room and kitchen, and through a separate door I can see a bedroom with a king-size bed covered in a black-and-white duvet and matching pillows.

"Make yourself at home," Henry says, toeing off his Converses. "I'll order some drinks. What are you in the mood for?"

"Alcohol," I reply vehemently.

He chuckles. "Any particular sort?"

"My relationship is over, Henry. I don't care what alcohol it is, as long as it makes me not care anymore."

He stares at me. "You've broken up with Cam?"

"After he walked out, I texted him and asked if he was coming back. He said 'No, I'm done.'"

"Did you message back?"

"No. I turned my phone off."

He frowns. "I doubt he means it's over. He probably just meant this evening."

My eyes sting. "I don't care. I've had enough. I've tried so hard, you have no idea, and he's just mean to me. I'm always the one who ends up apologizing because I can't stand the bad atmosphere. I'm a nice person. I don't deserve this. I deserve better than him. I don't want to be with him anymore."

Upset, furious, and heartbroken, I can't stop the tears, and they tumble over my lashes.

"Ahhh…" Henry sighs.

He directs me over to the sofa. "Sit there," he instructs. He passes me a box of tissues. "I'll call room service. We need alcohol, stat." He picks up the phone and dials.

I try to stop crying as Henry talks to the person on the other end of the phone. He asks for a bottle of Jameson, a bottle of London gin, and another bottle of vermouth. He knows I like dry martinis.

Then after he hangs up, he goes over to the kitchen and takes a few miniatures out of the minibar. He opens a can of G&T and pours it into a glass, opens a tiny bottle of whisky and tips it over ice, then brings them through to the living area.

"Here." He passes me the G&T and sits beside me. "If you want to get drunk, you're going to have to drink more than one an hour."

I have a big mouthful, cough as the alcohol sears through me, then have another.

"But don't drink it too quickly," he says hastily, taking the glass from me and putting it on the table.

I cover my face with my hands. "I just want it to stop. I don't want to be here anymore."

"Ah don't say that. You're breaking my heart."

I don't mean that I want to die, but I do want the pain to be over. I don't want to have to deal with Cam and his moods and problems. I want to stop being so unhappy.

The tears come for real, and this time I can't stop them.

"Come here." Henry holds up an arm. I turn toward him and bury my face in his neck. He lowers his arms around me, and I dissolve into wracking sobs that I couldn't control any more than fly.

He strokes my back and kisses the top of my head, and murmurs comforting things like, "Everything's going to be okay," and "It's all right, I'm here." I know I'm soaking his Henley, but he doesn't seem to care. He's big and warm, and he's holding me tightly. I wish I could stay here forever, safe and secure in his arms.

When was the last time Cam held me like this? I honestly can't remember.

My tears are just starting to die down when there's a knock at the door. I sit up and wipe my face. "I'll just go to the bathroom."

"Okay, it's through there." He gestures at the bedroom.

I rise and leave him to answer the door, go into the bedroom, and close the door.

He wore a suit to work today, so I'm not surprised to see it hanging on the outside of the wardrobe door. His discarded shirt lies over the top of his suitcase. I pick it up and press my nose to it. It smells of his cologne, something masculine, exotic, and dark—the scent of leather, wood, and incense.

I blink, embarrassed at the thought of him catching me sniffing his clothes, put the shirt down, and go into the bathroom. Yes, there's the bottle—Louis Vuitton's Nuit de Feu, no doubt several hundred dollars a bottle, knowing Henry. He's not ostentatious by any means, but he likes his expensive colognes, his Omega watches, and his sleek cars.

Next to the cologne is his razor, shaving foam, hair product, and toothbrush. Water pools on the floor of the shower, and the towel over the rack is damp. He had a shower before he came out, although he obviously didn't shave, judging by his five o'clock shadow. I feel oddly shy at this glimpse into his life.

I look at myself in the mirror and sigh. The kohl and mascara have run—I should have worn waterproof makeup. I look like a panda. Using the hotel's complimentary items, I remove it all. It's not the first time he's seen me *au naturel*, and he won't care.

When I'm done, I go out and discover Henry seated again, this time at the other end of the sofa. He's put the bottles on the coffee table, along with a jug containing a few ice cubes and a spoon. He's also retrieved a small box of chocolates and a tube of Pringles from the minibar.

"Everything a girl needs when she's had her heart broken," he says. He smiles at me. "How are you doing?"

"I'm okay." I sit back on the sofa. I finish off the G&T, cough, and hold my glass out to him.

He pours out a large measure of gin into the jug over the ice, adds a splash of vermouth, mixes it with the spoon, and pours it into my glass. "A bit rough," he says, handing it back to me, "but it'll do the job."

I have a mouthful and sigh. "God, that's good." I gesture to his glass. "You've got to keep up with me, come on."

He tips a large splash of Jameson into his glass and sips it. "Are you feeling better now?"

"A bit. Sorry about the…" I gesture at my face. "You know."

"You look beautiful," he says. "With or without makeup."

I blush and poke him with my toe. He just smiles.

We sip our drinks, and gradually I feel the tension fade from my spine. I put down my drink, lift my sari, and take off my sandals. Then I slide down on the sofa a bit and stretch out my legs, curling my toes over the edge of the coffee table. Henry watches me, but he doesn't say anything.

"You put the TV on if you want," I tell him. "Or some music."

"I don't mind the quiet," he replies.

Opposite us, he's opened the doors onto the balcony. I can hear people in the distance, outside one of the bars by the river, talking and laughing. The sound of ducks quacking and oars splashing in the water also rises to my ears.

I guess some people would find the silence uncomfortable, but I don't, and I don't think he does, either. He's very restful to be with. He stretches out his long legs, resting his glass on the arm of the sofa, and we look out at the setting sun, watching the light slowly fade.

We sit there, sipping our drinks, and my thoughts gradually settle, like silt that's been stirred up at the bottom of a stream. Eventually, though, I feel guilty for not talking, and wonder whether he's bored.

"Are you sure you don't want to go back to the bar?" I ask.

"Nah. Everyone will have gone by now anyway."

"Do you think James and Aroha left together?"

"Maybe."

I wrinkle my nose at him. "You never gossip."

"It's their business. I don't want anyone speculating about what I'm up to, so I don't speculate about them."

"Fair enough." I rest my head on a hand. "You're a very private person, aren't you?"

"You think?"

"I do. I didn't even know you were having trouble with Shaz until you'd been apart over a year."

He drops his gaze to his drink and has a mouthful of whisky.

"You don't have to talk about it now," I say awkwardly.

"I don't mind. You know what relationships are like. They rarely break overnight. Maybe they do if someone's having an affair or something, but mostly it's an erosion, like the sea eating away at the coastline."

I nod. "I know what you mean." It's the same with me and Cam—a slow, steady, painful breakdown.

I study Henry's face, which I know so well—his wide nose, generous mouth, and dark blue eyes. "Was the main reason you broke up because you can't have children?"

He swirls the whisky over the ice in his glass. "It was a symptom, not the cause. There were other factors."

I wait for him to elaborate. He doesn't. He sips the whisky, watching me over the rim of the glass.

I said he didn't have to talk about it, but he replied that he didn't mind, so I give in to my curiosity and continue. "You lived together for a while after you separated, didn't you?"

"It was a big house. She moved into the other wing, and the courts took the day she moved as the start of the two-year separation. We did try and rekindle it a couple of times, just because we were both so sad it had ended, I guess. But eventually she told me she'd met someone else, and she moved out a few days later."

"I'm so sorry she's pregnant now," I say. "I mean… well, you know what I mean. Not sorry for her, but sorry for you."

He sighs. "Ah, I'm pleased for her. They're getting married in a few weeks. She's happy now."

"But you're not."

He just shrugs. "I'm happy enough. I have a great job. I like my work."

"You're very successful in your professional life."

"Yeah. It's just my private one that sucks." He rolls his eyes.

I finish off my drink. I've had several glasses of mulled wine, the G&T, and now a martini, and I'm starting to feel loose and relaxed. While he pours me another, I study him, thinking how gorgeous he is. I wonder how many girls he's been with since Shaz. He hasn't talked about dating since he broke up with her, even though it's obviously been more than two years. I study him with a frown, puzzled. "Why aren't you dating anyone else?"

He doesn't reply. Instead, he finishes off the whisky in the glass, then leans forward to pour himself another measure. I watch as he picks up the box of chocolates, takes off the wrapping, and opens it up. "Go on," he says, "I know you want one."

I examine them. "If you're trying to distract me, it's not going to work."

He just sighs.

"I'm guessing you don't want one," I say, choosing a caramel truffle.

"That's correct."

"You're the only person I know who doesn't like chocolate."

"I'm sweet enough."

"Sweet isn't the word I'd use to describe you," I say with feeling.

"What word would you use?"

Tasty? Gorgeous? Mouthwatering?

He takes the lid off the Pringles, peels back the seal, extracts a pile, and takes a bite out of it as he waits for me to answer.

"Monster," I choose. "Nobody eats Pringles like that."

"Life's too short to eat one at a time."

I nibble the caramel truffle, enjoying the flow of soft caramel onto my tongue. "If life's too short, why aren't you on Tinder, dating a different girl every night?"

"Because I'd be a withered husk if I did that. I'm not twenty-one anymore."

I giggle. "All right, not every night, but once a week, say. You're young, single, and gorgeous. Every woman would swipe right on you. You'd be able to pick and choose."

He shudders. "I can't think of anything more horrific. Companionship is based on having common interests. You can't tell that from three keywords on a bio."

I eat the other half of the truffle, amused. "Companionship? You're practically Victorian, Henry. I'm talking about sex."

He leans back and sighs. Finally, his gaze rises to meet mine.

My heart skips a beat. "There is someone," I whisper.

He doesn't reply. He just sips his whisky, his gaze meeting mine over the rim of the glass.

I'm shocked at the way I feel at that revelation—as if I've been punched in the stomach.

"Who is she?" I ask.

He looks into his drink and sighs again.

"Have you told her how you feel?" I ask.

He shakes his head. "She's with someone."

"Do I know her?" I wonder if she works at Kia Kaha. Rachel, on reception? Or Clara, from accounts? She's gorgeous. Oh God, don't let it be Clara…

He meets my gaze again, though, and just tips his head to the side and gives me a look that's part exasperated, part amused.

I stare at him. And slowly, my jaw drops. "You don't mean… me?"

Chapter Four

Henry

I can see the exact moment the penny drops. It's as if someone's struck a match behind her eyes, and they flare with understanding.

"Of course it's you," I say. "It's always been you. Don't tell me you had no idea."

She shakes her head. "I thought maybe… but I didn't know…" She couldn't have looked more shocked if I'd stripped naked and run around the apartment with my tackle hanging out.

Ah, shit. She really hadn't guessed. And now the toothpaste is out of the tube, and it's not going back in.

We stare at each other for a long, long time. I have no idea what's going through her mind. Over the years I've seen her upset, puzzled, amused, indignant, and furious, but I can't tell from her expression now which of those she's feeling. Maybe all of them. Will she throw the gin in my face? Get up and leave? Cry? Laugh at me?

She doesn't do any of those things. She drops her gaze to her glass, finishes off the martini, then slides it over to me. "I think I'm going to need a lot more of those."

Trying not to show my relief, and conscious of her watching me, I mix her another, pour it into her glass, then top up my whisky. We both have a big mouthful, our gazes meeting again. We're sitting closer than we were before, not touching, with only six inches or so separating us. At least she hasn't slapped me.

"Are you serious?" she asks eventually. "You're not having me on?"

"No."

"You… have feelings for me?"

"I'm in love with you," I clarify. "I have been since the first time we met."

Her eyebrows rise, and she inhales. "You're in *love* with me?"

"Yeah." I let that sink in for a moment.

I shouldn't have told her. But although I'm blaming it on the alcohol, it's not the whisky's fault. I couldn't keep it in any longer. Eventually, I add, "Why else do you think Shaz and I broke up? She knew. She's always known. I tried to ignore it because you were with Cam, and I'd already proposed to her, and I knew you and I couldn't come to anything, but Shaz always knew."

Juliette looks so shocked it makes me laugh.

"Don't mock me," she says indignantly.

"I'm sorry, but your face is a picture." I force the smile away. "You really had no idea?"

She swallows hard. "I suppose I wondered, but I wasn't sure. You never made it obvious."

"Of course not. Alex would have hung, drawn, and quartered me. And…" I sigh. "You deserve better than me. I know you want children, and I can't give them to you."

Her expression softens. "So why have you told me now?"

I hold up the whisky glass and admire the amber Jameson. "Too much truth serum."

She brushes a hand over her face. "I wish you hadn't told me."

It wasn't what I expected her to say, and my heart sinks. She's about to be kind to me, tell me thank you, and she appreciates the sentiment, but that she doesn't feel the same way. Fuck, I think. Fuck, shit, arse. I've ruined everything.

Oh man. Alex is going to kill me.

But instead she says, "I've only coped because I've been able to tell him there's nothing between us."

My eyebrows rise. "What?"

She lowers her hand. "Cam's jealous of you. He's accused me of having feelings for you lots of times. That was what tonight was about, partly."

I stare at her. "Do you? Have feelings for me?"

She moistens her lips with the tip of her tongue and doesn't reply.

She does. My heart soars. Why else would he accuse her? Even if she doesn't want to admit it to herself, he obviously picked up something in the way she talked about me.

So why isn't she admitting it now?

"You and Cam," I say softly. "*Is* it over?"

She covers her face again. "Yes. No. I don't know."

It's not the reply I wanted. But I can't force her to say the words I want to hear. I can't force her to do anything.

I want to get angry, tell her how resentful I feel, how furious I am that she's still with this guy who treats her so badly. But she lowers her hand then, and there are tears in her eyes again, and my fury fades away.

"What happened with him?" I ask gently. "You seemed happy for a long time. What went wrong?"

"I've never talked about this," she says. "He made me swear not to tell anyone, and if he knew I was talking to you about it… of all people…"

"I won't say anything. You know I won't."

Her lips curve up a little. "I know." She swallows hard. "But… I'm still not sure I can tell you."

"Why?"

"It's very personal. Are you sure you want to know?"

She means it's about sex. Ah, jeez. I hate to think of her sleeping with anyone else. But I have to know, or how can I make it better?

I nod. I hope I don't regret it.

She has a mouthful of martini. I turn a little and lean on the back of the sofa, propping my head on a hand. My knees are almost—but not quite—touching hers.

"When he was a kid, Cam was sexually abused," she says.

I close my eyes for a moment. Oh fuck. It's worse than I thought.

When I open them again, she's looking into her drink, lost in thought. She gives a big sigh, exhaling as if she's been holding it in for a lifetime. "It was an uncle," she continues, "his mother's brother. It went on for three years, and nobody knew."

"Was it just him, or did it happen to either of his brothers?"

"Just him. He's the youngest. When his dad left, his uncle helped his mum out with money, and he threatened to stop helping if Cam told anyone."

"Christ."

"When he was eleven, his mum caught his uncle in the act, and she went ballistic. She took the boys and ran to the nearest police station. The uncle was arrested and eventually put away. This was in Dunedin, and she moved to Christchurch with the boys and started again. Took Cam to counseling. She was supportive and did everything she could to put things right. He doesn't blame her. But he's damaged, Henry. Terribly damaged."

I've never liked Cam much, mainly because I don't think I'd have liked anyone who was with Juliette. He's a bit lacking in the sense of humor department, he's superior, and he's often rude to Juliette, which I detest. But at this revelation, my heart goes out to him. It's already a horrific story, and I know there's more to come.

"Did you know from the beginning?" I ask.

She shakes her head and finishes off her drink. Without asking, I make us both another. I'm feeling the alcohol now, so I know she must be too, but you can't talk about this kind of thing if you're sober.

"For the first few years, things were okay between us," she says slowly. She takes the new martini from me and has a sip. "I mean… in bed. I wasn't his first, but he was mine, and I didn't know any different. Sometimes… he struggled to get an erection. But I assumed that was normal. Men aren't robots, right? He used to get frustrated and even angry, but I just said it didn't matter, and that we'd try again later. I figured it wasn't his fault, and that I had to be patient."

I lean on the back of the sofa again and sink my hand into my hair. Her face has reddened—she's embarrassed to admit this, but she obviously needs to talk.

"It got worse as time went on," she admits. "And gradually I began to realize that he couldn't get an erection unless I was…" Her gaze flicks to me, then away again. "In control," she continues carefully.

I have a big mouthful of whisky, half wanting to hear it all, half afraid to listen.

"I think I knew deep down that something was wrong," she continues, "but he wouldn't talk about it. Then, six months ago, he went away on a course in Auckland. When he came home, he said he wanted to talk. And he admitted he'd slept with someone else."

I didn't expect her to say that. My eyebrows rise.

She gives me a small smile. "I knew you wouldn't like that bit."

"He cheated on you?"

"Technically? Apparently not. He said he'd been talking to a sex therapist online, and she put him in touch with a surrogate partner."

"Sorry, what?"

"It's another kind of therapist who helps people who are uncomfortable with sex."

"Okay… And what did she do? I presume it was a she?"

She nods. "She was a specialist."

"A specialist in what?"

She hesitates. Then she says, "Stuff."

Outside I can still hear the people down below and music from the bar, but silence falls between us. She looks at me cautiously, obviously embarrassed about going into detail.

"Can you be more specific?" I ask eventually, when it's clear she's not going to elaborate.

She fiddles with a pleat of her sari. She's silent for a long time. And then eventually she admits, "In intimacy issues. They talked about how he felt out of control in bed. And she said she could help by showing him some things…"

"That was nice of her."

"So they went to bed."

"Seriously?"

"Yeah. And she showed him… things." Her gaze flicks up to mine, then away again.

I think about why she could be nervous about telling me. "Is he into pain?"

"Um… not really. Apparently she called it service-oriented submission."

We fall quiet again. I'm not shocked. Sex is often about the balance of power, and I understand how Cam might find it helpful to regain control over his past by exploring BDSM roles.

But I'm not concerned about Cam. I'm concerned about Juliette and the effect this is having on her.

"Did he use a condom?" I ask.

"Yes."

Well, that's something.

"He said he needed to know whether she could help him get an erection," she says.

"And did she?"

"Yes. I asked him if he wanted to break up. He said no. But he asked if I'd be prepared to do some of the things she did to him."

She looks away. Her face is scarlet. She looks embarrassed and humiliated. Clearly, she doesn't want to talk about what he asked her to do in detail.

"I'm guessing you said yes," I reply.

She nods tightly. "I didn't want to lose him. I wanted to help. So I made him go into detail. I wanted to know why he'd visited this woman, and what he wanted—what he needed. He told me everything. We talked for hours and hours. It was the most open conversation we'd ever had. He explained how, when I was in control, it helped him because being out of control was then his choice. Does that make sense?"

"Kinda."

"And it worked... for a while." Her gaze comes back to me then, though, and she looks utterly miserable. "But it's just gotten worse and worse. He can't get an erection at all now unless he's being..." She hesitates, unsure how to phrase it.

"Dominated?" I suggest.

She nods. "On my birthday we had this big argument because he asked me to do something, and I did, and he got so turned on he sort of got carried away, and he ended up finishing inside me without a condom even though I was asking him to stop, and I was really angry with him." She blushes scarlet—she doesn't want to tell me, but she can't stop herself. "Then, last night, he asked me to..." She trails off again. "Do something I didn't want to do," she says lamely. "I said no, and it blew up into another major argument. He ended up sleeping on the sofa. And this morning, when I attempted to talk about it, he was embarrassed and angry, and he said I obviously didn't love him, or I'd help him more. He called me names, said things that hurt me. But the thing is, it's all about him now. What he wants, what he needs. He never talks about what *I* want. What *I* need."

"Ah, Juliette..."

She's crying again now, tears running down her beautiful face. "And I don't know why but he's angry with me now, all the time, as if he's upset that I know his secret. And I have to do all these things I don't want to do, and in return he's resentful and cross with me all the time."

I sigh.

"He's so broken and inwardly focused that there's nothing left for me. I can't remember the last time he touched me lovingly." She dashes tears from her face. "His therapist told him that if I loved him I'd be understanding, and I do love him, or I did, anyway, but I can't cope anymore. I'm just not good enough for him. I'm not a big enough person."

"Stop it." I lean forward, slide a hand beneath her chin, and lift it so she has to look into my eyes. "It's not you. It's not your fault."

"But—"

I lower my hand, but I keep my gaze fixed on hers. "I'm not going to talk about Cam. What he requires in bed is his own business. I understand the therapist saying that a loving partner might wish to try things to help. But you shouldn't have to change yourself to please him, or do things you don't want to do. That's not fair."

"I've tried."

"I know."

"I really have." She presses the heels of her hands into her eyes. "But I don't want to do those things anymore."

"You don't have to."

"I just want to have ordinary sex without worrying. Does that make sense?"

"Of course it does. I understand, because I'm the same."

She lowers her hands and wipes her face. "What do you mean?"

"Sex with Shaz became all about making a baby. For two years we had charts marked with fertile periods and ovulation days and temperatures... And all the fun went out of it. There was no question of doing anything that didn't result in... ah... fluid ending up where it shouldn't, if you get my drift. It got to where I wanted to refuse to perform on the necessary days out of spite. And that's not me. It made me into a person I didn't want to be."

"Yes, that's it exactly." Her big brown eyes stare up into mine, pleased I understand.

We study each other for a long moment.

Eventually, she looks at her glass on the table, picks it up, and drains it. "I'm tipsy," she says. I think it's an understatement—we're both quite drunk.

"Yeah, me too."

She puts the glass down and wipes her face. Then she looks up at me again. Her gaze lingers on my mouth. "I used to think of you," she whispers. "I used to think that Henry wouldn't ask me to... do those things." She swallows hard.

"No, I wouldn't."

"In the real world, I'm confident and capable, and I don't like being told what to do. I know you all think I'm bossy, and I don't mind that. But in bed... I like to give up control. Does that make sense?"

"Yeah." My heart is pounding, and my voice is husky with desire. I want to touch her, but I'm not going to do it without her permission.

"I don't intimidate you?" she asks.

That makes me laugh. "I'm six-foot-four. I'm not easily intimidated."

"I just want to be..." She sighs.

"Worshiped?" I ask.

Her lips curve up. "Maybe a tiny bit."

"You should be."

"I want to be wanted. To be desired. Just once, for it to be about me."

"It should always be about you."

She blinks. "You said 'If you were my girl, I'd treat you like a queen.' Did you mean it?"

"One hundred percent." I move a little closer to her, still not touching.

Her gaze drops to my mouth. "I can't imagine what that would be like…"

We're both breathing fast. Oh Jesus, this girl… I've never wanted anything as badly as I want her right now. I put my arm on the back of the sofa so it's almost—but not quite—around her. The air between us is almost sparking with electricity.

She swallows, and then her eyes meet mine again. "I love the way you look at me," she whispers.

"How am I looking at you?"

"As if you want me."

"I do want you."

"As if you need me."

"More than I need air to breathe."

"Henry," she says, exhaling, and my name in her mouth is a soft caress that sends the hairs rising all over my body. "Would you… would you kiss me?"

I give a triumphant, short laugh. "I thought you'd never ask."

Sliding my arms around her, I lean back, pulling her on top of me, but twist at the last moment, and now she's half under me, pinned against the back of the sofa. She squeals, then laughs and looks up at me with eyes ablaze with desire.

Without further ado, I crush my lips to hers.

She moans against my mouth, her lips parting, and I slide my tongue against hers in a kiss that sends fire shooting through my veins. She wraps her arms around me, and I feel her fingers slip beneath my top and fan out on my back, eager to touch my skin, and I get an instant erection.

Whoa… steady, tiger. I have no doubt that she wouldn't complain if I thrust us both to a climax in minutes, but that's not what I want, and it's not what she needs. I don't know what's going to happen tomorrow, but I need to make the most of her while I have her right here, right now.

I lift my head and look down into her big brown eyes. When she tries to kiss me, I move back a little, out of her reach.

Her smile fades. "Are you having second thoughts?"

I laugh at how preposterous that statement is. "No. But we're not going to rush this."

She blinks a few times. "What do you mean?"

"I mean that we've got all night, and I have a lot of worshiping to catch up on."

Her eyes light up. We're tangled together, my legs between hers, one of my arms beneath her.

"You have an erection," she says. Her obvious delight at such a basic reaction makes my heart ache.

"And it's all down to you, baby." It's the first time I've used an endearment like that for her, and she looks at me almost bashfully.

"What do you want me to do?" she asks.

I kiss her. "I don't want you to do anything. Here's what's going to happen. I'm going to kiss you for a long, long time. Then I'm going to take your clothes off, slowly, and find out exactly how to unwrap you from that beautiful sari, so I can kiss every piece of skin as it's revealed. Then I want to see what you taste like, because I've fantasized about it for years."

"Oh," she says faintly.

"I'm going to take you to bed and make you come with my mouth. And then I'll make love to you for as long as I can manage it, until you can't think about anything but me."

She lets out something like a little squeak. I bend my head and brush my lips against hers, just touching.

"How does that sound?" I murmur.

"I don't want to be on top," she says. Her eyes glisten.

"Okay." I kiss slowly across her mouth, from one corner to the other. "I can think of plenty of other positions we can try."

That makes her laugh. "Just one will be amazing."

"Oh, I have lots more than one planned."

"You've thought about this way too much."

"You have no idea."

She giggles, then lifts her arms around my neck, her brows drawing together. "Just make me forget," she whispers.

"You're not even going to be able to remember your name when I'm done with you."

"Promises, promises." She sounds breathless with excitement.

"Absolutely, it's a promise. But first things first. Would you let your hair down?"

"My hair?" Her eyebrows lift. "Um, okay." She releases the two butterfly clips holding it up and tosses them onto the coffee table.

I watch as she unfurls the long, brown locks. She never wears it down, and so I had no idea how long it was. It's luxurious, like a strip of chocolate-brown silk, and as she pulls it straight, it reaches all the way to her hips.

I lift a strand, inhale the scent of it, then run it through my fingers. It's soft and silky. Ahhh… for some reason it really turns me on.

Her lips curve up. "You like?"

"I like. A lot." I slip my hand into it while I study her mouth. "I'm going to kiss you now."

"Okay."

"Try to remember to breathe. It's going to take a while."

She gives me a helpless look. And then, as I lower my lips to hers, she sighs, her breath mingling with mine.

Chapter Five

Juliette

I'm lying on the sofa, crushed beneath Henry, who's kissing me senseless, while the warm summer breeze blows in through the windows across us like a sirocco wind.

In the distance, one of the bars is playing old love songs, and strains of Dr. Hook's *A Little Bit More* drifts in with the breeze. Henry hums it, then starts laughing, and I giggle against his lips as he sings the wonderful, cheesy lyrics.

He's so relaxed and confident in his sexuality, evident in the way his erection sprang to life without any effort, so it seems, and is now pressed against my hip in all its glory. He wants me, and the thought brings tears to my eyes.

Mmm… he kisses like a god. I can't remember the last time I made out like this. *It's going to take a while*, he told me, and, true to his words, he kisses me with agonizing slowness, pressing his lips all over my face. He kisses my cheeks, my eyebrows, my closed eyelids, my nose, up my jawline to my ear, and beneath the lobe to my neck, which makes me shiver in his arms.

"You like that?" he murmurs, touching his tongue to the place where my pulse beats in my throat.

I sigh. "Yes…"

So he does it again, kissing down to the hollow at the base of my throat, then back up the other side, taking his time to touch his tongue to the sensitive skin there.

I lie calmly, but my mind feels like a pinball machine, the ball bearing shooting around at a million miles an hour. Is it over with Cam? I shouldn't be doing this until I'm sure. Cam is my partner. He's the only man I've ever been with. We rent an apartment together. I love him. At least I think I do. I've been faithful to him, and even though deep down I admit to having been attracted to Henry from the start, we've never come close to doing anything about it. Does it matter that I've thought about it? Especially over the last year or two? Does it count as cheating if it's all in the mind?

In Sanskrit, intention is called *Samkalpa*, and it's seen as more than mere thought—it's caused by desire, which directs you toward a purpose or goal. It means that subconsciously, I've always wanted

Henry. My desires have led me down this path. I've manifested this outcome. I came to this hotel because I knew this was going to happen. I'm fooling myself if I think anything different.

I think of the Rubik's Cube, me turning the sides, passing it to Henry, him completing the puzzle, then passing it back, our fingers occasionally grazing, exchanging a secret, hidden message, but never when Cam was around. In my mind, I cheated on Cam years ago.

Even though he cheated on me in every sense of the word, does that make it right to cheat on him physically? Am I trying to pay him back? The universe doesn't carry debts, and what you give is always returned to you. Karma has no menu—you get served what you deserve. Epithets run through my mind, but the outcome is the same—Karma isn't about tit for tat. I can't do this to punish Cam. I want to be a better person than that.

I'm not being fair to Henry either. I'm in such a muddle. My old relationship is still clinging to me like cobwebs. I should shake them free first, before I let him anywhere near me.

Henry lifts his head, obviously sensing something. He looks into my eyes. "Are you okay?" he murmurs.

"I'm not being fair," I whisper.

"To Cam?"

"Or to you."

"To me?"

I cup his face. "I'm a mess. I don't know what I'm doing."

He studies me for a moment. His hair falls over his forehead. I can still feel his erection against my hip. It's in proportion to the rest of him. Oh God… I have to fight not to groan. I'm only human. I can smell his cologne, mixed with the warm scent of his skin. I can taste whisky on my lips from where he kissed me.

This is nothing to do with Cam. It's all about me, and the man lying on top of me. I've wanted him ever since I met him. That's why I'm here.

His eyes flare, and I realize then that I've tilted my hips up to feel him.

He shifts so he's nestling between my legs, then rocks his hips so he grinds against me. "You look like you know what you're doing to me," he comments silkily.

A moan escapes my lips. He's cruel, but he's correct. I know what I want. I want his mouth on mine. I want him inside me.

"It's not fair to you…" I whisper.

He looks amused. "I don't care, as long as I get what I want." His gaze is direct, demanding. Ooh. I'd forgotten that the quiet, gentle Henry is also a rich, powerful businessman.

"You want me to stop?" he asks, rocking his hips again. The root of his erection presses right against my clit. "You've got to tell me."

I open my mouth to say the words, but nothing comes out.

His lips curve up a little more. He takes my hand and links my fingers with his. Then he lifts it above my head and pins it there. Bending his head, he presses his lips to the sensitive skin under my arm, and my nipples tighten in my bra.

"Tell me to stop, Juliette," he says, his voice husky, his breath hot on my skin, "and I'll stop."

I shudder. God help me, but I can't say it.

He looks back at me, and his expression is triumphant and a tad smug. "Good girl," he states.

"I hate you," I tell him.

He just laughs as he kisses down my throat again. "Yeah, yeah."

Ahhh… all those years of being so close to him and not being able to touch him… My desire has been contained and restricted, and now it overflows and begins to drown me. He kisses my mouth again and releases my hand, and I run my fingers over the short hair on the back of his head, feeling a surge of pleasure as he shivers. I'm affecting him as much as he's affecting me.

He kisses me for ages, until my lips feel puffy and tender, until I'm aching with need for him. My body feels as if it's a tuning fork that's been struck and is humming a single long note. I brush my hand down his back to the base of the Henley and slip my fingers beneath the material, desperate to feel his skin. He's hot, as if he has a temperature. Our desire is burning us both up. We're going to self-combust, and they'll find us days later, just a pile of ash amongst a scatter of clothes and shoes.

Eventually, he lifts his head. His pupils have dilated, and his eyes look almost black. He rises from the sofa, surprisingly agile for a big guy, and holds out a hand to me. I take it and let him pull me up. Ooh, the room spins a little.

"I'm tipsy," I tell him.

"Yeah, me too." He cups my face and brushes a thumb across my bottom lip. "You want me to stop?"

"God, no."

Laughing, he takes my hand and leads me into the bedroom.

The sliding doors here are open a little, and the room is warm and smells of the jasmine growing in pots below us. Fat Larry's Band is singing *Zoom*, a song that makes me feel happy.

"At last," Henry says, "I get to unwrap my perfect Christmas present."

I smile and turn my back to him. "Can you undo the safety pin there?" I gesture to my shoulder blade.

He does as I ask, sliding it out of the material and leaving it on the bedside table. "I've always wondered how you put a sari on," he murmurs.

"I'll show you. Hold this." I take the material over my shoulder and give him the end to hold. After undoing the pin at my waist, I move back a few steps, letting the silk pleats fall away. Then I turn around so the material unwinds, until eventually I'm left with the last loop tucked into my petticoat.

"Fascinating," he murmurs, folding the silk. To my surprise, he presses his nose to it briefly before he puts it on the table, the same way I sniffed his shirt.

Self-conscious now, I undo the tie of the petticoat, push it down, and step out of it.

He grabs a handful of the Henley behind the back of his neck and tugs it off, then runs a hand through his hair, which does nothing at all except show me the size of his biceps and nearly cause me to faint. We both have light-brown skin, but mine has cool, jewel undertones, whereas Henry's has golden earth tones, making me think of warm summer days by the beach.

He moves closer to me and kisses me as he undoes the buttons of my blouse. My heart hammers as he moves the sides apart to reveal my breasts in the white demi-cups. He pushes the blouse off my shoulders, then, keeping his gaze on mine and smiling, he slides his hands behind me, undoes my bra, draws the straps down, and tosses it away.

He pulls back the duvet, then lifts me up, wrapping my legs around his waist. Climbing onto the bed, he then lowers me down onto my back.

"You're the most beautiful woman I've ever met," he says, shifting to the side a little so he can admire me. He strokes a hand down to my breasts and studies them, his hot gaze like a laser burning into my skin.

"Henry!" I tease, my face flushing. "It's rude to stare."

"I'm admiring the view." He traces a finger around the areola. "They're lighter than I thought they'd be. Like caramel."

"You're not supposed to compare skin color to food."

"And milk chocolate," he says, ignoring me as he touches the tip with his finger. "I wonder if they taste as sweet as they look." He covers one with his mouth, and I feel his tongue brush over the sensitive skin before he sucks gently.

Pleasure ripples through me, and I groan.

"Mm," he murmurs. "They do." He looks up at me. "Want me to stop?"

I glare at him.

He chuckles and swaps to my other breast, brushing his thumb across the nipple so it tightens into a bud.

I squirm. "Ah... Henry..."

He trails the tip of his tongue around the edge, then closes his mouth over it and sucks. Ohhh... it's an amazing sensation, and I feel an answering tug deep down inside me.

He does this for ages, swapping between them, until both nipples are glistening, elongated, and throbbing. Then he lifts up and hooks his fingers into the elastic of my knickers.

He looks at me and waits.

Damn him—he's going to make me admit I want this every step of the way.

I nod, and he peels them down my legs and tosses them away.

Then, bare chested and gorgeous, he moves between my legs, hooks his arms under my knees, and tugs me down so I'm lying flat. Finally, completely brazen and uncaring, he parts my thighs and stares hungrily at me.

Looking up at me, he waits. I cover my face with my arms. "Yes," I hiss. "Please..."

He exhales with a sigh that turns into a groan, lowers down, and buries his mouth in me.

"Yeah..." He exclaims. "So sweet..."

I shiver as he slides his tongue through my folds and sighs. Parting me, he licks all the way down to my entrance, then back up to my clit, which he covers with his mouth. He sucks gently, and I shudder as pleasure ripples through me.

Lifting his head, he circles the pad of his forefinger slowly over the tiny button. "You're more beautiful than I could have imagined," he murmurs. "And you taste amazing." He buries his mouth in me again, and I slide my hand into his hair with a groan.

"Oh that's so good," I tell him, unable to stop rocking my hips to meet the movement of his tongue.

"Yeah, baby, tell me what you like. Softer? Harder? Faster? Slower?" He flicks my clit with the tip of his tongue.

"Mmm… slower… softer…"

He licks more slowly, long licks as if he's eating an ice cream, then sucks gently on my clit. At the same time, he teases my entrance with a finger, then turns his hand palm up and slides two fingers inside me. Ahhh… this guy is driving me insane.

"Good, baby?" he asks.

"Oh yes… Don't stop…"

"I won't." Now he knows how I like it, he keeps the rhythm going, stroking his fingers inside me, and licking and sucking until the tension starts to build.

I tighten my fingers in his hair. "Henry," I whisper. "Ohhh…"

"That's it, baby girl, come for me…" He presses his fingers up gently as he strokes them in and out—oh shit, I have a G spot?—and continues to lick and suck, and there's no way I'm going to survive that. It's intense, ooh, wow, a sudden tightening of everything, and then the pulses claim me, and I cry out with each one… Oh God…

When they finally end, I fall back, panting.

I close my eyes, feeling him shift, taking off his boxers. Finally, he moves over me. When I eventually open my eyes again, he's leaning over me, smiling.

He licks his lips, his gaze turning sultry. "You taste nice."

I blink slowly, hearing warning bells, way off in the distance. I'm more drunk than I realized. But it's too late now. I couldn't stop even if my life depended on it. I want this man desperately. I've had years of wondering, of fantasizing about him, even though I've hated myself for it, and now he's here, and I don't have to wait any longer.

He lowers to kiss me, and as he does, I wrap my arms and legs around him and tighten them. He laughs and falls on top of me.

"Steady," he mumbles, tangling his hand in my hair. "We've got all night."

"I can't wait, Henry." I move my hips, trying to encourage him to enter me, and moan as I feel the tip of his erection press against me.

"Jesus. Wait, I want to get you ready…"

"I'm ready now." I tilt my pelvis up. He enters me a fraction, and then, unable to fight it, he pushes forward.

We both groan as he slides in, right up to the hilt in one smooth thrust. Christ, he's so thick and hard. I can feel him all the way up. And it was so effortless.

"You're driving me insane," he says hoarsely.

I look up at him, into his gorgeous blue eyes, and clench my internal muscles so I'm gripping him. He blinks slowly, then begins to move with long, deep thrusts, almost withdrawing before burying himself back inside me again.

Oh he wants me, and I'm so happy I could cry. As he kisses me, I stroke up his arms, then across his broad back, feeling his defined muscles. He's so big—I love that. His mouth moves over mine, and then I part my lips and our tongues tangle, and we both groan again.

This was what I wanted—to be desired, to be needed. He's trying to take it slow, but I can feel the willpower it's taking him to hold back. And when he gives in to his body's urge to thrust and goes deeper, I moan against his lips.

He lifts his head, breathing hard. "Slowly," he scolds. "Let's make it last."

But I shake my head. "No. Please."

He sighs and kisses me. "All right, baby girl. Tell me what you want?" He kisses my nose. "What do you need?"

"I just want you to want me."

"I do, Juliette. Can't you tell?"

"Show me how much." I don't know how to make it any clearer. I'm too shy to tell him I want him to fuck me as if his life depends on it.

He looks into my eyes, and he must see the yearning in them, because he withdraws with a growl. Before I can complain, he moves off me, tugs my arm, and rolls me over onto my front. Then he pushes up my knee, positions himself between my legs, and guides himself down into me again.

"You should be careful what you wish for," he states, lowering down so his mouth is close to my ear. Then he pushes his hips forward and buries himself inside me again.

I moan and bite the pillow. Oh, in this position he's so deep…

"Like this, Juliette?" he asks silkily, beginning to thrust.

"Yes…" I whisper. "Oh God, yes…"

He wraps my hair around his hand and pulls it so I have to lift my head. "I can't hear you," he murmurs in my ear.

"Ahhh… yes…" I close my eyes. "Please…"

He gives in and starts to thrust properly, driving into me until his hips meet the back of my thighs with an audible smack.

I squeal and bury my face in the pillow again. He's hot and heavy on top of me, and I can't do anything as he thrusts inside me except lie there and take it, and it's so damn marvelous it makes me want to cry, and oh God I'm definitely drunk, but it's absolutely amazing and I can't stop now…

He slides a hand beneath me and tugs my nipple, and I clench around him.

"You're so beautiful," he whispers in my ear. "Do you know how long I've dreamed about this? Fantasized about having you at my mercy?" He slows down a little, driving me mad with his slow, leisurely thrusts. "I'd watch you in the boardroom, talking about everyday things, and I'd picture you like this, bent over the table, naked beneath me, your gorgeous hair spread over your back, and I'd imagine what your breasts and nipples looked like, and how you tasted…"

"Ahhh… Henry…"

"And I'd wonder what you sound like when you come, and how it would feel to know I'd given you pleasure…"

I groan. I can already feel it building inside me again. "Oh God…"

"Are you going to come for me again, angel?"

"Yes…"

He steps up the pace, pounding into me, and that's it—it's too much—I clamp around him and squeal as I clench, so powerfully it makes me see stars.

He doesn't stop, thrusting all the way through my climax, and I come and I come, so hard it almost hurts.

"Ah I'm so fucking in love with you," he says as he drives into me, "you're mine now, say it."

"Henry…"

"Say it."

I bite my bottom lip. I don't want to say it. But I didn't know it was going to be like this. He's usually so quiet and gentle, and I was unprepared for how amazing it feels to have his big, powerful body taking me, and how I feel overwhelmed not just from the pleasure, but from the thought that he wants me.

He thrusts harder. "Say it," he demands.

Tears run down my face. "I'm yours."

He slams into me a few last times, then stiffens. His hips jerk, and I feel him twitch as he comes, the muscles in his arms hardening to rock where he's supporting himself.

He groans as he empties into me, and then his breaths come in huge gasps as his body finally relaxes.

We stay like that for a moment, unable to move, like two wolves knotted together. Then, eventually, he withdraws and lowers onto the mattress, so he's facing me.

"Jesus," he says.

I can't move. I lie limply, tears trickling down my cheeks, looking at him helplessly.

"Ah, baby," he says. He reaches down, retrieves the duvet, and tugs it up over us. Then he says, "Come here." He puts his arms around me and pulls me close.

I curl up against him. He smells warm and sexy. I wipe my face as he strokes my hair. Half of me expects him to apologize for upsetting me, for demanding that I say I'm his.

He doesn't. But he does lower his lips to mine and give me a long, gentle kiss.

I snuggle up to him, and I feel his lips press against the top of my head.

"Go to sleep," he says, stroking my back.

And, worn out from the emotion and the pleasure, I do.

Chapter Six

Juliette

I come to slowly, the way night turns into day, with the sun gradually rising above the horizon. I open my eyes and discover I'm still lying on my front. Jeez—have I moved at all during the night? Oh, I did get up at one point to visit the bathroom. The room was still spinning at that point, and when I was done I just slid back into the bed and fell straight asleep again.

I'm looking at the window. The sliding doors are still open a crack. The breeze is cool now, and carries with it the scent of morning—fresh grass, and the smell of baking croissants and coffee. The sky is a beautiful blend of tangerine, coral, and lemon. It's early, then, sunrise, not even six. Thank God. It's our last day in the office, and I don't want to roll in late.

I'm lying with my arms tucked beneath me. I usually keep my hair in a braid at night, but this morning I can feel it lying over my skin like a silk blanket. The duvet rests across my hips.

Someone is stroking my back.

I close my eyes as what happened last night comes flooding back. Oh God, Henry.

Fuck, fuck, fuck. I let him bring me back to his hotel room. And I let him make love to me.

No, own up to it Juliette. Remember your whole internal debate about intention? You didn't 'let' him do anything. You made the decision to come back here. You knew perfectly well where it was going to lead. You're not a victim. You're the perpetrator of this crime.

Although… at this moment it doesn't feel like a crime. It feels like heaven, lying there sprawled on my front, so relaxed I'm almost comatose, with Henry's fingers trailing lightly over me. He touches my hair, moving strands of it aside to expose my skin, then when he's done, begins to stroke my neck with a finger. Beneath my ear. Down my throat. Around to the nape. Across my shoulders. Back to my nape. Down my spine. Up the sides of my ribs. Sometimes with one finger, and at other times with his whole hand, big and warm, brushing over my skin. Mmm…

After a while, he slips his hand beneath the duvet and continues stroking down. Over my bottom. Down the back of my thighs. Across the sensitive skin at the back of my knees. Then up again, stopping to circle a finger in the dip at the base of my spine before continuing up.

Over and over again. Until I'm like caramel warmed by the rising sun.

I screw my eyes shut. Oh dear God, I've got to stop him. He's turning me on, and that's not going to end well.

What do you mean, Juliette? Isn't an orgasm a rather nice way to start the day?

No! I can't give in again. In the cold light of day, I think about Cam, and I shrivel inside like a poked spider. Last night when he walked out, I asked if he was coming back and he said *No, I'm done*. I told myself it was all over, but this morning I know nothing is certain. It's not the first argument we've had, or the first time he's slept on the sofa or even at his brother's, and he's usually contrite and upset the next morning. We always make up. And now I've jeopardized a seven-year relationship with one simple act.

Henry strokes my back, continues beneath the duvet, then slides a finger down between my legs.

I inhale and rear up, turning to look at him. He gives a husky chuckle and says, "I knew you were awake."

He's lying on his side, head propped on a hand. His normally styled hair is all mussed. His jaw is covered with stubble. His eyelids are at half-mast. He's so gorgeous I think I might actually die from lust.

"Oh God." I sit up, pulling the duvet with me and tucking it tightly around my body.

"Morning," he says.

"What are you doing?" I demand.

"Enjoying myself." He smiles.

I swallow hard and run a hand through my hair. His gaze follows it, filled with amusement as I find the strands tangled. "You still look just-fucked," he says.

"You needn't sound so smug about it," I snap.

He just smirks. He obviously doesn't have an ounce of regret.

Well that's fine, because I have more than enough for us both.

"Where's my purse?" I demand.

He holds up something in his fingers. It's a breath mint. He smiles, the corners of his eyes crinkling. I have a phobia about having bad breath, and he would know I wouldn't want to kiss him without having a mint.

I'm tempted to refuse it, because accepting it admits I want him to kiss me. But my mouth tastes sour, and I know he's probably going to kiss me whether I have it or not, so I take it and crunch it, glaring as he grins.

"What are you doing?" he asks as I start scanning the carpet.

"Looking for my underwear." I spot my knickers and bend over to get them. Before I can pick them up, however, he slides an arm around my waist, lifts me, and flips me onto my back again.

"First things first." He hooks a leg over mine and shifts to half lean on me, pressing me into the mattress.

"No, no!" I push him. It's like shoving a brick wall. "I can't…" I look up at him, at the broad expanse of his chest, covered with a smattering of dark curly hair, his muscular shoulders, the hollow at the base of his neck. I can smell his cologne, warmed by his skin. I gather my courage and whisper, "I want to go," then wait for him to apologize and move off me.

He doesn't. "You're not going anywhere," he says. "Not until I've given you at least one orgasm."

Infuriated, I try to get up. In response, he grabs both my wrists and pins them easily above my head with one of his hands.

"Henry!"

"What?" He trails the forefinger of his other hand down between my breasts.

I inhale with indignation. "Let me go!"

He laughs. "No." He takes my nipple between his thumb and finger and tugs. Aaahhh… it sends an electric shock between my legs.

Anger flares inside me. "So you're going to hold me here against my will?"

"Yeah, you don't want this at all."

My eyes widen. Oh God, he thinks I'm playing. "I'm serious," I tell him as earnestly as I can, trying not to wriggle as he continues to tease my nipple. "This isn't a game." I'm going to have to be blunt. "This was a mistake, Henry. I'm… I'm with someone else, and I need to go home and sort out that relationship. Do you understand?"

I wait for comprehension to dawn in his eyes. For his expression to turn hurt, or even angry. I deserve it, and I expect it.

Instead, he tips his head to the side. His hair falls forward over his forehead. "Do you remember what you told me last night?"

Oh God. *You're mine now, say it. I'm yours.*

"No," I reply.

He lifts an eyebrow.

"I know this is all my fault," I tell him before I can think better of it, "but even if you thought I'd finished with Cam last night, you should be more understanding. I've been with the guy for seven years. I owe him more than this."

Henry's eyes gleam. Uh-oh. Maybe I shouldn't have said that.

His pupils have dilated. He nudges my knees apart with the leg that's resting on me.

"You think I'm going to let you go now I know how much you want me?" He moves his hand between my legs, and I gasp as he draws his fingers through my folds, then brings them up to his mouth and sucks them. "Now I know what you taste like?" He lowers his hand again and slips his fingers right down inside me. His lips hover over mine. "How it feels to be inside you?"

Ohhh… shit. This has been a huge mistake. I shouldn't have come here. He's not the gentleman I thought he was. He's a rogue in sheep's clothing. I was a fool to think I could sleep with him without there being repercussions.

He brushes his lips against mine, continuing to stroke inside me. "Do you know how much I want you?"

"I have an idea." I sound breathless, even to myself. "I have a broom handle poking my hip."

He chuckles and thrusts it against me. Jesus, it's enormous.

"Don't you want this inside you?" he asks silkily.

Oh God, I really do. I groan, my hips tilting up in spite of myself.

He brushes his lips over mine. "Tell me to stop, Juliette, and I'll stop."

I close my eyes. He's pressing up with his fingers, and ohhh… holy moly, I thought the G-spot was a myth, like Atlantis, but it appears to be real. At the same time his thumb circles over my clit. His fingers are making squelchy noises, but he obviously doesn't care. I squirm, but he doesn't let up, and my traitorous body responds. My internal muscles clench, and his breath hisses across my lips.

"Tell me you don't want me," he demands.

God help me, but I can't. Ohhh… this man… I've always thought him handsome, and found him attractive… but I didn't expect him to be like this… so commanding…

He kisses me, plunging his tongue into my mouth, and I lie there and let him, because I'm powerless to stop him. He kisses me like a man who hasn't kissed anyone for ten years, as if kissing me is the only thing he's ever wanted to do.

When he finally tears his mouth from mine and his lips sear down my throat, I'm seeing stars.

He places big, wet, hungry kisses, and then when he reaches the place where my neck meets my shoulder, he fastens his mouth there and sucks, hard.

I squeal, annoyed that it arouses me. "Henry!"

He just laughs though, withdraws his fingers, and rises up over me. While I lie panting and aching for fulfillment, he leans over and grabs his wallet from the bedside table, takes out a condom, rips off the wrapper, and rolls it on. He strokes the tip down through my wet, swollen skin and presses against my entrance. Then he leans over me.

"Tell me to stop," he says again. His eyes are blazing. He looks unashamed and unrepentant.

My eyes prick with tears, and my bottom lip trembles, but I can't bring myself to utter the words.

His gaze searches mine, and he must see my emotion, because for the first time a frown flickers on his brow. But he doesn't stop. Slowly, with our eyes locked, he pushes up my knees, then slides inside me. Once, twice, thrice, coating himself with my moisture. He only stops when he's up to the hilt, his hips pressed against the back of my thighs.

My lips part with a soundless groan, and my eyes close at the sensation of being stretched and filled. Oh God. To my absolute limits.

For a moment, he doesn't move. I give deep, ragged gasps as I struggle to adjust.

"Ooh…" I blow out a breath.

He bends and kisses me. "All right, baby?"

"No. You're enormous."

He lowers down. "No, I'm not. You're tight. Must be all those pelvic floor exercises you do."

"I didn't notice last night. Ohhh…" I suck my bottom lip as he pulls almost out, then slides back in. "I guess that's what being drunk does for you. Mmm…"

"And I'd gone down on you, and you'd already had one orgasm." He kisses me. "Sorry if I didn't warm you up enough."

"I'm plenty warm. You're just hung like a moose."

That makes him laugh. "A moose?"

"It's a saying."

"I thought it was a horse?"

"If we're being technical about it, the blue whale has the biggest penis. It's nearly ten feet long."

"Well, I'm not that big." He chuckles, kissing the corners of my mouth where they've curved up. "That's better." He kisses back to the center, then touches his lips to my nose. "Look at me."

I open my eyes. Oh… this is an entirely different experience from last night. Then, we were drunk, and it was dark, and it was as if I was dreaming, living out a fantasy. It was still cheating, but I could explain it away as due to the effects of alcohol, and the heat of the moment.

This morning, I'm sober, and it's light, and there's no hiding from what I'm doing. I'm fucking a man who isn't my partner. I've chosen to do this. I have no defense to argue. And I can't bring my mouth to form the word 'stop'.

His eyes seem very blue today, the color of the morning sky. Keeping his gaze fixed on mine, he begins to move inside me.

He continues at that pace for ages. Sliding in and out, gentle and rhythmic, while he looks into my eyes and occasionally kisses me. And all the time, his hands continue to stroke me, down my sides, over my thighs, up to my breasts, slowly teasing me toward the edge.

I'm completely defenseless against this man. I feel as if, last night, under the influence of alcohol, I revealed the code to the Tower of London, and today he's snuck in and stolen the crown jewels. I told him all the secrets of my heart, so he knows exactly how to infiltrate it, how to get around me. Oh, I'm a stupid, stupid person. But it's too late now, and I'm just going to have to deal with my foolishness.

He closes his eyes for a moment, and when he opens them again they're full of hazy desire. "Juliette," he murmurs, continuing to press his lips against mine. "Your name feels like a spell."

I shiver. "Abracadabra." I'm trying to be funny, to lighten the mood, to stop him saying things that trickle inside me and through me like sand in a jar of stones.

But he continues to say, "Juliette," as he kisses my mouth, and, "Juliette," as he grazes his teeth on my bottom lip, and, "Juliette," in a husky voice as he dips his tongue inside. "I've waited so long to be able to do this," he whispers, stroking a hand down to my breast. "I'm never going to be able to look at you again without thinking about being inside you."

Oh God, Alex is going to kill us both. He's vehemently against having relationships with someone you work with. How am I going to be able to sit across the table from Henry knowing he's thinking about this? And how can I focus on timesheets and appointments and patients ever again and not have this moment in my mind the whole time? He's searing himself onto my brain, branding me, and I'm going to see him, feel him, even when we're apart.

I'm still drunk. I must be. I'd never think things like this if I were sober.

He shifts up an inch, and now he's grinding directly on my clit as he moves, while he teases my nipple with his thumb. Ooh, yeah, that's working. He's going to make me come like this, with just penetration. Cocky bastard.

He's not immune, though, his eyes growing hazy as his hips speed up. "Ah, I want to make it last," he murmurs, "but you're too fucking amazing."

"I'm not."

"You are."

"Ahhh... I'm just me."

"I'm in love with you."

It's not the first time he's said it. "You don't know me," I tell him desperately, "not really. Ohhh... You're in love with a version of me you've created..."

"I know you better than you think."

"I'm... aaahhh... grumpy and bitchy and irritable..."

"And kind and generous and... fuck... so sexy..."

"Henry..."

He gives up any attempt at going slow, lifts up onto his hands, and thrusts hard. "Look at me," he says as my eyelids flutter closed.

I shake my head, trying to ignore the white-hot heat of him branded on my brain.

He sinks a hand into my hair and pulls my head back. "Open your eyes," he demands. When I do, I'm staring right at him. His blue eyes are blazing.

"You're mine," he states fiercely.

My lips part, but it's just to release a cry as I come, my belly tightening as I clench around him with hard pulses. He continues to thrust me through it, and then I'm able to watch as his climax hits. Jesus, the man is magnificent. I dig my fingers into his biceps, and they're like boulders, ooh, and he swells inside me as he comes, pushing forward and stretching me to the max... Holy fuck, I think he's trying to spear me to the bed... He gives a deep, husky groan, and I can't deny the thrill of pleasure that ripples through me at the thought that I've done this—I've made him feel good, and to hope that I'm the best he's had, that no other girl has made him feel like this.

Then the intensity fades, and we both drift slowly back down to earth.

Well, I don't drift. I land as if I've jumped out of a plane at three thousand feet without a parachute, the realization of what I've done hitting me as if I've landed with a smack on the concrete.

Henry blinks and focuses on me. I wait for him to look smug and self-satisfied, but instead his expression turns tender, and he gives me the softest of kisses on the bindi between my brows before withdrawing and moving to the side.

I roll away from him, facing the window. The sky is now the color of buttercups, and I can hear the distant sound of traffic and people having breakfast out on the street at the café. A nice, normal day outside.

Inside me, though, a hurricane is tearing through me, destroying everything in its path. Last night was forgivable. Today is not. I work with Henry. He's a colleague. Oh... What have I done?

I need to go home, shower and change, and pull myself together before I have to go work. He does something to my brain, tugs it out of whack, the way a magnet makes your watch lose time. I can't think this close to him. I need space.

Without looking at him, I get up, pick up everything except the sari, go into the bathroom, shut the door, and lock it.

I stare at myself in the mirror, and my eyes widen. He's given me a hickey on my neck. I glare at it as I pull on my underwear, blouse, and petticoat. The blouse covers the bite, but only just. The damn man knew what he was doing. It's as obvious as if he's written his name on there with a permanent marker for all to see.

I wrestle my hair into a braid that hangs over my shoulder, also covering the hickey, then sit on the toilet and put my face in my hands. It's not his fault that my relationship with Cam is fucked up and that

I'd drunk too much last night, but clearly Henry isn't going to make my life easy.

You think I'm going to let you go now I know how much you want me? Now I know what you taste like? How it feels to be inside you?

An erotic shudder passes through me, and I let out an audible groan. I need to go home.

Gathering my courage, I unlock the door and go out into the bedroom.

I expect to find him looking at his phone, but he's standing by the window, lost in thought. He's wearing a pair of black track pants, but he's still bare chested. He's done that on purpose, I bet. He's like a melting ice cream. I just want to lick him all over.

"Hey," he says, turning. "Would you like a coffee?"

"No, thank you." I pick up the folded sari and shake it loose. "I need to get going."

He doesn't reply. Instead, he stands there and watches as I loop the fabric around my waist and tuck it into the petticoat, pin the end to my shoulder blade, then start pleating the rest of the material, folding it back and forth between my fingers. My face heats under his calm gaze, but I continue pleating, pin the material at my waist, then adjust it so it hangs properly. Finally, I go out into the living room, find my sandals, and sit to put them on.

When I look up, he's standing in the doorway, his hands in the pockets of his track pants. We study each other for a long moment.

"You gave me a hickey," I tell him, lifting my braid and pulling aside my blouse to show him.

His gaze dips to it. If I expected him to look ashamed or regretful, I realize I'm going to be disappointed. His lips curve up, just a tiny bit.

"You did that on purpose," I snap. "You know Cam's going to spot it."

His eyebrows rise. "What do you mean?"

"He can't exactly mistake it for something else, can he? I can't say that I walked into a cupboard or something."

He pushes off the door jamb and walks toward me. "Juliette," he says carefully, "tell me you're not going back to him."

I open my mouth, but nothing comes out. I close it, swallow, then say, "I'm going home. I don't know if he'll be there." He won't be. I'm sure he'll have stayed over at his parents' house with his brothers.

"And if he is?"

"I don't know. I need time."

"Time to what?"

"Decide what I'm going to do."

He runs his tongue over his top teeth and puts his hands on his hips. "If you expect me to sit back and let you go, you can think again."

"Henry…"

"I want you, and I'm going to have you if it's the last thing I do."

"Stop it," I snap, trying not to look at his bulging biceps. "I didn't promise you anything when we went to bed."

"You said you were mine."

"That didn't count."

His eyes blaze. "Yeah, you tell yourself that."

Oh God, I've made a terrible mistake.

I've sometimes wondered how Henry fits into his group of friends. He's not as driven as Alex, or as smart as James with his two degrees, or as innovative as Tyson. He is personable and reliable—you know if you ask Henry to do something, it'll be done, in half the time you expected, and in an organized and efficient fashion. He's head of HR at the company because he's great with people, able to put them at ease. But I suppose I've always thought of him as… I don't know, passive, I guess.

I couldn't have been more wrong. He's not hesitant, indifferent, or obedient. He's quiet, single-minded, and determined. And that's just on the outside. I'm pretty sure that on the inside his thoughts and emotions are crashing into each other like particles in a hadron collider.

"Henry," I plead, "please don't make this difficult for me."

He lifts his eyebrows. "Did you think I'd let you walk out of this door and run back into his arms?"

"This isn't *Fatal Attraction*! What are you going to do? Boil my rabbit in a pot?"

We glare at each other. He's never angry, and his obvious fury makes my eyes prick with tears. "Don't be cross with me," I whisper.

At that, his expression softens, and to my surprise he comes forward and puts his arms around me. I stand stiffly for a moment, then rest my cheek on his shoulder, and let him hug me.

"I'm not cross with you," he says. "Never with you. I'm angry at the situation. Cam's not the only one who's been damaged by this."

His words shock me. I've never considered that what happened to Cam has damaged me, too. After all, it didn't happen to me, right? And it's not as if he's ever gone into detail. I couldn't have coped with that. I've just had to deal with the fallout, like coping with radiation poisoning long after the bomb has detonated.

But of course, Henry's right. The effect it's had on Cam, and trying to heal him through years of trauma, has had a huge impact on me.

His arms are warm, and he smells so good. I want to undress, to go back to bed with him, and stay there all day.

I move back. "I have to go."

I walk to the door. When I turn back, he's still standing there, hands in his pockets.

"I'll see you later, at the office?" he says.

I nod, open the door, and leave.

Outside, it's a beautiful summer's day. I don't look up at the blue sky and bright sunshine, though. I hurry along the pavement, heading for the apartment, lost in my own world. I want a shower, hot as I can bear it, and a cup of coffee, so strong you can stand the spoon up in it. And then I want to sit on the balcony and think.

On the way, my phone buzzes with a text. I take it out and see Henry's name, and my heart leaps.

I burn for you. I need you. I love you. Just so you know.

I stop walking, my body heating all the way through. Jesus, Henry! I press the heel of my hand to my forehead, closing my eyes for a moment. I can't cope with this. I need to get home.

I walk fast, not seeing anything around me. When I reach the apartment, I take the elevator up, go along to the door, and let myself in.

I'm lost in thought, and I'm therefore doubly shocked when the first thing I see is Cam sitting at the dining table, looking miserable and defeated, nursing a mug of tea.

Well… shit.

Chapter Seven

Henry

I'm just getting out of the shower when my phone vibrates on the sink, announcing the arrival of a text. My heart leaps with the thought that it might be Juliette, but when I glance at the screen, it states my nephew's name, Rangi.

I pull up the text. *Hey, Unc, are you busy atm?*

I text back. *Just having a shower. What's up, you okay?*

He comes back, *Dont spose youve got time for brekky?*

I see him a lot, but it's unusual for him to contact me this early in the morning. I'm tired and grumpy and have a hangover, but Rangi is more important than my own comfort, so I reply, *Sure. The Flying Saucer, fifteen minutes?*

See you there, he says.

I go into the bedroom, stop, and glance at the bed. It's impossible not to think about what happened there last night and again early this morning. I stare at the pillow, thinking about the way I moved Juliette's long brown hair aside to reveal the soft skin of her neck. I recall the light-red bruise of the hickey and feel a mixture of emotions—shame, guilt, and smugness. I shouldn't have done it. But I'm glad I did. I want Cam to see it. I don't want to make her miserable, but the only way I'm going to get her is for her to end her present relationship, and if that helps… well, I'm not going to regret it.

She won't go back to him, surely? Not after what we had?

You're mine now. Say it.

I'm yours.

My heart was thrilled at the time. Now, the words sound hollow.

I need time.

Time to what?

Decide what I'm going to do.

I told her back in March that I'd broken up with Shaz. If she had feelings for me, surely she'd have made them obvious to me over the last nine months? Maybe it was just physical for her. One night, born out of misery and unhappiness, and she's intending to stay with Cam and continue to sit next to me in the boardroom as if nothing's happened?

Ah, shit. Henry, you fucking idiot. And if you refuse to accept it, it's going to be your fault that your working relationship is ruined.

I'm not going to think about it now. I'll have to wait and see what happens after she's spoken to Cam.

Even though this isn't a business breakfast, I decide to go straight to the office afterward, so I don a navy suit, put on my Apple watch, pocket my phone and wallet, and glance one last time at the bed.

I walk the short distance to the café, trying to put Juliette to the back of my mind.

The Flying Saucer is one of my favorite places to have breakfast. Posters hang on the walls of famous movies like *The Day the Earth Stood Still* and *Close Encounters of the Third Kind*, and models of UFOs and little green men adorn the counter and tables. They do a fantastic coffee and a terrific cooked breakfast, and I come here a lot.

Rangi is already outside when I walk up, and we exchange a bearhug. He's nowhere near as big as me, but he's tall for sixteen, and on the way to developing an impressive build. His black curly hair needs a cut, and his jeans are ripped in a couple of places, but maybe that's just fashionable, I don't know.

Christ, I sound old.

"Come on," I say to him gruffly, "what are you going to have? Full English?"

He nods eagerly, and we order two breakfasts, coffee for me, and a Coke Zero for him. Then we find a table near the window and sit opposite each other.

"You look great, bruh," he says, gesturing at my suit. "Smart as."

I smile. "Thanks."

"And you paid using your watch!"

I show him my Apple Watch, and how I can change the face to match the color of my tie.

"That's so dope," he says, impressed.

"I could get you one for Christmas," I suggest casually. "Be a good excuse."

But he shakes his head, the shutters coming down over his eyes, as they always do. "Nah, I'm good."

I don't say anything, leaning back as the waiter brings over my coffee and his Coke. I have a big mouthful, enjoying the rich, creamy taste of the latte.

"So," I say, "what's this about then? I was surprised to see you before midday."

Usually that would have earned me the finger, but he just leans on the table and fiddles with the top of the can. "I got a problem."

"Okay..."

He chews his bottom lip. Then, eventually, he says, "Ellie thinks she's pregnant."

I stare at him, frustration and exasperation sweeping over me. "You fucking idiot."

His shoulders droop. "I know," he mumbles. "I'm sorry."

His apology dissipates my anger. Ah, the poor kid called me because he needed to talk, and he thought I wouldn't pass judgment on him.

I sigh, thinking how young he looks, with his bum-fluff facial hair. Technically, he's old enough to have sex, and sixteen-year-olds can get married in New Zealand with consent from a Family Court Judge. But he's still a child really, too young to vote or buy cigarettes or alcohol.

"I'm sorry," I say gently, "I shouldn't have said that. You shocked me, that's all. I still think of you as the kid I used to let win at Mario Kart. I can't believe you're old enough to make a girl pregnant."

He gives a short laugh and rubs his nose.

"All right," I say. "Give me the details. How far gone is she?"

"What do you mean?"

"Well, what makes her think she's pregnant? Has she taken a test?"

"I don't think so."

"How late is her period, then?"

He looks embarrassed. "I dunno."

I survey him with a frown. "Bro, you do know how babies are made, right?"

"Yeah." He fidgets. "Sort of. We did all the sperm and egg thing in Health class."

"Well, that's something. You know about ovulation and periods?"

Another blank, embarrassed look.

I grit my teeth. My fucking brother should have explained this to him.

"Did you use a condom?" I ask.

"She said it was okay if I pulled out."

"Jesus, only if you've got a superhero's reflexes. That's really dangerous, because if you mistime it, the first fraction of ejaculate contains the most sperm." I roll my eyes at his baffled look. "The first spurt of cum has the Olympic medalists doing the crawl to the finish line."

He looks appropriately embarrassed. "Oh."

"And if a girl ever says she's using the rhythm method, which means she's calculating when she ovulates—when the egg leaves the ovary—just remember that sperm can live inside a woman's body for five days."

"Fuck."

"I know. That's why it's best to use a condom every time you have sex."

"Okay."

"Look, she needs to take a test. You can buy one in the pharmacy. I'll take you there after breakfast and get you a couple, and you can give them to her, just in case she can't get one herself." God help me if she hasn't told her parents and they find out I'm involved.

He frowns at me. "How do you know so much about all this?"

I lean back as the waitress arrives with our breakfasts. Once she's left, I add salt and pepper, then say, "Just because we're not the ones having the babies, we should still know how it all works. But in answer to your question, when I was with Shaz, we tried to have a baby for a few years. When it didn't happen, we had to work out the best time to have sex to make sure we did it in the fertile window—the time around ovulation. But it turned out I can't have kids."

He stares at me. "Seriously?"

"Yeah." I stare at the plate for a moment, trying not to think about the doctor's meetings, the monthly disappointments, the arguments, and the tears. Feeling tired, and very hungover, I stab the fried egg with my fork.

"I'm sorry, bro," he says. "I didn't know."

I shrug and cut into the sausage. "It was a long time ago now."

"Is that why you got divorced?"

"Partly, yeah."

"Couldn't you have, you know, adopted or something?"

"She wanted her own kids." I gesture at his plate. "Tuck in."

He cuts up his sausage, obviously still thinking. "How do you know you can't have kids?"

"The fertility clinic tests both of you, and they discovered I have a low sperm count."

"How do they do that? Do they inject your balls or something?" He winces.

"No. They test your cum."

"How?"

Jesus, it's too early in the day for this conversation. I hope nobody's listening. "You have to jerk off into a cup."

"Oh dude, seriously?"

"Yeah." I try not to laugh at his obvious dismay. "You can do it at home on your own. It's not like a doctor is standing there watching with a clipboard. You just have to take it to the clinic within sixty minutes. It's a bit embarrassing handing it over, but they're all very professional about it." I smile as he continues to look horror struck. "If you've made a girl pregnant, hopefully it means you won't have to do it."

"I'm so sorry," he says. "I didn't know you had to go through all that."

I shrug. "Anyway. Let's say Ellie does the test and she is pregnant. First of all, you should know that up to forty percent of pregnancies end in miscarriage, so even if the test is positive, it's possible that might happen."

He stops with his fork halfway to his mouth. "Forty percent?"

"Yeah. But let's assume that doesn't happen, and she stays pregnant. Have you talked about what she'll do?"

"What do you mean?"

"Whether she'll have the baby, Rangi. Or whether she'd want to terminate the pregnancy."

His eyes widen. "She wouldn't do that."

"She's sixteen. She has her whole life ahead of her, as do you. A baby is a huge tie. And even if she doesn't want one, her parents might pressure her to have an abortion because of that."

"They can't! You can't kill a baby just because you don't want it!"

"Ah, Rangi, come on, man. Don't go down that road. You have absolutely no say in it, so you need to keep those thoughts to yourself, do you hear me?"

He stares at me, breathing heavily. "It's my baby, too."

"It's not a baby, it's an embryo, and then at nine weeks it'll be a fetus, and it stays that way until it's born. Then it'll be *your* baby, and you'll get to do all the fun stuff like change nappies and pay child support. That's how it works."

He glares at me. "I don't care what you call it. It's alive. It's still murder."

Irritated now, I point my fork at him. "Stop it, and grow up. It doesn't matter what you or I think."

"Do you agree with abortion?"

"Our personal thoughts are irrelevant. We don't get to have an opinion on this."

"Why?"

"Because it's her body. She's the one who'd have to go through nine months of pregnancy. Who'd have to breastfeed it, care for it, and have her life turned upside down for it. Whatever happens to you, the effect it would have on her would be tenfold. So you don't get to influence her. It might feel unfair, but your role in it is over. It's the way it is, and part of being a man is learning to deal with it. Do you understand?"

He stares at his breakfast, chest heaving. Then, gradually, the fight goes out of him, and he flops back in the chair, covering his face.

"This fucking sucks," he says from behind his hands.

"Yeah." I pile the sausage, bacon, and a fried egg onto the toast, slap another bit on top, then bite into it like a sandwich. "Welcome to adulthood."

He lowers his hands and stares moodily at his Coke, then eventually sits up and continues eating his breakfast, copying me and making a bacon and egg sandwich.

"Are you going to tell your dad?" I ask.

"I might as well wait if she's going to get rid of it," he grumbles. Then he sighs. "He's going to fucking kill me."

I nod sadly.

"Will you be there?" he asks. "When I tell him?"

"Ah, bro. It'll just make it worse if he knows you told me before you told him."

"I guess." He picks at the bacon. "I hate that he's like that with you."

"Yeah, me too."

"Was he like it when you were kids?"

"Not so much. He was just your typical bossy older brother. He thought I was a pain in the arse. It was when I went to Greenfield that he really found it hard."

"You don't talk much about that," Rangi says.

"It makes your dad angry, so I don't tend to speak about it."

"You went there when you were fourteen, right?"

"Yeah."

"What made you go?"

"I was in trouble a lot at school. I'd been suspended three times for smoking weed, and then I fell in with a bad crowd, and got into trouble with the police. I had to attend a meeting with the school board who were going to decide whether to expel me. Grandpa died when I was twelve, so Grandma had to take me on her own. She was terrified, so our school counselor asked if there were any teachers I got on with who might attend with us. Well, I hardly ever went to school, but I did like my computer teacher, and he agreed to come."

Rangi's eyes are wide—I've never told him about this. "What did he say?"

"He stood up for me—the first time in my life anyone had done that. He said I was a good kid at heart and just needed positive role models and the opportunity to shine. He suggested they put in an application to a residential specialist school he knew of called Greenfield, and they agreed. It was the best thing he could have done. It turned my life around."

"What was it like?"

"It's up near Hanmer Springs, close to the mountains. It was run by a few people, but I mostly dealt with a deacon called Atticus."

"It was a church school?"

"No, but he believed that if we give boys strong guidance and positive role models, they'll grow up to be good men. He believed in developing kids' self-belief and sense of worth, and concentrating on their wellbeing through these creative, recreational, and social programs. I thought it was either going to be a military-style camp or some religious school that I knew I'd hate. But it wasn't anything like that. We went on something called adventure therapy, like a wilderness program in the mountains. We had team-building exercises, and a lot of group therapy. It sounds like bullshit, I know. We didn't—don't—talk in our family, and Atticus said that men should be encouraged to talk about their feelings, and our fears, hopes, and dreams."

"You liked it there?"

"Yeah, I loved it. Atticus had a knack of helping kids discover what they were good at. When he found out I loved computers, he asked the guy who taught our IT lessons to give me extra tuition in the evenings. I just took to it and flourished. I stayed until I was eighteen, and then they encouraged me to go to university. Nobody in my family had ever gone before, and of course we had no money, but they showed me how to apply for grants and loans, and explained that I'd have to work in the evenings. I wasn't sure I'd ever be able to pay all the loans back. But I studied all day and worked in a bar every evening, all the way through uni. And I met Alex and the others, and… well, you know the rest."

"And that's why Dad resents you?"

I nod. "I hadn't accounted for Tall Poppy Syndrome."

"Huh, yeah," he says.

In New Zealand and Australia, it's the name given to a tendency to criticize and resent those people who are successful, and it hit my family big time. Both my siblings are jealous that I had the opportunity to better myself. It doesn't matter that I've worked incredibly hard to get where I am. They see it as pure luck, and even though I've offered to share my success with them and help them financially, both of them have refused, saying they don't want charity, and don't need my help.

My brother, Philip, is especially resentful. Older than me by four years, he has four children, all by different women, and he struggles to support them with the money he earns from his job driving delivery trucks around the South Island. I want to help, but you can't force people to accept money or advice, so even though it grieves me to see him and his kids living on the edge of poverty, there's not much I can do about it.

I do try to help Rangi where I can. We have to be careful, because if Philip discovers I've bought Rangi anything or given him money, he hits the roof, and Rangi's the one who pays the price for his father's temper. But, unknown to my siblings, I've opened trust funds for all my nieces and nephews for when they come of age, so I'm hopeful that Rangi will at least have some money to set himself up with whatever he wants to do once he turns eighteen.

And he'll certainly need it if Ellie decides to keep the baby.

"Come on," I say, "eat up, and we'll go and get the pregnancy tests."

Rangi sighs and tucks into his sandwich. "I wish I could have gone to somewhere like Greenfield."

I finish my coffee, watching as he mops up some ketchup with the toast. It's not the first time I've had that thought. I broached the subject with Philip once, but he soon shot me down in flames, saying his boy was doing fine and didn't need some specialist school giving him ideas above his station. But Rangi reminds me of me at that age—he has a smart brain, but he's caught in a never-ending cycle where he feels he has few positive options, coming from an area of high unemployment, high crime, poverty, poor health, and a less-than-great education. I'd hoped I'd be a good role model for him, but Philip is determined that Rangi won't follow in my footsteps, and as the boy isn't mine, there's not much I can do, until Rangi comes of age, anyway.

This might be a turning point, though. Philip's going to be furious that Rangi has knocked a girl up, and it might be the one thing that convinces him that Rangi might make better life choices if he went away.

First things first, though. We need to work out whether Ellie is pregnant, and if she is, what she's going to do about it. Then we can start making decisions about their future.

As we leave the café and go out into the bright sunlight, I think about that young girl, whose whole future now rests on whether a line appears in a box on the test. I doubt that her parents are rolling in it. It's possible that they might agree to look after the baby while Ellie goes to university and finds a career, but I very much doubt that's going to happen.

As we walk down to the pharmacy, I think of Juliette, who did everything 'right'—she's smart and resourceful, she found a boyfriend with a successful job and stuck by him, she went to university and got herself a great job, and she's done exceptionally well for herself. And yet she's still unhappy. Life is always a struggle, but having a baby at such a young age will make it so much harder for Ellie, and not much fun for Rangi either.

The light's too bright and it's making my head ache. Relieved when we get to the pharmacy, I steer Rangi over to the right aisle, buy him two pregnancy tests and several packs of condoms.

"You pee on the stick and a line shows in that box if you're pregnant," I tell him.

"I pee on the stick?"

I think my head is going to explode. "No, I meant…" I sigh. "She does," I say as patiently as I can, telling myself that you're not born knowing these things. Was I ever that clueless, though? "Now fuck off and get it done. Call me when you have a result."

We have a final bearhug and I watch him go, then turn and head toward the car park. The last thing I feel like doing is working. Was

Cam there when Juliette went home? Has she spoken to him yet? What decision has she made? My heart begins racing, and my mouth goes dry. Please God, don't let her have gone back to him. Don't let me get so close, and then make me lose her again.

Chapter Eight

Juliette

Cam gets to his feet as I enter the apartment. He's wearing the clothes he wore last night, he's unshaven, and his hair's a mess. Before I can say anything, he walks across the room and puts his arms around me.

"Thank God," he whispers in my ear. "I thought you weren't coming home."

I stand there, stiff as an ironing board. Cam is not a hugger, and usually shrinks from physical affection. I've learned over the years that the small things mean more where he's concerned, like holding hands, for example. So this is huge for him, and shows the extent of his fear.

Normally I'd have lapped up this meager display of love, but all I can think about is Henry—lying in bed, stroking me, his fingers never leaving my skin; kissing me as if his life depended on it; moving inside me so gently, while his eyes watched me, drinking in my pleasure. I know I must smell of his cologne and the scent of his warm skin. I haven't brushed my teeth, and despite the mint I had, I can taste whisky, which I rarely drink. I feel coated in him, my pores oozing him.

After about ten seconds, and recognizing I'm clearly not going to respond, Cam drops his arms and moves back. We stand there and stare at each other for a long time.

"Where were you?" he asks eventually.

Such a small question. With such a potentially lethal response.

My whole future rests on what I say next. Tell the truth. Or lie. It's such a simple decision. But the pressure of answering feels as heavy as uranium, and just as dangerous. The words in my mouth are nuclear bombs ready to drop and blow us both sky high. I've constructed them. I've loaded them onto the plane. Now all I need to do is press the button to release the doors, watch them fall, and observe their destruction.

But I can't. I don't want to be responsible for detonating them and destroying our relationship. I'm a coward, and I'm frightened of change. Things aren't right between me and Cam, but I have a good life, and I'm not sure I'm willing to risk everything for Henry. He's a wonderful guy, and he should have women clambering over each other to get to him. But the thing is… I want children. And Henry can't give them to me.

There are options, of course. Sperm donors and IVF and adoption. But it's one thing to be in a partnership and discover you can't have children. It's another to enter a relationship willingly with that knowledge.

And anyway, although last night was amazing, I don't know whether Henry and I are suited. Whether we'd last once the first blaze of passion wore off. He's so quiet and private, and I know very little about him. He might drive me mad when I get to know him. I might drive him mad, despite his declaration that he's in love with me. It's a huge risk when I'm already in a stable relationship with a man I love.

Do I still love Cam? I'm not sure, but I did once.

"I stayed in a hotel," I say, which isn't a lie. *Yeah, Juliette, you tell yourself that.* "I didn't want to come home."

He shoves his hands in his pockets and looks at the floor. "I'm sorry," he says.

It's a rare thing for him to say. "I appreciate the apology," I tell him. "But it doesn't make everything right."

"I know."

We stand six feet apart, but it feels like six miles.

"I didn't think you were going to be here when I came home," I admit.

"I only stayed at Mum's for an hour. I kept thinking about you. I texted you again, and I tried to call, but it kept going to voicemail."

"I turned my phone off. I'd had enough."

He nods as if to say he understands why.

Silence falls between us. My neck suddenly tingles, as if Henry is reminding me of the love bite he placed there. I wrap my arms around my middle, full of shame and guilt and misery.

"It's the first time you've ever not come home," Cam says eventually.

"It's the first time I've not wanted to."

Our eyes meet. Something shifts between us, as if the tectonic plates are moving beneath our feet. He's realizing how bad this is. How fragile our relationship is right now.

"Are you staying?" he asks.

"I need to have a shower and go to work."

"I don't mean that. I mean are you staying with me? Or are you leaving me?" His brows draw together.

My throat tightens. "I don't know."

Silence falls between us once more. His eyes have lit with fear again.

"I don't want you to go," he says eventually.

"Then you should be nicer to me." I mean to sound sassy, but a little hiccup in my voice makes it come out pathetic.

"I know." He runs a hand through his hair and sighs.

"I know you have issues, but you can't keep taking out your frustration and misery on me, Cam."

"I know."

"I deserve better."

"Yeah, I know. It's all my fault. I'm an arsehole, and I don't deserve you. I deserve to be on my own."

"No," I exclaim, "don't do this. You always do this. You always turn it so it's about you."

"But I'm the one at fault."

"I don't care. I don't want to talk about what you've done wrong and how you need help." I'm getting hysterical, but this argument is following the same pattern it always does, and I don't know how to stop it. "This is about me. What *I* want. What *I* need."

"All right. Tell me, then. Tell me what you want me to do."

I swallow hard. What you want *me* to do. It's still about him.

If you were my girl, I'd treat you like a queen.

Tears rush into my eyes. "I'm going to have a shower," I say, and I walk out of the room. I go into the bathroom, close the door, and lock it. Then I sit on the toilet seat and burst into tears.

I cry for a good five minutes, and then the sobs finally die down. Standing, I switch on the shower, then take off my sari, trying not to think about Henry unwrapping me with such obvious delight. I strip off the petticoat and my underwear, then get into the shower.

Slowly, I wash my hair, remembering his fascination with how long it is, and how soft. Then I wash my body with the shower puff, trying not to remember his hands moving across my skin in the early sunlight.

I feel as if I'm slowly washing him away, and the thought makes me so sad that I start crying again.

When I finally come out of the shower, I dry myself, then stare at my reflection. I have shadows under my eyes, and I look miserable. I have to get ready for work, and I don't want Henry or anyone else to think I've been crying.

It would be easier to phone in sick, but today is the office Christmas party and officially the last day of work before Christmas, and I have to go in. So I do my face carefully, using the time to calm down, applying foundation and powder, outlining my eyes with kohl and black mascara, then applying a scarlet bindi sticker between my brows.

I try not to think of the way Henry kissed me there.

I look at the hickey on my neck and remember his deep groan as he sucked the tender skin.

Ah… jeez.

Finally, I dry my hair, then twirl it into a tight rope and pin it up in a ballerina-style bun. It's a harsh look, especially with the way I look so wan with big dark eyes, but it feels appropriate today.

When I'm done, wearing a bathrobe and turning up the collar to hide the hickey, I unlock the bathroom door and go out into the bedroom.

Cam is there, as I knew he'd be, sitting on the edge of the bed, leaning forward, his hands in his hair, although he straightens when I come out.

"Are you okay?" he asks. "I heard you crying."

"I'm fine." I collect a scarlet sari from the drawer—I'll take it with me and put it on before the party. This morning I'll just wear a top and leggings. I retrieve them and some fresh underwear, and go back into the bathroom to put them on, not wanting to do it with Cam watching.

When I come out, his gaze skims down the tight white top with its high collar and the black leggings. "You're losing weight," he says.

I sit on the edge of the bed and pull on a pair of flat sandals, not answering. When I stand and go to walk out, he moves to intercept me.

"You look stunning," he murmurs, tucking a stray strand of hair behind my ear. "You're so fucking beautiful."

"Don't." I step backward, away from his touch. It's ridiculous, but I feel disloyal to Henry. *I'm so fucking in love with you*, he told me. Oh, I've got myself into such a mess.

Cam and I study each other for a long moment. Seven years is a long time to spend with one person, and I know his face almost as well as my own. He's a handsome man, and I've always loved his thick dark-blond hair, his Roman nose, and his sensual mouth. Do I still love him, though? Or has he killed all the feelings I had for him?

"Have I lost you?" he asks softly, pain in his eyes.

My eyes prick with tears, but I fight not to let them fall. "I don't know."

"So there's still hope?"

"I don't know. I'm angry, Cam. I know you have problems. And I'm sorry for what happened to you. But you seem to resent me for it all, and I can't deal with that."

He shoves his hands into the pockets of his jeans and hunches his shoulders. "I know. I'm sorry."

"Yeah, we're all sorry, but they're just words. It doesn't make it right."

"I know."

"Actions are what matter. This isn't what I want out of a relationship."

I just want to be…
Worshiped?
Maybe a tiny bit.
You should be.
I want to be wanted. To be desired. Just once, for it to be about me.
It should always be about you.

"I want to feel as if I'm the most important thing in my partner's life," I say desperately. "I know maybe that sounds selfish and egotistical, but I'm tired of being the last thing on your To Do list."

"That's fair." He moves a little closer. "Let me try and put it right."

I frown. We've argued a lot in the past, but this is the first time he's ever accepted that he needs to change. That he's realized I might actually walk away.

"Don't throw away seven years," he says. "We've worked hard to get where we are."

He's right. I shouldn't throw away seven years with him for Henry. Two and a half thousand days versus one night? The math doesn't work.

But the reality is that Henry made me feel wanted and valued last night, more than Cam has done in all the time we've been together.

"I've taken you for granted," Cam says. "I've taken what we have for granted. I won't do it again. Just let me try to put it right."

I bite my bottom lip. "I don't know. I've got to get to work." I walk past him into the living room.

He follows me out. "Just tell me you'll come home tonight," he says. "Please."

I pick up my purse and keys and head for the door.

"Please," he says again. "I'll cook dinner. I'd like to talk. Just… come home."

I hesitate with my hand on the door handle. I've invested seven years in this man, and I don't want to admit that it was all a waste of time. Maybe he can change, now he knows I'm not prepared to continue being his metaphorical punchbag.

Is this what I want? Right now, I can't think clearly.

"All right," I say, because I can't think how else to answer. I live here. Where else would I go?

"Thank you."

I go out, and close the door behind me.

*

When I get to my car, I'm shaking, and I sit there for a few minutes, trying to recover. While I'm there, my phone buzzes with a message. My heart leaps as I think it might be Henry, but it's just my mum, sending me a song on Spotify that she thinks I'd like. She adds a message, *How did the party go?*

I let out a long sigh, then text back, *Um…*

Mum: *Oh dear. What happened?*

Me: *Cam and I had an awful fight, and he left the bar.*

Mum: *Oh no. What about?*

Me: *Oh, just stuff. But I was miserable, and I got drunk, and…*

Mum: *AND WHAT?*

Me: *I went back to Henry's hotel.*

She knows all the guys I work with, and I think she's also guessed that I like Henry.

Mum: *OMG what did you do?*

Me: *You want me to draw a picture?*

Mum: *JULIETTE!*

Me: *Don't shout. I have a hangover.*

Mum: *Are you okay?*

My eyes water. *Not really.*

Mum: *Aw, taupuhi.*

It's Māori for darling, and it's what she always calls me.

Me: *I'll be okay. I'm just nervous about seeing him at work.*

Mum: *Was it… you know… good?*

Me: *It was pretty terrific, Mum. He told me he's not going to let me go easily, either.*

Mum: *How do you feel about that?*

Me: *Mixed. I went home thinking it was all over between me and Cam, and he was there.*

Mum: *Did you tell him?*

Me: *No. I couldn't. He said he's sorry for making it hard for me, and he wants us to try to work it out. Now I don't know what to do.*

She doesn't come back for a minute. I sit resting my elbow on the windowsill and my head on my hand, feeling miserable.

Eventually, a text pings up.

Mum: *You remember what I told you when you were a teenager?*

I give a small smile. *Find a man who smudges your lipstick, not your mascara?*

Mum: *That's right. Now you just need to work out which one's which.*

I swallow hard. I have no idea. At the moment I feel like bawling my eyes out when I think of either of them.

Me: *I've got to get to work.*

Mum: *All right. Let me know how you get on.*

Me: *Will do.*

I toss the phone onto the passenger seat, start the car, and head into the traffic.

By the time I get to Kia Kaha, it's gone eight thirty. I park out the front, next to Henry's precious BMW. He doesn't let anyone drive it but me. Jesus, why I didn't I realize what that meant before now?

I'm in love with you. I have been since the first time we met.

My head's pounding. I need some Panadol. I have some in my office. I get out, lock my car, and, carrying my bag with my sari, head for the building.

Everything in Kia Kaha reminds me of Henry. I walk into the lobby and look at the beautiful stained-glass windows, the painting of Ranginui and Papatūānuku on the wall, the fountain surrounded by green plants and rocks, and feel as if he's all around me, watching me. It makes a shiver run down my back.

The senior management team always meets first thing for a brief catchup to discuss the day ahead. Normally I'd walk past the boardroom to get to my office, but I know Henry will probably already be there, and if he's not, he's going to be in his office, so instead I turn left and skirt the main secretarial office and head for the treatment rooms.

Once I'm in my office with proper brick walls, I feel as if I can breathe a bit easier. I say good morning to Rose, the secretary who works for the physios, drop my bag off, make myself a coffee, and sit behind my desk to check through the morning's post and my emails, although I end up just staring into space.

I jump when Rose puts her head in and tells me they've all gathered and I should head for the boardroom.

Collecting my cooling coffee and laptop, my heart hammering on my ribs, I walk past the guys' empty offices.

We don't have designated places around the boardroom table, but we often sit in the same seats—human habit, I guess. Alex is at the head of the table with his puppy, Zelda, lying by his feet, Tyson is sitting next to James on Alex's right, and Henry is, as usual, sitting on the other side, with the chair next to him vacant.

Summoning my courage, I go through the automatic doors into the room and say, "Morning guys."

"Morning," they all say back, watching as I approach the table. I pull out the chair next to Henry and sit, then fuss Zelda as she comes up to say hello.

Tyson clears his throat. "I was just talking about the Sydney conference."

I nod and open my laptop, type in my password, pull up Word, and open a new document. I put my phone on the table and adjust the angle of it. Then, finally, I glance at Henry.

He's watching me. As he sees me look up, he smiles. Oh my God, he looks amazing. He's wearing my favorite suit of his, a navy British-cut, with a white shirt and a light-blue tie. He looks crisp and formal, like a fucking soldier. *Thank you for your service, sir.* Ahhh…

I glance around the table. James is talking to Tyson, but Alex meets my gaze as I look at him.

He lifts an eyebrow.

My face burns as if I've been lying in the sun for a fortnight. Jesus, talk about a guilty complex.

He notices, and his lips curve up, just a tiny bit. Embarrassed at the thought that he knows what happened, I tear my gaze away and study my laptop. Did Henry tell him? Or is he just assuming?

"Would you like a coffee?" Henry asks me softly.

I look back up at him. I still have a third of a cup left, but it's lukewarm. "Yes, please," I murmur.

He gets to his feet, goes over to the table against the glass wall, and starts making me one. I fidget with my phone, trying not to think about how Cam never offers to make me a drink unless he's having one himself.

Henry brings the cup back and places it before me, and takes his seat again. He picks up the Rubik's cube and completes it while James and Tyson talk. Then, quietly, he places the finished cube on the table between us.

It's just a toy, a plastic cube, but I know it's a peace offering, as tender and gentle as a single rose. Without looking at Alex, I can see him watching us. If I ignore the cube, he'll know something's up. But accepting it means I'm accepting the gesture. I'll be telling Henry that things are all right between us.

I should ignore it. Tell him without having to say the words that things aren't all right, that I regret what we've done. But I can't. It's pathetic and needy, but I want him on my side. I don't want him to stop looking at me as if he wants to undress me with his eyes. I want his support, his affection. It's dog in the manger, and I hate myself for it, but I can't ignore the cube any more than fly.

Swallowing hard, I pick it up and begin turning the sides, muddling up the colored cubes. I hear his soft sigh, and I know he understands. I can smell his cologne, and almost feel his body warmth. Only hours ago, he was kissing me, and he was inside me, telling me he's in love with me.

Oh God, what am I going to do?

Chapter Nine

Henry

Christ, what on earth happened when Juliette got home this morning? She's scraped all that magnificent hair up into a tiny, tight bun—I have no idea how she's managed that—and she's wearing black leggings and a white top that clings to her figure, revealing that she's definitely lost weight over the past few months. The top has a collar she's turned up, presumably to hide the hickey I gave her. She looks pale and thoroughly miserable. I can't help but feel relieved that it probably means all isn't rosy between her and Cam, but I feel bad that I might be the cause of some of her unhappiness.

James and Tyson are talking, but Alex is watching her as she turns the sides of the cube. He looks at me then, and frowns.

Feeling like a naughty schoolboy, I study my laptop, pretending to find whatever article I was reading fascinating.

"Do you think it's worth us actually taking one of the patients to Sydney?" Tyson asks. "Juliette, what do you think?"

She's silent, and we all look at her to find her lost in thought, still turning the Rubik's Cube.

When I first came into the boardroom this morning, James was making himself a coffee. He looked fed up, and when he'd finished stirring his drink, he tossed the spoon onto the table with a clatter that illustrated his frustration before he saw me.

"How are you doing?" he asked me.

"As well as you, by the look of it," I replied.

"Yeah," he said. That was the extent of our conversation, but it was enough to tell me that last night with Aroha hadn't gone as planned, either.

Now, he glances at Alex, who's tapping on the table with his pen, then back at me, grimacing as he silently acknowledges our shared culpability.

Tyson clears his throat. "Juliette?"

Her head snaps up. "Oh. Sorry?"

"I was just wondering if it was worth taking one of your patients to Sydney for the conference? First-hand experience, you know?"

"Oh, um, maybe. Although a series of case studies might be less trouble."

"Yeah, true."

She finishes turning the cube and slides it across to me. I glance at her hand, with its long, slender fingers, remembering how they slipped beneath my Henley and splayed on my back, exploring my muscles as I kissed her. She meets my gaze, and we stare at each other for about ten seconds as my heart rate slowly climbs.

Then she lowers her eyes. Sighing inwardly, I pick up the cube and start doing it again.

Alex begins going through what's happening today, and I try to listen, but it's impossible to concentrate with Juliette beside me, silent and obviously unhappy. It doesn't help matters when a text pings up on my phone from Rangi.

I pick it up and glance at it. It just says two words. *She's pregnant.*

I sigh, and only realize it was audible when James says, "What's up?"

"I saw my nephew this morning. He told me he thought his girlfriend was pregnant. I bought him a test, and he's just texted to say it was positive."

They all groan, and Juliette says, "Oh no."

"How old is he again?" James asks.

"They're both sixteen."

"Silly fucker," Tyson says.

"Yeah. He's a good lad, and he's not stupid, but honestly, the education these schools are giving them… He seemed puzzled as to how it happened, then told me he used the withdrawal method."

They all snort.

"And then when I bought him the pregnancy test, he asked whether he had to pee on the stick or whether she did."

That makes them all laugh. It's good to see Juliette smiling.

"What's he going to do?" she asks.

"Dunno yet. I'll go and see him later."

"Okay, I don't have anything else," Alex says, and the others shake their heads.

"The party starts at one," Juliette states. "You're all expected to be there."

"Yeah, yeah." James gathers his stuff and heads out.

Tyson watches him go, then says, amused, "What happened with him and Aroha last night?"

"Don't know," Alex replies. "He won't talk about it."

Tyson chuckles, closes his laptop, and leaves the room.

Juliette and I stand, but Alex says, "Henry, a moment, please?"

Juliette picks up her laptop and, without saying anything else, follows Tyson out. The doors slide closed behind her.

I look at Alex. He's leaning back in his chair, turning his pen in his fingers.

"Are you still on to play Santa at the party?" he asks.

I sigh. "Yeah."

"Okay."

I look at my laptop screen for a moment. He doesn't say anything, just continues to watch me. Eventually, I lean back and meet his eyes.

"What happened last night?" he asks.

"It's none of your business."

"It is if it affects Kia Kaha." He gives me a direct look. "You know the company's policy on relationships at work. We have to set an example to the staff, and it doesn't look great if we're having one-night stands or getting sued for sexual harassment."

"Jesus Christ. Juliette's not going to sue me."

"I'm just saying we need to be careful."

I get up and close my laptop. "I'm Head of HR. If I need to report anything, I'll have a meeting with myself."

He points his pen at me. "Stop with the sarcasm and sit down. This conversation isn't over."

The senior management team are all on equal footing at Kia Kaha. It's true that it's kind of unspoken that Alex is in charge, but we've never discussed it, and we've certainly never voted him as our leader.

I'm older than him, too, even if it's only by a few months, and I bristle. "Don't fucking tell me to sit down like a five-year-old."

"Stop acting like a five-year-old and I won't treat you like one."

"You really want to do this? I'm two inches taller than you and about twenty pounds heavier."

"Yeah," he says sarcastically, leaning forward, "because what we need to do in a boardroom with glass walls is wrestle like a couple of teenagers."

We glare at each other. Then, eventually, he leans back and says mildly, "Anyway, I dance like a butterfly. You'd have to catch me first."

That makes me give a short laugh. Blowing out a breath, I lower into the chair, flop back, and give a heavy sigh.

"So it *was* a one-night stand?" he asks.

"No," I reply.

He lifts an eyebrow.

"Probably not," I add. "The jury's out."

His expression softens. "What happened with Cam?"

"I thought it was over. So did she, I think. I haven't spoken to her this morning, so I don't know what happened when she got home. I'll go and talk to her in a minute."

"Is that a good idea?"

"Alex, I really don't need your help with this."

"Oh, I think we both know that's not true. Look, don't come down too heavy on her."

I remember my words to her: *You think I'm going to let you go now I know how much you want me?* I try not to wince.

"I'm not going to let her slip through my fingers when I know she wants to be with me," I tell him.

"She's been with the guy a long time. And we both know Juliette. If you want her to do something, the best way is to make her think she came up with the idea herself."

My irritation fades. I thought Alex was only concerned about the company, but I should have known better.

"Just be careful," he says softly. "I know how you feel about her, and this isn't going to end well if you try and force her hand."

I sulk, but I know he's right. "When did you become all wise and holier than thou?" I grumble.

"Last night," he says, and smiles.

My eyebrows rise. "Did you and Missie..."

He shakes his head. "I walked her home, and I was the perfect gentleman. Mainly because her mother and son were in the house." We exchange wry smiles. Dating was a lot easier when we were at uni!

"She's coming over for dinner tomorrow, though," he adds, and his eyes sparkle.

"Ah, I'm pleased for you, bro. Are you asking her to the wedding?" Our friend Damon is getting married after Christmas, and we're all flying up to attend it. All our invitations state we're welcome to bring a plus-one.

"Yeah, I might well do that," he says. "What about Juliette? Do you think she'll bring Cam?"

I go cold at the thought. "Jesus, I hope not." Frowning, I get to my feet. "I need to talk to her."

"All right. Like I said, give her space. You might have to wait for her to sort things out."

I walk to the doors, then hesitate. "Waiting isn't my strong point."

"I've waited a whole year for Missie," he says, gathering up his things. "Hardest thing I've ever had to do, so I sympathize, but she'll be worth it."

"Hmm." I run my tongue over my top teeth, then head along the corridor.

I want to tell him that I've waited six years for Juliette, but it's not the same as he and Missie. I was with Shaz for much of that time, and Juliette was with Cam, so it wasn't waiting in the truest sense. And although I told Juliette that my marriage was over in March, there were no signs of her leaving Cam, so I assumed she wasn't interested in me.

Technically, I haven't been waiting for that long. So why does it fucking feel like it?

I drop my laptop off in my office, then continue to the treatment block. She might be in an appointment, in the middle of strapping a patient into MAX or THOR—the robotic exoskeletons. But as I approach the area where the physios are based, I hear her in her office talking to Rose, and my pulse picks up.

I stop in the doorway and lean on the door jamb, waiting for her to finish her conversation. She doesn't spot me at first, and it's only when Rose smiles at me that Juliette turns. I watch her inhale sharply, then drop her gaze to her desk and shuffle papers about as she tries to gather her wits. Rose gives me an amused look, obviously realizing something's going on, then says, "I'll get that typed up by midday."

"Thanks," Juliette says. "Um…" She looks up in alarm as Rose goes to leave.

"Yes?" Rose asks.

Juliette obviously can't think of a way to keep her in the room, and mumbles, "Nothing."

Rose meets my eyes, tries not to laugh, and goes out.

I close the door behind her, and Juliette's eyes widen. "Don't do that," she says. "People will talk."

"No, they won't. We have meetings all the time. That's your guilty conscience talking."

She glares at me, then shuffles her papers again. "Probably," she admits grumpily.

I walk over to the window. This office looks out onto what we call The Square—an appropriately named area of lawn with carefully tended trees and flowerbeds, and garden benches where members of staff sometimes have lunch. I take the cord to the vertical blinds and pull it to close them.

"What are you doing!" she exclaims.

"Relax. I'm not about to do you on the desk." I tip my head to the side and study her, taking in her small, high breasts in the tight top, and her shapely thighs in the leggings. "Probably."

"Henry!" She walks around the desk so it's between us.

I chuckle. Then my smile fades at her obvious distress. "What happened this morning?" I ask, sitting on the edge of her desk.

She wraps her arms tightly around herself, like a shield. "Cam was there when I got home."

Fuck. "What did he say?"

"He asked where I'd been." She swallows hard. "I told him I'd stayed in a hotel because I didn't want to go home." She meets my gaze for a moment, then looks down at the floor.

She didn't tell him about me.

"You're staying," I say flatly. A statement, not a question.

She doesn't reply for a moment. Then she says, "I think it's the first time he's ever understood that I might leave. He said he realized he'd taken me for granted, and he wants to try to put it right."

I don't say anything, my heart sinking.

"He asked me not to throw away the seven years we've had together. And he asked me to go home tonight, so we can talk some more."

Silence falls between us. I try to slow my breathing as my chest heaves. She stares miserably at the floor.

Eventually, I say, "You don't look like a woman whose partner has told her she should be worshiped. That he's going to treat her like a queen."

She gives me an exhausted, wry look.

"Has he said he won't ask you to do the things you don't want to do in bed?" I get up and walk around the desk to stand before her. She doesn't move away, but she does study me warily.

I fix her gaze with mine. "Did he tell you that he wants you? Desires you? That he's going to devote every minute to loving you?"

She flinches as I turn her words from last night on her, but doesn't answer, which informs me that he hasn't said anything like that.

Instead, she says, "He needs me."

"Are you prepared for things to continue the way they were?" I demand.

"No," she says.

"Do you think he can change?"

"I don't know." She presses the heel of her hand between her brows, over her bindi. "I just feel that I have to try. I owe him that, don't I?"

"Are you really asking me?"

She gives a short laugh and lowers her hand. "No."

"You've given him seven years and plenty of chances to change, and to treat you the way you want—no, you deserve—to be treated. But he hasn't. You don't owe him anything."

She trembles, giving a shaky sigh, and rubs her nose. I'm so frustrated, I want to shake her, to force some sense into her. But instead I can only stand there, aching for her, feeling as if she's on a raft caught by a riptide that's going to sweep her away.

I wait for her to turn, or even order me to leave.

But she doesn't. Instead, she moves forward the short distance that's separating us and rests her forehead on my shoulder.

Shocked, I stand there for a few seconds, not sure how to respond. As she doesn't move away, though, I slowly lift my arms around her.

Moving up close, she turns her head and rests her cheek on my shoulder. Aaahhh… she feels small and slight in my arms, and I feel an overwhelming urge to protect her.

I rub her back, moving my hand in a circle, and she nestles against me and sighs, almost purring. It strikes me then—this girl is touch-starved, hungry for affection, obviously having had to live for years with a man who abhors physical contact.

And that's how I'm going to win. Because I have oceans of tenderness and love to give her.

"Ah, baby," I murmur, continuing to stroke her back. "I'm sorry you're having to go through this."

"It's so hard…" she whispers.

"I know."

In business, if there's something I want, I'm not shy in using my money, my influence, my position, or my physical size to walk in and take it. But I think of what Alex said: *don't come down too heavy on her*. I can't force her hand. So I'm going to have to come at it some other way.

"I'm sorry about the things I said yesterday," I tell her softly. "I'm used to getting what I want, and I don't like being told no."

She gives a small laugh. "I know. And I'm really sorry too. I'm just so mixed up. I've liked you for so long, and last night was amazing. But I shouldn't have done it. I… I don't want to lose you."

I push aside my instinct to force her to choose between us. If I do that, I'm pretty sure she's going to choose him.

Instead, I say, "You won't lose me. I'm frustrated because I think we'd be really good together, but I'm not about to sever all connection with you if you don't leave him. I'm your friend first. I'll always be there for you."

Is it true? I don't know. If she stays with him, I think something inside me might actually die, withering away like a tree without sunshine or rain. I don't know if I can continue to work beside her every day, knowing she's going home to a guy who doesn't love her the way she wants to be loved.

But right now, she needs my love and support, and I have to be the bigger guy.

I'm six-foot-four; I'm always the bigger guy. I'm fucking used to it.

"Oh God," she says. She turns her head and rests her forehead on my shoulder again. Then she moves back. Her eyes are wet, and she dashes the tears away angrily. "You don't mean that," she snaps.

"I do."

"I don't believe you. You're not that honorable."

"Hey, I'm exactly that honorable."

"Henry! Stop it! Stop being nice to me. I can't deal with it. I can't think when you're close to me." She backs away. "You do something to my brain—you scramble the signal." She presses the heel of her hand to her temple. "There's more to a relationship than heat and passion and excitement."

Anger flares inside me. "Yeah, you keep telling yourself that."

"Not everything is about sex."

I walk up to her, and continue walking as she backs away, until she bumps into the wall. I press up against her, and she gasps as I lower my head so my mouth is a fraction of an inch above hers.

"Are you sure?" I demand.

She studies my mouth, moistening her lips with the tip of her tongue.

"Tell me you don't want me to kiss you," I ask roughly. "Tell me to stop."

A little sound escapes her, a combination of a sigh and a whimper, but she doesn't speak. She just lifts her gaze to mine, tears glimmering on her lashes, a helpless look in her eyes.

I crush my lips to hers. She lifts her arms around my neck, sliding her hand into my hair, and moans, opening her mouth. I slide my tongue against hers. Ahhh… fire shoots through me, giving me an erection in seconds, and I thrust my hips, rocking so I press into her soft flesh through her thin leggings.

Her fingers clench in my hair. I cup her breast and rub a thumb across her nipple, and she shudders. At that point, I'm completely oblivious to anything but her. My whole world has shrunk to this office, this corner, this woman, and I want to be inside her more than I've ever wanted anything in my entire life. I don't know what I'm expecting to happen—whether I intend to turn and lock the door and take her there, on the desk, or up against the wall—I'm not thinking rationally, or sensibly, and I'm certainly not thinking about Alex and his cautionary words.

But suddenly she tugs my hair and tears her mouth away from mine, and she gasps, "Stop!"

I step back, dropping my hands. My chest heaves with deep, uneven breaths. She dashes the back of her hand across her mouth, looking up at me with accusatory eyes.

"You need to leave," she whispers.

I rest both hands on my hips and glare at her. I don't want to go. I want to stay and fix it. I want to kiss her until she admits she loves me and we're meant to be together.

But I know I've behaved badly. This isn't the way. I promised I was her friend first, and I'd be there for her. *Is this helping her, Henry?*

"I'm sorry," I start saying, but she turns and walks away.

"Please go," she says. "I've got work to do."

I hesitate. Then I turn, open the door, and walk out, closing the door behind me.

Chapter Ten

Juliette

Oh God.

I collapse into my chair, shaking all over, put my elbows on my desk, and cover my face with my hands.

I can still feel the heat from his lips, as if they've seared into my flesh. This guy is going to give me third-degree burns all over if I don't stop kissing him.

I'm so ashamed. I was just starting to convince myself that last night was a terrible mistake and that it would never, ever happen again, and then Henry comes into my office and within five minutes I'm letting him kiss me senseless.

What the hell has happened to my willpower? I normally have a lot of self-discipline—when I decided I was going to give up sugar for a month I didn't touch a grain for the whole twenty-eight days. When I agreed a few years ago to run a half-marathon for charity, I got up at five a.m. every morning to train. So why does it all fly out the window whenever Henry West walks into the room?

The problem is that I told myself I only slept with Henry to punish Cam, but it's not true. I like him. And I like the way he makes me feel. I love the way he looks at me. I love the things he says to me. I like everything about him.

Find a man who smudges your lipstick, not your mascara.
Now you just need to work out which one's which.

I press my fingers to my lips. It's not that easy, Mum. There are other factors to take into account.

I'm not a Hindu *per se*, but my father taught me about Hindu beliefs as I was growing up, and they took seed inside me. Hinduism tells us of the importance of *Ahimsa*—the principle of non-violence and compassion towards all living beings. We're not supposed to cause physical or mental harm, and we should be kind and empathetic to others. It also teaches us *Dharma*—the moral and ethical duties and responsibilities we should follow, which include righteousness, duty, and proper conduct.

Is it *Dharma*, Juliette, to cheat on your partner with your colleague?

Does *Ahimsa* involve doing something that will hurt Cam terribly if he finds out?

Not everything is about sex.
Are you sure?

My phone buzzes, announcing a text. I glance at it and see Cam's name. Oh, holy fuck. I lean forward and bang my forehead on the desk. These men are going to drive me insane.

I pick up the phone. Hopefully it'll be a loving message that'll bring me to my senses.

How does cheesy pasta sound for dinner tonight?

From Cam, that's as loving as a romantic message. But it doesn't have the same effect on me as the text Henry sent this morning. I pull it up.

I burn for you. I need you. I love you. Just so you know.

Disgusted with myself, I toss the phone on the desk and lean back in my chair. I'm the worst human being that ever lived. In fact, I'm not even a human being. I'm an insect. Or an amoeba, floating in primordial soup and somehow still managing to get its knickers in a twist over the amoeba swimming next to it.

The intercom beeps, and I lean forward and press the button. "Yes?"

"Your first appointment is here, Juliette."

I sigh. They're early. I need to get my head into gear. "Thanks, Rose." I get to my feet, grab my white coat, and pull it on. It's my last day in the office today. I have two appointments this morning, but then this afternoon it's the office party, and after that we break for Christmas. I won't have to see Henry for a few days—not until we go to Damon's wedding. Cam is supposed to be coming with me to that. I grimace. Henry is not going to be happy about it, and Cam isn't exactly going to be ecstatic either. He doesn't really like any of the guys I work with, Henry least of all.

I'm not going to think about it now. Leaving the office, I head for the main treatment room, and decide to lose myself in work.

*

I keep myself busy all morning. At twelve-thirty, I take my sari to the bathroom, pin it in place, touch up my makeup, and then head for the main office workroom. The food has arrived, and the office staff has laid out the sandwiches, sushi, hot savories, mince pies, Christmas cake, and a hundred other things on several tables, along with bottles of bubbly and orange juice. Christmas music is already playing, and laughter and conversation rings throughout the building.

At one o'clock, I round up James, Tyson, and Alex, who are all still working, and bully them into the workroom. They start circulating, thanking the staff for their hard work during the year.

I've organized the Secret Santa, and not long after, Henry appears wearing a Santa suit and begins handing out the named presents. I move around the room, avoiding him, but of course eventually he has to come over to me.

"Here you go," he says softly, handing me a present with my name on it.

I don't look at him. "Thank you."

He hesitates. I don't look at him, though, conscious of Alex standing not far from us, and unwrap the gift. Henry goes to say something, but in the end he walks away, over to the next person.

I study the book about the New Zealand national netball team, the Silver Ferns, my vision blurring, and swallow hard as Alex walks up to me.

"Nice," I say brightly. "Haven't read this."

"How are you doing?" he asks.

"Great." I ball up the paper and toss it into one of the nearby black rubbish bags.

"Everything all right between you and Henry?" he asks.

"Mind your own business," I snap. He lifts an eyebrow, and my face heats. I lift my chin. "If you want to know if it'll affect our working relationship, it won't."

He frowns. "Hey, give me some credit. I'm worried about you."

Oh God, these guys. Why do they have to be so nice to me?

He dips his head to try and catch my eye. "Are you still with Cam?"

"Yes," I reply, because Henry is my work colleague, and I'm not supposed to have feelings for him.

Alex sighs, though. "Aw, Juliette..."

"Don't..." Fighting back tears, I take the book and walk away.

I try to enjoy the rest of the party, but it's impossible when I feel so miserable. Everyone else's high spirits eventually get to me, and I slip away, back to my office, collect my purse and laptop, and then head out to the lobby. Nobody will notice I've gone.

That proves to be a lie though, as I head for the front doors, only to hear someone call, "Juliette!" behind me.

I stop and turn, and sigh to see Henry—minus the Santa suit—jogging toward me. He slows as he nears, and stops a few feet away.

We study each other for a long moment. I'm conscious of Rachel sitting behind the reception desk with a glass of bubbly, out of earshot, and we're also visible to everyone in the workroom through the glass walls.

"Are you going home?" Henry asks.

I meet his eyes and nod.

He frowns, but it's not a glare. It's more a look of concern or worry. "I know you said he wants to talk," he says. "And that's fair enough. But… don't sleep with him."

His gaze locks onto mine like a heat-seeking missile, and I can't look away. Was it really only this morning that we were making love? That he told me my name feels like a spell in his mouth? That he said *I'm never going to be able to look at you again without thinking about being inside you?*

I haven't been fair to him, but even so, he shouldn't ask me something like that. Cam is my partner, and Henry can't demand that I don't go to bed with the man I've lived with for seven years.

"I have to go," I tell him. "I'll see you on the twenty-eighth."

"Juliette." He calls as I begin to walk away. I stop and glance over my shoulder, knowing I'm going to cry if he asks me again.

"*Meri Kirihimete,*" he says. It's Māori for Merry Christmas. He holds out his hand. On it is a small velvet box.

I lift my gaze to his warily. "No," he scolds. "Not yet anyway." He gives me a mischievous look. "Go on, open it."

I should refuse it. But I don't. I take it from him and crack the lid.

It's a pair of earrings. They're in the shape of lotus flowers, an important Hindu symbol. They could be silver studded with cubic zirconias, but I know Henry better than that. They'll be white gold or platinum, and they'll be diamonds.

"I haven't got you anything," I say, my voice little more than a squeak. We take part in the Secret Santa and don't tend to buy each other gifts.

"You've already given me the best Christmas present I could ask for," he says. "It was fun unwrapping it." He smiles.

He looks so handsome standing there, his hands in his pockets, a twist to his lips. His hair is flopping over his forehead. But his blue eyes are gentle.

I should say I can't accept the earrings. I should give them back to him.

My eyes prick with tears. "*Meri Kirihimete*," I whisper.

Clutching the box, I walk through the door, and out into the sunlight.

*

I get home before Cam, who's also having his office party today.

I go straight into our bedroom and put the velvet box with the earrings into my bedside table without looking at them again. Then I go back out into the living room.

The apartment is quiet and a bit stuffy. He prefers to put the aircon on, but I like to open the windows, even though I appreciate that city air isn't the same as being in the country. I open the sliding doors onto the balcony, then go back in and through to the kitchen, and pour myself a glass of white wine.

I take it through to the living room and stand in the middle of the room. It's relatively quiet—music drifts up from a balcony below, some cheesy ballad from the seventies. It makes me think of Henry singing Dr. Hook's *A Little Bit More* and chuckling while he pressed kisses all over my face. I close my eyes and sway a little, remembering when I said *It's not fair to you.*

I don't care, as long as I get what I want, he replied.

Sighing, I have a large mouthful of wine. I shouldn't have slept with him. Twice. I groan out loud. It was such an idiotic thing to do. I've changed our relationship, and I can't undo it, like when you mix different colored paints on a palette. You can't turn purple back into red and blue, or orange into red and yellow. It's done. All I can do is paint a new picture with the color I've ended up with.

Still dancing to the music, I finish off my glass of wine.

Then I pour another one.

I wander through the apartment, looking with fresh eyes at the life that Cam and I have built together. Furniture, mirrors, paintings, throws, crockery, glasses. Paid for out of our joint bank account. The product of a shared life, as impossible to divide as the paint.

How many people stay together because it's too difficult to break up? Because they can't face the notion of dividing up the items they've taken a lifetime to collect? Or they just can't summon the strength they know it's going to take to end it?

That's not why I'm here though, I remind myself. I'm not staying because of shared plates or bedding or towels. I love Cam, and I've invested seven years in making this work, and I don't want to throw it all away because a handsome guy gave me an orgasm. Or two. Or three.

But then that's not fair to Henry, because even though I accused him that not everything is about sex, and he said *Are you sure?*, that's not what last night was about. Or not only, anyway. It was about comfort, and solace, and friendship, and... love? Yes, maybe about love, too. Just a different kind of love from that which I have with Cam. Cam loves me—I have no doubt about that. But our love is like the Egyptian pyramids, constructed over time, built stone by stone with hard work and determination. Not beautiful exactly, but impressive nonetheless. My relationship with Henry is more like an ice sculpture, something created in hours that is breathtaking but fleeting, and won't be around this time tomorrow.

Or is that unfair? I've known him almost as long as I've known Cam. We have a solid friendship. I'd trust him with my life. I would say I love him, as a brother.

No, not quite as a brother.

Would you rather be with a pyramid or an ice sculpture?

I want both. I want Cam to be like Henry, to be open and affectionate. To tell me he loves me with all his heart. To do romantic things like buy me flowers and jewelry. To leave me notes that say I love you on the bathroom mirror. I want his friends to say he talks about me all the time. For my girlfriends to be jealous of how he treats me.

I want him to send me texts that tell me he burns for me.

I wish... I wish he'd ask me to marry him. But he told me when we were first together that he thinks marriage is outdated and pointless, and he'd rather spend the money on the apartment. I didn't argue, because technically he's right. What's the point of marriage? Of wasting thousands of dollars on a wedding and a dress that can only be worn once, when we could spend the money on something we really need? Rings are an outdated symbol of ownership, he said, a medieval stamp of possession and jealousy like a chastity belt.

But there's something about the thought of a guy asking you to be his wife that just gives you the tingles, right? Or is it just me?

He sometimes says he loves me, but I don't feel it. I want to feel his love. Is that too much to ask?

I finish off the wine and pour myself another.

I didn't know about his abuse when I started seeing him. But when he told me, I made the decision to stay, to help him work through it. What kind of person does it make me now if I say I'm leaving him because I can't cope? It's not his fault. He's experienced this terrible thing in his past, and he deserves to be with someone who'll work with him to help him through all the aftershocks it's caused. Is that person me? I want it to be me. I don't want to end the relationship because it's too hard.

It's just… I wish he was… normal. There, I said it. It's a horrible word, I know it is. Cam is normal—he's a normal guy who's had abnormal things done to him. But I wish he experienced love and sex the way other men seem to. I wish he looked at me, and desired me, and his body responded the way it should do, without caveats and complicated displays of power and control.

Henry didn't blanch when I hinted at what Cam has asked me to do in the past, but I could sense his indignation and resentment. He said *You shouldn't have to change yourself to please him, or do things you don't want to do. That's not fair.* But surely, when you love your partner, you listen to their problems, and you try to help?

It was such a relief, though, to have Henry kiss me, and to feel his erection, and to make love with him in such a straightforward, simple way. With no humiliation, no embarrassment, nothing except desire, pure and clear, like the air at Lake Tekapo in the middle of the mountains, where there's so little light pollution that you can see the Southern Lights.

I wish—

I'm cut off mid-thought as I hear a key in the lock. I turn guiltily, even though I'm just standing there with a glass of wine, and watch as Cam comes into the room.

"Oh," he says, looking surprised. "I didn't think you'd be home yet." He's carrying a couple of bags of groceries, and he walks through to the kitchen and puts them down.

"I left work early as it was the last day," I tell him.

"Yeah, me too." He walks into the living room and stands a few feet away. "I wasn't sure if you'd come home."

"I'm here."

He nods, looking into my eyes. His are a very pale green, much lighter and cooler than Henry's dark-blue ones.

Oh God, when will I stop comparing everything about him to Henry? I drop my gaze and have a big mouthful of wine.

"I might get myself one of those," he says, and goes back into the kitchen to pour himself a glass.

No kiss. No hug and a 'hello darling, it's so nice to see you.' My heart aches for it. But it's not Cam's way.

I could go up to him, slide my arms around him, kiss his back, tell him I've missed him. But I know what'll happen. He'll stiffen, then move away to put something in the fridge. And I couldn't bear that rejection right now.

As he starts unpacking the groceries, he says, "I've got some garlic bread to go with the pasta."

"That'll be nice."

"Sit down," he says, "put your feet up. I'll get started." He turns the oven on and begins filling the kettle.

This is how he expresses affection, I tell myself as I sit down. It's one of the five love languages, isn't it? Words of affirmation, acts of service, giving gifts, quality time, and physical touch. Cam's number one is definitely acts of service. He tells me he loves me by cooking, cleaning, tidying, and doing chores, and he appreciates it when I do the same for him. He's also happy for us to spend time together—watching TV, going for a walk, playing computer games.

But he doesn't give gifts. He doesn't tell me he loves me. And he doesn't touch me, not in the way I want to be touched.

"How was your day?" he asks as he puts the pasta on, then begins to peel an onion.

"Not bad, thanks." I tell him about my morning appointments, and a bit about the Christmas party. "How was yours?"

"Pretty good, actually. They had a seventies theme so there was lots of dancing to Saturday Night Fever and ABBA. And plenty of flares."

"You should have stayed if you were enjoying it."

"No, I had something much more important to do." He smiles.

I curl up on the sofa and rest my head on the back. The wine is starting to have an effect, my limbs and spine beginning to loosen. I'm not going to think about Henry and what happened at the hotel. I'm going to practice mindfulness, and think about right here, right now.

I watch Cam cook, which he does capably and fluidly, frying the garlic, chopped onion, and chicken, adding spices, cream, and cheese while he tells me about an article he read today about the captain of the All Blacks. He couldn't cook much when I met him, but he's enjoyed learning techniques over the years, and even though he doesn't exactly tackle soufflés or consommé, he's better than Henry, who openly admits he even burns toast, and has a chef come in to prepare his meals every week.

Nope. Not going to think about Henry.

I rest the wine glass against my cheek to cool my hot skin, and sigh.

When the pasta is cooked, Cam tosses it in the cheesy sauce to coat it before serving it with a sprig of parsley. I rise and lay the table, carry through our dishes and cutlery and the green salad he's prepared, and we sit opposite each other to eat.

"This is lovely," I tell him truthfully, taking small bites of the chicken and pasta.

"Yeah, not bad," he says. "I think I got the recipe nailed now."

We're polite as strangers, circling each other, just observing. We've had enough arguments that we both know how this works. It takes a while for the heat of an argument to die down. For hurt feelings to subside, and for forgiveness to take their place.

He knows he's hurt me, and that at the moment our treaty is fragile, so he steers clear of any topics that are likely to cause problems. We talk about what we're doing the next few days. I've bought most of our Christmas presents for both our families, but there are a couple of things we need to get, and we also need to wrap them all. Cam suggests we shop tomorrow morning, then spend the afternoon wrapping together while we play some Christmas music, and I agree.

Sunday is Christmas Eve, which we're spending with my parents and my brother. Then on Christmas Day we're going over to his parents' place. His brothers and their wives will be there, too. Then we've got a couple of days alone before we fly up to Wellington.

"Is Henry going to the wedding?" Cam asks.

I stop with my fork halfway to my mouth. My face heats.

Oh shit. I should've known this was going to happen.

JULIETTE AND THE BILLIONAIRE BOSS

Chapter Eleven

Juliette

"Why did you ask that?" I demand.

Cam looks down at his dish and spears a piece of pasta. "I just wondered."

"Of course he's going. All the guys are going." Flustered and upset, I drop my fork with a clatter. "Why would you bring him up now, when we're trying to move on?"

"I'm sorry." He puts down his own cutlery. "I shouldn't have said that. I don't know why I did. I'm jealous of him, I guess. I know you like him." He massages his head. "I've got a headache." He gets up and takes our dishes out to the kitchen, then opens the Panadol and takes two with a mouthful of water.

He hesitates, then he opens the fridge and extracts two chocolate desserts he must have bought at the supermarket. He brings them back to the table and puts one before me, then sits.

"I'm sorry," he says softly. "I shouldn't have said that. Just ignore me. I'm being grouchy. Come on, eat your dessert and then we'll go and watch a movie."

I stare at the chocolate pot, boiling with resentment, guilt, and shame. But he's apologized, and I can't say anything because I don't want to draw attention to how I'm feeling. I have to move on with this or it's all pointless. I have to learn not to react to every little thing he says. I need to let things wash over me.

I peel the lid off the pot and begin to eat.

"I wonder how much money they've spent on this wedding," he says. "I bet it's a small fortune. Paying for all their guests to spend three nights in a hotel. All that food and drink. And they're hiring a whole set of staff for the event, aren't they?"

"I believe so."

"Crazy waste, don't you think?"

I eat a spoonful of the pudding. "Some might say it was romantic."

He snorts. "Yeah, the same people who spend three times the going rate on a bouquet of roses on Valentine's Day."

I put down my spoon. I know his thoughts on it. But this is the kind of thing I need to talk to him about. How's he expected to put it right if I don't tell him how I feel?

"You're right," I say slowly. "They do charge more for flowers and chocolates and in restaurants in the middle of February. It is highly commercialized. But the thing is that most people still buy their loved one a gift because it makes them feel good."

He studies me thoughtfully. "Are you saying that's how you feel?"

"Maybe. It's nice when your partner buys you gifts." I try not to think about the earrings in the box in my bedside table.

"I do buy you gifts," he says, a tad hurt. "I've got you something nice for Christmas."

"I'm sure you have, and that's really nice, thank you. But sometimes it would be cool if you got me something when it wasn't my birthday or Christmas to show me you were thinking of me."

"I think of you all the time," he says.

I swallow and pick up my spoon, then carry on eating. I remind myself he bought these puddings because he knew I liked them. He does buy me things. He does think about me. It's me who's at fault because I'm judging what he does and expecting him to change to suit me. My expectations are too high, and I'm being unfair.

When we're done, we go and sit on the sofa. He puts on *Love Actually*, which we've seen half a dozen times, but it feels like a silent acknowledgement that we need some Christmas spirit, and so I don't complain.

We sit side by side, Cam with his arm stretched out along the back, almost, but not quite, around me. I curl up next to him, and we watch the movie from beginning to end.

The only time we speak is when Cam asks me if I want another glass of wine, and I decline.

When it's over, I tell him I'm tired and he says he is too, so we go into the bedroom and get ready for bed. While he's in the bathroom, I put on my pajamas, then go into the bathroom when he comes out.

I let down my hair and braid it, take off my makeup, and go back out into the bedroom. He's already in bed, reading on his phone. I slide in beside him and lie back.

He puts down his phone and rolls onto his side to look at me. "I'm sorry," he says.

I look up at him. "For what?"

"Everything." He looks sad. "I… I do love you, you know," he says falteringly.

It's a big admission for him to make. He doesn't say it often, so I should feel thrilled. But I don't. He says it, but I don't feel it.

Then he leans forward and kisses me.

I freeze. We haven't made love since my birthday on the tenth. We tried a few nights ago, but it ended in disaster.

He cups my face and turns it toward him, pressing soft kisses across my lips. Then he moves his hand under the duvet to the bottom of my pajama top and slides his fingers beneath the hem, onto my belly, and moves them up.

Henry. Oh God, Henry, Henry, Henry.

I roll away from him and sit up. "I can't do this."

"Can't do what?"

"This, Cam. Not now. Not tonight." I get to my feet, panicking. "I'll sleep in the spare room."

He stands too, and for once his eyes flicker with emotion. "You need to make an effort as well," he snaps.

I hunch my shoulders and wrap my arms around my middle. I feel angry and defensive and guilty and so, so lonely, all rolled into one. "I know."

"This isn't all about me," he says.

I don't say anything.

"How long are you going to punish me for?" he asks.

"Why, are you enjoying it?" I bite my lip, but it's too late to stop the words. Shit, shit, shit. *You fucking idiot, Juliette.*

He gives a short, humorless laugh. "How long have you been waiting to say that?"

I brush a hand over my face. "I shouldn't have said that."

"No you shouldn't," he says angrily. "Not everyone likes their sex vanilla."

My eyebrows rise. "I'm not vanilla."

"Yes, Juliette, you are. And that's okay, there's nothing wrong with that, but there's nothing wrong with wanting to experiment either. Lots of people enjoy power play—it's really common."

"Is that what she told you?"

"Oh, and the gloves are off. Yes, she did say that I was wrong to feel bad about wanting to experiment and try different things." He runs a hand through his hair. "Look, I'm just saying that I'm not a freak, and I don't appreciate being treated like one. I do have… problems, but, as I tried to explain before, seeing Vanessa was my attempt to try and work out what to do about them."

I go stiff as a board.

He sees my face and rolls his eyes. "Don't go ballistic just because I said her name."

"You've never said it before."

"It's just a name."

It is, but for some reason it makes her horribly, alarmingly real. Before, she was just a nameless, faceless symbol of his problems. When he came home after seeing her and we talked about it, he was very careful not to say anything about her—he only talked about himself. I did my best to block her out of my mind, trying to see her as a therapist who was trying to help him.

But suddenly I see her as what she was—a living, breathing woman who talked to him about our personal life, who took off her clothes with him, and who did the most intimate things to him, and let him do them to her.

"The things you want me to do," I whisper, "I don't think I can do them."

Frustration flickers on his face. "Jesus, it's not like I'm asking you to torture me or anything. Lots of people tie the other person up and use vibrators on each other, and—"

"You're not just asking me to lovingly arouse you, Cam. You're asking me to..." I press my lips together. "It's not the what, it's the how. It's... it's so clinical and cold."

"It's not! It's sexy!"

"Not to me. I'm sorry, but I can't be the person you want me to be."

"You're still talking as if I'm a fucking freak! It's such a small thing. You're overreacting big time."

"I'm not overreacting."

"You just need to loosen up a bit."

I don't say anything. He's spiraling past the point of no return, and I know where this is going.

"You're fucking frigid," he yells. "And I'm sick and tired of having to live with someone who makes me feel like a freak because I don't just want to have sex in missionary with the lights out."

I don't respond. Anything I say will only make this worse.

He waits for me to speak, his jaw working with fury and resentment. When he realizes I'm not going to take the bait, he picks up his phone. "I'll sleep in the spare room," he states. "I guess it's what you think I deserve." He walks out, closing the door a little too loudly.

I sink onto the bed and let out a big breath. I feel as if I've been punched in the stomach. The rich dessert has mixed with the wine, and I feel a bit sick. I take deep breaths, fighting against the despair that threatens to overwhelm me.

When the sickness subsides, I turn to sit back against the headboard and pull the duvet up close around me. My eyes prick with tears, and it's hard to swallow.

I think about Cam in the spare bedroom. This has happened often enough that I know this won't end until I instigate it. Usually, after a while, I get up, go into his room, slide beneath the duvet, and cuddle up to him. He'd be stiff and resentful for a while, but if I were to say I'm sorry and nuzzle up to him, eventually he'd let himself be talked around. Normally I do it because I hate atmospheres, and I want things to be better.

Tonight, I stay where I am. Fuck him.

It's an easy thing to think, but I'm shaking. We've had arguments a lot worse than this, but for some reason I feel more upset than angry, like I normally do.

I know that arguments are necessary in relationships. They rebalance the power dynamic when one person is taking advantage of the other, and they usually clear the air, even if they're horrible at the time. But tonight it doesn't feel like that. It feels as if what we had is fragmenting, tearing apart at the seams.

I've tried so hard to make it work. And I know he's right—he's not a freak, and lots of people experiment in their sex lives. Why can't I do what he wants?

You shouldn't have to change yourself to please him, or do things you don't want to do.

Oh, Henry…

My phone buzzes on the bedside table. I glance at it, and my heart skips a beat as I see a green banner that tells me I have a text waiting. From Henry.

Heart racing, I open it. It says just two words, *You okay?*

I press the fingers of my left hand to my lips as I reply with my right. *Not really. Why did you message me?*

Henry: *I'm worried about you. Has something happened?*

Me: *We've just had an argument. He's gone into the spare room.*

I hope he doesn't gloat or sound smug. I couldn't bear that right now.

Henry: *Ah, I'm so sorry.*

Tears blur my eyes, then tip over my lashes. I brush them away as I reply.

Me: *It was horrible.*

Henry: *Arguments always are.*

Me: *He knows right where to slide the knife.*

Me: *Not literally btw.*

Henry: *I should hope not. And of course he does. That's what happens when you're with someone for a long time.*

Me: *Do you think it always has to be like that?*

Henry: *No. I think if you truly love someone, even in an argument, you choose not to breach their defenses.*

I lean back tiredly, sliding down the pillows a little. I shouldn't be texting him. Communicating with Henry is cheating on Cam, no matter what form the communication takes. But right now I don't care. I'm hurting, and he makes me feel better.

Henry: *Do you want to talk about it?*

Me: *It was the usual stuff. He accused me of being vanilla. He said I make him feel like a freak because I only want to have sex in missionary with the lights out.*

Henry: *I literally LOL then.*

Me: *Don't laugh at me.*

Henry: *Honey, I'm not laughing at you. The point is that I wouldn't care if you did only want it in missionary with the lights out. It would be amazing, every time.*

I swallow hard, trying not to cry.

Me: *He said I was frigid because I don't want to experiment, but it's not that.*

Henry: *I know.*

Me: *I can't seem to explain to him what I want.*

Henry: *You explained it to me very well. To be worshiped.*

Me: *It sounds so pathetic and needy. But is it so terrible?*

Henry: *It's what you deserve.*

Me: *I miss you.*

Henry: *I miss you too, sweetheart. More than you could ever know.*

I wipe the tears from my cheeks.

Me: *I'm sorry.*

Henry: *You've nothing to be sorry about.*

Me: *I'm stringing you along and it's unfair.*

Henry: *No it's not. You can talk to me whenever you want. Your relationship is in its death throes, and I want to help, but unfortunately you have to deal with it yourself.*

I read the words several times, then lie back and look at the ceiling. Is he right? Is my relationship with Cam over?

Henry has skin in the game—he's going to say that because he wants it to be true. But he's been through it. He knows how it feels.

It might seem obvious to him, but it's not to me. I feel so muddled, caught up in duty and obligation and what I should and ought to do. It's never just the two of you in a relationship, is it? My dad likes Cam a lot, and he would be devastated if we broke up. Mum is ambivalent and she likes Henry, but she'd still be upset. I'm not keen on either of Cam's brothers and I doubt they're that bothered about me either, but his parents both like me, and I get on very well with his mum, which I know is rare. And there are our friends and colleagues, who are all used to our relationship. Cam is a solid partner, with a good job—even if he hates it—and a decent income. He has lots of friends, he's good at sports, and he's well liked. Everyone would think I was crazy for letting him go, even if it was for Henry.

But in the end, I'm the one who has to live with him. I'm not happy. And I don't know that I can put it right.

I look back at my phone. Henry's texted again.

Henry: *I'm sorry, I shouldn't have said your relationship was over. And I shouldn't have told you not to sleep with him. I speak before I think. I have no right to ask you for anything.*

Me: *Ah, it's okay.*

Henry: *I want you so badly. But I keep forgetting that I can't give you children. And I know you want them.*

Tears trickle down my cheeks. He's right. I would like children. I'd like to be able to experience being pregnant and going through childbirth.

Henry: *I don't want to go through what I went through with Shaz again.*

Me: *I understand.*

He doesn't reply. After a while, I text again.

Me: *Why didn't you try IVF?*

Henry: *Things were already going wrong between us by the time it was brought up as an option.*

He doesn't elaborate. Was it something to do with me? I remember what he said last night. That he's been in love with me since the first time we met. *Why else do you think Shaz and I broke up? She knew. She's always known. I tried to ignore it because you were with Cam, and I'd already proposed to her, and I knew we couldn't come to anything, but Shaz always knew.*

Me: *Why is life so complicated?*

Henry: *I don't know.*

We're both quiet for a while. Then he messages again.

Henry: *What are you going to do?*

Me: *I'm not sure. But I think you might be right.*

I send it and pause, then send another few in quick succession.

Me: *I think it's nearly over.*

Me: *I didn't want to admit it. I wanted to fight it. But I think it's inevitable.*

Me: *You said when a relationship ends, it's often a slow erosion.*

Me: *That's how it feels.*

Me: *I think I just need time.*

Me: *And I don't know what it means for you and me.*

Me: *There are lots of factors.*

Henry: *Like children.*

We pause.

Me: *Yes. That's one.*

Henry: *It's a big one.*

We pause again.

Me: *Yes. But it would be different for us, right? We'd know about it going in. You and Shaz didn't.*

Henry: *True.*

Me: *Would you still like children? Or does what's happened before mean you don't want them at all?*

Henry: *It's not that I don't want them. But I wouldn't want to put you through all that waiting and disappointment. It nearly killed me last time. I don't want to do that to you. Or to myself.*

Me: *I understand. But you'd consider IVF?*

Henry: *Yes. Would you?*

I lie back, looking up at the ceiling again. My heart bangs against my ribs. It's a huge thing to ask, and we're not even in a relationship. Cam wants children, and he'd probably be able to give me them. But is that a reason to stay?

It's so hard. I know Henry relatively well. We're good friends, and we're obviously attracted to one another. He's hardworking, funny, wealthy, driven, and gorgeous—lots of reasons he'd make a good husband. But are we compatible as a couple? There's no way of telling yet, and it's a huge thing to discuss having children and IVF when we've only had one night together.

I look back at my phone. He's waiting for an answer, and I don't have one. I'm still living with Cam, under the same roof, and I need to finish one relationship before I embark on another. It's not fair to keep Henry hanging on. But all I can do is be honest.

Me: *I think so. I just need time to figure it all out. Is that okay? I'll understand if it isn't.*

He's quiet for a moment. Then eventually he replies.

Henry: *I've waited this long for you. I can wait a few more - what? Days? Weeks? Months?*

Me: *I don't know, but not months. It's just that it's Christmas, and there's Damon's wedding, and it's just a horrible time to break up.*

Henry: *There's no good time.*

Me: *Yeah, I know. I'm being unfair to you. I realize that.*

Henry: *It's all right. I've been there. I understand.*

I start crying.

Me: *I'm so sorry.*

Henry: *Look, you know where I am if you need me.*

Me: *Okay.*

Henry: *Just take care of yourself.*

It feels like an ironic thing to say when I feel sick and my head's banging like a bass drum.

Me: *I'll see you on the 28th?*

Henry: *Are you bringing Cam?*

Me: *I don't know.*

I can imagine him gritting his teeth and closing his eyes in frustration. I feel terrible. I should tell him that I'm going into the spare room now and I'm going to tell Cam it's over. But I can't, three days from Christmas. I just can't.

Henry: *Okay. I'll see you then. One last thing.*

Henry: *I'm in love with you. Remember that.*

I shake my head and give a short laugh.

Henry: *Meri Kirihimete.*

Me: *Meri Kirihimete.*

I turn off my phone and put it on the bedside table.

Before I lie back, I open the drawer and take out the velvet box.

Bringing the box beneath the duvet, I crack the lid and study the lotus flowers. They're absolutely beautiful.

After a while, I close the box again, but I don't put it back in the drawer. I curl up with it still in my hand, turn off the light, and slide down under the duvet.

I've forgotten to close the curtains. The moon hangs outside, almost full, like a silver bauble.

I open the box and watch the diamonds glitter like little fragments of moonlight.

I fall asleep holding it, thinking not of the man who's sleeping twenty feet away, but of the one with the dark hair that falls across his forehead, and a pair of dark-blue eyes blazing into mine.

Chapter Twelve

Henry

Despite my stomach feeling as if I've swallowed a box of butterflies, I keep myself busy for the next two days. I've neglected my garden over the past few weeks, and so I slap on my scruffiest shorts and tee, some sun lotion and an old hat that Shaz hated and tried to throw out, and spend a pleasant few hours digging, weeding, planting, and trimming.

My house near Sumner Beach has arguably one of the best views in Christchurch, out to sea across Pegasus Bay toward the Kaikoura Ranges. It cost me five million dollars, and even now, six months after I purchased it, it still takes my breath away when I walk into it. It's constructed so it appears to levitate out into the ocean. It has four bedrooms, four bathrooms, three living rooms, a gym, a steam room, and a lap pool, as well as a beautiful garden that is my pride and joy. It's far too big for me, but I love the space and the way that when you're sitting on the deck, all you can hear is the cry of the gulls and the splash of the waves far below.

So far, none of my friends or family has been to the house. I'm sure they think it's strange that I haven't invited them, and I do plan to have a housewarming party one day, but at the moment I'm reveling in the peace of it all. When I was with Shaz, there were always people popping in—mainly her friends and family, and I hated that we were never alone. Now, I can live my life the way I want, and that happens to be by myself, in total silence.

Sometimes I play music, of course, or watch the TV. But more often than not, the evenings will find me sitting on the deck or in the living room, reading, enjoying the peace and quiet, which is such a relief after the busy-ness of the office.

As Head of HR, I have to deal with recruitment and professional development, and compliance with employment laws and legal issues. But often I'm involved with people's lives—with conflicts, disputes, and disciplinary actions. Although I'm a computer engineer at heart, I've had plenty of training to deal with these matters, and I know I'm considered by everyone at Kia Kaha to be calm and capable when dealing with other people and their problems.

So why, right now, do I feel as if I'm struggling and out of control?

I suppose there's one crucial difference. I'm not in love with every employee that comes into my office.

On Christmas Eve, I take the meal out of the fridge that my chef prepared for me this morning and put it in the oven to heat. While I'm waiting, I pour myself a glass of red wine and take it onto the deck, and sit there watching the sun sink slowly toward the hills to the west. Out to sea, a few people zoom about on jet skis, and several boats return with the day's catch.

I've had invitations to go out this evening, but I declined them all, not in the mood for socializing. Tomorrow I'll go to my mother's, because it's what you do on Christmas Day, but I've been feeling the need for solitude while I do my best to stop swimming against the current and let Fate take over.

It doesn't come naturally. I'm the sort of guy who likes to be in control. At work, if an acquisition or merger was about to take place, I'd be doing my best to speak to everyone involved, to answer questions, to prompt them to take action, or to try and influence them one way or another so the outcome went the way I hoped.

With Juliette, I can't do that. I'd like to. I want to message her every five minutes, tell her how I've been dreaming about her smooth light-brown skin, and how I picture kissing down over her breasts and belly until I sink my tongue deep into her warm, moist flesh and taste the sweet nectar of her arousal.

I want to march around to her apartment, take Cam by the scruff of the neck, throw him out onto the street, then lift Juliette into my arms and carry her back to the car so I can drive her over here and have her all to myself.

I fantasize about that for a few minutes.

Then I sigh. I'm playing the long game here. She knows she's near the edge of the cliff, and she's panicking about taking the step off, even though I've told her I'll catch her. If I try to push her, I'm convinced she'll backtrack and tell me she's not going to leave. So I've just got to sit here and wait, and fight the stomach ulcer I think I might be developing.

The timer on my watch buzzes, so I go indoors, retrieve the meal from the oven, add the pots of yogurt and hummus that Anton prepared, and take it outside. It's slow-cooked Lamb Shawarma, a Middle-Eastern dish, with lemon rice pilaf, and flatbreads because he knows I like them. I tuck into it while I look out at the summer sky and watch the gulls diving for fish.

I wonder what she's up to now. I know she's at her parents today. She's close to her mum—has she told her about me? That would make it too real, though. I'm sure she hasn't told anyone.

I've purposefully not messaged her, wanting to give her space. As a result, I haven't heard from her for two days. Not even a text. I know I have to prepare myself for the possibility that she won't leave Cam. She's mentioned that they've argued about me, which means that he's jealous, which also means he's prepared to fight for her. They've obviously got their problems, but it's much harder to leave a struggling relationship than it is to stay.

And, of course, there's the issue that we've touched on only briefly, but that lurks beneath the surface like the submerged rocks out to sea. The fact that I can't have children.

She asked if I'd consider IVF, and I told her yes. And I would, if it meant I could keep her. But if I'm honest with myself, the thought of it depresses me.

It's not that I don't want children. I'm not sure I can have my heart broken every month for another two years, that's all.

Even though it was my fault, Shaz never blamed me. She never used it as ammunition, even when things were bad, and I was thankful for that. But the truth is that every month when her period started, the accusation would be in her eyes. I'd have failed her again. I wasn't enough of a man to fulfill my only real purpose for being here in Nature's eyes—to procreate and continue the line.

Yeah, I know it's more complicated than that, but it's Christmas Eve and I'm alone and feeling sorry for myself. It strikes me that it probably wasn't the best idea to decline all the invitations, but it's too late now. I'm stuck with my own company whether I like it or not.

I finish off the wine, and pour myself another glass.

I've worked hard for everything I've achieved in my life. I've worked my way up from almost nothing to become a successful, wealthy businessman. I'm well-respected in the community, and, I like to think, well-liked. Without bragging, I'm pretty sure I know half a dozen girls I could have asked out who would have been thrilled to date me. So why am I so fixated on the one woman who's fighting me like a kingfish on a fishing line? They're known to put up a fierce fight when they're hooked, and they're a sought-after trophy fish here in New Zealand.

Is that why I want her so badly? Because she's putting up a fight, and she belongs to another man? Because she's beautiful and exotic, and I'd be proud to parade her on my arm to all my friends, family, and business acquaintances?

But even though it would be easier to tell myself this was the case, because then I could tell myself to grow up and move on and find someone of my own, it's not the truth. I'm in love with Juliette, the woman I've known for six years, because she's kind, and spirited, and generous, and funny. She's not perfect. She can be frank and honest, and some people find her blunt. But I like that I never have to excavate her sentences to reveal some hidden meaning. I had to do that with Shaz all the time, and it frustrated the hell out of me. But Juliette is an open book, and I love that about her.

I finish off the last mouthful of rice, put my feet up on the chair opposite, pick up my wine glass, and close my eyes.

We tell ourselves we're civilized now, and a world removed from the cavemen and women who lived by their instincts so long ago. But we're not that different, not really. I believe women are equal to men intellectually, and they're probably superior to them in many other ways. But as a man, I feel a responsibility to provide for my partner. To look after and protect her. And to get her pregnant. It seems like such a small thing to ask, and it's impossible not to feel like a failure when you can't. It makes me feel less than a man. It's humiliating and embarrassing to admit my failing to other people, which is mainly why I didn't tell anyone for over a year after Shaz and I began to live apart.

I especially didn't want to tell Juliette. She's mentioned having kids before, and I was convinced it would be the end of anything ever happening between us.

A couple of nights ago, when we texted and she told me Cam was sleeping in the other room, and she asked me if I'd consider IVF, I replied *Yes* because I don't want to lose her. But I also added, *Would you?* It took her a long time to come back with: *I think so. I just need time to figure it all out.*

No girl wants to know going into a relationship that it's going to be a struggle to conceive. So I wouldn't blame her if she told me she wasn't interested.

SERENITY WOODS

Hell, if I was a bigger man I'd tell her to get on with her life and forget about me. I should find myself a girl who doesn't want kids or who can't have them herself, and that way I wouldn't have to worry about it.

But I don't want Juliette because I want her to have my babies. I want Juliette because I want Juliette. How do you tell yourself to stop wanting something?

On the table, my phone buzzes, and a green banner announces the arrival of a text. I glance at it, and my heart leaps to see her name. Next to it is the picture I took of her one day at the office, saying I needed it for my contact list. She was wearing a blue sari, the rich color complementing her skin and making her glow. I see it every time she texts me, and it always makes me smile.

I smile now as I open the text, although my stomach does a strange flip at the sudden thought that maybe she's messaging me to tell me she's decided it's over between us.

Juliette: *Hey, how are you doing?*

Me: *Hey you. I'm okay. You?*

Juliette: *I've gone for a walk to pick up a couple of bits for Mum from the supermarket.*

Me: *Are you alone?*

Juliette: *Yes. Cam's playing pool with Dad and Antony.*

She's told me a little about her family. Her Indian father, Krish, is the youngest son of five boys, and, after graduating as a doctor in New Delhi, he traveled to New Zealand and met and fell in love with her Māori mother, Marama. I've met Marama a few times, and she's a lovely woman, very clever, and a teacher of philosophy at the University of Canterbury. She told Krish she'd marry him, but that she didn't want her children brought up with any particular religion or culture, because she wanted them to be free to make up their own minds. It means that she's encouraged both of her children to be free thinkers, which is one thing I love about Juliette.

Antony is her brother. I know he was named after a character from a Shakespeare play, just like Juliette was. I also know he's gay, and that at least one of Cam's brothers has made a derogatory comment about that. I'm sure she's not looking forward to Christmas Day because his brothers are going to be there.

Me: *Are you okay?*

Juliette: *Not really. I miss you.*

My heart leaps.

Me: *I miss you too. More than I would have thought possible.*

Juliette: *Can I call you?*

Me: *Of course!*

I wait a second, and then press the button to answer as it begins to ring and hold it to my ear.

"Hello?" I say.

"Hey." She sounds breathless, although whether that's because she's talking to me, or if it's because she's walking fast, I don't know. I can hear traffic, which confirms she's outside. "I'm sorry," she continues, "I don't have long. I just wanted to hear your voice."

"That's okay. It's great to talk to you." I look out across the sea, watching the gulls wheeling in the marmalade-colored sky. "I haven't messaged you because I didn't want to make things difficult for you. But I have been thinking about you."

"I know. I appreciate that. But I've thought about you non-stop." She speaks quickly then, as if now she's started, she can't control the words. "I know I shouldn't, but I have. I'm obsessed with you, Henry West. You've possessed my mind and my soul. I can feel your kisses all over my body like a brand. When I close my eyes, I can see you and hear you. I can smell your cologne. I can taste you. What have you done to me? Have you cast a spell? Why can't I get you out of my head?"

Slowly, my lips curve up. "My work here is done."

"Oh God, I hate you."

I sigh, and eventually she sighs too.

"I don't hate you," she admits. "I should, but I don't."

"I'm glad."

"Do you still want me?" she asks in a small voice.

"Every second of every minute of every day."

She doesn't say anything for a moment. I think she's fighting against tears.

I feel a surge of protectiveness, and I'm jealous of Cam, because he gets to go home with her, and I don't.

"Are you sleeping with him?" I ask, unable to stop myself.

"No. He's staying in the spare room."

"Good."

She gives a short laugh then. "I won't, until I figure this all out."

"I'm glad to hear it," I say, but my heart sinks a little, because her words imply she still hasn't made up her mind.

"I wish it hadn't all blown up over Christmas," she says. "I know you're right, and there's never a good time, but it seems worse, somehow, at this time of year."

"I imagine it's very common. Families squished in together, forced to have fun. That's never going to end well."

"Where are you?" she asks.

"At home."

"Are you going out tonight with the guys?"

"Nope. I didn't fancy company. I need to get a dog."

She laughs. "So you haven't got a hot date, then?"

"Nah. The girl of my dreams is otherwise engaged."

She doesn't say anything, but I have a feeling she's smiling.

"I should go," she says. "I hope you have a nice day tomorrow with your family."

"It's going to be a nightmare, but thanks for the thought."

"Will Rangi be there?"

"Yeah."

"Has his girlfriend decided if she's keeping the baby?"

"I have a feeling I'll find out tomorrow, which could prove good entertainment."

"Well, good luck."

"You too."

She hesitates. "See you soon."

"Yeah, bye." I end the call.

I put the phone on the table, go inside, and fetch a tumbler, some ice, and a bottle of Islay malt I was saving. Fuck special occasions, I need a good whisky.

After returning onto the deck, I pour myself a generous measure. Then I sit, slide down in my seat, and prop up my feet.

I sip the very expensive 1964 Bowmore, tasting mango, peach, pineapple, and grapefruit, the colors of which are reflected in the evening sky.

I'm still there when the rich colors have faded, and the stars are popping out on the black velvet, filling the sky with diamonds.

Chapter Thirteen

Henry

The next day, I arrive at my mother's house at one o'clock. She said I could come at any time, but I know dinner will be around two, and an extra hour with my family is about all I can handle.

It's nothing to do with my mum. Beth Rewi is fifty-five, with short graying hair and let's be polite and say a curvaceous figure. She's a nurse, working part-time at a hospice, and she's practical, no-nonsense, but kind. She married Teariki Rewi only five years ago, after eleven years of being single. Outwardly, they act as if they're celebrating their Golden Wedding Anniversary soon, bickering like an old married couple, but I've seen the way they look at each other when they think nobody's watching, and there's plenty of sizzle left on that barbecue, let me tell you.

The problem is my siblings, both of whom drive me insane. My sister, Liza, is twenty-five and with two children by different fathers. My brother, Philip, is thirty-two, with four children by different mothers. Both of them look ten years older than they are, and Philip has already lost most of his hair. Come to think of it, I'm actually a tiny bit relieved that I'm infertile.

They're both here today, along with all their children, except Rangi, I discover a few minutes after arriving. Philip informs me he'll be along soon, though.

The house is hot and noisy, the kids all tired from having risen at six a.m., hyperactive from having eaten way too much chocolate, and bored, even though they've brought most of their new toys with them.

I greet them all with big hugs, though, and after Mum insists she doesn't need help in the kitchen, I join them in the garden to play Swingball and rugby, to push the smaller ones on the swings, and to hold my two-year-old niece's hands while she jumps on the outdoor trampoline, her feet barely rising an inch.

Teariki is in charge of the *hāngi*—the traditional Māori oven which consists of stones heated over a fire in a pit at the bottom of the backyard. Large wire baskets lined with foil containing all kinds of food have been cooking for hours, and he begins uncovering them and testing to make sure it's all cooked properly before getting Philip to help him carry them over to the large table on the deck.

I'd offer to help, but I know from experience that Philip will say no, that he's perfectly able to cope without my help, so I concentrate on keeping the kids amused.

Rangi arrives ten minutes before dinner is due to be served. In the process of tossing the rugby ball to another nephew, I glance over and see him leaning against the wall, watching me, and instantly I can see there's something wrong.

I lob the ball to Nikau, then walk over to Rangi. "Hey bro." I duck my head to catch his eye. "How's it going?"

He studies the Queens of the Stone Age logo on my new T-shirt which James bought me for Christmas. His jaw is knotted. "She's getting an abortion next week," he announces.

I blow out a long breath. "Ah, man, I'm sorry."

"She doesn't want one. Her mum's making her do it."

"Dude, that sucks, but I can understand why. She's only sixteen."

"It's fucking murder," he yells.

"Jesus, keep your voice down." I grab his arm and pull him away from the house. "It's Christmas Day," I snap. "Now is not the time."

He wrenches his arm away, sullen and mutinous. "I don't care."

"Well, I do. Grandma has worked hard to make dinner today, and I don't want you ruining it."

His gaze meets mine then, and his eyes are filled with tears. "She wants the baby, and so do I. Why does she have to get rid of it?"

"Because you don't know what you want at sixteen. Neither of you have any idea how this is going to impinge on your life. It's what happens when you're children—you have to let adults make the decisions for you."

"I'm not a child. Did you think you were a child when you were at Greenfield?"

I don't reply, because my answer would be no, and I'd have decked any adult who suggested it.

"Look," I say quietly, "after dinner, why don't we go for a walk and have a chat about it?"

He scuffs the floor with his shoe. "All right."

"Good lad. Now come on, it's Christmas Day. Baby in the manger and all that. It should be a day of celebration."

"I made a baby," Rangi says, "and he won't get to be born. What would Jesus say about that?"

I'm beginning to regret getting up this morning. "Grab the fucking rugby ball and come and play with the kids with me."

He does, albeit sullenly, and we toss the ball about until Mum yells that dinner's ready.

We sit around the table and tuck into the feast. She's done herself proud this year. The trays from the *hāngī* contain chicken, lamb, pork, fish and some shellfish, potatoes, kūmara or sweet potatoes, cabbage, pumpkin, and stuffing. Mum's also prepared a big watercress salad and fried bread, and there are steamed puddings with custard for dessert.

There's plenty of alcohol, and because it's Christmas, Rangi, who's the oldest, is allowed to have a beer. He drinks it—a little too quickly—and helps himself to another. Nobody else notices, but I frown as I finish my dessert. He returns to the table, and continues pushing his dinner around with his fork.

I've brought my guitar, and I strum *Po Tapu*—Silent Night, and *Harikoa*—Silver Bells, and then *Te pukeko i te rakau ponga*—A Pukeko in a Ponga Tree, which is our version of the *Twelve Days of Christmas*, the kids all joining in.

I manage to get all the way up to Five Big Fat Pigs before it all goes tits up.

"For God's sake," Philip says to Rangi, "what's wrong with you? You look like you've been sucking a lemon."

Still strumming, I glance at them. Rangi doesn't reply—he just glares morosely at the table.

"I asked you a question," Philip demands.

Rangi looks up, and his eyes meet mine. I give a small shake of my head. His chest heaves, and then he looks back at his father.

"Ellie's pregnant," he says.

I stop strumming. All the adults and the kids who know what it means stare at him. The toddlers look around at the rest of us, obviously sensing trouble brewing.

"What?" Philip thunders.

Rangi pushes his dinner away. "Her parents are making her have an abortion, so you don't have to worry."

Mum presses her fingers to her mouth.

Teariki frowns and says, "Rangi. That's not an appropriate topic at the table."

"Of course it's not," Rangi shouts. "We're supposed to be celebrating the birth of Jesus, aren't we? Not the murder of a baby."

Rangi's sister, nine-year-old Kaia, says, "What's an abortion?"

Her mother, Hine, snaps, "Rangi! Not at the table!"

He's upset, though, and he's not about to behave just because his stepmother—who he's always disliked—is demanding it. "We both want the baby," he says. "Why should she have to get rid of it?"

"Because her parents obviously have more sense than she does," Philip snaps. "You fucking idiot," he says to his son, filling me with shame, because I said the same thing. "You couldn't keep it in your pants, could you? I knew she was a slut."

A heartbeat passes as everyone stares at everyone else with varying degrees of horror, and then Rangi springs for his father across the table. He lands on Philip and knocks his chair backward, and Philip's feet shoot out, hitting the table. Glasses and plates of half-eaten food fly everywhere. The toddlers start crying, Kaia screams, and Mum yells, "Henry! Do something!"

I get to my feet, walk around the table, grab the back of Rangi's tee, and haul him off his father.

"Stop it!" I snap as he struggles to get free. I frog march him over to a seat, push him down, and say, "Sit there."

Teariki helps Philip up. Embarrassed and furious, he straightens his clothes and strides over to his son.

"How dare you hit me!" he yells.

"All right." I position myself between them. "Easy, now."

"Get out of my fucking way." Philip pushes my chest, but although I'm younger than he is, I'm six inches taller and a whole lot heavier, so I don't move.

"He's upset, that's all," I say, holding Philip back with a hand on his chest. "Don't make it worse."

"Get your fucking hands off me." He gives me a right hook that connects with my temple, making me see stars for a moment.

"You piece of shit!" I hit him back, and he stumbles and goes down.

"Enough!" Teariki yells. "I want everyone to calm down."

Mum gets up. "Liza, can you take the children indoors please."

"Aw…" they all say, wanting to watch the show, but Liza and her husband ferry them all inside, and soon we hear the strains of music from *Moana* drifting from the TV.

Mum comes to stand next to Teariki. He helps Philip up, the four of us forming a semi-circle in front of Rangi.

"I can't believe you," Mum says to all of us. "Fighting on Christmas Day, in front of the children." She glares at Rangi. "You are sixteen now, a full-grown man, and you should know better."

"He called Ellie a slut," Rangi says tearfully. "I love her."

She puts her hands on her hips and studies him for a moment. Her expression softens. Then her gaze slides to me and Philip. It hardens again. "And as for you two… you're supposed to set an example to the children!"

"He started it," I mumble.

"Henry," she scolds, "Good Lord, what are you, twelve? If the two of you can't act like grownups, you can both leave now."

Philip ignores me and gestures at his son. "He announced he'd made a girl pregnant at the dinner table," he says. "I'm sorry if I reacted badly, but I was a bit fucking shocked."

"Stop swearing," she snaps, holding up a finger. "We were all shocked, but let's face it, it's not the first time it's happened, is it?" She lifts an eyebrow.

Oh shit, I'd forgotten—Philip got Rangi's mother pregnant at sixteen, too.

He doesn't say anything, but his gaze drops to the deck. I frown, thinking about the fact that he was eighteen when I went to Greenfield. Rangi was two by then, and Philip had to get a job. He'd ended up driving a delivery van, as it was the only thing he could find. He didn't have the opportunity to better himself. There was no invitation to Greenfield for him, no adventure therapy or team-building exercises, no help to get into university. Mum hadn't taken her nursing qualification back then, and so she wasn't in a position to help him financially. For Philip, life has been one long struggle, made worse by having four children he can't afford. Mum's right, he's not really in a position to criticize Rangi when he's done the exact same thing four times.

She looks back at Rangi. "I'm sorry, love. How far along is she?"

"Eight weeks," he says. He glances at me. "Her mum helped her figure it out."

Philip frowns. Then he looks at me. "Wait… what? You knew?"

Rangi realizes his mistake and sends me a guilty look.

Ah, shit.

"He came to see me," I reply, knowing there's no point in denying it. "She'd told him she was pregnant and he didn't know what to do. I bought them a pregnancy test so they could confirm it. That's all."

His eyes blaze with fury. He looks at his son. "Why did you go to him? Why didn't you come to me?"

"Because he knew you'd react like this," I reply.

"Shut up, I'm not talking to you."

"Philip," Mum scolds. "Enough. Let's concentrate on Rangi. He didn't get Ellie pregnant on purpose, and he hasn't done it to spite you. It was a mistake, and he's obviously upset about it."

"At least you got to keep your baby," Rangi says to his father.

"Yeah," Philip replies, "what a great decision that turned out to be."

"Philip!" Mum is horrified. Rangi looks crushed. I look at Philip, gutted for Rangi, but he refuses to meet my gaze.

"We should go," Philip says. "I don't want to spend one more minute in his company than I have to." He shoots me a look then, and it's full of bitterness.

"No," I say, "you stay. The kids haven't even finished their dinner. I'll go." I walk over to Mum and give her a hug. "I'm sorry," I murmur. "It was a lovely meal."

"You don't have to go." Her eyes glisten.

"He'll cool down if I leave." I nod at Teariki, then I stop in front of Rangi. "Bro," I say. "Do you want to come with me?"

Rangi looks up at me, then at his father.

"Stay where you are," Philip tells him.

"Henry," Mum says, "don't make it worse."

But I can see the pain in the boy's face, and I'm furious with Philip for implying he wishes that he hadn't kept Rangi.

"You're sixteen," I say to Rangi. "You're old enough to leave home without his consent, if you want to."

Rangi looks at his father again.

"Don't you fucking dare," Philip says. He jabs a finger at me. "He's my boy, not yours. It's not my fault you're a fucking Jaffa." Jaffa—a seedless orange. I should take comfort in the fact that he's chosen to pick on my infertility because I have no other weaknesses, but funnily enough I don't find it comforting.

His eyes gleam, and his lips curve up. He knows he's hurt me.

"Fuck you," I whisper fiercely, fighting the urge to pummel him. He's not worth it. I'm not going to lower myself to his level.

Instead, I look at Rangi. "Are you coming?"

He gives me a helpless look. "I can't." He's too frightened of what Philip will do if he goes.

I go over to Mum, give her a hug, nod at Teariki, then head for the door without another look at my brother.

Outside, I get in my BMW, and within a few minutes I'm on the State Highway, heading toward Sumner Beach.

I spend the first five minutes of the journey cursing myself. At Kia Kaha I'm known for my calm, unflappable manner, but that's only because the people I deal with at work are unable to penetrate my armor. Philip, however, knows exactly where to insert the blade and how deep to drive it.

I remember Juliette's text about Cam: *He knows right where to slide the knife.* I replied: *of course he does. That's what happens when you're with someone for a long time.*

Do you think it always has to be like that?

No. I think if you truly love someone, even in an argument, you choose not to breach their defenses.

I know that the fact that Rangi confided in me hurt Philip, but that's not my fault. I didn't wound him on purpose. If I wanted to stick the knife in, I could—I'd mock his lack of education, his inability to earn a decent wage, the fact that none of his kids respect him, that none of the women he's fathered children by have been faithful to him. But I don't; I choose not to breach his defenses because he's my brother and I love him.

Clearly, though, he doesn't feel the same way about me.

I'm twenty-eight, a successful, grown man, and long past the age where I need to earn the respect of my big brother. On paper I've surpassed him in almost every way, and nobody would say he's more successful. And yet I feel stuck in our childhood relationship, constantly trying to earn his approval and love.

I do it for my mother, and because deep down I've always hoped that if I could break through his resentment, we'd be able to share the positive sibling relationship I've always wanted.

Well, he can slide into poverty and misery for all I care. I'm fucking done with him.

The traffic is relatively light, and it only takes me fifteen minutes to get home. I slide the car into the garage, go into the house, kick off my Converses, grab a bottle of whisky, and take it out onto the deck. I pour a generous amount into the tumbler, throw myself into a chair, and knock back half the glass in one go.

Then I slide down in the chair and look out at the ocean.

My life feels as if it's slipping away from me. How can I be so in control in business and so fucking useless in my personal life?

My marriage broke down, and at twenty-eight I'm already divorced. I'm unable to father children. I haven't dated for two years, because I'm obsessed with a woman who belongs to another man, and she's showing no real signs of leaving him for me. My father died. My brother hates me.

I earn a fortune, I live in a mansion, I have three cars, a couple dozen tailor-made suits, handmade leather shoes, and the biggest, most expensive iPhone, but it's Christmas Day, and I'm sitting here, about to get drunk, alone.

So which of us, really, is the most successful?

Ah, Juliette…

I let out the longest sigh I've ever given, finish off my whisky, and pour another glass. I'm drinking too much lately, but it's the only way to numb my misery. It's weak, though, and I despise myself for it. Tomorrow, maybe I'll start doing something about it. Today, I just want to forget.

I can't forget her, though. She captivated me the first moment she walked into the bar, and it's only gotten worse over the years. Now I'm obsessed, or, more correctly, possessed. She's bewitched me. Bedeviled me. It's all her fault.

But of course it's not. Until we slept together, she hadn't done anything to suggest she was interested in me except mess up the fucking Rubik's Cube. And then I seduced her, and made her cheat on her partner, and now I'm making her life a misery, hounding her while she tries to stay loyal and faithful like any good partner should.

#PityPartyAndYou'reNotInvited.

I wonder what she's doing right now?

I mustn't contact her. I've already ruined my own family's Christmas Day; I can't ruin hers too.

I have another whisky instead.

Then one more.

The sun's going down, and I'm more than a little drunk by the time I text her.

Juliette, I miss you, I yearn for you, I burn for you, I can't stop thinking about you, I know I shouldn't message you, I know I should leave you alone, but I can't, you're in my heart, my body, my soul, you're haunting me, every time I close my eyes I can see you, your skin, your hair, your eyes, I can taste you, I remember what it was like to be inside you, to hear you say my name when you came, I love you, I want you, I need you.

I type the last word and press send, not giving myself time to think.

Then I throw my phone on the table and reach for the whisky bottle again.

Chapter Fourteen

Juliette

"Nice earrings," says Cam's mum, Kathy.

I touch the diamond lotus flowers in my ears. "Thank you."

"Where did you get them?"

"We had a Secret Santa at work, and someone bought me these. I think they're only cubic zirconia, but they're really pretty."

"They are," she agrees. "Would you like another glass of wine?"

"No, thank you."

"Well you're a cheap date this Christmas," she jokes, because I only had the one glass with my dinner.

"I've got a bit of a headache," I admit.

"I'm not surprised," she says, glancing with amusement at her husband and sons. They're playing Call of Duty on the PlayStation, and they're accompanying the firing of the guns and the commands of the soldiers with their own ramped-up yelling and laughing.

"Still," she says, "they're having a good time."

I glance at Cam, who looks the most relaxed I've seen him in months. Today, he's happy, here with his family, unplagued by the fears and doubts that normally shadow his thoughts.

I'm getting through the hours as well as I can. Kathy's nice enough, but she suffers from depression that's not well managed, and when it's bad she struggles even to get out of bed. Today she's bubbly enough, but I know that when her boys leave she's going to crash and be unable to do even the most basic tasks, and I'm not looking forward to that.

Alan and Peter's wives seem unfazed by the fact that their husbands have regressed to fourteen-year-olds, and they're sitting together, talking about some soap opera they both watch. Both of them are pregnant, and they talk incessantly about babies, making no effort at all to draw me into the conversation.

Normally I wouldn't care. I'd read a book, or talk to Kathy, relaxed enough in my own skin not to mind that I don't feel like a part of this family. But today I feel agitated and unhappy. I miss my friends—Alex, James, Tyson, Gaby, and Aroha. And I miss Henry. Oh God, Henry.

I'm not resentful because Cam and the boys are playing video games—all the guys I know have consoles and play regularly—I often play with them, for God's sake! But my friends are all educated, and they have a great sense of humor. They're constantly making clever jokes, and I'm always in stitches when we play.

I know how snobbish that sounds, but I can't help it. Peter is also a delivery driver, and Alan works in a hardware store. I shouldn't mock them—they have jobs, and I'm sure they work hard. But we played Trivial Pursuit once, and the only questions they came remotely close to getting right were in the sports category, and then only the most recent ones. They have no idea about or interest in other countries, other cultures, politics, or the arts. In fact they laugh at people who enjoy classical music or art history or literature.

Cam is different in that he did go to university, and he's an accountant, so he's pretty smart, but when he gets with his brothers, who are both older than him, he reverts to their childhood relationship and joins in with their mocking until I want to scream.

I think of the trivia night and what fun we had once Cam and Cassie left. About how we bickered about the answers, and all the jokes we told. Cam hates our banter, and thinks the guys are elitist and trying to shut him out. They're not, because they're all decent, kind men who've done their best to welcome him into our group of friends, but Cam has shut himself out, then complains when he can only look in from the outside.

I watch the guys playing now, and the two women sitting talking to Kathy, and wonder if I've done the same. I have tried to fit in here. I really have. But I just don't.

I'm the misfit. I'm the one who wanders through the corridors of these relationships like a ghost.

I want to go home, but I know that after they've finished playing, they'll want to watch a movie, and there'll be turkey sandwiches and more drinking and awful, obvious jokes until everyone stumbles to bed blind drunk. We're staying here tonight, but I can't go to bed at seven p.m., and I can't sit and read a book on my own because that'll look rude, so instead I have to join in with the conversation, and watch the movie, and just hang in there until the day's finally over.

Cam finally wins whatever battle they were playing, and he whoops and punches the air.

"Aw, Pete," his wife complains. "You suck."

"Only my girl knows what it's like to be with a real man," Cam teases.

"Yeah, well, it runs in her family," Pete says. It's a reference to Antony being gay.

Alan and their father snigger. Cam sends me an apologetic look, but he doesn't berate his brother, and Pete just glances at the others, who try not to laugh, and fail.

My face flames. If it was just the two brothers, I'd have called them out on their rudeness. But it's Christmas Day, and I'm in his parents' house, and I know that if I make a fuss, everyone's going to blame me for spoiling the atmosphere, not Pete.

My heart aches with resentment and frustration. I think of Henry with his family, and wonder if he's having a better time. I miss him so much.

Today I'm wearing jeans and a red tee with a white Christmas bauble. It's unusual for me—normally I'd wear a sari on a special day like this—but I wanted to wear something with a pocket so I could keep my phone in it. Now, it buzzes against my butt, announcing the arrival of a text.

It could be anyone. But somehow, I know it's Henry, our thoughts reaching out through the ether, finding each other.

"Just going to the bathroom," I announce.

Nobody reacts. I'm not sure anyone even heard me.

I walk through the house to our bedroom at the other end, go into the *en suite*, and close and lock the door. I take my phone out of my pocket, put down the lid of the toilet seat, and sit. I tap the screen. The green banner pops up with a small photo of Henry's face that I took earlier this year at Tyson's wedding. He's looking at me, his lips twisted and his eyes gleaming, which I'm sure now means he was thinking about what I look like naked.

I tap the banner and read his message.

When I'm done, I put the phone down, lean my elbows on my knees, and cover my face with my hands.

My heart hurts. It feels as if someone is squeezing my brain in their hand.

His message is heartfelt, and full of hurt and pain. He doesn't sound as if he's forgetting about me while he has a great time at his family's. He sounds drunk, miserable, and lonely.

And it's all my fault.

I'm not to blame for his infertility, for his marriage ending, or for the fact that he hasn't dated in two years. I've never led him on, or promised him anything—Jesus, I wasn't even convinced he was into me until the trivia night. But when I slept with him, I opened Pandora's Box, and now neither of us can get our obsessive thoughts back inside it.

I miss you, I yearn for you, I burn for you…
You're in my heart, my body, my soul…
I love you, I want you, I need you…

Hot tears prick my eyes so badly it hurts. I fight not to let them fall—I'm wearing kohl and I don't want to go out looking like a panda—but it makes my throat hurt to hold the emotion back.

How does he know exactly what to say to make me hunger for him?

I look at the message again, my thumb hovering over the keypad. I shouldn't message back. I shouldn't encourage him. I'm here with my partner, and it's Christmas Day, and I hate myself for cheating on him again.

I believe that if you're contacting someone who isn't your partner with a message that you wouldn't want to show them, it's inappropriate. It's how I've been brought up, and it's almost impossible to change the way you were programmed when you were a kid.

Messaging Henry back would be cheating on Cam. Because if I showed Cam what Henry has just sent me, it would hurt him terribly. And I still love him. At least I think I do. Don't I? Or do I love Henry? Is it possible to love two men at the same time? In different ways?

My love for Cam is—or at least, has been up until this point—solid, dependable, protective, comfortable, content, supportive, affectionate, and committed.

My love for Henry is… electrifying. Passionate. Exciting. Obsessive. All-consuming. Maybe even feverish. It's new love, which isn't the same as old love. I know that. And it's unfair to compare one with the other.

But it's too simplistic, because that's not all I feel for Henry. I trust him more than I do Cam. Is that a strange thing to say about my partner? I respect Henry more, too. I know he'd never cheat on his girl. And whatever Cam says about the sex surrogate being a therapist, I can still only see what he did as cheating.

Cam is like the moon—he only reflects back the love I give him. I'm not sure he's ever shown me any love of his own.

Henry is like the sun. He sears me with blistering heat—but that's not all. He brings me warmth and brightness, and makes me feel positive, enthusiastic, and joyful. He gives me solace and support. He nourishes my soul, which, I realize with some surprise, Cam has never done.

And then I think about the fact that Henry can't give me children, and press my hand over my heart. I know he doesn't want to go through IVF. He had two years of monthly disappointments, and I know he's afraid a repeat of that experience could kill whatever feelings we have for one another. But it doesn't have to be like that, right? If we were to support one another, and deal with it together, we could get through it.

And if he were to decide he couldn't do it, what then? Do I turn my back on a relationship with him to have one with Cam—or some other man—just because I want to be pregnant one day? Is having a child more important than having a loving, supportive relationship? Oh God, what a question to have to ask myself.

He knows how hard this decision is for me. *I know I shouldn't message you, I know I should leave you alone.* He understands. And it's in my hands. If I were to tell him now that I'm not leaving Cam and it's over, he wouldn't contact me like this again.

I think about us sitting next to each other in board meetings, me mixing up the Rubik's Cube, him doing it again and passing it back. Those silent conversations we've had for years, telling each other we're thinking of one another, although we've been unable to voice our feelings.

Cam is my partner, my lover, my confidante, but I've never felt about him the way I feel about Henry. And he's never felt about me the way Henry feels about me, I'm sure of it.

Duty. Responsibility. Coulda, shoulda, woulda.

Passion. Warmth. Solace. Support. Love.

I'm not a Hindu. Or a Christian. Or a Pagan. I don't worship Brahma or Vishnu or Shiva or Jesus or Hecate or Papatūānuku. I pick and choose what I want from different religions to form my own belief system based on moral codes like love, peace, wisdom, and truth. I don't care what other people think about that. Physically, socially, I'm a mishmash of cultures, and my belief system is the same.

I've read some of the Vedas, a good portion of the Bible, researched a lot about Māori gods, and also about Paganism. And from everything

I've learned and read, one image jumps into my mind right now. It's from the Tarot—card sixteen of the major arcana, called The Tower in most decks. The picture shows a tower that's been struck by lightning, tumbling down, shaken to its foundations, with people falling to their doom. It symbolizes change, upheaval, and chaos, which I'm certainly experiencing right now.

But it also refers to the rebuilding after a catastrophe. Christchurch itself has suffered several horrendous earthquakes. One caused its magnificent cathedral to crumble, and I've never seen such a sad sight as the remnants of that sacred site. When a building has been so badly damaged, you have to destroy it, right down to its foundations. Only then can you start to rebuild it. You'll never be able to recreate the original. You can only hope to construct something new, maybe even better, in its place.

That's what's happening to me now. The night of the summer solstice was the lightning strike, and now it feels as if everything is falling down around my ears. But I realize it has to, in order to create a better future. I have to destroy, in order to rebuild.

I sit with my hand over my mouth for a while, letting that thought sink in.

I read the message one more time. Then I type a reply.

Me: *Hey, sweetie.*

He replies almost immediately. *Hey! I didn't expect to hear from you tonight.*

Me: *How could I not, after that message?*

Henry: *Ah, shit. I regretted it as soon as I pressed send. I know you don't need all that right now.*

Me: *It was exactly what I needed.*

Then, quickly, I add:

Me: *I miss you so, so much.*

Me: *And just so you know, you're not the only one who's obsessed.*

Me: *I think about you night and day, with all my heart.*

Henry: *Are you trying to make me cry?*

I give a short laugh.

Me: *Maybe!*

Henry: *I don't need much provocation tonight.*

Me: *Why? Has something happened? Where are you?*

Henry: *Home. I had an argument with Philip. It ended badly.*

Me: *Oh no, Henry.*

Henry: *Ah, it's done. It's just sad. All endings are sad, aren't they?*
Me: *They are.*
Henry: *I wasn't implying anything with that or trying to force your hand.*
Me: *I know.*
Henry: *How are you doing?*
Me: *I have a headache, and it's been a rotten, awful day.*
Henry: *I'm sorry.*
Me: *But soon it'll be tomorrow, and tomorrow is another day, right?*
Henry: *Yeah.*
I hear movement outside, and someone tries the door handle.
"Honey, I'm sorry about what Pete said," Cam calls out. "Come on, don't turn it into a big thing."
"I'm on the toilet," I call back. "Give me a minute."
His footsteps walk away.
I look back at my phone.
Me: *I've got to go. I just wanted to say thank you for the message, and please, hang in there. I'm nearly done.*
Henry: *Ah, baby.*
Me: *I love you.*
Henry: *I love you too.*
Me: *See you soon.*
I turn my phone off, and slide it back into my jeans.

*

True to form, we watch a movie—some action flick that takes no brain power at all—while we eat our turkey sandwiches. Afterward, the guys decide they want to play another PlayStation game.

I say that my headache is quite bad, and I'm going to bed. Nobody—least of all Cam—bats an eyelid.

Actually, I do have a headache, and I am quite tired. I take off my makeup, get into bed, and fall asleep quickly.

I jerk awake when the bedroom door opens. I don't move, though, but lie with my eyes closed, listening.

Cam has slept in our spare room for the last three nights. That's not possible tonight because all the spare rooms are taken in this house, so we have to share a bed. I didn't tell Henry that.

I lie still, waiting. I can't hear him moving about, though. Like most guys, he normally bangs about opening cupboards and drawers, even though he thinks he's being quiet.

A whole minute passes. I count the seconds in my head, fighting the urge to turn over.

Then, eventually, I hear the door close again.

I wait for him to go into the bathroom. But I don't hear anything, and something about the way the air in the room is still tells me he's not there.

I turn over. He's gone out again. Probably back to the living room, to sleep on the sofa.

I roll onto my back and look up at the ceiling. My eyes prick with tears. I'm upset that I'm relieved, and also because I feel a deep, overwhelming sense of sadness.

All endings are sad, aren't they?

Turning onto my tummy, I bury my face in the pillow, and close my eyes.

*

The next day, after breakfast during which Cam and I don't meet each other's gazes, we Uber back to the apartment.

We don't say much in the car. Cam looks out of his window, and I look out the other side, watching the shops and apartments flash by.

When we get home, we let ourselves in, and he takes the bags through to the bedroom. I go into the kitchen, feeling suddenly nervous. I put on the kettle, more for something to do than because I want a drink.

Cam comes back out and leans a hip on the worktop.

"Do you want a cuppa?" I ask.

"No, thanks."

I study the kettle, then switch it off. Finally, I turn and look at him.

"I think we should talk," he says.

"Okay."

He doesn't say anything, though, and we look at each other for a long time.

"Why did you sleep on the sofa?" I ask eventually.

He slides his hands into the pockets of his jeans. "I know you were upset about what Pete said. I didn't think you wanted me in the bed."

"It wasn't just what Pete said. It was the fact that you didn't stand up for me. You should have told him it's not acceptable to make fun of my brother. Of anyone who's gay, in fact. Christ, Cam, this is the twenty-first century. How can you just keep quiet when someone says things like that?"

He studies the floor. I still think he's handsome, in a softer, less rugged way than Henry. He looks tired, though, and worn down.

"I think we need to be honest," he says.

"Okay."

"I don't know how to put right whatever is wrong between us." He takes a deep breath. "I know I fucked up by seeing Vanessa, because even though I feel that she helped me, I know you see it as cheating. And I get why. I just wish you could understand my motivations."

"I do."

"Then why can't you deal with it? Why do I feel as if you're accusing me, every time you look at me?"

It suddenly seems very quiet. I can't hear anything—no traffic, no voices. It's as if all that exists is me and him, in this room.

There's no place to hide anymore. We can't paper over the cracks any longer. They're getting too wide and too deep.

"Honestly?" I say eventually. "Because I don't know that I can get over what you did."

His frustration boils over. "Just because you're so fucking perfect. You never put a foot wrong. You don't understand what it's like for us lesser mortals to have to deal with the shit that life throws at us."

"I'm not perfect, Cam."

"You act like you are, and it's incredibly hard to live with sometimes."

"I'm not perfect." I take a deep breath. It's time. "On the trivia night, when you left… I went back to Henry's hotel."

Finally, after coping with days of fallout, the nuclear bomb explodes.

Cam stares at me. "What?"

"I stayed the night with him."

He's quiet for a moment. Then he says, "You mean on the sofa?"

"No. We slept together."

His jaw drops. "You had sex?"

"Yes."

He turns and walks into the living room, and stands by the sliding doors, staring down at the street.

After a while, I follow him in. I feel better now it's out in the open. I don't have to hide it anymore.

"Were you drunk?" he asks eventually.

"Yeah, a little bit. But that wasn't why I slept with him. I was upset, and angry, and sad, and lonely. And he made me feel better."

He turns from the window. "Are you paying me back? Is that what this is? Tit for tat?"

"Did I want you to understand how hurt I feel? Maybe. But that was only a small part of it. I like him. He makes me feel good about myself. He wants to be with me."

"Do you want to be with him?"

I swallow hard. "I think so. Yes."

He presses his hand on his chest. "Fuck," he says. "Jesus. I swear, I heard a crack just then. You've actually broken my fucking heart."

I press my fingers to my mouth. It's an unfair thing to say, because he cheated first. But I know then that he doesn't see what he did as cheating. He really thought he was trying to get help for himself, and for our relationship.

I'm not sure what I expect him to do. Yell at me, I guess. Scream. Cry. Throw accusations at me. Call me names.

But he doesn't do any of that. Instead, he sinks into one of the armchairs, puts his face in his hands, and starts crying.

For a moment, I just stand there, shocked. I've seen him display a whole range of emotions, from fury to resentment to embarrassment to being curled up with laughter. But he's never cried in front of me. Not once. Not when his dog died a year after we met. Not when his grandfather died a year later. Not after any of our arguments. Not even when he told me about his abuse.

But now he's crying for real—not just a tear trickling over his lashes, but full-grown, heart-rending sobs.

"Cam..." I go over to him and put a hand on his head. "Come on, don't cry..."

He doesn't stop, though, and eventually I lower down onto my knees and put my arms around him.

"I'm sorry," he says, his voice hoarse.

"It's okay."

"I can't bear it," he whispers. "I don't want to lose you."

My own eyes prick with tears. "Aw, come on…"

"I love you so much."

Tears run down my cheeks. "I know."

"I don't tell you enough. I find it so hard, I don't know why. The words just won't come out. When you say I love you, you're giving the other person the power to hurt you."

"That's true, but that's the beauty of a relationship. Trusting that the other person *won't* hurt you."

"I know, but it's so hard. I've built this wall around myself, around my heart, and I'm too afraid to let anyone in. It's the only way I can cope."

I move back as he lowers his hands and wipes his cheeks. His green eyes glisten.

"I understand," I say. "I know how hard it is for you. But the thing is, I need someone who will tell me he loves me. Who'll respond when I touch him. Who isn't afraid to hold me and show affection. I'm sorry, but I've tried so hard, and I just feel so lonely."

"I know." He meets my eyes. "But what if I was to try harder?"

"Cam… come on. We've tried so many times to make this work."

"I know, but this is the first time I've really understood that I'm going to lose you if I don't change."

I don't say anything, brushing a hand over my face. Oh God, this is so hard.

"I love you," he says. "For Christ's sake, don't throw away seven years for a fucking one-night stand."

I bristle, just a little. I suppose it was a one-night stand. But it felt so much more than that. A culmination of years of hope and longing.

"I don't think we can get over the problems we have," I say. "Maybe we could try if it was just about communicating better, but I think the issues we have in the bedroom are too hard to overcome."

"Don't say that. I'll change."

"Cam…"

"I swear, I'll change. I won't ask you to do any of those things. I shouldn't have gone to see Vanessa, I shouldn't ask you to change for me. I know that. We'll work together. We'll talk about it, and spend more time on foreplay. I'll work really hard."

I think about Henry. How easy it was with him. We didn't have to work at anything. It just happened, and it was such a relief.

"I'm not going to let him take you," Cam says fiercely, and I know then that he could see I was thinking about Henry.

"It's not up to you," I say desperately.

"You're my girl," he says. "And he's a thief who's snuck in during the night. I'm not going to let him steal you away from me. I'm going to fight for you, Juliette. I'm not just going to let you go."

I didn't expect this. I thought he'd be mad that I'd slept with someone else, and that he'd either ask me to leave, or walk out. I thought once I told him that it'd be easy. Oh God, I was so wrong.

It's my turn to cry then.

Chapter Fifteen

Henry

I don't hear from Juliette for two days.

That worries me. After our text message on Christmas Day, and her saying *I'm nearly done*, I thought the next time I heard from her, it would all be over. But nothing.

I leave it until the twenty-seventh, and then I text her.

Me: *How are you doing?*

But she doesn't reply.

I know then that it's not good news. Something's happened to stop her leaving. Cam? Almost certainly.

Maybe the guy's got bigger balls than I thought.

I don't hear from Philip, either, and although Rangi does text me, they're monosyllabic messages that nevertheless tell me a lot about the atmosphere at his house.

I spend the days at home alone, and, getting irritated with myself for being morose and for drowning my sorrows in alcohol, I start on a health kick. I stop drinking, put away all the junk food, tell my chef that I only want healthy food from now on, and draw up a fitness plan. I start swimming every morning and evening, and I work out in my gym, too, giving myself a punishing routine that leaves me exhausted and aching.

It's probably the wrong time to start because I'm about to head to Wellington for Damon's wedding. But it gives me something to concentrate on.

So the hours pass, as they always do, and eventually it's Thursday, and it's time to head for the airport.

I catch an Uber, and when I arrive, I make my way to the private gate, where The Orion—Kia Kaha's plane—is waiting. Alex is flying Missie up in his helicopter, but Gaby, Tyson, and James are already here. We board the plane, Gaby and Tyson sitting beside each other on one side of the aisle, James and I sitting across the table on the other side.

I'm nervous. I have no idea if Juliette's even coming still, or whether she's bringing Cam. I study my phone, my mouth going dry, and then my pulse speeds up as I hear her talking to the flight attendant behind me.

She walks down the aisle, and I look up as she passes me.

"Hey," she says to nobody in particular.

"Hey, Juliette," Gaby, Tyson, and James reply.

She slides across into the seat by the window opposite Tyson. Today she's wearing long, loose, white pants and a white vest with a wave pattern in various shades of orange that suit her light-brown skin. Her hair is pinned up in a bun with a Māori bone comb. A glittery orange bindi sits between her brows.

Making herself comfortable, she puts her purse on the seat next to her, and settles in. Only then does she glance up at me.

She gives me a small, brief smile. Then she looks away, out of the window.

"No Cam?" Gaby asks her.

Juliette doesn't look at me. "No, his brother is over from the UK, and he decided he wants to spend some time with him."

Gaby nods and asks her something about the wedding, and the two of them continue to talk. I study my phone, even though I'm not seeing what's on the screen.

So she's still with him, then. But he's not here. What does that mean?

I can't ask her in front of everyone, though. I can only hope that at some point over the next three days I'll be able to find an opportunity for a private conversation.

At that moment, there's another voice behind me, and I see a look of alarm appear on James's face. It's Aroha, and, judging by his expression, he wasn't expecting to see her.

She sits next to me, and I exchange an amused look with him, acknowledging that we're both in the doghouse. It could have made for a very awkward flight, but to be fair, Aroha is pleasant and obviously keen not to make a fuss. The hour passes quickly, and soon we're landing in Wellington and making our way to the minivan that's come to take us to Damon's parents' house, Brooklyn Heights. It's a mansion really, high on top of one of the Wellington hills, an absolutely gorgeous place.

Once we arrive, we make our way to the top terrace where we're greeted with drinks and food. Everyone's there, including all the guys from Auckland with their girls, and soon Alex and Missie arrive, and the mood is very jovial.

SERENITY WOODS

But Juliette pointedly avoids me, and I don't get a chance to talk to her.

After lunch, we're taken to the hotel, and as a group we sign in and make our way up to our rooms. She's on the same floor as me, but at the other end of the corridor, and she walks away with her case without another word to me. Sighing, I go to my room and let myself in. We don't have long before we have to leave, so I start getting ready. Today is Belle's hen party and Damon's stag night, and there's a lot to get through, so I do my best to put Juliette to the back of my mind and concentrate on helping Alex—who's Damon's best man—to make sure that everything goes to plan.

First of all, we have a paintball game. I'm not great at paintball because I'm so big—I'm easily spotted, and my coveralls are soon covered with multicolored blotches of paint. But we have a great time, and the camaraderie is high as we return to the hotel.

We all go to our rooms to shower and change, and then it's back to Brooklyn Heights. We're taken to the lower terrace, which is where the pool is. The girls are on the top terrace having a beauty spa, but they'll be joining us on the middle terrace later on tonight for a special show. They don't know yet, but the guys are all performing a song for them, a kind of half-striptease to the Kiwi band Paua of One's sexy song, *I Scream*. Alex came up with the idea about a month ago, and since then we've secretly come up with a routine for the song, which we've all been practicing. Once we have a couple of drinks down us, Alex organizes a couple of trial runs, which leads to much laughter, but is a lot of fun.

We watch a movie—*Extraction 2,* played on a projector onto a big screen, while we have a barbecue and a swim if we want to, or just lie on the loungers and doze, because we're all heading toward thirty and getting old. The food is amazing—not just burgers and sausages, but steaks, kebabs, and a huge kingfish, as well as a dozen different salads, coleslaw, and homemade bread. There's plenty of alcohol, too—beer, whisky, gin, whatever's your poison. I put aside my fitness plan for a few days, eat what I want, and have a couple of whiskies, although I'm careful not to drink them too quickly, and I have a glass of water in between each one, because it's going to be a long night.

The sun slips slowly toward the horizon, and it's nearly set when Alex announces it's time to start getting ready for the entertainment. He's already dressed in our 'costume'—a smart black suit, white shirt, and black bow tie, and while the rest of us get changed into similar attire, he heads up to the middle terrace, where the girls are apparently already seated.

We know he's begun his comedy routine when we hear laughter and cheers.

"I don't envy him," I mumble, a tad anxious about standing up in front of a group of women, even though I know them all.

"He was very nervous," Damon says, amused, "although you'd never guess. He hides it well."

We're all ready now, and I have to admit that we look smart in our matching suits. For the first time since the plane landed, I let my mind linger on Juliette. She'll be in the audience tonight, watching our routine. How will she react when it's time for us to choose our partners? Will she accept me? Or will she turn away? I'm anxious about it, but I keep it to myself, and I follow the others as we head up the stairs and wait behind the stage for Alex to finish his routine.

He told us that he was going to remove a piece of clothing if he couldn't make them laugh. He had confidence in his ability as a comedian, but privately I guessed that the girls would do their best to force him to strip, and that certainly seems to be the case, judging by the cheers. I can hear him teasing Missie, telling her jokes, and we all laugh as he begs her not to make him strip completely.

Then there's a loud cheer, and a relieved Alex announces, "Luckily, it's time for the real entertainment. Thank you, ladies, you've been a terrific audience."

Damon grins at us all and says, "Oh well, here we go!" He walks onto the stage, goes up to the mic, and says, "Dude, what the fuck? You were only supposed to tell jokes."

"They made me do it," Alex mumbles, pulling his trousers, shirt, and waistcoat on before sitting on the edge of the stage to pull on his socks and shoes. "It's a feral crowd, I'm telling you."

While Damon talks to the audience, the rest of us give supportive fist-bumps, then head out onto the stage, forming a line. It's dark now, with one spotlight on Damon and another on the DJ to the side. A heavy bass beat starts, while colored lasers jump into life.

The song—*I Scream*—is famous throughout the country, and the girls all cheer as they recognize it. I'm not surprised it earned an Explicit tag. The lyrics are filthy, but they're perfect for what we're planning to do.

We start moving to the beat, and Damon moves closer to the mic and says, "Let me hear you scream…"

The girls all scream in response, and he smirks as he begins to sing, telling them how the hot sun is going to melt their ice cream.

As he states that it's time to strip, we start unbuttoning our jackets, and the girls all scream again. I can see Juliette, sitting a few seats to the right. She's clapping and cheering with the rest of them, and although I can't be certain, I'm pretty sure she's watching me.

We join in and sing with Damon, and I make sure to direct the words at her.

"Take it, take it, take it inside,
Gonna take what I give you, gonna open wide,
Gonna melt on my tongue, gonna taste so sweet,
Girl I'm coming for you, are you coming for me?"

As one, we let our jackets drop and toss them into the audience. The girls scream, and we all laugh as we sing the chorus together.

"Ice cream, you scream, scream for me,
Love every flavor in your recipe,
I wanna lick your chocolate and strawberry,
Ice cream, you scream, scream for me!"

Every time we say the word scream, the girls all do as they're told.

We strip off our waistcoats, then finally our shirts. And then, as the guitarist goes into a wild break, we jump off the stage and each go up to one of the girls.

I walk up to Juliette and hold out a hand. "You gonna dance with me, baby?" I ask her.

To my relief, she takes my hand and lets me pull her up. I slide my arms around her, and she lifts hers around my neck.

"Lie down baby, and open wide," I tell her, "Want you to take my ice cream all inside…"

She laughs and looks into my eyes, and I lose myself in her hot gaze, as we dance to the music, our hips swaying together. Her eyes aren't cold, and they're still filled with longing.

"I've missed you," she mouths, as it's almost impossible to talk above the pounding music.

"I've missed you too." I smile, sliding my hands around to her butt and naughtily giving it a quick squeeze.

She giggles, still moving with me, and I want to do more—I want to kiss her, and stroke her, but the guys are heading back to the stage, so I release her reluctantly and join them, where we sing to the final part of the song.

The girls cheer, and we all take a bow, relieved and disappointed in equal measure that it's over. But immediately the DJ starts playing another song. It's Nine Inch Nails' *Closer*, and so we shrug on our shirts and head back down to the girls.

I dance with Juliette for a few songs, and then Alex declares we should all change partners. I'm disappointed, but it's all in good fun, so I dance with Aroha, and Missie, and Huxley's wife Elizabeth, and Mack's wife Sidnie, and all the others, to old and new songs.

I see Juliette from time to time during the evening, but there's no chance to talk. It's two a.m. before people start heading off. We all say goodbye and get into two minivans, but I discover that Juliette is in the other one. We seem destined not to be together.

When we arrive at the hotel where most of the guests are staying, we crowd into the elevators, then get out at our floors.

I see Juliette coming out of the other elevator. She glances at me, gives a small smile, then turns away and continues talking to Aroha as they head along the corridor in the other direction.

I turn and look at James, who purses his lips. "Sucks being single," he says.

Aroha revealed at lunch today that he fell asleep on her when they were making out after the trivia night. I could tease him about it, but I'm hardly in a position to make fun of him for being single.

"Yeah." I sigh. "Goodnight."

"The van's picking us up at 2:30 p.m., right?"

"Yeah." It's the wedding rehearsal tomorrow, followed by a buffet dinner and more partying.

"Okay, see you then," James says, and he goes into his room.

I walk to the next one, wave my key card over the front, and go inside.

I toss the key card onto the table and walk into the room. It's a standard hotel room, with a king-size bed in the middle, a sofa and a chair, a widescreen TV, and an ensuite bathroom. I could have paid to upgrade to one of the suites on the top floor, but everyone else is staying on this floor, and besides we're not spending much time in our rooms, so I was happy to stay here.

After the excitement and buzz of the evening, I feel oddly flat. I've drunk more than I intended; it was impossible not to when Huxley was constantly topping up our glasses when we weren't looking. So I'm feeling low because I'm tired, as well as because I didn't get a chance to talk to Juliette. I'm still none the wiser about what's been happening in her life. Maybe I should have demanded she come with me at the Heights so I could take her off somewhere quiet, but that's not my way.

I remove my jacket, waistcoat, shoes, and socks, grab a bottle of water from the fridge, and drink a third of it in one go. I sit on the sofa for a moment, intending to check my emails and social media for five minutes before I go to bed.

I've just opened Instagram and I'm smiling at a photo that Mae Chevalier has posted of Damon standing on the stage singing when there's a knock at the door.

Eyebrows rising, and wondering whether James has decided he needs a drinking partner, I go over to the door and open it.

It's Juliette.

My eyes widen. "Hey!"

She moistens her lips with the tip of her tongue and glances nervously over her shoulder. She doesn't want to be seen. "Can I come in?"

"Of course." I move back, opening the door. She slips past me, eyes downcast, and walks into the room.

Heart pounding, I close the door behind her, then follow her in.

She walks past the bed, glancing at it briefly, then stands in front of the sofa. She wraps her arms around her middle—a defensive stance, her shoulders hunched. This evening she's wearing a long, light-gray dress that sparkles in the light. Her eyelids also sparkle with glittery eyeshadow.

I rest my butt on the desk that stands against the wall. "Are you okay?"

She gives a short nod.

"You want a drink? Wine? Coffee?"

She shakes her head. "I know we didn't get time to talk today, and I felt I owed you an explanation for why I haven't messaged over the last few days."

"Okay."

She lifts her gaze to mine then. "On Boxing Day, when we got back from Cam's parents' place… I told him about us."

I stare at her. I had not expected her to say that.

"Shit," I say.

Her lips curve up, just a little.

"What did he say?" I ask, my whisky-addled mind trying to run through a thousand different options.

"He said I'd broken his heart." Her lips twist. "He was absolutely gutted, as I knew he'd be of course. I… I thought he'd go ballistic. Scream and shout at me. Call me names. Probably walk out. But he didn't. He… he cried."

Oh fuck. The clever, clever bastard.

"He said he didn't want to lose me. And that I shouldn't throw away the seven years we've spent working our relationship for my one night with you."

I fold my arms and don't say anything.

"He said he wasn't going to let you steal me away from him. And that he was going to fight for me." She stops and swallows hard.

Fuck, shit, wank, bollocks, cunt, arse. That motherfucker, gaslighting her into believing they have a golden relationship, and I'm out to ruin it.

"Right," I say.

"He begged me to stay. To talk to him about what needed to change."

"Which I'm guessing you did."

"I was very confused. So yes, I stayed. And we talked, almost non-stop, for two days."

She falls quiet for a moment.

"Did you sleep with him?" I ask.

She shakes her head.

The tight hand that had gripped my heart releases it, and I exhale. Still, I'm not out of the woods yet. "And? Have you come here to tell me this is it?"

"No," she says. "We talked, and we talked, and we talked. About everything. We were totally honest. And I think, if one thing had been different, we might have been able to make it work."

"What was the one thing?"

"It was you, Henry," she says softly. "Over those two days, it became clear to me. I didn't sleep with you to punish Cam. Or because I was sad, or lonely. I'm sure those things played a part in it. But that wasn't the reason."

She moves closer to me and looks me in the eyes. "I went to bed with you because I wanted you. I've wanted you for years, since the first time we met. I've pretended I haven't, because you were with Shaz, and I was with Cam, and I thought it wasn't meant to be. But I couldn't deny it any longer. And I told him the truth—that I'm in love with you, and I want to be with you."

I release the breath in a whoosh. My heart's thundering. I want to dance, cheer, sweep her up in my arms.

But something doesn't feel right. Why hasn't she called me? And why does it feel as if storm clouds are still circling over our heads?

"This morning, I told him I wanted to go to the wedding on my own," she says. "I said we needed time apart. He was really upset about it. He cried, again. Begged me to stay. He actually got down on his fucking knees." For the first time, anger flares in her eyes. She didn't like that. "But his brothers are still here, and I said he should spend some time with them, because we both need to think about what we want. He said he knows what he wants, but he agreed to give me space if I would agree to talk again when I get back."

She hesitates. "He wanted me to promise that I wouldn't talk to you. I refused. I said you were a friend and I wasn't going to ignore you. He got angry and said I was being unfair, because we needed to take you out of the equation. And I said I couldn't do that. I kept thinking about an image I had in my mind on Christmas Day, that when a building has been so badly damaged, you have to destroy it, right down to its foundations, so you can rebuild it again. I know I've got to do it. I've got to destroy that relationship so I can start again with you." Her bottom lip trembles. "But he's making it so hard for me. I thought when I told him about us it would all be over, but he keeps tugging on my heartstrings, and telling me that what we have is worth fighting for… And I just feel so incredibly, heartbreakingly sad…"

My brow furrows, because I remember how it felt when Shaz and I decided it was finally over. Even though it's a relief, it's so, so hard to believe the person you dedicated your life to is no longer going to be yours. You feel as if it's all been a massive waste of time. You tell yourself repeatedly that it could work if only you tried harder, loved each other that little bit more. I can see the torment Juliette's going through, and my heart aches for her. How can I get angry when she's obviously trying so hard to end it?

"I'm so confused," she whispers. "Everything's going around and around in my head, until I can't decide what to do or what I want. And I know it's unfair to you, and I'm so sorry…"

We stand there like that for a moment. And I realize I can react in two ways.

The first way is to tell her I understand, and that I'm going to give her time to think about it, and come to the decision at her own pace. To be humble and considerate, kind and gentle, tender and supportive, and just hope it all works out.

That hasn't worked well for me so far.

Or I can do it the other way.

Fuck it. Carpe diem, right?

Chapter Sixteen

Juliette

Henry has listened to everything I've said, barely speaking, his eyes flashing every now and then as I say something that obviously upsets or angers him. As I stand there miserably, having come to no conclusions at all, I wait for him to get annoyed with me and either give me an ultimatum, or declare he's had enough and say that, if I want Cam, I can fucking go and be with him then and stop dangling myself like a carrot in front of his nose.

But he doesn't. I can see thoughts passing through his mind like fish in a glass tank, but he waits quietly, his blue eyes studying me while he has his silent debate.

He looks so gorgeous tonight. I can't believe he stripped off on the stage with all the other guys. It was quite possibly the hottest thing I've ever seen, watching them all slide off their jackets and waistcoats and unbutton their shirts. I could no more have refused to dance with him than flown to the moon.

And now, his hair is flopping over his forehead, his eyes are sleepily tired, and he has a dark shadow of bristle on his jaw. He's barefoot, and his shirt is only held together by two buttons in the middle, so I can see his chest hair. The smell of his cologne rises to my nostrils, warmed by his skin. My fingers itch to slip beneath the cotton and creep up his back, but I can't do that, because he's not mine, and I have no right to touch him, and oh jeez I'm so fucking miserable because I want this man and I can't have him.

What's he going to say?

His arms are still folded, but as I watch, he lowers them, his hands resting on the edge of the table he's perching on. He tips his head a little to the side, and he fixes me with his steady gaze.

"Oh, I think you know what you want," he says. "You wouldn't be here if you didn't."

My heart stutters, and for a moment I can't breathe.

He pushes off the table and stands, then closes the distance between us, moving right up to me, until we're only an inch apart. He's so tall, and even though I'm wearing high-heeled sandals, he towers over me, so imposing with his wide shoulders and broad chest.

He lowers his hands and rests them on my hips, low down, almost on the outside of my thighs. Then he begins to gather up the material of my dress.

Keeping his gaze on mine, his lips curving up as my eyes flare, he continues to gather until he reaches the hem. My heart is now thundering so loudly I'm amazed he can't hear it.

Once again, he's shocked me. He's such a nice boy. Deep down, I thought the best I could hope for was a hug, and for him to tell me everything's going to be all right, and maybe, if I was lucky, he'd give me a comforting kiss.

Instead, he pauses and waits for me to give my assent. When it comes—because I'm helpless to do anything other than nod—he lifts the dress up my body. Automatically I raise my arms, and he draws the material up over my head, then drops the dress onto the sofa.

He inhales. The only underwear I'm wearing is a white lace thong.

"Jesus Christ," he says, eyes widening. "Are you trying to give me a coronary?"

That makes me laugh. "I wasn't expecting you to strip me." Despite my amusement, my eyes prick with tears, because he's looking at me as if he's not eaten for two weeks and someone has just placed a juicy steak in front of him.

He's having trouble tearing his gaze away from my body, but eventually he lifts his eyes to mine, and his expression softens.

"You're so fucking beautiful," he murmurs, cupping my face. He says it with such feeling, as if he's discovered a flower in the desert.

"You still want me?" I whisper.

A gorgeous smile spreads across his face. "*E mutunga kore ana taku aroha ki a koe*," he murmurs. It means 'my love for you is endless.'

A tear spills over my lashes and runs down my cheek. He observes it, then leans forward and touches his tongue to it, lapping it up. Fuck, why's that so sexy?

He kisses my bindi, my cheek, my nose, down to my mouth. Then he proceeds to kiss the living daylights out of me.

Ohhh… the way this guy kisses me… covering every inch of my lips, from one corner to the other… tilting his head to change the angle… slanting his lips across mine… and then sliding his tongue into my mouth with such sensual slowness that it sends bells ringing as if it's time for Sunday service.

He's just getting going when he lifts his head and looks at my hair, then pointedly at me.

"You want me to take it down?" I ask, and he nods and takes a step back to watch.

I slide out the Māori bone comb. Then, one by one, I take out the Bobby pins holding my bun in place. There are a few, but I don't hurry, informed by the heat in his gaze as it skims down me that he's enjoying the view.

Now I'm here… now I know where this is going, and that he still wants me… a strange calmness descends on me. He's right—I know what I want. Cam's muddied the waters over the past few days, but the surety I felt in the bathroom on Christmas Day—the moment where I knew I could only build my life with Henry once I let my old relationship die—returns to me now. I'm not cheating on Cam, because this is my new life. My body wants Henry, and my mind wants him too. It's foolish to believe anything else.

Gradually, I release the strands of hair, and I let them unfurl and fall to my waist in waves. Henry moves forward again and sinks his hands into it, then returns to kissing me, his fingers weaving through the strands.

"So soft," he whispers, pressing kisses up to my ear. "So silky." He touches his tongue to the lobe and then sucks it gently, making me shiver. "*Ka nui taku aroha ki a koe.*" It means 'I love you so much.'

"*Ko Hinemoa, ko āhau,*" I reply softly. It's a Māori proverb that means 'I am just like Hinemoa, I'd risk all for love.' Hinemoa was the daughter of a great Māori chief who fell in love with a man called Tūtānekai. Because he wasn't rich or powerful enough to ask for her hand in marriage, he loved her from a distance. Neither realized their love was reciprocated until eventually she swam across the lake to be with him.

He lifts his head to look at me, obviously realizing the way our story kind of mirrors the tale.

"I'm swimming," I tell him. "I will get there."

His eyes shine as he slides one hand onto my hip and holds my other hand, and then he softly sings the first verse of the well-known folk song that tells their story, called *Pōkarekare Ana*.

"*Pōkarekare ana, ngā wai o Waiapu, whiti atu koe hine, marino ana e.*" 'They are stirred, the waters of Waiapu, but when you cross over, girl, they will be calm.'

He twirls me in a circle, then brings me back into his arms for the chorus. "*E hine e, hoki mai ra, ka mate ahau, I te aroha e.*" 'Oh girl, return to me, I could die of love for you.'

Oh God, this guy is killing me.

Bending, he lifts me in his arms, wrapping my legs around his waist. Suddenly full of joy that I haven't felt in so long, I crush my lips to his. I run my hands through his hair, loving the feel of the short strands on the back of his head and the way the top bit curls slightly beneath my fingers. Then I cup his face and brush my thumbs across his cheeks, adoring his manly stubble.

"You're going to give me bristle rash on my thighs," I tell him, and he laughs with the same unadulterated joy that I'm feeling.

"Presumptuous," he says, taking me over to the bed. He pulls back the duvet, then climbs on and lowers me onto my back.

"You're not going to go down on me?" I pout.

He lowers on top of me, deliciously heavy, and touches his nose to mine. "You really think I'm going to finally get you into bed again, and not taste you?" His voice is low and sultry; I can hear the hunger in his words. I shiver, and he groans. "Every time you do that, I get a little bit harder." He kisses down my neck to my breasts and covers one of my nipples with his mouth.

I arch my back with a moan. I'm not sure I believe he can get any harder. His erection is already like an iron bar pressed against my thigh, and I shudder at the thought of it sliding inside me.

"I've dreamed about this," I whisper as he swaps to the other breast. "Every night. You haunt me, Henry."

"Good." He sucks hard.

"Ooh!"

He leaves my breast and kisses back up to my mouth—big, hard, wet kisses. "I want you to have no other thought in your head but me," he demands. "During the day, and in your dreams. When someone says my name, I want it to make you clench inside as you think about me making you come."

"Jesus." I think I'm going to faint.

"I'm going to give you so many magnificent orgasms, you won't be able to look at me without thinking about climaxing," he says. "I'm going to make you sound like Meg Ryan in *When Harry Met Sally* for ninety-nine percent of the day."

"Only ninety-nine percent?" I ask, panting, as he kisses up my neck.

"You're allowed a one-percent lapse of concentration in a dire emergency." He chuckles and kisses my lips again. "Once you're mine," he says fiercely, "I expect to be a part of every thought you have."

"I'm already yours," I say, meaning it.

He moves back and looks at me. "No, you're not. Not yet. But you will be. And it's going to be amazing. Just me and you, out at Sumner Beach, making love on the deck and on the kitchen table and in the bath and on the bed." He kisses my nose. "Or wherever else you choose to live with me. I don't care. I just want to be with you."

My head spins. I purposely haven't drunk much for the past few days, wanting to try and keep a clear head, so it's not alcohol—it's Henry talking about us living together. If I've given any thought past leaving Cam and putting that relationship behind me, it was to presume I'd have to find a place of my own and live there for a while, as I dated Henry and we got to know each other more intimately. But he's talking as if he wants me to move in with him right away.

Wow, talk about fast forward. Is that what I want? I can barely catch my breath. I've never been to his house, but I'd love to see it. Alex told me it cost Henry five million bucks. I bet it's magnificent. But to live there, with him? Right now?

We get on well, but working together isn't the same as living together. Maybe he's untidy, or has lots of irritating habits. And I'm hardly perfect; perhaps after a few months of getting to know me he'll grow to hate all the things he thinks are quirky and amusing right now. I can't just move from one relationship to another without stopping at the border to show my passport.

And yet… I imagine living with this man… eating together, watching TV together… being a couple, in front of our friends and family. And sleeping beside him every night… making love with him whenever I feel like it…

And sex… oh God, what about sex? It's not going to be complicated. I won't have to find ways to dominate him to turn him on. It's going to be pure and sweet and lava hot.

At that moment, he tugs me down the bed, takes my hands, and pins them above my head, and I laugh.

"What's so amusing?" he asks, looking down at me.

"I was thinking I probably won't have to dominate you to turn you on."

"Yeah," he says with a laugh, "never gonna happen. You'd better get used to that."

"You don't fancy being a sub?"

"Nope." He kisses down my arm, along the sensitive skin from my elbow to my armpit, then licks all the way up it.

"Jesus, Henry! Gross."

"I am gross. I am disgusting and perverted. I am going to lick every inch of your skin, and taste your sweat, and stick my tongue in all the darkest places of your body."

"Oh my God."

"There's not going to be a single piece of you that I won't explore, so I hope you're prepared, my beautiful Hinemoa." He lifts up to look at me again. "You want out?"

I shake my head.

He lifts an eyebrow. "You're going to be permanently exhausted."

"Don't care."

"You'll have to be buried in a Y-shaped coffin."

That makes me laugh. "Bring it on."

He smiles. "I'm so incredibly happy right now."

"How drunk are you?"

"Just the right amount." He begins to kiss down my body. "I need to taste that sweet body."

"Okay, but I don't need a running commentary."

"Oh I'm definitely going to give you a running commentary. I am now kissing your beautiful breasts." He presses his lips across them. "Now I'm going to suck those soft nipples, and you're going to moan." He takes one in his mouth and fulfills his promise, and, despite my indignation, a quiet moan escapes me.

"Perfect," he says. "Now I'm going to kiss over your soft belly and down to your amazing pussy."

"Argh, don't call it that."

"My sweet, sweet kitty." He hooks his fingers into my thong. "Hardly worth it," he mumbles, sliding it down my legs and over my feet. He presses his nose to it and inhales, his eyes meeting mine.

"Henry!"

Still holding it, he moves between my legs and pushes up my knees. "Look at you, all swollen and glistening for me."

"Oh my God."

"Beautiful, moist, and juicy. Like fucking nectar." He lowers the thong between my legs. Then, to my shock, he presses it against my entrance and, very, very slowly, pushes the material into me.

I gasp. "Henry!"

He ignores me. Once the material is all inside me, he gives me a hot glance, then carefully extracts the thong again. I groan at the sensation of the material being drawn through my sensitive, swollen folds. He lifts the thong to his nose and inhales, then, as I stare at him, he places it in his mouth and sucks it as he pulls it out again.

"Jesus," I mumble. "You're completely depraved."

He tosses the item away. "I thought you should know what you're letting yourself in for. Now, open your legs."

Still blushing at what he did, I press my knees together and give him a rebellious look.

He leans over me again and stares down into my eyes, giving me the kind of look he gives me in the boardroom when I've been sassy to him. "Okay, let's get one thing straight. In bed, I'm in charge, and I expect you to do as you're told."

"Are you always this bossy?"

"Yes. And you can be as much of a brat as you like, but you should know now, I'm always going to win."

"Ooh," I say, linking my arms behind his neck. "Challenge accepted."

He gives a short laugh. Then he bends to kiss me. "We're going to have so much fun. But tonight it's late, and Huxley made me drink too much, and I just want to enjoy myself. Is that okay?"

I nod.

"So you're going to be a good girl and open wide for me?"

My face heats again. "Are you determined to make me blush?"

He begins to kiss down my body again. "You're going to have to get used to that."

I sigh and cover my face with my arms as he lowers down between my legs and pushes up my knees. I feel him part my folds with a hand on either side, and a pause tells me he's admiring the view, which makes me blush even more.

But then he dips his head and slides his tongue down into me, and all other thoughts flee my mind.

I ascend to the stars glittering out in the night sky as he slides two fingers inside me, and as he licks and sucks and teases my clit with the tip of his tongue until I'm writhing and gasping on the bed.

As everything begins to tighten, he lifts his head and waits a few seconds before starting again. He does that a few times, edging me toward the cliff, and then finally, when I'm trembling and begging for release, he closes his mouth over my clit and sucks, and this time he doesn't stop.

Every muscle inside me contracts, and I cry out with pleasure, clamping around his fingers as the pulses hit. Six, seven, eight… ooh, they seem to go on forever… but eventually they stop, and I fall back onto the pillows.

He withdraws his fingers and sits up. "I'm never going to wash again," he announces, brushing his hand over his face and inhaling.

I huff a sigh, knowing it's pointless to object.

Smirking, he straddles my hips, then unbuttons his shirt, slips it off his massive shoulders, and tosses it onto the floor. Keeping his gaze on mine, he unbuckles his belt, then slowly slides it out through the loops of his trousers.

When it's out, he folds it in half. "Do you like being tied up?" he asks mildly.

I swallow hard. "I don't know."

He smiles, then tosses the belt onto the floor. "Something to think about." He undoes the button of his trousers, then slides down the zipper.

I can't help it—as if it's a magnet and my eyes are made of iron, my gaze drops to his black cotton boxer-briefs.

"Oh," I say in a helpless, squeaky voice.

He pushes down the elastic of his underwear, releasing the erection that is straining toward me, eager for action. Fuck me, he's massive.

He closes a hand around it and gives himself a couple of slow strokes. Then, leaning forward, he takes my hand and moves it down.

He wants me to touch him. First, I slide my hand down into myself. I'm swollen and slippery, and I coat my fingers with the moisture there before closing them around him. As I stroke him, my hand glides over the soft skin that coats the iron-like bar.

"So hard," I murmur, exploring the feel of him, the ridges and veins, the smooth, velvet head. "Can I taste you?" I whisper, my voice husky with longing.

But he shakes his head, leans over to retrieve his wallet, and takes out a condom. "Not tonight. My willpower isn't that great, and I want to be inside you." He glances at me as he tears open the packet. "Don't pout."

"You got to taste me."

"Yeah, but you can have multiple orgasms. I'll be asleep in five seconds after my first, so I have to make the most of it." He smiles as I laugh and rolls the condom on. Then, before I can protest, he grabs me and rolls onto his back, bringing me with him.

"I don't want to be on top," I remind him, feeling a touch of panic. Cam always preferred me on top as it made him feel subservient, and I don't want to be reminded of that.

But Henry says, "Doesn't mean you're in charge," and with that he takes my hands in his, then lifts his arms above his head, pulling my hands with them. It forces me to lean forward, bringing my breasts up to his face, and without further ado he latches on to one of my nipples and sucks.

"Ooh, fuck." I close my eyes, impressed by his adeptness. For a big guy, he's pretty damn smooth.

He swaps from one nipple to the other, licking and teasing with his teeth and tongue until I can feel pleasure rising inside me again. Eventually he releases my hands and slides his fingers from the back of my knees up my thighs to my butt. Curving an arm over my thigh, he slips his fingers down into my moist skin from behind and explores there for a while before finally drawing some of the moisture up between the cheeks of my bottom. Then he teases the tight muscle there with a finger, making me gasp and moan in equal measure, until I'm quivering with need.

Lifting up, he flips me easily onto my back again.

"You weren't kidding about being disgusting and perverted," I accuse, panting.

"Nothing about you is forbidden to me." Propping himself on one hand, he uses the other to guide the tip of his erection inside me. Once he's there, he leans either side of my shoulders and looks me in the eyes. "Relax."

"Oh my God, that's impossible."

"Why? This isn't our first time."

"I was drunk last time. Now I'm aware of how big you are."

"And you're very wet. You'll be fine. Deep breath in, baby girl."

I do as I'm told, inhaling. I hold it for a moment, then as I breathe out, he slowly slides inside me.

"Oh!" I bite my bottom lip and screw up my nose.

He stops. "Relax," he says again, amused.

"I'm trying." I breathe in, then out, and he withdraws a little, then pushes forward again.

Slowly, he sinks into me, deeper and deeper, and each time I'm convinced there's no more to go, and each time he says, "Just a little more," until finally his hips meet the back of my thighs, and I feel absolutely full and stretched to my limits.

"Good girl," he says, his voice husky.

"Oh my God."

"You feel amazing." Looking down at where we're joined, he withdraws all the way.

"We just got there," I complain.

"Yeah, but the process was fucking hot, and I want to do it again." He lowers a hand and strokes the tip of his erection up though my moist skin so it rubs on my clit a few times, then presses it back inside me. Once again, he pushes forward. It's a little easier this time, and just takes three thrusts until he bottoms out.

He lifts his hand to my breast and plucks the nipple. I clench around him, and we both groan.

"So tight," he whispers, his voice almost a squeak.

Keeping my gaze on his, I purposely tighten my internal muscles in my best Kegel exercise.

"Aaahhh!" He closes his eyes. "Have mercy."

"I'm going to milk you dry, Henry West. So get working."

He opens his eyes and meets mine, and they lock together as he starts moving inside me.

It's late, we're tired, and we're both hyped up, so I doubt it's the most beautiful sex we're ever going to have, but it's a hundred percent pure electrifying sensation, as we both focus every ounce of awareness on the place where we're joined.

Once he's fully lubricated and I've relaxed a bit, he moves more easily inside me, and he speeds up the pace of his hips until he's thrusting hard.

"This isn't going to take long," he confirms as he plunges down into me. "I apologize in advance."

"Go for it," I urge, already feeling the approach of an orgasm, especially as he moves up an inch so he's grinding on my clit. I'm pretty sure he's hitting my G-spot too, and when I cry out, "Oh my God, yes, right there," and he gives an appreciative, "Yeah," I realize he likes me being vocal, and I give in to the urge to tell him how much I'm enjoying it, with plenty of, "Oh yes, harder," and, "That feels so good," and, "Oh God, fuck me, hard as you like."

Suitably encouraged, he goes for it with enthusiasm, and we fill the air with the sounds of sex, moving together and driving each other onward toward the final goal.

He gets there a second before me, his hands tightening into fists on the mattress beside me, his eyes closing with a fierce frown as his lips part in a deep groan, but I have no time to appreciate his climax because I'm coming too, clamping around him with incredibly strong pulses. We exclaim, both crying out, and by the time we finish, our skin is damp and we're sticking together, tired and exhausted and sated.

I open my eyes and look up into his, which seem black tonight, the pupils huge.

"Fuck," he says.

"Yeah."

"You've drained me dry. I don't think there's a drop of fluid left in my body."

I giggle. "They'll discover us like a couple of mummies in the morning."

He snorts and withdraws, disposes of the condom, then falls onto the bed beside me, on his stomach. "Five seconds," he mumbles. "I did warn you."

I roll onto my side and kiss his temple. "Go to sleep. You deserve it."

"I'm better when I'm not drunk and it's the right side of midnight."

"You were pretty good anyway." I stroke his hair. "Sweet dreams," I whisper, watching the moonlight coat his dark hair with silver.

"Mmm." He's already nearly asleep.

I pull the duvet up over him. Then, quietly, so I don't disturb him, I slip out of bed and go into the bathroom, taking my phone with me.

I tap the screen, and my heart sinks. A green banner displays a text from Cam.

Miss you, it says. *Can't wait to see you again soon. x*

Guilt pokes me, casting a shadow over the beauty of my time with Henry. Tiredly, I dismiss the text, then turn off my phone again.

When I'm done, I go back into the bedroom, switch the lamp off, then slide under the duvet and curl up next to him.

He's warm, he takes up more than half the bed, and he smells amazing.

I kiss his arm, and I'm sure I see his lips curve up before I close my eyes.

Chapter Seventeen

Henry

Someone murmurs in my ear, "I'm going to take a shower," rousing me from the depths of a dark slumber.

"Mmph." Still in the mists of dreamland, I figure I've conjured up the soft skin and low voice of the woman I love. I imagine I feel the person move off the bed and hear the bathroom door closing.

Then my eyes spring open. Juliette!

I blink a few times, trying to reboot my brain. I'm lying on my front, facing the window. Light streams through the gap in the curtains, a bright buttery yellow, so it's past sunrise—six-thirty maybe? Seven? I lift my head and turn it to the other side. The bed is empty, but the indentation in the pillow and the sheet are a sign that I didn't dream her.

I push up onto my elbows, pull her pillow toward me, and bury my face in it. It smells of her perfume and the sweet scent that is all her.

Jeez, I was so tired last night, and inebriated. I can only remember about sixty percent of everything that happened, and I have a feeling my performance was distinctly less than average. It's Huxley's fault, plying me with whisky. Well, I'm not drinking today. *Have some willpower, dude.*

I debate whether to wait until she comes out, then decide the opportunity to savor a wet, slippery Juliette is too good to be missed. I rise, yawn, stretch, collect my phone and—with a smirk—a condom, then go over to the bathroom door. I can hear the shower going. And she's humming. That's a good sign.

I knock, open the door a crack, and say, "Can I come in?"

"Yes," she calls back. "I'm in the shower."

I go in. She's in the cubicle, her body visible as a light-brown shadow through the steamy glass walls. I look at myself in the mirror and wince. My stubble is too untidy to be anything close to designer. My eyes are slits. My hair is all over the place.

"I need to pee," I mumble. "Do you mind?"

She laughs. "Fire away, sunshine. As long as you don't mind me watching." She clears a patch of steam, and her brown eyes appear, lighting with amusement as she spots my hair. "Feeling a little hungover, are we?"

Deciding it's too late for pride, I leave my phone and the condom on the sink, lean on the tiles behind the toilet, and pee. I hear her laugh as it goes on forever, and sigh. When I'm done, I flush the toilet, wash my hands, then pick up my phone. I bring up Spotify, choose The Cure's *Friday I'm in Love*, and set it playing. Then I walk over to the shower and open the door.

"It's occupied," she says, giving me a mischievous smile.

"That's the least of my worries." I get in, forcing her to move into the corner of the cubicle, and close the door behind me.

"There's no room," she complains, although by the way her eyes have widened, I don't think she's bothered.

"We'll just have to stand very close together." I tip my head back under the spray and soak my hair, then look down at her.

"Ooh," she says. "You're all shiny."

"So are you." Her smooth light-brown skin glistens as water runs down it. "Have you washed your hair yet?" She shakes her head. "Can I do it?"

She smiles. "If you want."

I tip some of the complementary hotel shampoo onto my hand, smooth it onto her hair, and massage it in. She hums to the music as I glide my fingers through the strands, and then I turn her so her back is to the spray and rinse her hair clean.

"My turn," she says when I'm done. "You'll have to bend a bit."

I dip my head so she can wash my hair, then let her rinse it, enjoying the movement of her fingers across my scalp.

Afterward, I hold her hand in mine and slide the other arm around her waist, and we dance to the song together beneath the water, both singing the lyrics. She laughs, and my spirits lift in a way they haven't for a long time.

"*Taku toi kahurangi,*" I tell her. It means 'my precious jewel.' I kiss her ear. "*Me te mea ko Kōpū ka rere i te pae.*" 'Your beauty is like Venus rising above the horizon.'

She lifts her face, and I lower my lips and kiss her. When I lift my head, her eyes are glistening.

"*Tum meri zindagi ho aur meri jaan tum men basti hai,*" she says.

"Is that Hindi?"

She nods. "You are my life and my soul resides in you." She smiles. "It's a bit soppy."

"I like soppy."

"I can see that."

I stroke up her spine, and she sighs, slides her arms around me, and rests her cheek on my shoulder. The music changes to Elton John's *Rocket Man*—it just happened to be the next random track on my liked songs playlist. As we continue to dance, and then we sing the chorus together, I carry on stroking her back. Up to the nape of her neck. Across her shoulders. Along her arms. Back to her shoulders. Down her back. Across her hips.

She draws circles on my back, across my shoulder blades, down my spine, exploring the lines of the muscles. It is sexy—she's wet and naked, so there would be something wrong with me if it didn't turn me on—but there's also something therapeutic about touching each other in this way. We're getting to know one another. I explore the tiny hollow at the base of her spine. The way her figure curves inwards above her hips to her waist. My thumb finds the small mole on her ribs beneath her left breast, and then a few moments later the other one on her shoulder. She touches the scar on my hip that I got when I came off my motorbike in my early twenties.

My stomach rumbles, and she laughs.

"Sorry," I say. "I'm starving."

"You're always starving."

"True."

"I've never met a man who eats as much as you do and still manages to stay trim."

"I have a healthy appetite." I nuzzle her ear.

"There's no time for that," she scolds.

"There's always time for that." I cup her face and kiss her, and she sighs, opening her mouth to accept my tongue. She tastes minty—she's cleaned her teeth. She gives a soft moan, which sends hairs—and everything else—rising across my body.

I kiss her for a long time, my hands skating over her body, and for the first time I stroke her breasts. When I tease her nipples with my thumbs, they tighten and glisten like wet pebbles in the ocean, and I bend to suck them, trying different pressures until she clenches her hands in my hair and exclaims, "Oh!"

Fired up now, I move her into the corner of the cubicle, and she gasps as I back her up against the cool glass. I kiss down between her breasts, lower onto my knees, and follow the trails of water over her tummy and the soft skin of her mound. Lifting one of her legs over my shoulder, I slip my tongue down into her, and her long, breathy exhale fills me with joy.

"Henry," she whispers, "oh my God…"

As I begin to arouse her with my tongue, I bring up a hand to join in the fun, moving my fingers beneath her. She parts readily for me, already swollen and slippery, and, palm up, I slide two fingers inside her, curving them toward me and pressing gently to find her G-spot. The clench of her fingers in my hair tells me when I've found the target, and I massage it as I continue to flick my tongue over her clit.

It doesn't take long for her to reach the point where her breathing becomes ragged and her legs start to tremble. After withdrawing my fingers, I get to my feet, open the cubicle door, and retrieve the condom from the sink.

"Oh, you came prepared," she says, watching me tear off the wrapper and toss it away, come back in, and roll the condom on.

"Like I'd expect us to get in the shower and be all wet and slippery and not have sex." I spin a finger in the air. "Hands on the glass."

"Seriously? There's not enough room—"

I take her by the shoulders, turn her around, and place her hands on the glass wall, then tap her foot with mine. "Spread 'em, girl."

She widens her stance, mumbling something. I move until my back is against the glass, pull her with me so she's bending more at the waist, then guide the tip of my erection into her. It takes a bit of maneuvering to get the angle, but eventually I push forward and slide slowly into her.

"Ahhh…" Her hands curl into fists on the tiles, so I stop and let her adjust.

"All right, baby girl?" I stroke her back, then around her ribs to her breasts and tug her nipples.

She groans and moves her hips, coating me with her moisture, then pushing back so I slide into her a little more. Letting her do it at her own pace, I continue to caress her, enjoying the sensation of her silky skin beneath my fingertips as gradually she impales herself on me, until our bodies are touching, and I'm right up to the hilt.

"Ohhh…" She shudders. "Wow."

"Good girl," I tell her, bringing my hands down to hold her hips. "I'll take over from here." I pull almost out, then thrust in again, and she groans.

Turned on and fired up, I set up a fast pace, and Juliette can't do much except hang on for the ride. She leans her forearms on the glass to steady herself, and I lose myself in her soft, wet body, only half conscious of the water spray pouring over us, filling the air with clouds of steam.

At first she lets me lead, her body a little tense, but gradually she relaxes and throws herself into it. She pushes back against me, and I slide a hand around her hips and find her clit, then circle the pad of my middle finger over it as I continue to thrust.

It doesn't take long, only a few minutes, until we're both panting. I hold her hips again and thrust hard… ah jeez, I'm so close… come on Juliette… and she lowers her own hand between her legs, which I love, and arouses herself until eventually she cries out and clenches around me. I give in to the climax I've been struggling to hold onto, and come hard, driving us both over the edge, our bodies locking together and turning to stone for a few moments before we both gasp and go limp.

Her legs tremble, and I quickly slide an arm around her waist to catch her before she falls.

"Careful." I withdraw, turn her, and hold her tightly.

"My legs are all wobbly."

"Mmm. Mine too. Come on." I turn off the shower, grab a towel, then lead her out. After getting rid of the condom, I wrap my arms around her and hold her as I gently rub her skin with the towel until she's dry. Then I lower her onto the toilet seat and towel her hair until it stops dripping.

"You okay?" I ask, lifting her face so I can look into her eyes.

She nods. Her eyes are huge.

I kneel down before her and cup her face. "Are you sure?"

She smiles. "I'm fine. It's just… that was a first! Kind of blew me away." Her gaze searches mine, her eyes filled with wonder, and then she lowers her lashes, slightly bashful.

She's never had shower sex? I'm puzzled, but I don't want to ask her about it. I don't want discussion about Cam and what they used to do to become a part of our life. Maybe spur-of-the-moment sex like that put too much pressure on him, and he was unable to perform.

"Is there a comb in there?" she asks, gesturing at the box of complimentary items.

I extract one in a paper sheath and pass it to her, and she begins to comb the tangles from her hair while I dry myself. When I'm done, I tuck the towel around my waist and start running hot water into the hand basin. I splash some onto my face to open up the pores, smooth on some shaving foam, then take out my razor and begin to shave.

After a few scrapes, conscious she's not said anything, I glance at her. She's finished combing her hair, and she's now watching me.

I rinse the razor. "You all right?"

She nods. "Just admiring the view."

I smile and draw the razor up my neck again. "You like what you see?"

"Very much." She gets up and walks to stand behind me, then draws her fingers up my arm. "I hadn't realized you'd taken this all the way up."

I look at the *kirituhi*—which literally means 'skin art'—or the tattoo that curls up my arm to my shoulder. She traces a finger over the *manawa* or heart lines that represent my life journey, and the *koru*—the curled silver fern symbols—that represent my *whakapapa*—my genealogy. The she examines the other patterns—the *pakati*, like diamonds of a dog-skin cloak, which are representative of warriors, battles, courage, and strength; the *unaunahi*, which are fish scales that represent abundance and health; and the figure of the *manaia*, or spiritual guardian.

"It's beautiful," she says. She has a similar one, although it's much smaller, and just on her forearm. She touches the largest koru at the top of mine. "Does this represent your father?"

I nod and continue shaving, moving up to my cheeks.

"Will you tell me about him?"

I wash the razor in the water. "What would you like to know?"

"What was his name?"

I shave carefully around my upper lip. "Edward."

"West?"

"Yeah."

"That's where your connection to George Henry West comes from?"

"Yeah." George—whose Māori name was Kāi Te Rakiāmoa—was the first pilot of Māori descent to join the Royal New Zealand Air Force in 1936.

"Do you mind talking about him?"

"Dad?"

She nods.

I rinse the razor again. "There's not much to say."

She slides her arms around my waist and kisses my shoulder. "I have a feeling that's not true. I know he died in a boating accident, but I think there's more to it than that. I'd like you to tell me the rest. But I understand if you'd rather not."

I pause. Then I finish the last few strokes, empty the water, and rinse the sink as I think about how much to tell her. I turn and rest my butt on the unit and dab my face with the towel while she watches me.

As a rule, I'm a lone wolf. I don't talk about stuff. Many Māori are close-knit, and they deal with problems together, but I've never been like that. As much as I love my family, I cope with my problems on my own; I always have.

But that was part of the issue with my relationship with Shaz. She said I was too closed off to her; that I didn't talk to her enough. And I don't want to start off my relationship with Juliette—if there is going to be one—the same way. It doesn't come naturally, but I do want to talk to her more.

I take a deep breath and say, "If I tell you all of it, you have to promise me not to tell anyone else."

Her brow furrows. "Why?"

"Do you promise?"

"Of course."

"I haven't told anyone else this."

She stares at me. "Not Shaz?"

"Nope. No one."

"Okay. I promise. Of course I won't tell anyone if you don't want me to."

Despite her vow, I'm loath to talk. It's not a pretty story, and I'm not sure whether it's going to make her question her promise not to say anything. But I've promised now, and I discover, with some surprise, that I want to confide in her.

"Do you need to rush off?" I ask.

"Not till ten. I'm meeting Gaby."

It's only seven thirty. "Come on," I say. "Why don't we finish getting ready, order some breakfast, and make a coffee, and then I'll tell you everything?"

Leaving her to dry her hair, I go out and pull on a tee and a pair of track pants. Then, after checking what she'd like, I ring room service and order a continental breakfast for two, including two lattes from the barista. It's going to be around thirty minutes before it arrives, though, so in the meantime I make us a couple of coffees with the machine in the room.

Just as I'm adding milk, she comes out, fresh-faced and beautiful. "I'll have to go back to finish getting ready for the rehearsal," she says. "Hopefully nobody will knock on either of our doors to check on us!"

She obviously doesn't want anyone to know about us yet. Our relationship feels like newly wet cement. I want to write my name in it, so everyone can see at a glance that she's mine now, but it's not what she wants, and I'm just going to have to wait until she's ready.

"Can I borrow a tee?" she asks after.

"Sure." I watch her lift a couple out of my suitcase, and then she pulls on my black *Alice in Chains* shirt. It falls past her bottom, the sleeves coming to her elbows. I'll never be able to wear it again without thinking of her.

She sits on the sofa, and I think I've never seen anything as beautiful as the sight of her, backlit by the rising sun, sitting in my tee shirt, with her gorgeous brown hair tumbling around her shoulders. She begins to braid it loosely into one plait, her fingers threading the strands automatically the way women do, and she secures the end with an elastic, then lets it fall over one shoulder.

I put our coffees on the table and sit opposite her, elbows on my knees, hands loosely linked, conscious that I'm about to open up to her, and a little nervous about it. She observes me and says, "You look younger today. Without your suit, all ruffled and baby-faced."

I run a hand through my hair, then stroke my smooth jaw. "And I was thinking that I've never seen you without your bindi. You look like Hinemoa."

"*Haere mai*," she sings, which means 'welcome', widening her eyes and making the fluttering hand movement called *wiri* that Māori women do, which symbolizes shimmering waters or a breeze moving the leaves of a tree. It gives me goosebumps.

She smiles. Then she tips her head to the side. "Are you okay? I'm thrilled that you want to talk, but if you're worried about it, you don't have to tell me, you know."

"I do want to talk. I'm not used to it, that's all, and it doesn't come naturally." I have a sip of coffee. Where to start?

SERENITY WOODS

Chapter Eighteen

Juliette

I wait for Henry to start speaking. I'm still in shock. I can't believe he's choosing to tell me something that he didn't tell Shaz. I have no idea what he's going to say. I can see him picking through his words as if he's choosing a chocolate out of a box—not that he eats chocolate. He's always been like this—thoughtful, reticent, preferring to keep things to himself. That he's chosen to confide in me touches my soul deeply.

"I guess the first thing I need to do is explain about my childhood," Henry says slowly. "My parents' relationship was not a good one. My father drank a lot, and he and Mum used to argue about it. Occasionally—not often, but I do remember it happening—he'd be violent. He'd hit her, and he beat both Philip and me a couple of times. Mum would get really upset, and then he'd regret it in the morning and be ravaged by guilt and self-loathing."

I didn't know any of this. I listen with wide eyes at this glimpse into his past.

"When he died," he continues, "Mum told us he'd been drunk, and he'd drowned in a boating accident. She was resentful that he'd left her alone with three kids, and she refused to talk about it any further. As a result, I was a very angry young man. I got into a lot of trouble, and eventually I ended up going to Greenfield."

My eyebrows rise even more. It's a school for adolescents with problems, and I'm genuinely shocked that the rich, successful Henry comes from a background like that. "Oh, I didn't know."

"That's a story for another time," he tells me. "But anyway, Greenfield turned things around for me. I worked my socks off, ended up going to uni, met you and the guys, started Kia Kaha, and began to feel better about myself. So I decided to find out about my father. Mum still refuses to talk about him, so I had to do my own research. All I knew was that he'd drowned in a boating accident, so I decided to start with the coroner's report. The immediate family of the person who died is allowed to ask for the medical reports, the post-mortem report, the coroner's findings, witness statements, all that sort of thing."

He stops to have a mouthful of coffee, then continues. "The first thing I discovered which came as a shock to me was that his body was never recovered."

That surprises me. "Oh, really?"

"Yeah. I realized then that when we had the *tangi*, there was no coffin, it was just a memorial service. I feel dumb now that I didn't make the connection at the time, but I was only twelve, and nobody would talk to me about what had happened, so I just didn't think about it."

I think about that young lad, and how miserable and confused he must have been. "I'm so sorry."

"That's not the half of it," he says. "The police report relied on the statement given by Dad's brother, David, or Rawiri as he's known." It's the Māori version of David. "I vaguely remembered him," Henry continues. "He came to visit us in Christchurch a couple of times when I was younger, and I recall him being at the tangi, but Mum was upset and angry and refused to talk to him, and he left early, so I didn't get to talk to him, and I haven't seen him since. Anyway, I read that Dad was out fishing with Rawiri on the day he died."

I'm genuinely shocked that his mother hasn't told him the details of his father's death. "He saw it happen?"

Henry nods. "Rawiri's statement said the sea was choppy but not too bad, so they decided to go out, but about an hour into their trip, a storm blew up. They struggled to control the boat, and eventually Dad was swept overboard. Rawiri spent thirty minutes trying to find him, but Dad wasn't wearing a life jacket, and he just disappeared. Eventually Rawiri returned to the mainland and called the police. The coastguard spent several days looking for him, but his body never turned up."

"Oh, how awful."

"There was an investigation, but it didn't uncover anything suspicious. The coroner eventually ruled that the cause of Dad's death was accidental drowning, and the case was closed. Anyway, Dad's death certificate gave the place of his birth as Bluff." It's a town on the southernmost tip of the South Island. "I didn't know he came from there, but I did some investigating and found out that although Dad's parents had both passed away, Rawiri still lived there."

He has another mouthful of coffee. "So, I decided I'd go and see him. I thought he might like to meet his nephew, and that maybe he'd be able to tell me a bit about him. I didn't want to do it over the phone, so I flew down there and knocked on his door one morning."

"That must have been a shock for him."

He gives a short, humorless laugh. "You have no idea. When he opened the door, his face was a picture, completely stunned. I explained quickly that I was his nephew and just wanted to talk. It was clear he didn't want to. He tried to make all sorts of excuses. Normally I'd have backed off, but something made me persist, some sixth sense that told me it was strange that he didn't want to speak to me. I thought he would've been thrilled to meet his brother's son. But he looked terrified. It took me about half an hour to convince him to invite me in, but eventually he did, and we went into his living room. He sat there with his head in his hands, obviously upset. I tried to get him to talk, but he wouldn't. In the end, I asked why he'd looked so shocked when he opened the door, and he said I was the spitting image of my dad. I asked if he thought Dad had come back from the dead to haunt him."

He sips his coffee. "He said no. Because my dad wasn't dead."

I stare at him. "What?"

"Yeah. You can imagine my reaction. He said the two of them had faked his death."

I thought he was going to say the two men had had a fight, and Rawiri was somehow responsible for his dad's death. I did not expect this.

"It all came pouring out," Henry says. "He hadn't told anyone for sixteen years, and I think once he started, he couldn't stop. He said Dad called him one day and he was deeply depressed. It was after one of his drinking bouts, and he'd had a huge argument with Mum. He was unhappy, and he said he wanted out. Rawiri tried to convince him to just leave, but Dad told him if he did that he'd have to continue paying child maintenance, and he couldn't afford it, and he was thinking of taking his own life. So they came up with a plan. They'd go out in their boat and fake Dad's death, and then Dad would be free to start a new life without anything to hold him back."

"That's awful," I whisper.

"Rawiri had had sixteen years to think about it," he continues. "He was scoured hollow with grief and guilt. He said it was the only way he could think of to stop Dad killing himself, but when he went to the *tangi*, he saw what it had done to Mum and us kids, and he felt terrible.

He said he'd thought about coming to tell us many times, but one reason he hadn't was because he was still in touch with Dad."

My jaw drops. "He's still alive?"

"Oh, very much," Henry says. "He lives in Tauranga." It's a city in the North Island. "With his second wife." He sips his coffee, waiting for my reaction.

"Wait," I say. "So… if your mum thought he was dead, it would mean they didn't get a divorce?"

"That's right."

"Oh shit! So legally they're still married to one another?"

"Yep."

"So they're both committing bigamy?"

"Yep."

"Holy fuck."

"Yeah," he says with feeling.

We sit in silence for a moment as that sinks in. Jesus, what a predicament.

There's a knock at the door, and Henry says, "Breakfast, I think."

Just in case it's James or someone else we know, I run into the bathroom, but it is breakfast, and when I come out, I'm met with the mouth-watering smell of freshly baked croissants.

Henry adds a pot of the chopped fresh fruit to one of the bowls of muesli, pours over the milk, then sits back to eat it. I take one of the croissants, some butter, and jam, tear off a piece, and eat it slowly as my brain processes what he's told me.

"Bigamy is against the law, right?" I ask him.

He nods. "It carries a prison sentence of seven years."

"Wow. For all of them or just him?"

"It's complicated. Apparently it's thought to represent a threat to public morality, and to compromise the institution of marriage. If the spouse of the second marriage—Dad's second wife, in this case—was aware that he was still married, then they would both probably get two years. If she didn't know, and especially as more than seven years have passed, a judge would most likely find her innocent. The same for my mum and Teariki, although Dad would get the whole seven years."

He has a few spoonfuls of muesli while I eat my croissant, thinking.

"So, what did you do?" I ask eventually.

"I went to see him."

My eyes widen again. "What happened?"

"I went to his house and knocked on the door, but he wasn't there. He lives right near the beach, so I walked down to the sand, and then I saw him. He was with his wife and two of his kids. Apparently he has four now by her. Rawiri said he'd stopped drinking. He has a steady job. He looked happy."

"So what did you do?"

He stirs the muesli with his spoon. "I didn't do anything. I watched him for half an hour. Then I walked away, flew home, and didn't tell anyone."

"How long ago was this?"

"About two and a half years."

That shocks me. I'd assumed this had all happened recently. "Christ, Henry. Why didn't you tell Shaz?"

"My marriage was falling apart by that point. I was unhappy and lonely. I didn't talk to her enough at the best of times, and I wasn't going to start confiding in her when things were bad between us."

That's why he's telling me—because he feels guilty he didn't tell her. Māori men are often quiet and shy, and if you add to that his troubled youth and his anger and resentment toward his father for dying and leaving him, he's obviously grown up reluctant to talk about his feelings.

I try to imagine how that must make him feel. That his father didn't love him enough to stay. That he was so unhappy with his first family that he faked his own death to get away from them. God, what must that do to a man?

I put down my plate, get up, and go over to his armchair. He places his bowl on the table as I approach, then sighs as I sit on his lap, loop my arms around his neck, and give him a hug.

"I'm so, so sorry," I say, resting my lips on the top of his hair.

He doesn't say anything.

"It wasn't you, Henry," I say, stroking his hair. "Your father didn't leave because of you."

He still doesn't speak, but I know that's what he's thinking.

"He obviously suffered from depression, and maybe he was caught in a cycle of poverty and misery where he couldn't see a way out." I kiss his hair, thinking about my own predicament, and how sometimes it's so hard to separate yourself from a situation, even if you're unhappy.

His father would have known that if he asked for a divorce, he would have had to pay child maintenance for Henry's mum and their three children. He would have been tied to them, even though he knew he was making the family unhappy. As a poor man, he would have found it almost impossible to find a well-paid job he enjoyed, to escape on regular vacations, or even to indulge in expensive hobbies to take his mind off it. Alcohol would have become a crutch, and he would have seen his wife's and children's misery on a daily basis, and known he was the cause of it. In his father's eyes, he was helping his family by leaving.

But from Henry's point of view, his father didn't love him enough to stay. He's happier with his new family. And that has to hurt.

Why hasn't he told anyone? Surely he must be tempted to punish his father by revealing what he's done? It has to be a huge weight to bear alone.

But I know the answer, even as it springs into my mind. It would ruin his mother's marriage and his father's second marriage, and crush his siblings and his new half-siblings, who would be devastated to know what their father had done. Having to carry the burden of it rather than destroy all those lives would be a small price for Henry. He wouldn't even consider making himself feel better by offloading the information if it meant harming someone else.

He shifts awkwardly beneath me. His hands are resting on the arms of the chair, and he's not hugging me. He's regretting his confession.

I slide a hand under his chin and lift it so I can look at him. "I'm so glad you told me," I say.

His eyes harden, and his body stiffens. "Don't feel sorry for me," he says. "I don't want your pity. I'm not Cam."

Ooh, ouch. That stings. I know he despises Cam. Not the fact that he was abused, because Henry is a kind man who would always help those in need. But I'd guessed he dislikes how Cam treats me and takes advantage of me, and now he's confirmed it openly.

I don't blame Cam for being the way he is because he's been through a lot. But when it comes down to it, forgetting about his abuse, at heart he is a weak man who often takes the easy option, and who expects other people to sort out his problems.

Henry is a strong man with weaknesses. There's a huge difference. He's very proud, and he doesn't expect—and probably wouldn't—accept—help from anyone. He's a self-made man who's come from a troubled background, and who's worked extremely hard to get where he is. He has no time for people, especially men, who prey on others' weaknesses, who lack self-discipline, and who expect others to solve their problems for them. I have no doubt that he thinks Cam is gaslighting me and trying to guilt me into staying, and he's probably right.

I'm going to have to get used to dealing with Henry in a different way. He won't want me to sort out his issues. He's not the sort of guy to tell his girl everything that's going on in his head. That doesn't necessarily mean he's keeping secrets, just that he doesn't want to burden those close to him. He's jealous and possessive, and a little traditional and old-fashioned in how he thinks men should treat women. I don't think he hates Cam, but he definitely doesn't like him very much. So if I'm expecting him to be forgiving toward my previous relationship, I'm going to be very disappointed.

Actually, I'm amazed he let me go back to Cam after our night together. I'm surprised he didn't chain me to the bed and refuse to let me out of his sight.

Ooh. Mmm.

My lips curve up. He sees my smile and glares at me, and that just makes me smile more.

I get up, turn and lift a leg over him to straddle him, then sit back on his lap. Slowly, I slide down his thighs until our bodies are flush. He gives me a suspicious look.

I pick his hands up in mine. Then I move mine behind my back, bringing his with them, as if he's restraining me.

"Want to tell me off, Daddy?" I ask, batting my eyelashes.

He lifts an eyebrow, and his eyes flash. "Are you making fun of me?"

"No." I dip my head until my lips brush his. "Just acknowledging how it's going to be."

His glare vanishes and his eyes blaze. He tightens his arms, and I fall forward onto his chest with a laugh.

"You're mine," he says fiercely. "You hear me?"

"Yes."

"Not his."

"No."

"I don't want you going back to him again."

My smile fades. He might be old-fashioned and traditional, but I'm a modern woman, and I don't like being told what to do. My relationship with Cam is ninety percent done, but there are things we need to talk about, and I'm going to have to see him again.

But Henry has opened up to me today. He's revealed how out of control he is in so much of his personal life. He's learned that his father ran away because he didn't want to be with his first family. His relationship with his brother is damaged almost beyond repair, and he can't help his nephew. He couldn't give his wife a baby, which stretched his marriage like a rubber band until it eventually snapped.

And he knows he can't force me to leave Cam, and he's having to wait for me to sort myself out. It must be killing him.

"All right," I say softly, looking into his eyes.

His hands grip mine, so hard it hurts. "Do you mean that?"

I don't flinch. "You're going to have to trust me. Unless you want to bite me again?"

He blinks and then loosens his grip. Pulling my hands around to the front, he lifts my wrists to his mouth and kisses them. "Sorry," he mumbles.

I kiss his fingers.

He watches me, unfurls my hands, and kisses the palm. Then he puts his arms around me.

I lean on his chest, snuggling into his neck. Cam is not a good cuddler. Henry's terrific at it. Mmm… this is nice. And it's not just a quick hug either; Henry sighs, but shows no signs of wanting to release me.

"I should go and get ready," I tell him after a few minutes. "Gaby and I are going shopping."

"It's not even nine yet."

"I have to get ready."

"Five more minutes." He tightens his arms. He's not letting me go.

I smile and stay where I am.

Chapter Nineteen

Henry

When Juliette's gone, I feel a sudden surge of panic that it's going to be the last time we're together. Despite her agreement that she won't see Cam again, I know that's unlikely, and it's a horrible thought that he only has to snap his fingers and she'll go running back to him. Maybe that's unfair, but that's been the case so far. She cares for him, and he plays on that, no doubt telling her he can't live without her. I wouldn't put it past him to threaten to take his own life if she left. If he does that, I'll go and see him and save him the job. Fucking bastard.

Staying in my room isn't going to help my irritation, so instead I head up to the hotel pool and do some lengths, then go to the gym and run for half an hour. I meet James there, who's also presumably running off some angst, and Tyson, who's doing his daily exercises to strengthen his lower limbs, and the three of us agree to go and get some lunch together when we're done.

After lunch, feeling better now I've exercised and eaten, I head back to the hotel for a read—during which I examine the inside of my eyelids for half an hour—and then it's time to get ready for the wedding rehearsal.

Before she left this morning, Juliette made it clear that she wants to keep our relationship quiet for now. She said it was because she doesn't want to answer questions from the others about what's happening, but I'm convinced it's because she hasn't yet officially broken up with Cam. She knows she's going to have to do that if she wants to be with me, and she's trying to build up the courage to do it, knowing he's bound to object.

I wish Cam would realize it's over and tell her it's done, but equally I want her to be the one to do it. I want her to prove to me that she really wants to be with me, and not just because she's afraid of being alone. Leaving a long-term relationship is scary, especially when you're not sure if you'll ever find someone else. Juliette knows I'm here waiting for her, but to make it work, she needs to be the one to jump.

I can't fast forward things, though. All I can do is wait, and support her, and hope it all comes out in the wash.

*

Because we're groomsmen, James, Tyson, and I head up to Brooklyn Heights at two to join Alex, Damon, Saxon, and Kip, for a quick run-through of what's going to happen tomorrow morning before we all head up to the minivans with the rest of the family.

Alex takes me to one side and says, "I wonder if I can ask you a favor?"

"Sure," I reply.

"Kait's causing a bit of trouble," he says, referring to his mother. "Just making things a tad unpleasant. So I wondered whether you'd be able to... you know... escort her a bit. Unless you've got yourself another date."

"Nope," I reply, silently apologizing to Juliette in my head. "Of course, I'd be happy to help."

"Thanks," he says, relieved. He looks anxious, which is very un-Alex.

"You okay?" I ask, amused.

"Yeah. A bit nervous. Dunno why."

"It's a big day for Damon. You just want it to go well, that's all. And it will. He's a lucky guy having you for a best man."

That makes him smile. "Thanks, man."

I clap him on the back, then head toward Kait as I see her leaving the house. She's a movie actor, quite famous, slender and beautiful. I know she broke up with her boyfriend in LA a while ago, and she's here on her own. Her divorce from Alex's dad was extremely acrimonious, which was presumably why he said she's been causing trouble.

I can see a couple of women nudging each other as she passes, and I watch her dip her head so her hair swings forward to hide her face. Feeling a touch of pity for her, I approach her casually and say, "I don't think we've been introduced yet. I'm Henry West, one of the groomsmen."

"Hello, Henry," she replies, shaking my hand. "You work with Alex, don't you?"

"At Kia Kaha, yes."

"He speaks very highly of you."

"Well, that's nice to know. I'm here on my own, too." I offer her my elbow. "Want to sit together?"

She gives me a grateful look. "That would be great, thank you."

I lead her toward the minivans, hold her hand as she climbs the stairs, and sit next to her. I'm not the smallest of men, and I apologize for taking up more than my share of room.

"No worries at all," she says, her eyes meeting mine, a tad flirtatiously before she looks out of the window. I don't think it's what Alex had in mind when he asked me to look after her!

The vans take us to Old St. Paul's church, which is a beautiful building, built in a Gothic revival style, with large, colorful stained-glass windows and native timber columns. Alex told me that although it's consecrated, it's non-denominational, which means that any type of wedding can be held here, whether it's religious, civil, or LGBTQIA+. Damon and Belle are having a traditional Anglican ceremony, though.

When we arrive, Alex explains that Mik, the wedding organizer, wants to chat to the groomsmen, so I take Kait inside. She kisses me on the cheek, then sits in a pew beside Elizabeth Huxley. I wink at Elizabeth, who winks back and starts talking to Kait. Then I straighten and see Juliette in the pew behind. My heart skips a beat like a schoolboy faced with his crush. She's wearing a light-gray pantsuit with a white shirt—an unusual outfit for her, but she looks amazing. Her hair is up, and a silver bindi graces her brow.

She glances at Kait, then back at me and raises an eyebrow. Oh… she saw her kiss me, and she's jealous. I try not to laugh as I head outside, ready for Mik's brief chat.

As well as the groomsmen being there in the morning when Damon and Alex are getting ready, he gives us some ideas of how we can help on the big day: handing out the order of service sheets, greeting guests and showing them to their seats, and generally answering queries and running any errands the groom or best man might need.

After that, he matches us up with the bridesmaids—Tyson with Gaby, Saxon with his wife, Catie, Kip with his wife, Alice, James with Belle's friend, Jo, and me with Damon's cousin, Kennedy. I've met her several times before, and she's fun and friendly. She has a prosthetic arm, and she jokes about the lace gloves she's wearing tomorrow, and how she's had to have one made bigger than the other.

Mik lines us up behind Belle and her father, and we proceed down the aisle. The guys leave the bridesmaids once they reach the altar, and Mik tells us to take a place in the pews.

Juliette is on the end of one of the pews. She's next to Mack's wife, Sidnie, but there's plenty of room on the pew, so I go up to her and gesture for her to scoot along.

Mik's talking again, so she can't argue with me, but she sends me a glare as she moves up, forcing everyone to shuffle along. I squeeze in beside her, and she huffs.

"Cozy, isn't it?" I murmur.

"Thought you'd go and sit beside your new girlfriend," she whispers back.

"Alex asked me to look after her," I tell her.

"Oh." She looks a little mollified.

Smiling, I face the front, and we listen to Mik as he runs through the ceremony.

When the rehearsal is finished, it's time to head to the minivans to return to Brooklyn Heights. I hesitate as we wander outside, wishing I could sit with Juliette, but she's not my girlfriend, and even though we're good friends, I need to be careful about how much time I spend with her. Disappointed, I join Kait again, and we travel back together. She's pleasant enough, and at any other time I'd have enjoyed flirting with a movie star, but I'm still a little hungover, tired from the party last night, and restless from not being able to be with Juliette, so I'm not great company.

"You're very much the strong, silent type, aren't you?" Kait says with amusement when, after arriving at the Heights, we head down to the top terrace for cocktails.

"I'm sorry." I smile. "I'm a bit distracted."

"Women troubles?"

I sigh. "Unfortunately, yes."

"I thought as much. There's no way a good-looking guy like you was going to be single. Besides which, you're Alex's age and far too young for me." She winks at me, then leans forward conspiratorially. "Is she here?"

"I couldn't possibly comment."

"That means yes. Is she the rather striking dark-haired woman with the bindi?"

My eyebrows rise, and she laughs. "It's written all over your face when you look at her. What's her name?"

"Juliette," I admit reluctantly. "And she's sort of still with someone, so it's a secret."

"My lips are sealed, darling. She's been shooting daggers at me all afternoon, though, so I'm guessing she's a tad jealous that you're with me." She lifts up onto her tiptoes and whispers in my ear. "Shall we make her jealous?"

I give a short laugh. "That's a bad idea on so many levels."

"Oh well." She kisses my cheek anyway. "That might be enough to get the ball rolling."

I chuckle and accept a couple of cocktails from a passing waiter. "Come on, before you cause any more mischief."

It's a buffet dinner today, and we wander around the food stations, helping ourselves to meats, cheeses, fruits, and seafood—Kait hardly choosing enough to feed a rabbit, while I pile enough for two people onto my plate. We find a seat with some of the others, and eat looking out at the glorious view across Wellington and its harbor, while the sun beams down.

I try not to keep looking at Juliette, giving her the space she wanted. It's a beautiful day, and after a decent dinner and a cocktail or two, I feel more relaxed. I'm going to make sure to drink plenty of water during the evening, and I steer clear of the rich desserts and help myself to fresh fruit, taking it back to my seat to nibble as the day wears on.

The sun is heading toward the horizon when Alex stands up to give an informal speech, followed by Damon. Music starts playing after that, and people begin dancing.

"Would you like to dance?" I ask Kait.

"Aren't you supposed to dance with Kennedy?" she says, amused.

"She'd much rather dance with her husband," I scoff, getting up and holding out a hand.

"Thank you," she says, looking genuinely surprised. "I'd love to."

I lead her onto the area in front of the DJ, and we start dancing. We chat while the music plays, talking about the day, and our hope that the wedding goes well tomorrow. When the song comes to an end, James comes over and asks if he can have the next dance, and I smile and let him step in.

I can't see Juliette anywhere or I'd ask her to dance, but I take the opportunity to head up to the house and visit the bathroom. When I'm done, I wash my hands, then open the door to head out.

"Oh!" I exclaim as someone pushes me back into the bathroom and closes and locks the door behind them. It's Juliette, and she looks pretty mad.

"Hello," I say, amused.

"Don't you 'hello' me." She pushes me up against the wall. "Are you enjoying yourself out there, flirting with the rich and famous?"

"I told you, Alex asked me to look after her."

"You don't have to be so enthusiastic about it," she says. Her cheeks are flushed. She looks absolutely amazing.

I know I should remind her that she's the one with a partner, and the one who wanted to keep us a secret. But behind her jealousy, misery flickers. She knows she's being unreasonable, and she hates herself for it.

"You know you're the only girl for me," I tell her, tucking a hand under her chin.

She knocks it away. Then she starts unbuckling my belt, keeping her gaze on mine.

I lift my eyebrows. "What are you doing?"

She doesn't reply, just finishes undoing my belt, then flips open the button at the top of my suit trousers. "You think you're the only one who gets to make demands?" she says.

I don't say anything, my thermostat rapidly rising.

She slides her hand into my trousers and cocks an eyebrow. "Oh, are you finding it exciting to be locked in a bathroom with a girl?"

"Not with any girl," I tell her, my voice husky. "Only with you."

She likes that. Her face flushing, she moves up close to me, massaging my rapidly growing erection. "You're mine," she says.

"Okay," I admit happily.

"Only I get to do this," she says. And then, to my astonishment, she sinks to her knees before me.

"Juliette!" I'm genuinely shocked. "People will be waiting to use the bathroom…"

"I don't care. I saw you eating pineapple. I want to make sure I'm the only one who gets to take advantage of it." Somewhat feverishly, she lifts the elastic of my boxers over the erection that has sprung to life and takes me in hand.

"Oh. Uh… We shouldn't…" My words trail off as she looks up at me and closes her mouth over the tip. "Ahhh… holy fuck."

Over the two years that Shaz and I tried to get pregnant, it was out of the question for my precious baby-making fluid to end up anywhere but where it needed to be, so it's been a long, long time since I've experienced this.

Juliette murmurs as she slides her lips down the length of my shaft, and I groan and let my head fall back, closing my eyes. Jesus... that feels good. I swell in her hand, and she moves back as she strokes me, giving a short laugh. "You're so big," she says, eyes sparkling. "You're going to make my jaw ache." Despite the protestation, she does it again, and this time she takes me deep in her mouth, brushing her tongue across my sensitive skin.

Oh, it feels heavenly, and I couldn't stop her for a million dollars. I slide a hand behind her head and look down at her through hazy eyes, turned on by the sight of her lips around me, and the way she looks up at me with an adoring gaze. She adds more moisture so her hand can slide easily up and down, then licks all the way up the shaft before closing her mouth over the end again, and applying gentle suction, making me groan.

She does this for several minutes, accompanied by throaty moans that make my hair stand on end. At one point, she moves back and murmurs, "Okay baby?"

"Great," I say, close to panting.

"Anything you want me to do?" she asks, still stroking.

Ohhh... this girl... "Underneath," I mumble.

Obediently, she slides a hand down to cup my balls and massage them, then slips a finger back a little to stroke the sensitive skin behind them. Ahhh... yeah... that's hitting the spot...

She continues to lick and suck while she does it, and, unsurprisingly, it doesn't take long before I feel my climax start to approach with the tightening of all my muscles deep inside.

"Ah, careful," I hiss, "I'm going to come..." I wait for her to move back, but she doesn't... she just keeps sucking, taking me as deep as she can... and that makes me lose my shit completely. My climax hits with the force of a bullet train, and, when I realize she wants me to come in her mouth, I hold her head and let it happen, again and again, feeling her throat muscles contract around me as she swallows it all down.

When I'm done, she gives me gentle kisses, cleaning up with her tongue before tucking me back into my boxers and getting to her feet.

Then, to my surprise, she slides her arms around my waist and gives me a hug.

"That was nice," she whispers.

I blow out a long breath as I hug her back. "Understatement of the year."

"I'm sorry." She lifts her head and kisses me. Then, clearly amused, she kisses me again. "Aren't you going to complain?" she asks when she moves back.

"I don't have the energy."

She chuckles. The flashing jealousy in her eyes has vanished, and now they only show affection. "Thank you," she says.

"Thank *me*?"

She smiles. "I'm sorry, I shouldn't have gotten jealous. It was just seeing you with Kait—she's so beautiful and confident."

"She's also the same age as my mum."

She laughs, then fiddles with my tie. "I know I don't have the right to complain…"

"You have every right," I tell her simply. "I'm yours, one hundred percent. It doesn't matter that we can't tell everyone yet. I'm wholly yours, and I always will be."

She hugs me again. "Can I come to your room again tonight?"

"I was hoping you would."

She sighs. "Do you think we can get away with one dance together?"

"I think it would be odd if we didn't, don't you?"

"Yeah." She gives me a squeeze. "All right, I'd better go out."

"You first. I'll follow in a minute."

She opens the door and peeks out, then gives me a final smile before walking away.

I close the door for a moment and look at my reflection in the mirror above the hand basin and watch myself blow out a breath. I did not expect that this evening!

*

We do dance together, more than once, because everyone changes partners, and nobody else is paying any attention to us. It's a beautiful evening, the sky the color of summer fruit, and I'm surrounded by my friends, who are all in love and happy with their girls.

One day, I promise myself, I'll dance with Juliette, and everyone will know she's mine. Tonight, though, I keep the secret close to my heart, and just drown in the love in her eyes.

*

We get back to the hotel in the early hours. I go to my room, and ten minutes later, answer the door when she knocks. She comes in, and this time the door has only just closed before our mouths meet and the clothing starts coming off. She's naked by the time we reach the bedroom, and it takes me two seconds to join her.

This time, after her performance in the bathroom, I'm determined to make it last for her, and I spend ages taking the time to arouse her, kissing her soft skin, stroking her all over, and eventually going down on her. I make her come once, then, because she tastes so good, a second time, before rolling on a condom and finally sliding inside her.

I want to wipe away any memory she has of Cam. I can't avoid the things she used to do with him because I don't know what they all are, and anyway most of them are fun in one way or another, and I'm not going to deny myself the pleasure of her body in any shape or form because that means it belongs to him, and I'm not having that.

So, taking it slow for a while, I try different positions, letting her get used to being with me. Me on top. Her on top. From behind, on all fours, lying down. I let her adjust to me each time, then thrust inside her with long, purposeful strokes, and just when we're both starting to feel the heat rising, I switch position.

"Ahhh…" Eventually she gives a half-sigh, half-groan, when I flip her onto her back once more and slide into her. "Please…"

"Please what, Juliette?" Leaning forward, I lift one of her legs over my shoulder so I can drive into her more deeply.

"Oh fuck… let me come… please…" She lowers a hand between her legs, but I push it away.

"When I'm ready." I cup her chin and lift it. Her eyes are feverish and slightly unfocused. "When you come," I tell her, "I want you to keep your eyes open."

"I'll try."

"You'll do as I tell you. I want you to look at me and realize that you belong to me, and no other man is allowed to touch you like this. Ever. Do you hear me?"

She nods, her lips parting as her orgasm approaches.

"Only I get to make you come," I tell her, my voice hoarse with passion. "Say it."

"Ahhh… Henry…"

"Say it."

"Only you," she whispers.

Satisfied, I give in to the urge to thrust hard, and moments later she cries out and comes, looking up at me with hazy eyes as she pulses around me. I continue thrusting, feeling heat building inside, and our eyes lock as my climax hits. Ohhh… Juliette… I want to do this to you every day of every month of every year for the rest of eternity… I don't ever want to let you go.

Chapter Twenty

Juliette

We lie for a while as our heartbeats slow, outlined by the moonlight. I rest on Henry's chest, and he traces patterns on my back with light fingers.

"How's your nephew doing?" I ask.

"Not great." He sighs. "His girlfriend is having the pregnancy terminated next week. Happy New Year, eh?"

"Aw. And he doesn't want her to?"

"He said she doesn't either. I don't know whether that's true and she's getting pressure from her parents, or if she's just saying that because she doesn't want to hurt his feelings."

"Poor kids. Sixteen's no age to have a baby."

"No. He's very upset about it. On Christmas Day, I told him to stop making a fuss because it should be a day of celebration. He said, 'I made a baby, and he won't get to be born. What would Jesus say about that?'"

"He's got a point."

"I know. That's what makes it so hard. You gotta support the girl, no question. Pro-choice and all that. But it's tough. Still, won't ever be a problem for me personally."

I turn my head and rest my chin on my hand. He has one arm tucked under his head, and we survey each other quietly.

"Elephant in the room," he says.

I kiss his chest. "Yeah."

"Have you been thinking about it?" he asks.

"Yeah."

His hand stills on my back. "And?"

"Am I right in thinking you'd rather not go through IVF?"

"I'd rather not. But I would, for you."

I rest my lips on his skin. I'm deeply touched. After everything he's been through, he'd still do it for me.

It's such a shame, though. I'd rather him do it because he really wants children. I'm sure the urge to have them is what carries most couples through the regular disappointments. If he's reluctant going in, and the first round doesn't work… what then?

Ohhh... life is so hard sometimes, so complicated. And it's ridiculous, because we haven't even dated properly. Hell, I haven't even finished my old relationship. Talk about run before you can even crawl. The last thing we should be discussing is having a family.

But we're not like Rangi and his girl—we're not sixteen. We're heading toward thirty, and although there's still plenty of time, his infertility is a cloud hanging over us that is going to force us to look at things differently.

"How do you feel about not being able to have kids?" I ask.

He studies me, his eyes like silver discs in the moonlight. "I'm not used to talking about it."

"Really? Shaz never asked?"

He shakes his head and resumes drawing on my back. "It's hard not to see it as a failure," he says eventually. "It's the whole reason for existence, isn't it? Procreation. Continuing the line. If Darwin had his way, I'd have been weeded out long ago."

I blow a raspberry.

"I'm serious," he says. "If we were a prehistoric tribe, I'd have been sitting in the shadows without a woman, all skinny because they wouldn't give me any food."

"Bullshit. Even if you couldn't knock up the women, you'd still be running the place, bossing all the cavemen around and telling them they'd used up their holiday quota."

That makes him laugh. "Yeah, maybe."

"We've advanced a long way from procreation being the major reason for existence. So many people, like James, choose not to have children nowadays, but that doesn't mean they don't deserve to live. You contribute to mankind in a huge way. You enrich people's lives, including mine. Darwin can go fuck himself."

"Yeah, all right."

"I'll get that put on a T-shirt for you."

He laughs again.

I kiss his chest. "Can I ask you a question?"

"Of course."

"Did you ever talk about having a sperm donor with Shaz?"

"No. We never really got that far. Things were going wrong between us before we got to the IVF and donor discussion."

"So... what do you think about it?"

He hesitates. "I don't know. Donor children can access details of the donor when they're eighteen."

"Ah, I didn't know that."

He shifts on the pillow. "I suppose it's no different from adopting and the adopted child wanting to find their real parents."

"True."

"I'd need to think about it. It's pretty much like bringing up someone else's child."

"Well, in the donor case it would be half mine."

"I suppose." He doesn't sound enthused.

I draw a finger through his chest hair. "What about having a personal donor? Someone we know and trust?" I chuckle at the look on his face. "You don't like that idea?"

"I'm not letting Alex or James knock you up."

"You know the donor doesn't have sex with the woman, right?"

"Even so. That would be weird."

"Do you think so?

He hesitates, clearly struggling with the idea.

"I've changed my mind," I say with amusement. "You are a Neanderthal."

"Okay, look, say that I wasn't infertile, and Gaby and Tyson came to me and asked if I'd donate for them? Wouldn't it be weird to watch her get pregnant with my sperm? And when the baby was born, every time I looked at it, I'd think that baby's mine. Don't you think that would haunt me? And Tyson?"

"I don't know, I think being a donor is an incredibly generous thing to do. Especially for someone you know well. I'd much rather a friend do it than a stranger."

"I'm afraid we'll have to agree to differ on that one."

I smile. "I can tell you're a Scorpio."

"What the hell does that mean?"

"You're a very jealous man, aren't you?"

His smile fades, and he looks away, out at the dark night.

I push myself up. "Oh, what did I say?"

He sighs. "Nothing, it's okay. It's something Shaz accused me of a lot. We had terrible rows about it."

"Who were you jealous of?"

"A guy she worked with. I was convinced something was going on between them. She always insisted nothing happened."

"Do you believe her?"

"Possibly, although she's now married to him and she's expecting their first baby, so…" He shrugs.

"Oh fuck, Henry, seriously?"

He just sighs.

I cup his face. "I'm so sorry."

He kisses my hand. "I thought I was going mad. That's why I have a very low tolerance for gaslighting. It's one of the worst things a partner can do to you, in my opinion."

He's talking about Cam. I know Cam definitely does it to me—he talks as if I'm crazy when I say that he cheated on me with that surrogate. He's made me feel as if I'm going mad in the past. I'd forgotten about that.

Henry draws up the duvet, and I snuggle up to him, and soon we're both drifting off to sleep.

Deep down, our talk hasn't solved the issue. His infertility lies like a bolster between us, and it doesn't matter how much we talk about it, or if we choose to ignore it, it's not going away.

A sperm donor clearly isn't something he'd consider. I don't want to force him to have IVF, and even though he's said he'd do it for me, I'd feel guilty if he doesn't really want it. I think I could convince him to adopt, but I would love to have my own children. I've always dreamed of being pregnant one day, and I'd be heartbroken if I couldn't be.

I suppose it comes down to what I want more. My own children? Or Henry?

Outside, the moon shines its calming light on us. I'll worry about it tomorrow. Tonight, he's here in my arms, and I'm going to make the most of the moment.

*

The next morning, I head back to my room after breakfast. Henry is going over to Brooklyn Heights later to be with the other guys, and I want to take my time getting ready. I have a bath and wash my hair, then take a long time drying it and coiling it into an intricate bun. After that I do my makeup—lots of kohl on my eyes and shimmering eyeshadow, and I choose a blue bindi to wear between my brows.

As the time to leave nears, I pull on my petticoat and my new pale-blue vest, and slip on my silver high-heeled sandals. I have a new, special sari today, and I retrieve the fabric from my bag with care and unfold it reverently. It's also pale blue with a slightly darker blue strip on each long edge, and it's embroidered with silver thread in clusters of flowers. It's absolutely beautiful, and I know Henry's going to love it.

I drape it around myself, pleat it, and pin it, doing it a couple of times until I'm happy with it. Then I add my matching blue earrings, bangles, and necklace, and finally I'm good to go.

I head down to the foyer at 2:15 and meet the others heading to the church. We all get into the minivans and arrive just after 2:30.

As we leave the van, I see Henry at the front, helping people down. My heart skips a beat. Ooh, he looks amazing. Like the other groomsmen, he's wearing a black morning coat over a dark-gray waistcoat and trousers, and a silvery-gray tie.

When I get to the front of the van, he looks up, and my heart lifts as an amazing smile lights his face.

"Hello," he says, holding out a hand to help me down. "Wow. Look at you."

I step down carefully and look up at him. "You look yummy," I tell him softly.

He laughs. His eyes are very blue today. "And you look absolutely stunning, you gorgeous thing. Come on. I don't care what anyone else thinks; I'm escorting you into the church."

I let him, because I can't deny him when he looks so good, and I slide my hand through his arm and walk down the path and into the church. We stop at the top of the aisle, and I take in the view of the guests starting to gather like colorful birds in their finery. Flowers decorate the end of each pew, and someone's playing the organ, filling the church with uplifting music.

Damon's mother, Mae, comes over, and Henry reluctantly releases me. I haven't had much chance to speak to her yet, and she smiles as she kisses me on the cheek.

"You look so beautiful," she says.

"You too," I reply sincerely.

"No Cam this weekend?" she asks.

I swallow, not looking at Henry, but conscious of him standing next to me, silent and gorgeous and disapproving. Panic fills me, and I can't think what to say. "No, his brother is visiting from the UK, and he decided to stay with him," I blurt out.

"That's a shame," she says, "you make such a lovely couple. I'm sure he's missing his girl. Well, I can see you're in good hands! Have a great time." She smiles and moves on.

Henry slides his hands into his pockets, glowering. He didn't like Mae calling me Cam's girl.

"Sorry," I say awkwardly.

"Why aren't you married?" he demands. "To Cam, I mean."

I look up at him in surprise. "Because he's never asked me."

He frowns. "Why not?"

"He doesn't believe in it. He says rings are an outdated symbol of ownership and possession."

"Yeah," he agrees. "That's what so fucking amazing about them." His eyes are like lasers, burning through mine as they lock onto them. "Marry me," he says.

My jaw drops. "What?"

"You heard me."

"Henry…" I pull him to one side and speak in a fierce whisper, conscious of the guests coming into the church. "We haven't even dated properly yet."

"We're hardly strangers. I've known you for six years. I bet I know you better than he does."

Someone says his name, and we glance over to see James beckoning him outside.

"Coming," Henry calls. He looks back at me. "Cam has never married you. He has no claim on you. You're not his. You're mine, and I intend to put a ring on your finger so he and everyone else can see that."

With a final glare, he walks away and disappears through the door.

I stare after him, stunned into silence. I feel as if I've been blasted all over with a blowtorch. My legs are wobbly. I feel a bit faint. Any thoughts I had that this was a little fling, an affair that would soon be over, rapidly vanish. I feel exultant, panicky, excited, and oddly upset, all rolled into one. He wants me, and that thrills me, but it's too much, too fast, when I haven't even said goodbye to Cam.

"Hey you! Wow, you look gorgeous." It's Aroha. "You okay?" she asks, concerned.

"Um, yes. I got a bit hot in the van and I feel lightheaded."

"Come on," she says, sliding her arm through mine. "Sit with me and we can gossip about everyone's outfits."

I smile and let her lead me to the end of a pew, and it's cool there, the deep-red carpet covered with beautiful jewels cast by the stained-glass windows. Gradually my heart rate slows as I sit and listen to the music and chat to Aroha about how gorgeous the women are in their dresses and the guys are in their suits.

The pews fill up, and Damon and Alex take their places at the front. They both look nervous, but I see Alex nod to James at the back and whisper something to Damon, and his whole expression changes, his face lighting up, so I presume Alex has told him that his bride has arrived.

Belle walks down the aisle, and we all inhale at how beautiful she looks in her wedding gown. I watch her blush as her father hands her to Damon, and see his answering smile. I feel a strange twist deep inside. How can Cam say this is outdated and unnecessary? Even if you're not religious, what can be more touching and affirming than standing before your friends and family and declaring that you love this person and you want to stay with them for the rest of your life?

Behind Belle, the groomsmen leave the bridesmaids and take their places in the pews. This time, Henry sits on the other side from me, which I'm kind of relieved about. I've already compared him to the sun, and I feel myself turning to a crisp when he's in the vicinity. I adore that he's larger than life, passionate and fierce in his affections. It's what I've always wanted—to be admired and adored. But I need time. Robert Burns said 'My love is like a red, red rose,' and I feel the same, except my love for Cam is dying, and I'm waiting to snip off the dead bloom. A new one will grow, and I can already see the shoot. But it takes time to turn into a bud, and then a new flower. It needs careful nurturing, sun and rain. It'll happen. But you can't rush these things, and Henry needs to accept that if he wants to be with me.

Still, as I watch Damon slide a ring onto Belle's finger, I remember Henry's insistence that *You're not his. You're mine, and I intend to put a ring on your finger so he and everyone else can see that.* Will we be standing here one day, before our friends, promising to love one another till death parts us?

Emotion rushes through me, and when I glance at Aroha, I see her eyes glistening, too. There's magic in the words, in the rings, in the motes of dust dancing in the jeweled light, and in the happiness that everyone's feeling today. I lift my face, hoping some of it lands on me.

*

After the service, we go outside for the photos. Henry's kept busy organizing guests, and I have a feeling he's also giving me a little space. So I mingle and chat, and then we make our way to the vans, which take us all back to Brooklyn Heights. Today it's a sit-down do, and place names dictate where we sit. Henry's on the same round table as me, but across the opposite side, so we don't get much chance to talk.

Later, after dinner and the speeches, we all head down to the next terrace where there's a live band and a DJ, and the dancing is soon underway. I dance with the girls, while the sun slowly sets and the fairy lights flicker on. And then after a while, the music changes to Eric Clapton's *Wonderful Tonight*—an oldie but a goodie—and couples slowly take to the floor. I watch Damon and Belle in the center, arms around each other, talking and laughing as they turn to the music. Alex dances with Missie, James comes and takes Aroha's hand, and Gaby and Tyson turn together.

When Henry comes up to me and holds out his hand, I don't hesitate to slide my fingers into his and let him lead me onto the dance floor. He holds my right hand and rests his other hand on my waist, and I rest my left hand on his shoulder, and we start moving to the music.

After a while, he slides his hand around to my back, pulling me a little closer. I look up at him, and his eyes are gentle.

"Hey," he murmurs.

"Hey."

His thumb strokes my hand where he's holding it. "I want to say I'm sorry," he states.

"What for?"

"Coming on a little strong."

I inhale, then let out a long breath.

"I know you need time," he says. "And I know I can't force things."

I look into his eyes, my heart swelling with feelings for him. "Thank you."

He continues to study me as we move from side to side. "That doesn't mean I've ruled out handcuffing you to the bed."

I giggle. "Fair enough."

He grins. Then he sighs and pulls me close. "Nobody's watching," he says. And he's right—everyone's caught up in themselves. So I rest my cheek on his shoulder and enjoy being close to him.

"I just want more," he murmurs. "Sex is great. It's fantastic. But I want more than that. I want to be with you. I want to hold your hand in public, and go out for dinner together. To wake up with you every morning and go to bed with you every night."

I don't say anything to that, because what could I possibly say? It's all I've ever wanted, and it's up to me to make it happen.

*

The next few hours are filled with dancing, eating, drinking, and laughing. It's great to be around all my friends, and to make some new ones. I haven't spoken much to Saxon and Kip's wives, and so I spend some time chatting to Catie and Alice, and promise to visit them both next time I'm in Wellington.

I don't dance with Henry again, but I watch him throughout the evening. He moves through the crowd, checking that everyone has drinks, handing out shawls to some of the older guests as it grows cool, and asking women to dance, so nobody's left sitting on their own. Luckily, Kait has found herself a partner for the evening, a lawyer by all accounts, so Henry's obligation there has finished. But he dances with grandmas and maiden aunts and single moms and teenage girls, and I can see they're all half in love with him by the time he takes them back to their seats.

I start thinking about what might happen when we get back to the hotel. I shouldn't go to his room again. But I will. I know I will. I won't be able to resist the opportunity to get him into bed again. Just thinking about it makes a shiver run through me.

Maybe I'd be more reluctant if I'd heard from Cam. If he'd called or messaged me, telling me he loves me and that he can't wait for me to come home. But my phone is silent, the love we had so cool now it's practically frozen over.

When we get back, I'm going to tell him that we're done.

I make the decision as I watch Henry dancing with one of Damon's aunts, making her laugh as they turn around the dance floor. I want my future to be with Henry. With a man who loves me with all his heart, and who wants to dedicate his life to making me happy. Maybe that's selfish, but I don't care. I've spent too long being unhappy, listening, trying to understand, and talking, talking, talking. I don't want to talk anymore. I just want to be loved.

And once that realization hits me, I know everything's going to be okay.

Chapter Twenty-One

Henry

I'm in my room for over fifteen minutes before there's a knock at my door.

My heart races as I open it. "Thought you weren't coming," I say as casually as I can when she slips past me.

"People kept arriving," she replies. "It's busy out there."

I close the door and follow her across the room. She's still wearing her sari, wrapped up like a beautiful Christmas present for me. My heart swells at the knowledge that she came—she wants to be with me.

She goes up to the window and looks out at the view. The city lights sparkle like stars. In the hotel across from us, where the occupants haven't drawn their curtains, we can see into the rooms, catching a glimpse of people going about their lives—eating, talking, watching TV.

"It was such a magical day, wasn't it?" she whispers. "Damon and Belle looked so happy."

"Yeah, I'm glad it went well for them."

She turns to face me. "You were magnificent."

I smile, touched by the compliment. "Well, thank you."

"I mean it." She moves closer to me, rests her hand on my chest, and begins to undo my shirt buttons, her eyes turning sultry. "I watched you dancing with all those women, and I just kept thinking, in a few hours' time, his mouth is going to be between my legs."

Heat sears through me as if I've drunk a bucketful of lava. "Damn straight."

She laughs and splays her hands on my chest as I pull her toward me and crush my lips to hers.

I've watched her all day, moving through the guests, beautiful and exotic as a tropical flower, and I'm hungry for her. But when I go to undo the pins holding her sari in place, I make myself go slow, not wanting to damage the precious fabric.

I unwrap her deliberately, making her turn in a circle as I peel the material from her, revealing her pretty blue vest and petticoat. As I undo the tie of the petticoat, she glances over her shoulder and says, "We should draw the curtains."

I shake my head, loosening the tie and lowering the petticoat so she can step out of it. "I want everyone to see us and think how lucky I am to be with such a beautiful woman."

"Oh," she says, her eyes widening. I take the bottom of her vest and peel it up her body, revealing that she's not wearing a bra, and I toss the vest aside. Now she's just wearing a small, lacy pair of knickers, and I soon divest her of those, leaving her naked except for her high-heeled sandals.

Moving her so she's up against the glass, I then drop to my knees in front of her. "Henry!" she scolds, genuinely shocked, but I lift one of her legs over my shoulder, dip my head, and slide my tongue into her warm flesh.

Oh man, she's already moist and swollen, and I groan as I lick through her folds and circle my tongue over her clit. Her fingers tighten in my hair, and she says, "Oh my God," but she doesn't push me away. Encouraged, I move a hand beneath her, turn it palm up, and slide two fingers inside her, and she lets her head fall back onto the glass and gives a long, heartfelt moan.

She was obviously telling the truth when she said she's been thinking about this for a while, because it doesn't take long at all to reach the point where her breaths turn uneven, and I know she's close to the edge. I love making her come with my mouth, but I'm keyed up and hot for her, and so I get to my feet, grab my wallet and extract a condom, release my erection from my boxers, and roll the condom on.

"Here?" she says with a gasp.

"So everyone can watch." I lift her up and wrap her legs around my waist. Then, pressing her back up against the glass, I lower her until I feel the tip of my erection enter her. I hold her there for a moment and kiss her until I feel her relax a little. Then I lower her down, a centimeter at a time, until she's completely impaled on me.

"Ah, fuck." She tips her head back on the glass, fighting for breath.

"All right, baby?" I kiss her jaw, her ear, and her neck, doing my best not to move as I wait for her to adjust.

"Mmm… yeah… oh that's good."

My lips curving up against her skin, I start to move with long, rhythmical thrusts, kissing her all the while, nice and slow, until we're both coated in her moisture, and I'm slipping easily inside her.

Only then do I begin to speed up. It's impossible to hold back, and I know she's not far from coming anyway, so before long I give in to the urge to thrust hard, driving deep inside her and grunting with pleasure each time I sink into her softness.

"Oh God, Henry," she says, pressing her hands against the window and leaving hot prints on the glass. "Oh, oh, oh…"

"Come for me," I demand, speeding up, and she tightens her legs around me and cries out, driving me insane. "Fuck, yeah…"

She comes with a squeal, clenching so tightly that I give a helpless groan. I thrust her all the way through it, hanging on as long as I can, then come too, shuddering and sighing, and filled with joy at just having her here, in my arms, and being inside her.

I hold her there for a while, as our bodies calm. Then, gently, I withdraw from her and lower her legs to the ground.

"I'm all wobbly," she whispers.

"Me too." I quickly dispose of the condom, tuck myself back in, and zip up my trousers. I pick her up and deposit her on the mattress, and strip off my clothes. Then I slide under the duvet and gather her up in my arms.

"Do you think anyone saw us?" she whispers.

"Almost certainly." I chuckle. "I hope they enjoyed the view."

"You are so wicked."

"You could have said no."

"Like you'd have taken any notice."

I kiss the top of her head. "Maybe we should have a safe word, just in case."

"Pineapple?" she suggests.

I look up at the ceiling. "No. Something else."

She's quiet then, and I wonder whether she's thinking about the time she once suggested to us all in the office that we have a safe word in the bedroom. It obviously meant that she and Cam had used one, and at the time I remember feeling a flare of jealousy.

She lifts up and leans on my chest to look into my eyes. "It wasn't for me," she says, so clearly she was thinking about it.

I take a strand of her hair and run it between my fingers. "Okay." I guess she's saying that it was Cam's safe word for whatever he asked her to do to him. Jesus. Each to their own and all that, but I'm old fashioned enough to believe it's the guy's job to please the girl, and I don't like to think of what she's had to go through. No wonder the poor girl looks haunted half the time.

"I want to say goodbye to that life." She speaks vehemently. "All this time I didn't know why I was so unhappy, but you've shown me what love can be like, and this is what I want."

"You can have it as often as you like," I tell her. "I'll just have to eat more steak."

That makes her laugh, and she snuggles up to me again. "I love the way you are," she murmurs, drawing a finger through the hairs on my chest. "You're so warm and open."

"Huh."

"What?"

"Shaz always said I was a closed book."

"I don't think of you like that. I know you don't want to burden people with your problems, but that's different to hiding things. I don't find you secretive. And I like that."

I skate my fingers over her back, loving the warmth of her body close to mine.

"Why the big sigh?" she says.

"I'm sad to be going back tomorrow. It's been a good few days."

"I know what you mean. But I'm glad in a way. I want to get things sorted."

I don't reply, because I don't want to demand to know when she's going to talk to him, and what she's going to say. I don't want to push her. But when sleep overcomes us, I dream of losing my way in a misty forest. The future is unclear, and all I can do is hope.

*

Juliette

The next day, we fly home. When we get to Christchurch, we walk out of the airport with the others and wave goodbye to Gaby and Tyson.

"What's going on with James and Aroha?" I ask when they stay behind to chat.

"He told me she's in some kind of financial trouble, so she's going to be coming into the office in the New Year to help us prepare for the conference."

"Oh yes," I say, "I forgot about Sydney. It's about three weeks away, right?"

"Yeah, but we've got a lot to do for it. I'm going into the office tomorrow actually and so's Tyson, I think, to get started on it."

I tuck a strand of my hair behind my ear. I wish I could kiss him, but I'm conscious that someone could be watching, so I restrain myself.

We stand there awkwardly, just looking at each other, a world of emotion passing between us, but unable to vocalize it. I want to promise him that this will all be over soon, but my coming conversation with Cam is looming like a tidal wave. Something tells me he's not going to take it lying down. He's going to make it difficult for me, and I can't think about anything past that.

"When's your first day?" Henry asks.

"Next Monday, the eighth." The office is officially closed before then, although the guys are all going in to start work on the conference.

"Okay. Will I see you before then?"

"I hope so." It's the best I can do.

He frowns. "Are you feeling okay? You look tired."

"That's because someone wore me out last night," I scold. Then I sigh. "Just a bit of PMS." It's the truth—I'm due around Thursday, and I feel achy and tired, and my boobs are tender. Although I acknowledge that might also be from all the action I've had over the last few days.

"Ah. I'm sorry," he says.

"Eh, it's no big deal. Well, I'd better go. Stay in touch, okay?"

"Yeah. Take care of yourself."

I watch him walk over to his Uber and get in, and before long it's pulling away.

With a sigh, I get into mine, and the driver's soon heading into the city. The gray sky mirrors my mood. It's New Year's Eve tonight, and I wish I could spend it with him. But he told me he's heading over to his family, hopefully to patch things up with his brother, and I'm going over to my parents' house. So it's a matter of waiting until I've sorted myself out, and we can finally be together.

When I get to the apartment, I let myself in. It's cool and quiet, and Cam's not there, to my relief. I unpack and put some washing on, make myself a cup of coffee, then take it to the sofa and pull out my phone. It's time to call Cam.

I don't want to break up with him over the phone, but it would be impossible to do it in person. I'm just not strong enough. So I'm going to have to do my best.

My stomach churns, because I know this isn't going to be easy. I feel sick, and I'm already near tears. Not, I think, because I'm breaking up with him, but because I can't bear to face the emotional recriminations and blackmail I know are coming. But there's no way around it. I have to do it. For Henry.

I dial his number and wait, heart pounding.

He answers after a few rings. "Lettie!" It's his pet name for me. I've never liked it.

"Hey," I say softly.

"Are you back?" he asks.

"Yeah, got in about half an hour ago."

"I'm so sorry I haven't called you," he says, "but I didn't want to spoil the wedding for you."

I frown. "What do you mean?"

"It's been an awful few days here. Jesus, where to start? Alan left on Thursday, and Pete flew out on Friday morning, so Mum and Dad were already a bit low. I was going to go back to the apartment, but I decided to stay on a day or two and spend some time with them. Then yesterday we got a call from Alan's wife—he had a heart attack on the fucking plane, just before it landed."

My jaw drops. "A heart attack? He's only thirty!" I'm not totally surprised—Alan is overweight, smokes, does no exercise, and drinks like a fish, but even so, it's still quite shocking.

"I know, what are the fucking odds? They rushed him to hospital and he's having surgery today."

"Jesus, I'm so sorry. How's your mum?"

"Well that's the thing…" I hear footsteps and the sound of a sliding door opening—he's going into the garden. The door slides shut before he speaks. "She totally lost the plot yesterday. So upset. We had to call the doctor to come and sedate her. She's a bit better today, but it was awful—she was hysterical, crying non-stop."

"Oh no."

"Can you come over?" he asks. "You're so good with her, there's something calming about you. She'll be better if you're here."

I cover my face with a hand. It's a terribly selfish thing to think, but this couldn't be more awful timing. What kind of person would it make me if I tell him I'm breaking up with him now?

"I'm sorry," he says, "I forgot to ask, how was the wedding?"

I flush as I think about the nights I've spent with Henry, his hot mouth searing my skin. The way he had me up against the window, in full view of anyone who cared to look. Oh this is so hard. Why, when I'm with Henry, do I know he's all I want, but as soon as I'm with Cam I feel as if I've cheated on him?

"It was fine," I say. "Look, I'll pack a few things and come over. I'll be there in twenty."

"Thank you," he says with relief. "I've missed you so much, you know."

I can't return the sentiment. "I'll be there soon, bye."

I end the call, toss the phone onto the table, flop back onto the sofa, and cover my face with my hands. This is so fucking shit. I'm just the worst person in the universe. Henry is expecting me to end it today. What's he going to think when I tell him I'm going over there? I'm not going to start our relationship off with a lie. I'm going to have to tell him.

On cue, my phone buzzes on the table, and when I look at the screen I see it's a message from him.

Thanks for a great time. Miss you already. Happy New Year.

Fuck, fuck, fuck.

I pick up the phone and dial his number. Then I lie back with a cushion over my face.

"Hello?" he asks. "That was quick."

I take the cushion off. "Hey. Where are you?"

"At home. Going over to my folks in a few hours. What are you up to?"

I hesitate.

"What's happened?" he says immediately.

Tears sting my eyes, and I press my fingers to my mouth. "I rang Cam to tell him it was over, and he told me his brother's had a heart attack in Sydney, and his mum's had a breakdown. He wants me to go over there, and I couldn't bring myself to say no. I'm so sorry." I burst into tears.

I wait for him to get angry. To accuse me of leading him on. To say that if I don't tell Cam it's over today, I can forget about a future with him. To tell me I'm weak, and I don't deserve him.

But it's Henry I'm talking to, and so he doesn't say any of those things.

"Baby," he says, "don't cry. Come on, of course you couldn't tell him now. Go and help sort things out. You'll know when the time is right."

I try not to sob. "Don't be nice to me."

"Aw, hey, everything's going to be fine. Just don't have sex with him, okay?"

I give a short laugh. "Yeah, all right."

"I've been there, remember? I know it's hard. It doesn't end with a blare of trumpets. It's more like you're sailing away from shore where someone's playing music. You think you're out of earshot, and then you hear strains of music on the wind. But one day you won't be able to hear it anymore. You'll get there."

I draw up my knees and rest my forehead on them. "How can you be so possessive one minute and so understanding the next?"

"I'm not saying I won't be yelling every swear word I know when I end this call. I'm frustrated. But with Cam, or Fate, or life I guess, not with you."

I wipe my cheeks. "Can I call you later?"

"Any time, sweetheart. I'm always here for you."

"I hope you have a good New Year's Eve."

"Yeah, well, I'm not holding out much hope. But you never know."

"Thank you."

"Take care of yourself, you hear me? I love you."

"I love you too," I say softly. "Bye." I end the call.

I sit there for a moment, letting my thoughts settle. And I realize he's right. Just because I'm going over to help Cam doesn't change anything. Our relationship is still done. It would be cruel to end it right now when he's suffering. Once things have settled a little, we can have a conversation, but until then I need to be a human being and do what I can to help his family get through this difficult time.

The washing has finished, so I put it in the dryer, then pack a few things just in case I decide to stay overnight. When I'm done, I head for the door and turn to look around at the apartment. Without the lights on, it seems dark and gloomy. It feels as if something has died in it, and I guess that's kind of the case. Love faded away here, leaving only sadness, and the air is heavy with it.

I go out of the door, and close it behind me.

Chapter Twenty-Two

Juliette

New Year's Eve is a complete washout, and the next few days are, frankly, horrendous. Cam's brother has a coronary artery bypass graft, but he ends up with a surgical site infection, and he's very unwell. Cam's mother, Kathy, is beside herself with worry, in hysterical tears most of the time, and ends up having to be sedated again. She is calmer when I'm there, so I stay with her for much of the time, reading to her, and just letting her talk when she is a bit calmer.

Alan's wife, who's now eight months pregnant, is unwell and struggling, which just upsets Kathy more. She wants to go to Australia to help her, but Cam's Dad tells her he's not letting her go in her mental state, which leads to her having more hysterics. In the end, Cam offers to fly over there, and he leaves on the second of January, which makes things both easier and harder. Easier because I don't have to tiptoe around him. But harder because there's no chance of us talking while he's away and I'm here with his parents. When I do talk to him, he constantly says things like, "I'm so glad you're there," and, "What would we do without you?" so there's no possible way I can tell him or his parents that I'd rather be elsewhere.

I'm incredibly tired and exhausted by this point. Kathy is nice enough, but she's not my mother, and I find her hysterics irritating, even though I feel sorry for her. I miss Henry so much it hurts. I want this to be over, but it shows no sign of ending right now.

And then on Thursday, after I've made yet another lunch for everyone that goes uneaten, my phone rings. To my surprise, I see that it's Alex.

I answer it and walk out into the garden. "Hey, you!"

"Hey," he says.

"Happy New Year!"

"Yeah. Sweetheart, where are you?"

Sweetheart? That startles me. Despite being one of my best friends, Alex is not the kind of guy to use endearments like that. "Uh… I'm at Cam's parents' place." I haven't told him or any of the others about Cam's brother, and I doubt Henry has either.

"Honey," he says, "I've got some bad news."

My heart skips a beat. Not Henry?

"We heard this morning that James's sister Maddie has died."

I stand still as the world shudders to a halt around me. For a moment, I'm sure the birds stop singing and the sun goes behind a cloud.

I know Maddie and have met her many times socially. She had a baby a few months ago, and I was aware that she was suffering from postnatal depression, and that James was going over to see her a lot to help her out. Oh, poor James.

"Oh my God," I whisper. "How?"

"She fell off a cliff near where she lived."

"Jesus."

"Yeah."

"She didn't… jump?"

"We don't know yet."

"Oh no, Leia?"

"She's fine. She was in her pushchair at the top. A couple who were walking by found her and called the police. Two officers came here to tell James."

"Oh how awful. How is he?"

"In complete shock. He's gone to identify the body."

Tears spring into my eyes at the thought of having to do something so horrendous. "Is he on his own?"

"No, no, Henry's with him."

I feel a rush of relief. If Henry's there, everything's going to be fine. "I'm glad about that."

"Yeah, me too. James has to pick up Leia afterward, so Aroha's gone with them, and she's going to look after the baby for a while."

"That was kind of her."

"Yeah, a real coup that she just happened to be working here. Anyway, I said I'd call and let people know. I'll ring as soon as we know anything more."

"When do you think the funeral will be?"

"No idea. I imagine there'll be a police investigation and a coroner's inquiry until they sort out the cause of death, so it might be a while."

"Okay. Well, thanks for calling me."

"All right, speak soon, okay?" He ends the call.

I stand there, listening to the birdsong that's started up again. I'm trembling a little. I wasn't close friends with Maddie, but James is like a brother to me, and I can only imagine what he's going through. Did she take her own life? Oh God, I hope not. It's awful either way, but an accident is one thing; knowing your sister was so unhappy that she killed herself is another. James will blame himself, and it won't be an easy thing to get over.

As far as I know, he and Maddie don't have any brothers or sisters. Their mother is dead, and their father lives in Australia. They have no other close family here. What will happen to the baby? Poor little Leia. I know Maddie wasn't in touch with the father, but I guess he'll have to be contacted. Will he want her? If he doesn't, what will James do? He's always said he doesn't want kids. I can't picture him bringing up a baby, especially when she's not his own.

I'd like to talk to Henry, but I don't want to interrupt him while he's with James, so I just send him a text, telling him I'm sorry and that I'm thinking of them.

He calls me around six. Seeing his name on the screen, I go outside again, not wanting Cam's parents to hear the call.

"Hello?"

"Hey," he says. "It's me." He sounds tired.

"Hey, sweetheart. How are you?"

"Shattered. What a fucking awful day."

"God, I'm so sorry." I sit on the edge of the deck, looking down the garden. "How's James?"

"Upset. Angry. Devastated. Pretty much what you'd think. He had to go and identify her body."

"I'm guessing it was her?"

"Yeah. I can't even think how awful that must have been."

"What about Leia? Did you pick her up?"

"Yeah. She's fine. We took her back to his house, and Aroha's with her now, thank God. She's got it all in hand. I'm so relieved she was there."

"She's got her head screwed on right—she'll be good for him."

"Yeah."

"Are you okay?" I ask softly.

"Yeah. I feel gutted. I can't believe Maddie's gone. Twenty-eight is no age."

"Do you think she took her own life?"

"James thinks it's possible because of her postnatal depression. I don't know. I don't think she would have left Leia alone on the top of that cliff if she was going to jump. But who knows? Either way, it fucking sucks."

"It does. I'm so sorry."

He sighs. "We're going around to see him tonight—me, Alex, and Tyson. We'll commiserate and get him drunk."

"And yourselves, no doubt," I tease.

"Probably." He doesn't laugh. "I miss you," he says. "So fucking much."

I press my fingers to my mouth. "I miss you too."

"How's it going over there?"

"It's awful. Kathy's hysterical most of the day. Roy just yells at her to calm down, and that makes her worse."

"How's Alan?"

"I think he's improved a fraction."

"When's Cam back?"

"Saturday. I might try to talk to him then. God, what an awful start to the year."

"Yeah. All right, I'm going to have a shower, then head over to James's."

"You're not driving?"

"No, I'll Uber." I can hear the smile in his voice.

"Take care of yourself," I murmur.

"You too. Love you." He ends the call before I can echo the sentiment.

I go back into the house to hear screaming from Kathy's room, and Roy yelling at her to calm down. I press a hand to my forehead. I want to just walk out, go back to my apartment, and grieve on my own. But I promised Cam I'd stay and help his mum, and I don't have the heart to abandon her when she's so upset.

Taking a deep breath, I head for the bedroom, mentally rolling up my sleeves for the fight.

*

The next day, Gaby calls me to say she and Tyson are going around to James's if I want to join them. When I tell Kathy I'm going out for a few hours, she collapses into tears, and in the end Roy gives her more pills and tells me to go.

I Uber over to James's, relieved to be out of the cloying atmosphere, and, despite the sadness of the situation, excited to see Henry. When I arrive and walk into James's house, Henry is the first person I see, and while Gaby goes up to hug James, Henry and I have a quick cuddle which goes unnoticed as everyone greets everyone else.

"How are you doing?" he asks, tightening his arms around me.

"Shit," I reply. "I miss you."

"Yeah, I miss you too."

That's all we have time for, but it's wonderful to be back with my friends. We sit out on James's deck and eat pizza and reminisce about Maddie, and I have a cuddle with Leia as he discusses the options for what to do with her.

I look up and see Henry watching me. I lift Leia's hand and wave it at him, and he gives a smile, but it's a sad one. Is he thinking about Maddie? Or about the unresolved issue we spoke about in Wellington—about us having children of our own? I'd sort of forgotten about that in the heat of everything that's been happening, but the problem is still there, and it's not going away.

Not long after that I get a text from Cam. *Any chance you could head back soon? Dad says Mum's asking for you.*

I don't want to go. I want to stay here with my friends, get drunk, tell stories about when we were young and carefree, then go home with Henry, make love to him for hours, and fall asleep in his arms. But at the moment that option seems further away than ever.

Heavy with responsibility, I say goodbye to everyone and head for the door. Henry comes with me on the pretense of getting himself a glass of water from the fridge, and we pause in the lobby, standing a foot apart.

"You okay?" he asks. "You look exhausted."

"I am. God, this week. I just want it to be over."

"I know what you mean."

I think about Maddie, and my eyes water. "I can't believe she's gone."

"Me neither. It feels unreal."

I reach out and rub his upper arm, just because I want to touch him. "I'm glad you were there for James. You're such a rock."

"I wish I could be there for you." His blue eyes are sincere, without any anger or resentment that I haven't left yet. "I'm sorry you're having to go through all that."

"It's really hard. Kathy needs me, and I know if I walk now, it'll kill her. What kind of person would it make me to turn my back on someone in need?"

I look back at him, and his expression has softened. "You're a lovely girl," he says. "And I know that Hindu philosophy suggests selfless service and adherence to your moral and ethical responsibilities are important for spiritual growth. That's commendable. But I think sometimes duty is so ingrained in you that you forget we all have our own paths to walk. Our own crosses to bear, if you don't mind me mixing up our religions. Kathy has to learn to cope emotionally with what's happening to Alan and his family. Buddhists say pain comes from resistance to change, right? She needs to develop coping mechanisms and learn to accept that bad things are going to happen, or she won't be able to deal with these major problems that life throws at us going forward."

My face heats at the thought that he thinks I'm enabling her. "What am I supposed to do when she's screaming the house down and threatening to hurt herself because she's so frightened and unhappy? Roy and Cam can't deal with her—should I just walk out and leave her?"

"She needs proper medical help. You're not her doctor or her therapist, and she's not your mother."

"She's a human being, and she needs me right now."

"I understand, and I admire you for the way you care about people. But all the time you're there, Roy and Cam will leave it to you, and nothing will be solved. Sometimes it's okay to put your own needs and desires first. Sometimes you have to."

I wipe away a tear that falls over my lashes. Is it true? Is duty so ingrained in me that I end up taking over and not letting people walk their own path?

"I have to go," I tell him, because my head hurts, and I need to think about this.

"All right. Take care of yourself." He pulls me toward him and gives me a hug.

I bury my face in his T-shirt for a few seconds. He smells warm and familiar, and I want nothing more than to stay there and let him comfort me.

But in the end, I move away and say, "See you soon," before I slip out of the door into the dark night.

I return to Kathy and spend over an hour calming her down and getting her back to bed before falling exhausted into the spare bed. I check my phone before I settle down. No message from Cam, who might be at the hospital. But there is one from Henry.

E kore e mimiti te aroha mōu. It means 'my love for you will never wane.'

Eyes stinging, I text back. *E kore e ea i te kupu taku aroha mōu.* 'Words can't express how much I love you.'

He texts back a line of hearts. I smile as I turn my phone off, but the smile fades as I curl up under the covers. The sentiment is wonderful, but they are just words. Deep down, I feel queasy with anxiety. Something has to give, and I can feel it coming.

It takes me a while to fall asleep, and when I do, I dream about gray skies, and thunder rolling around the hills.

*

With Alan finally appearing to be on the mend, Cam comes back from Australia, tired and weary. When he walks in, he flicks me a quick smile, then goes through to talk to his mum. No hug, no passionate declaration of how much he missed me.

Both of us start back to work on Monday, but we shoot off to his parents' house at lunchtime and at the end of the day to fight the fire that's constantly burning there. It feels as if we're caught in a never-ending loop. Kathy is in a real downward spiral mentally, barely able to lift her head from the pillow without dissolving into tears or panic. Cam calls to make her a doctor's appointment, but the surgery is run off its feet at this time of year, and the first appointment he can get is in a week's time.

When he tells me that, my frustration boils over, and the two of us have an argument in the garden that inevitably turns personal. I announce that we're not a couple anymore—we're like roommates who have no physical contact at all, to which he gets angry and replies that he didn't think I wanted him to touch me, and by the time Roy comes out to yell at us to stop because Kathy can hear us, we're both close to tears and exhausted.

Things get worse when Alan's wife calls Cam Wednesday lunchtime in a panic to say she's started having contractions. Her family lives in Melbourne and she's not close to them anyway, and Alan is still at least a week away from being released from hospital. I go back to work, taut as an elastic band that's been twisted to breaking point. I've hardly seen Henry, who's been closeted with Tyson, working on the conference, and my period still hasn't started so I'm achy and miserable and tired and exhausted.

And then, that evening, when I arrive at his parents' place after work, I'm preparing dinner for us all when Cam comes into the kitchen.

"Em rang again," he says, massaging the bridge of his nose. "They've taken her to hospital because her blood pressure's up."

I stop where I'm draining the pasta and say, "Oh no. It's not pre-eclampsia?"

"Borderline, I think. She's really upset. I think we need to go over there, so I've booked two tickets for Friday. We can be there then for both of them, and we can stay at their place so it won't cost us anything."

I put down the colander. "What do you mean, 'we'? I can't go."

"I need you, Lettie. You've got to come with me."

"Well, for a start, what about your mum?"

"I know, I might try to get a nurse in or something. But I need you."

"You need me because I'll organize everything," I say, a little hysterical. "And anyway, I'm working."

"Alex will let you have the time off," he says impatiently. "This is important."

"Cam, the funeral is on Friday. I have to be here for that."

"This is more important," he insists.

I meet his gaze. "Not to me."

We stare at each other for a moment. I can see it's only just occurring to him that saying goodbye to Maddie is more important to me than his brother and his wife. I've shocked him.

"I thought Hindus believed in reverence to their husbands," he says snarkily.

"I'm not a Hindu," I snap back. "You know that. I like to respect my father's culture sometimes, that's all. And you're not my husband, which was your decision, I have to point out."

He glares at me.

"Anyway," I continue, ignoring the churning of my stomach that tells me he's partly right, and I should go with him to support him, "a person's duty is also toward their friends. I need to be here for the funeral. I want to be here to support James."

"You mean you want to be here with Henry."

My face burns. "Actually, I want to be here for all my friends. They're all upset and suffering." I think about what Henry said, about people needing to develop their own coping mechanisms, and that sometimes it's okay to put your own needs first. I'm not being selfish. This is important to me, and I'm upset that Cam can't see why.

Now is the moment where I should tell him it's over. We haven't been a couple for weeks, not really. We're hanging onto the dregs of this relationship, and I'm tired, and I want it to be over.

But there's one final reason I can't let go of it. One more thing I need to sort out before I make the jump.

I swallow hard. "Look, you should go and help Em and Alan. I'll stay here and keep an eye on your mum until you get back."

His lips thin, and his eyes harden. "Right," he snaps. "I should have guessed you'd put me last."

My jaw drops. "All I've done since New Year is put you and your family first," I yell back.

He holds up a hand and says tiredly, "All right, don't get hysterical."

Me? I'm so speechless I can only stare at him as he walks away. In the background, Kathy is crying, and I hear exhaustion in his voice as he goes into her room to calm her down.

I'm done. I'm so done. My eyes blur with tears as I finish getting the dinner. I wish I could just walk out. Tell him I'm not coming back, and not have to put up with this misery anymore.

Oh, Henry. I dash the tears away. I want to feel his arms around me. I want to lie in the morning sunshine and have him stroke my back again while he sings songs to me in Māori. I want to feel his lips on mine.

Whoever's up there, watching over me, please let it come to pass. Give me courage.

And please…oh God, please, by all that's holy… make me not pregnant. Because if I am, I don't know what I'm going to do.

Chapter Twenty-Three

Henry

It's getting late, and Rangi still isn't answering his phone, so in the end, I call Philip.

"What do you want?" he demands.

"Hello to you too." I clamp down on my irritation, determined not to let him rile me. "I can't get hold of Rangi, and I wanted to make sure he's okay."

"He's fine." Philip talks curtly. "He's in his room, being emo and listening to music."

"Did Ellie go ahead with the termination?"

"Yeah, apparently it's all done, thank God. Maybe he'll pull his fucking socks up now and sort himself out."

I frown, sad and angry at my brother's lack of compassion for his son. "Come on, Phil, have a little heart. The kid's grieving. He had no say in the matter and now he's lost his girl and his baby, as he sees it." Ellie's actually only fifteen, and her parents have forbidden her from seeing Rangi again.

"I should have guessed you'd take his side."

"I'm not taking sides. I—"

"I've gotta go." He ends the call.

I toss my phone onto the kitchen table, grab a bottle of water from the fridge, and head out to the pool. The sun is setting, and the water is the color of cranberry juice beneath the beautiful sky. I drink half the bottle, strip off my tee, then dive into the water and swim the whole length of the pool before emerging to rest my arms on the side.

If I set sail from the beach below and went east in a straight line, I'd probably hit Chile. For a moment I imagine being on a boat, alone, on the Pacific, with just the sun and wind for company, where nobody could contact me. That sounds like heaven. Except for the fact that I don't know the first thing about boats or sailing, and I'd probably drown before I even left the harbor.

I let out a long sigh. There's just over a week until the conference in Sydney, and I've got tons of work to do. James has been into the office once or twice, but he's obviously tied up with what's happened with Maddie, and the funeral tomorrow, so he hasn't been able to contribute much to preparing our presentation. Alex is busy covering for James and getting Kia Kaha up and running ready for the company to reopen on Monday. So it's been down to Tyson and me to work everything out. It's meant working fourteen-hour days, eating lunch at our desks, and coming home most nights exhausted and with a headache. But I've welcomed the work, because it's taken my mind off Juliette. A bit.

She's still with Cam. I know she's not having the time of her life, though. Although I haven't seen much of her at work, she texts me a lot and occasionally calls me, and it sounds as if things are horrendous with Cam's family. She's also exhausted and feeling the strain, but she won't listen when I tell her she has to put herself first sometimes. I understand that she's been brought up to have a deep-rooted sense of community, and it's important to her to help people, but she doesn't want to be with Cam, and all this is doing is delaying the inevitable.

I can't push her, though. All I can do is get on with my own life and hope she sorts things out in the end.

I wish she was here. My body aches for her, and so does my heart. I hate to see her suffering like this. I want to help and comfort her, to take her to bed and help her forget. At night I dream about her soft mouth and her light-brown skin and her silky hair. But like Rangi, my hands are tied, and all I can do is wait.

I'm tired, and it's going to be a big day tomorrow. At least I'll be able to see her, and she's told me that Cam won't be coming to the funeral, so that's something.

I swim lengths for half an hour, get changed, have dinner, answer some emails, write up some notes while I half-watch a movie, and then go to bed at nine-thirty, unable to keep my eyes open. I'm asleep within about five minutes of my head hitting the pillow, and it's not even properly dark.

Jesus, I'm getting old.

*

Friday dawns dull and gloomy, kind of fitting for a funeral. I dress in a dark suit and tie, and head over to James's house around one o'clock. The funeral's not until three, and he's hired caterers to organize the wake, but I know guests are going to be arriving soon, and I offered to be there to help.

He looks pale but composed, and Aroha is gorgeous in a white blouse and black pencil skirt. She's dressed Leia up in a red frock with hearts on it, though, with a matching headscarf, and the baby is like a red rose in a concrete city.

Most people are going straight to the funeral home, but some of his family turn up, and soon I'm busy making sure everyone has a drink and a seat, greeting others as they arrive, and liaising with the catering company so that everything runs smoothly. Alex, Missie, Gaby, and Tyson arrive around two, also wanting to be with James, and I can see he appreciates his friends being around at such a difficult time.

Juliette arrives not long after. I watch her get out of the Uber, and stand in the doorway to greet her as she approaches.

"Hey," I say softly.

To my surprise, she comes right up to me, slides her arms around me, and gives me a big hug. "Mmm, I've missed you so much," she whispers.

"Aw, me too." I tighten my arms around her. She's lost weight over the past few weeks, emphasized by the black dress she's wearing, and she feels slight and fragile in my arms.

"I thought white was the traditional color of mourning for Hindus," I say.

"I'm not a Hindu," she says. "If I was, I wouldn't be here." Not explaining that mysterious comment, she moves back. "You look nice."

"Thank you."

She looks up at me. "It's really strange—I can feel confused and emotional and all over the place, but when I see you, it feels as if everything's going to be okay."

"It will be. We'll get there."

A frown flickers on her brow, but she just says, "How's James?"

"He's hanging in there."

"I'll go and see him." She gives me a small smile, then walks inside.

I watch her go, wishing she was mine, and I could stay at her side today. But she's not, and so I turn away to greet the next guests, hoping that if nothing else I get to spend some time with her later.

*

The funeral goes as well as can be hoped. Afterward, I stay by James's side, steering him through the crowd before delivering him to the car with his father and stepmother, make sure that everyone has transport back to the house, then head off with Alex and Missie.

When we get back, the catering staff have everything in hand, and begin serving drinks. I look for James, but he's vanished. I approach Aroha and say, "Do you know where he is?"

"I saw him going around the house to his room," she says. "Is he okay?"

"Leia's father turned up at the funeral home," I tell her. "I don't know what he said to James, but he went white as a sheet afterward."

"I'll go and see if he's okay." She holds Leia out to me. "Can you take her for a minute?"

"Oh. Uh. Okay." I take the baby from her, and she walks off into the east wing of the house.

Conscious that I'm holding Leia like a rugby ball, I put her up against my shoulder the way I've seen Aroha do, and the baby snuggles up to me. She's sucking on a dummy, but she doesn't seem sleepy. She looks up at me with her big turquoise eyes. They're the same color as James's—the color that Maddie's were. I feel a sudden sweep of grief. Maddie will never get to see her daughter grow up. God, that's so incredibly sad.

I walk to the window that overlooks the garden. It's raining, and I immediately see a fantail jumping from branch to branch in the lemon tree. The *piwakawaka* is said to be a messenger between the living and the dead, and it makes me catch my breath. Maybe Maddie hasn't gone entirely. Surely, if it was at all possible, she'd stay around Leia to keep an eye on her?

"It suits you."

I turn at the voice to find Juliette smiling at me. At my querying look, she gestures at Leia.

"I didn't really have a choice," I say gruffly.

"You look like a natural."

I glance down at the baby. She looks back, the dummy moving up and down as she sucks.

"She's very small," I say.

"Everyone's small next to you," Juliette states. She steps back, holds up her phone, and takes a photo of me. "For my own private collection," she says.

I shift from foot to foot, awkward and uncomfortable. "You want to take her?"

Her smile fades. "Sure." She lifts Leia out of my arms and coos to her, a natural, like women often seem to be.

I look away, out at the garden. The fantail has gone, and it's raining more heavily now.

"She's so beautiful," she says, kissing the baby's hair. "So James is going to bring her up as his own?"

I nod. "He's a bigger man than I am."

She lifts her gaze to me. "You wouldn't do it, if you were in his shoes?"

"I don't think so. I wouldn't want to bring up another man's child." I've already told her that I wouldn't want her to have a sperm donor, so it can't come as a surprise to her.

Our eyes meet. Hers are shining, and she seems to be having trouble holding back tears as she drops her head and kisses Leia's hair again.

I go to reply, but James comes out then, Aroha at his side. "Let's get this party started," he says, and he grabs a drink and heads to the middle of the room.

He gives a speech about Maddie, makes everyone laugh, starts some music playing, and bids everyone to eat, drink, and dance.

I don't talk to Juliette much for the rest of the afternoon. She always seems to be somewhere else, in the middle of a conversation. Once it stops raining, I play rugby outside with Saxon, Kip, Alex, and Huxley, and afterward I sit on the deck and chat to some of the others as the sun begins to head toward the horizon, hoping to catch up with her before the end of the day.

But later, when people start saying they're leaving, I look around for her and realize she's gone.

When I eventually get home, it's late, and I'm tired after the emotion of the day. I haven't drunk today, wanting to make sure I was able to help James if he needed me, so for the first time I pour myself a whisky and sit out on the deck.

Rangi finally messaged me this afternoon. I asked how he was doing, and he came back with one word. *Shit.* The poor kid. He's in his last year at high school, with no job prospects, no brilliant future to speak of. I wish I could do something, but Philip will do his best to dissuade his son from accepting my help.

I message him back, saying I'm always here for him and that he can message or call me anytime if he wants to talk.

Then, feeling lonely and sad, I text Juliette. *It was good to see you today. Hope you're doing okay. X*

But she doesn't message back. We often send each other little texts—jokes, memes, songs—and it's only now that I realize they were the same as the Rubik's Cube—a private communication that said far more than what was actually contained in the message. And I miss it. I miss her. She's been with me, in my heart, for so long, and now she's been snuffed out like a candle flame, and all that's left behind is smoke.

I'm tempted to call her—Cam is in Australia, after all—but I know she might be in bed. It's late, and she was tired, too. But I can't help but think she just doesn't want to reply.

She's slipping through my fingers, and there's nothing I can do about it. I'm not just infertile, I'm fucking impotent, helpless in what feels like every area of my personal life.

It's starting to rain, so I go inside and stretch out on the sofa. My New Year's resolution not to drink too much is already down the drain, so I pour myself another and welcome the slow, relentless slide into oblivion as the rain patters on the deck and drums fingers on the window, its reflection like tears on my skin.

*

The next day, Saturday the thirteenth of January, I wake up annoyed with myself for giving in to alcohol last night. I swim and work out for a while, trying to make up for it, eat a healthy breakfast of muesli and fresh fruit, then get in the BMW and head off to James's again.

Today the guys are coming around and we're working on the presentation for the conference together. The girls—Missie, Gaby, Aroha, and Juliette—are going shopping together, partly in an attempt, I think, to cheer themselves up after the difficult day yesterday.

When I arrive, Alex and Missie are already there, and I join Alex and James at the dining table and set up my laptop. Gaby and Tyson arrive soon after, and the guys are just settling down and the girls are getting Leia ready to leave when Juliette turns up.

It's a warm summer's day today, and she's wearing a light-blue tee and a pair of denim shorts. Her legs are long, brown, shapely, and smooth. She's pinned her hair up in a bun, and she has only the lightest of makeup on today. She looks about five years younger, and absolutely gorgeous, and she makes my heart ache.

"Hey," she says to the room in general. She meets my eyes and flicks me a smile, but she doesn't approach me. "Ready, gang?" she asks the girls.

"Yep, good to go," Aroha replies, picking up Leia in her carry seat, and with cheery goodbyes they all head for the door and go out. The door closes behind them, and there's a few seconds of silence in the room.

Then Tyson blows out a breath. "Right. Beer and PlayStation, guys?"

We all laugh and take a chair at the dining table. We might well have a play later, but we're not eighteen anymore, and we all want to get the work done first.

"First of all," Alex says, "James, we want to put forward the idea of Henry going to Sydney with Tyson next weekend. You've had a tough time and we thought you might need some time off."

James looks at me. "You wouldn't mind?"

I shake my head. I'm not as natural a public speaker as James, but I'm not bad, and Tyson and I work well together. "Not at all."

"Then that would be great, thank you. I could do with a rest."

"Right," Alex says. "That's settled. Let's get stuck in."

We work until one, then make ourselves some sandwiches and sit out on the deck with a can of Coke Zero. And it's then that James reveals that he's asked Aroha to marry him, ostensibly to secure Leia and make sure her lowlife birth father doesn't get his hands on her, and he announces he's paying her a million dollars to do it.

I'd seen him kiss her at the funeral, so I'd assumed he was developing feelings for her, but he's now implying it was all a ruse. Shocked at his idiocy, I say, "You do realize what an insult that was?"

He frowns. "The money, you mean?"

"Yeah."

"Why? I couldn't just ask her to marry me for nothing, could I? It's a two-year commitment, minimum."

"You fucking idiot."

James stares at me, obviously baffled, and says, "I don't understand."

"Don't worry about it," Alex replies. "It'll all come out in the wash." He winks at me. Oh… He thinks James likes Aroha. Ah, that puts a different perspective on it.

We joke with James about the *Droit du seigneur*, which is the right of the lord to have sex with any female subject, especially on their wedding night, and he bears it in good humor. But as the conversation moves on, I wonder whether Alex is right.

I was the first of our group of friends to get married. Now they're all following in my footsteps—Tyson got married last year, Damon at Christmas, Alex is sure to propose to Missie soon, and now James—the eternal bachelor—looks as if he might be settling down.

Hopefully they won't all follow me out of the exit.

Lost in thought, I only half hear James tell Alex to follow him to his office to get something, and when I look around, I discover myself alone with Tyson, who's sipping his Coke, looking out at the garden, although he glances over and smiles as he sees me looking at him.

I have nothing but admiration for him. Confined to a wheelchair at twenty-two, he could easily have given into depression and resentment at his bad luck. And he was low for a while, there's no doubt about it. But Gaby stuck by his side, and the rest of us were determined to help him walk again. Once we discussed the idea of the exoskeleton and the creation of Kia Kaha, he never looked back. He did his physio, never missing a day, and worked his butt off, determined to stand next to Gaby at the altar, which he did last year, bringing a tear to every eye at the wedding.

He walks somewhat stiffly, and occasionally uses a cane if he's having a bad day, but it never seems to faze him. He's a good-natured guy.

"You're sure about Sydney?" he asks.

"Yeah, of course. It'll be fun."

He nods, turning his can in his fingers. "Alex thinks it'll do you good to get away," he says softly.

My eyebrows rise. "Oh?"

"Tell me to mind my own business if you want," he says, "but it's obvious that something's going on with Juliette."

I inhale, then give a long sigh. "It's complicated."

"It always is." He tips his head to the side. "Is she still with Cam?"

"Like I said, it's complicated. He's in Australia at the moment—his brother had a heart attack, and his wife is about to have a baby. Juliette's looking after his mum, who had a kind of breakdown."

"Jesus."

"Yeah. I don't think they're *together* together, if you know what I mean. But she hasn't broken up with him, either. I'm just waiting, hoping she'll work it out."

"That's tough for you, man."

I shrug. "It is what it is." I look up as Alex walks back through the living room and joins us.

"James is just coming," he says, "and then we'll get started again."

Tyson gets to his feet and heads off to the bathroom, and Alex and I start clearing up.

I glance at him as he stacks the plates. "Tyson said you suggested I go to Sydney because you thought it would be good for me to get away."

"Yeah." He picks up some of the rubbish. "I know you and Juliette are having trouble."

"How did you know?"

His eyes meet mine. "You haven't given her the Rubik's Cube since she started work on Monday."

My eyebrows rise. I'm surprised he's picked up on that. But he's right. Since she came back, we haven't done it. I don't know why. But something's awry between us. I suppose I shouldn't be shocked that he's noticed. We've all worked together for years, and he's pretty astute.

"She'll get there," he says. "Hang in there."

My throat tightens, and I look away. "I dunno. I thought she was done with him, but then his brother fell sick, and now… I feel like I'm losing her." I don't normally talk like this, and I'm embarrassed to admit it, but I don't know what to do.

"She has a strong sense of duty," he says, "and Cam's brother falling ill has knocked her for six. But she's not the sort of woman to stay in a failing relationship. He's let her down, and eventually she'll walk away."

"Maybe." I crush my can with a hand. "But I'm tired of things being out of my hands, you know?"

"Yeah, I get that."

"I know this is the reason you hate relationships at work. But I'm not waiting forever. If she stays with him… if she doesn't leave soon… I can't continue to work with her."

He sighs. "Yeah, I know." He scoops a few crumbs onto the plate on the top of the pile. "What would you do?"

"I'm not sure. I was thinking about helping out at Greenfield."

His eyebrows rise. "Working there, you mean?"

"Yeah. Atticus—the deacon who runs it—has asked me if I'd consider leading some of the adventure therapy sessions. It would be cool to help out some youngsters. Maybe even work there full time."

He nods slowly. Then his lips twist. "Kia Kaha wouldn't be the same without you."

"You'd be fine."

"Come on, the building was all your idea. There's more than a little of your heart left in the walls."

"I dunno. It's pretty fractured at the moment. I think maybe it needs some time to heal, you know?"

He goes to reply, but James and Tyson are heading back to the dining table, and so we rise, go back in, and take our places.

But I see him look at me a few times as we work during the afternoon, lost in thought.

I know all of them would be incredibly sad if I left the company. But how can I continue to work there, seeing Juliette at the meeting every morning, knowing how close I came to having her? And knowing that I lost her?

I just can't do it, and unfortunately it's looking more and more like a reality with each passing day.

Chapter Twenty-Four

Juliette

When I leave James's house, I sit in my car for a moment, not starting the engine. It's getting harder to be with Henry and not be with him, and I can feel something building, like a thunderstorm about to break. My head hurts, and I don't feel well, and the last thing I want is to go back and listen to Kathy's hysterics. So I ring Roy with the intention of telling him that I'm going to stay at my apartment for the night. But he tells me Kathy has had a particularly bad day, and he sounds angry and frustrated, so in the end I drive around there, my sense of duty too strong to fight.

As soon as I walk in, though, Roy gets a beer out of the fridge, puts on the TV, and leaves me to handle Kathy alone. Gritting my teeth, I run her a bath, as that normally helps to calm her down. But even though she gets in, she's too low to wash herself, so I end up helping her. I wash her hair, then help her out, dry her and her hair, and get her dressed in her nightie. Finally I put her to bed, and I sit by her side as she cries and says she's sorry, until she eventually falls asleep.

Exhausted and frustrated, I go into the living room. Roy is sitting there watching an old comedy show, laughing and swigging his third beer.

I go over to the TV and switch it off.

"Hey!" He sits up and glares at me.

"You can't do this," I tell him resentfully. "You can't just leave me to deal with Kathy. It's not fair. She's not my mother, and I'm not a nurse. I have a life to live."

"So do I," he snaps.

"But she's your wife! You married her, Roy. She's your responsibility."

He sits back, looking moody and sullen. "What if I don't want that responsibility anymore?"

I stare at him. "What do you mean?"

"This isn't why I got married. She's supposed to look after me. I'm the one who goes to work, who pays the bills. It's her job to run the house, not lie in bed moping. I didn't know it was going to be like this. I don't want to be married to her anymore."

Panic fills me. Normally I'd have ripped into him for his misogynistic attitude, but if he leaves Kathy, the burden of her care is going to fall on Cam's—and therefore my—shoulders.

"All right," I say, taking deep breaths and trying to calm down. "I understand how you feel, and it's natural to have bad days and to feel like this. But I know you don't mean it. You love her, and you just want her to be better."

He lifts his chin. "I don't love her anymore. She's just a fucking millstone around my neck." He picks up his beer and walks away, out of the sliding doors into the garden. Shocked, I can only watch as he disappears into his shed—his Man Cave—and closes the door.

I sink onto the sofa. I'm shaking now. What am I going to do? I don't want this responsibility. But I can't just leave.

Feeling sick, I call Cam. It's early evening in Sydney, and he answers after half a dozen rings.

"Hello?"

"It's me," I say.

"Hey. I'm at the hospital."

"How's it going?"

"Okay. Alan's improving. And Em's contractions have stopped. They think they were Braxton Hicks. I'll be taking her home soon."

"Oh, well, that's something."

"How about you? How's your day going?"

I cover my face with a hand. "Not great."

"Why, what's happened?"

I tell him what his father just said.

He snorts. "He's just fed up. He'll get over it."

"I don't know, Cam, he looked pretty serious."

"He wouldn't leave her."

I take a deep breath. "Cam, I need you to come home. I can't deal with this. I don't want to deal with it."

"I can't, you know I can't. I've got to make sure Alan and Em are all right."

Tears prick my eyes. "I don't want to do this anymore."

I hear him inhale, and then he gives an audible, frustrated sigh. "Don't do this to me. Don't get hysterical."

That makes me angry. "I'm not hysterical. I'm tired and frustrated. These aren't my parents."

"No, maybe not, but when you're in a relationship you help each other out, right?"

"That's true, but what am I getting out of it, Cam? Tell me. What's in it for me?" Tears run down my cheeks.

He's silent for a long moment. I don't speak, though, and eventually he says, "All right. I'll come home. I'll try and book a flight tomorrow."

I wipe my cheeks. "Thank you."

"Can you stay there tonight?"

"Yes, I'll stay."

"Thank you. You know I appreciate everything you do."

This is always how it is. He drives me to the edge, then spends the next few days pulling me back from it. I'm so tired of it. So tired.

"I've got to go," he says, "Em is waiting for me. I'll let you know what flight I get."

"All right. Bye."

"Bye." He ends the call.

Leaving Roy in his shed, I go to bed. Before I turn off the light, I check my phone.

There's a message from Henry. *Love you. Miss you. Want you. Always x*

Everything that my partner should be saying to me. Oh God, that hurts so bad.

Another text pops up as I'm watching. It's a link to a song on Spotify—Bill Withers' *Ain't No Sunshine*. I press play, turning the volume down so it's just a murmur.

Bill wonders where his girl has gone, and tells us there's darkness every day she's away, and tears run down my face again.

I don't know what to say to Henry. So instead I just send him a heart. Then I turn off the phone and the light.

Within minutes, I fall into an exhausted sleep.

*

The next morning, as soon as I open my eyes, I know I'm in trouble.

I barely make it to the bathroom before I throw up, vomiting whatever's left in my stomach into the toilet. I retch and I retch. When I'm finally done, I rinse out my mouth and sink onto the toilet seat.

I sit with my head in my hands for a few minutes. Then I get up, go into the bedroom, and retrieve my purse. I take it into the bathroom and extract the pregnancy test I bought yesterday, and read the instructions. Apparently it's ninety-nine percent accurate.

With shaking hands, I take off the wrapper and pee on the stick. Then I let it sit there while I wash my hands.

After the longest three minutes in the history of mankind, I check the result. In the box is one clear word.

Pregnant.

I sink back onto the toilet seat. I knew, of course. My cycle is a little longer than average, but even for me, forty-two days is extreme. Realistically, I'm around ten days late.

I'd hoped that all the hassle of the past week—the grief and shock following Maddie's death, and the stress of looking after Kathy and dealing with Cam—might have been the reason I was late. But I should have known better. All week, I've been hoping my period might appear, hoping that the symptoms—sore breasts, tiredness—were just a sign of PMS. But deep down, I knew.

And now I'm in love with one guy and pregnant by another. I don't love Cam anymore. I'm convinced of that. But it's not just about me now. I have to think about the baby.

I wouldn't want to bring up another man's child. Henry's words ring in my head. Ever since he said that I've felt a sense of futility settle deep inside me. He's not going to want me if I'm having Cam's baby. He isn't a choice for me anymore. My choice is now Cam or nobody. Stay with a guy in a broken relationship. Or bring up the baby on my own.

And now I start crying for real.

*

I ring Alex and call in sick. He's concerned, but obviously hears the emotion in my voice and doesn't press me. "Take as long as you want," he says, "and let us know if we can do anything."

Half an hour later, I get a text from Henry. *Hey, Alex said you're unwell. How are you doing?*

I can't keep ignoring him, so I message him back. *Yeah, just a bit under the weather, that's all. J.*

I send it before I can add a kiss.

He doesn't come back.

I cry again.

*

I get up and go through to the kitchen. Roy's there, eating a slice of toast and drinking a cup of tea, but when I walk in, he picks it up and leaves the room. Heart sinking, I put more toast on, butter a slice and make a cup of tea, and take it through to Kathy. She's awake, lying there pale and listless.

"When's Cam coming home?" she asks.

"Soon," I promise. "A day or two."

"I miss him," she whispers.

"Yeah, well, it won't be long now."

"You do still love him, don't you?" she asks me.

I stare at her, shocked by her query, and unsure how to answer. I don't want to upset her, but I'm not going to lie. "Don't you worry about that," I tell her. "Eat your toast and then let's see about getting you up and about." I leave the room before she can push me further.

Cam messages me mid-morning to tell me that Em is home and doing well. Alan is being released Wednesday, and he wants to wait so he can bring him home too. So he's booked a flight home for Thursday.

I don't want to wait that long, but I don't have a choice. I feel bad for making him come home when Alan and Em could probably do with him staying there, but I need to talk to him, and I need him to be here and sort his parents out. So I stop myself from doing what I'd normally do—tell him to stay as long as he needs—and just text back *Thank you, see you then.*

*

In the end, I speak to Alex and decide to take the whole week off. Most of the staff don't start until next week, and my deputy, Claire, is happy to start the ball rolling for me and begin scheduling appointments, so it's not absolutely necessary that I go in. I need to sort myself out first. I need to speak to Henry. More than anything, I want to talk to him. But this is Cam's baby, and I owe it to him to tell him first. I need to see his reaction, and then I can decide what I'm going to do.

I also need to sort out Kathy and Roy. I have to get this sorted, or it's going to be an unbearable burden for me. I go with her to her doctor's appointment, and she doesn't argue when I suggest I go in to see him with her. I tell the doctor how bad she is and that she needs help now. He does everything he can. He takes it seriously. Ups her meds. Talks to her about the importance of taking them every day. Tells her she needs to look after herself with diet and exercise. Refers her to a psychiatrist. Recommends a new therapist. Gives me a phone number to call if things get bad.

But none of it seems to get to the root of the problem. It'll be weeks, if not months, before she gets her appointments. She's overweight and miserable, with terrible self-esteem. She's in no position to think about diet and exercise, and she forgets her meds unless someone is there to remind her to take them. How do you make someone care about themselves?

I should be angry with Roy for leaving me to deal with it, but on Wednesday evening, after the doctor's appointment, I sit down with him to tell him about it, and for the first time he opens up and begins talking. He tells me how she's been like this for most of their married life, which is over thirty years. He's spent much of that time managing her, trying to get her to take her meds, encouraging her to eat well and exercise, and she does well for a while, then hits one of her bad patches and plummets, and there's nothing he can do about it. Without him having to say it, I can tell they have no physical relationship, and I can see he's lonely and he's reached the end of his tether. And how can I criticize him for that when I feel the same?

"Cam takes after his mother," Roy says, surprising me. "I'm sorry about that."

We study each other in the quietness of the evening. The sliding doors are open, and I can smell grass from where he mowed the lawn earlier today.

"This is hard on you," he says. "And it's not fair."

I swallow hard. "It's not your fault."

"It's nobody's fault. Not even Kath's. But it sucks." He finishes off his beer. "You should get out while you can."

I stare at him, shocked, as he gets up and goes out, down to his shed.

Is he right? Is this going to be me in thirty years if I stay with Cam? He doesn't suffer from depression in the same way as his mother, but there are definitely similarities. It's only now that I realize how I've had to handle him for seven years. How I tread on eggshells sometimes to try to keep the peace. How hard I've worked to keep our relationship going. How I'm the one who gives, and all he does it take. And if I complain, he gaslights me and says I don't understand him and I'm unsympathetic.

I was so close to leaving him. And now, even if I walk out, I'm tied to him for the rest of my life by the mistake we've made.

I lean back on the sofa and rest my hand on my belly. And it occurs to me then for the first time. I could terminate the pregnancy.

I sit there for a moment and let the thought settle over me.

It's too late for the morning after pill—the last time I slept with Cam was back in December. I know that because it was on my birthday—December the tenth. So it would have to be an abortion.

I could do it without telling Cam or Henry. Just go down to the clinic, pop a pill, and let nature take its course.

I cover my face with my hands. Ahhh….

Hindus believe in the principle of *Ahimsa*, or nonviolence toward all living things. Abortion is only allowed to save the mother's life. But I don't consider myself a Hindu. Or a Christian. Or a pagan. My DNA, my culture, and my faith is a mish-mash, and I pick and choose the bits from it that I like and that I feel fit me. So where abortion is concerned, I've always been pro-choice. I believe it's better to terminate a pregnancy than to bring an unwanted baby into the world.

But now? It's one thing to tell others what you believe. It's another to carry out the act yourself.

I'm responsible for this baby. If I terminate the pregnancy, it'll be my choice. What was it that Henry told me that Rangi said? *I made a baby, and he won't get to be born. What would Jesus say about that?*

I press my fingers to my lips as tears well in my eyes. It's just baby hormones, I tell myself. Pull yourself together. You're a fucking professional woman with a career. You're in control. You're not one of those women who cry at the first sign of trouble.

But just the thought of there being baby hormones in my system is enough to make the tears impossible to stop. My body is already preparing itself to have this baby. Do I have the right to end the pregnancy?

Oh jeez, I can't think like this. Anyway, I know that something like forty percent of all pregnancies end in miscarriage. Women often think they're late and then their period starts, and they don't realize they've actually miscarried. It's still very early for me. There's no point in panicking yet.

But Cam's home tomorrow. If I'm going to terminate it without telling him, I need to make the decision before he gets here, because I know what I'm like. I can't keep a secret, and I'm going to have to talk to him about it.

So I sit there, going around and around in circles, while it slowly gets dark and I have to get up and shut the doors to stop the moths flying in.

*

The next day, Cam arrives at ten a.m.

He's exhausted. Alan came home yesterday, and Cam was busy all day, ensuring their cupboards were stocked, making his brother comfortable, and reassuring them that he'd be back soon.

"I'll have to go back next week," he tells me. "Em just can't cope, and the baby's going to come real soon."

"What about your job?" I ask, frowning. "You can't keep taking time off work."

He doesn't reply for a moment. Kathy is in bed. Roy is in the shed. It's just me and Cam in their living room.

"I quit," he says. "On Monday."

I stare at him, jaw dropping. "What?"

He studies his hands. "My boss told me I couldn't have the time off. So I had to."

I'm so shocked, I can't think. "Cam, we've got bills to pay."

"I'll get another job. I was looking around in Sydney. There were several jobs there I could walk straight into." He finally meets my eyes, resentful, challenging. He's trying to force my hand.

"What about your parents? You can't leave them, Cam. Your mum is in a terrible mess, and your dad's had enough of looking after her."

"I'm going to talk to them about them moving out with us. She'd be much happier there, nearer to Alan and Em and the baby."

He's figured it all out. He's obviously been thinking about this for a while.

"What about me?" I ask softly. "How do I fit into all this?"

He rolls his eyes as if it goes without saying. "I want you to come with me." I think it's the most unromantic thing he's ever said, and that's saying something.

My hand creeps to my stomach without meaning to, and before I can stop myself, I say, "I'm pregnant."

His eyebrows lift. "What?"

"I'm pregnant. I found out on Sunday."

We stare at each other for a long moment.

"Is it mine?" he asks.

I nod.

"How can you be sure?" he demands.

"Because Henry can't have children. He has a low sperm count. He spent two years trying to get Shaz pregnant. And anyway, we used a condom. But the last time you and I had sex, we didn't, remember?" It was the night of our first big argument, so I know he won't have forgotten.

He continues to stare at me. "Shit."

I give a short laugh, and my eyes sting. "Is that all you can say?"

"Well, it's not great timing. But we'll make it work, I guess."

I'm speechless with frustration. I don't know what I'd expected, but something more than this. I wanted him to look excited. To hug me and say it was amazing news. Something, anything to give me a reason to stay.

I get to my feet and go over to the window, wrapping my arms around myself defensively. After a moment, I turn to face him.

"I don't want to move," I tell him. "My family and friends are here."

"We can make new friends together."

"I happen to like my old friends. And my mum and dad would be devastated if I moved to Australia. They're going to want to see their first grandchild." Probably their only one, too, as Antony is gay.

"I can't stay here," he says helplessly. "I want to go. And I'd hoped you'd support me."

"What about you supporting me, Cam? Why is it always the other way around? I don't ask you for anything. I have a career. People I love. Why should I give them up for you?"

"Is this about Henry?"

I don't reply for a moment.

"It is," he says angrily, getting to his feet. "Jesus."

"It's not about him. I don't think I have a future with him. But it is about the fact that he makes me feel wanted. He makes me feel cherished. And you don't."

"I'm sorry. I know things need to change. Come to Australia with me. We'll go to Melbourne. You can study there. Let's start over again. You, me, and the baby. Perhaps we'll be able to make it work. But I can't do it here. I don't want you to see Henry anymore."

"You're making me choose?"

"Yeah," he says. "Maybe I am. I think that's fair. Don't you?" He walks over to stand in front of me. "This is our baby. Mine and yours. For its sake, we should try to make it work, don't you think?"

Oh God. This is so hard.

What am I going to do?

Chapter Twenty-Five

Henry

On Friday, I'm at home packing, ready to leave for my afternoon flight to Sydney, when my phone rings. My heart lifts as I see Juliette's name on the screen. I haven't spoken to her since last Saturday, and although we've messaged each other occasionally, it's been far less frequent than normal. I know things are hard for her at home, so I've tried to give her space, but it's been tough.

I answer the call with a mixture of emotions: pleasure, hope, and a touch of anxiety. "Hello?"

"Hey, it's me."

"Hey, sweetheart." I put down the shirt I was about to pack and walk out onto the deck. "How are you doing?"

"Okay. Not too bad."

"I'm glad you rang. I was wondering how you are. I'm guessing you've been busy."

"Yes. Henry, I… I need to talk to you."

I go still, and my heart seems to shudder to a stop. "Oh?"

She's silent for a moment. Then she says, "I'm pregnant."

Slowly, my heart collapses in on itself like a dying star.

I give a short, humorless laugh. "The one thing I can't do for you. Fuck me."

"I'm so sorry."

I run a hand through my hair. I'm having trouble breathing. My chest hurts. Ah, jeez, I think I'm having a fucking coronary.

"He… he wants me to move to Australia with him," she says, her voice husky. "He says he thinks if we have a fresh start, maybe it'll work out."

He's taking her away from me in every way he can.

GG, Cam. Good Game. You won. You motherfucking, cunting, shitting, pissing, fucking arsehole of a bastard.

"I hope you'll be very happy," I say.

Then, before I can think better of it, I draw my arm back and throw my phone as hard as I can. It sails away, turning in the air, and I watch it plummet down onto the rocks, where it breaks into a million pieces that scatter into the ocean.

"Fuck it!" I yell so hard it hurts my throat. Ah, bollocks, now I'm going to be hoarse for the conference. *And* I don't have a phone.

I sink onto the wooden deck, my back against the window, draw up my knees, and put my head in my hands. Over the last few days, I've repeatedly told myself that I haven't lost her. That it's not too late. I've reassured myself that I was doing the right thing in giving her time and letting her come to the conclusion on her own that we were meant to be together.

I should have gone over to see her and dragged her back here by her fucking hair.

But then what would've been the point in doing that? Cam hasn't forced her to stay with him. Well, maybe there's an element of that with the pregnancy, but I assume that was accidental. The fact is that Juliette is a grown woman. She had a choice. And she's chosen him.

Ahhh… that fucking hurts…

I tip my head back on the glass and look up at the gray clouds. I think about my phone and wince. That was childish. What must she be thinking? I should have finished the conversation like a man, congratulated her on being pregnant, told her I understood why it made sense to stay with the father of her baby, and ended with an 'I'll always be here for you,' type of comment. A promise that we can continue to work together and be friends.

But it's not the truth, is it? She's going to be leaving the company, well, leaving the country. The only time I'll get to see her will be if she comes back to visit her family, or if I go to Sydney and ask if she wants to meet up. And what would be the point of that? Would I really want to see her with her new baby, happy in the glow of motherhood, in her new life?

And realistically, we can't stay in contact. In the past I'd told myself we were just friends, but it's always been a lie. Shaz didn't know that Juliette and I messaged each other every day, and I'm betting Cam didn't either. We've had a six-year affair, and it wasn't fair on either of our partners. And it wasn't fair on ourselves. If she's going to be truly happy, we need to make the break.

Hey, if *I* want to be happy, we need to make the break.

For the first time, I think about a future without her. For two years, and maybe more, I've dreamed about ending up with her. But it's not going to happen. She's never going to be mine. It's time I put her behind me. I need to start dating again. Meeting other women. There's somebody else out there for me. Someone I can love, and who'll understand me. Who'll make me glow inside the way she does.

But I don't want anyone else. I want her.

I'm furious. And so fucking upset I want to either bawl my eyes out or hit something really, really hard, multiple times. Or someone. Preferably whose name starts with a C.

The last thing I want to do is go to the conference. But I can't get out of it now. I check my watch—I can't look at my phone because I threw it in the ocean—and see that I have thirty minutes before I have to leave the house.

I need to finish packing. And I have to go buy myself a new phone and SIM card.

But instead I continue to sit there and watch the seagulls, fighting back tears, wondering if my heart will ever feel whole again.

*

When my Uber pulls up at the airport, Tyson is sitting on one of the outside seats, looking at his phone. He stands as I get out and retrieve my case and flight bag, and I walk over to him.

"You're late," he says. "We need to check in. I was beginning to wonder if you were going to make it."

"Sorry."

"I've texted you, like, eight times asking where you are."

As we head into the airport, I say, "My phone's not working. I need to get myself a new one."

"Not working how? Run out of charge?"

"Don't want to talk about it."

He glances at me, then just says, "Okay."

We check in, put our cases on the conveyor belt, then shoulder our flight bags. Now we have a three-hour wait.

We head toward the flight lounges, find a phone shop, and I purchase a new iPhone and a SIM card. I transfer over my old number and turn the phone on, and I wait for it to sort itself out. We're flying Emirates First Class, so we head toward Manaia Lounge, where there are leather armchairs, a bar, and places to eat.

It's late for lunch but neither of us has eaten much today, so we order a steak sandwich and fries each and treat ourselves to a beer, then take a seat opposite each other at one of the tables.

I study the new phone. I have a heap of texts, and I scan them quickly. Nothing from Juliette. Am I surprised? Did I really think she'd message me back after I hung up on her? Even so, my spirits sink. I'm such a fucking idiot.

"Tell me something I don't know," Tyson says, and I realize that I said the words out loud. "You wanna talk about it?" he asks.

"No."

He leans back in his chair and has a swig of his beer. "You sure you don't wanna talk about it?"

I look up at him. In general, guys don't talk to one another about relationship issues, but Tyson is different. What he went through with his accident has made him look at life differently, and he's much more open than the rest of us. When he was first confined to a wheelchair, I went around to his place with Alex, James, and Damon. After a few whiskies, he admitted that although Gaby was determined to stay with him, he was worried he'd never be able to function in a normal way sexually again. It was a very frank discussion, and it was a major reason for the creation of Kia Kaha. We all understood that being able to have sex was as important to him as being able to walk, and it led to us all knowing more about sexual function.

As a result, he's more likely to want to talk about personal issues, and so the fact that he's asking me now isn't really surprising.

Still, I'm not interested in analyzing what's gone wrong, and so I say, "I'm sure."

He gives me a frank look. "Dude, I'm not going to spend the weekend with you when you've got a face like thunder. Spit it out. I'm guessing it's something to do with Juliette?"

I glower.

"What's happened?" he asks.

I give a long, heartfelt sigh. "It's a long story."

"Bro, we've got three hours."

So I start talking. And to my surprise, when I start, I find I can't stop.

I tell him about what happened on the trivia night, and then about the wedding. He doesn't look shocked, and so I'm pretty sure he's already guessed what's been going on.

But when I tell him about the events of the past two weeks, about Cam's brother and mother, and the stress that Juliette has been under, he frowns. And then when I finally explain about the phone call this morning, he tips his head back and gives a long, heartfelt sigh.

"Shit," he says.

"Yeah. And Cam told her they should stay together for the baby, and he wants to move to Australia. So that's that."

"And what did you say?"

"I said, 'I hope you'll be very happy,' and I threw my phone into the ocean." I roll my eyes at the look on his face. "Yeah. I know."

"So you didn't give her a chance to reply?"

"Uh, no."

"So you don't know whether she's told Cam she wants to stay with him?"

"Well, I assumed she's going to. She's had weeks to leave, and she chose not to. I can't imagine she will now that she's pregnant."

"Hmm."

I massage the bridge of my nose. "I just wish I'd finished the conversation better. I know we're not going to be able to stay in touch when she goes to Oz, but I want her to know that I don't mean her ill."

"Why don't you call her?"

I study the new phone. "I don't think she'll want to talk to me."

"I'm sure she's feeling lonely and heartsick right now. You should at least apologize and tell her you're not angry anymore."

I sigh. "Yeah, all right." I get up and wander over to the window as I dial her number. My heart begins to race, and my mouth goes dry at the thought of speaking to her.

But it goes straight to voicemail, and my heart sinks.

I'm about to hang up when I turn and see Tyson watching. He's right. I do need to apologize.

"Hey, it's me," I say softly. "I just wanted to talk to you and say I'm sorry for hanging up on you like that. It was childish, and I regret it. Hopefully we can catch up when I get back from Sydney. Take care of yourself. You can always call me if you want to talk. Okay, well, speak to you soon. Bye." I hang up awkwardly. It wasn't my best speech, but at least I tried.

I go back to Tyson and sit down. "It went to voicemail, so I left a message."

"Good, well done." He picks up his own phone. "Okay, well I'm going to give Gaby a ring before we leave. Don't eat all my fries if they turn up."

"Would I do a thing like that?"

He grins and walks off to call his wife.

I'm glad I called Juliette, but I feel uneasy. It's rare for her not to answer her phone. I hope she's okay. But there's nothing I can do about it now. She's not my responsibility. She's Cam's, and I have to get used to that.

I watch Tyson talking to Gaby, feeling more than a little envious as he smiles somewhat bashfully, then laughs at something she's said.

Our food arrives, and I steal a couple of his fries. Serves him right for being so fucking happy.

*

Juliette

On Saturday morning, I'm sitting in the corner of the coffee shop in The Garden Hotel, sipping a latte, when Gaby walks in. She spots me and comes over, and I stand up to give her a big hug.

When she moves back, she gives me an appraising look, but she just says, "You want anything to eat?"

"No, thanks."

"Okay. I'll just get a coffee." She goes up and places her order, then comes back and sits opposite me. "Thanks for agreeing to see me," she says.

I study my coffee. She rang me last night and asked to meet up. Initially, I said no, but she told me that Tyson had called her, and he'd been speaking to Henry, and she said, "Girl, I know you're in trouble. Please, talk to me."

It wasn't long after my call to Henry, and I'd been too upset at the time, so I suggested we meet up today. I'd half-dreaded having to see her and go through it all, but now I'm here, I find myself quite relieved to be talking to a friend who has nothing but my best interests at heart.

"I'm sorry to be so cloak and dagger," I reply.

She looks around. "Why are we meeting here?"

"I'm staying here."

Her eyebrows rise. "Why?"

"I knew Cam would come around if I went to the apartment, and I don't want to see him. I need some time alone."

"Aw," she says, her forehead creasing. "Sweetie. I know you're pregnant—Henry told Tyson. Come on, tell me. What's going on?"

I explain everything. That Henry and I have been seeing each other. About Cam's brother and mother being unwell. And that Cam wants us to stay together for the baby's sake, and that he wants to move to Australia.

"There is a university in Melbourne that offers a Masters of Clinical Prosthetics and Orthotics," I tell her. "He'd rather go to Sydney, but he said he'd compromise and move to Melbourne for me."

She tips her head to the side. "Do you want to go?"

"The course sounds interesting."

We study each other for a moment.

"Do you still love him?" she asks.

I bite my lip and look away, out of the window. It's a blustery summer's day, and the clouds are scudding across the bright blue sky. It's just gone ten—Henry and Tyson will be starting their presentation soon. I hope it goes well for them.

I look back at her. "Not in the way I used to."

"Do you love Henry?"

"Yes," I say, without hesitation.

"Well, then. You deserve to be happy, sweetie."

I swallow hard. "But he told me he wouldn't want to bring up another man's child."

He rang me yesterday and left a message. It was wonderful to hear his voice. He apologized for hanging up on me and said he hoped we could catch up when he gets back.

But he didn't say anything about the baby, or tell me he still wants to be with me. All he said was that he'll always be there for me, and while that's sweet, it's not enough.

She sighs, then leans back as the waitress delivers her coffee. "Thanks." She adds a sweetener and stirs it. "Tyson didn't mention that."

"I doubt Henry told him. I don't think he's proud of his opinion. When he was talking about James adopting Leia, he said, 'He's a bigger man than I am.'"

"You've spoken to him about his infertility?"

"Yes, we talked about IVF. He said he'd do it, but I could tell he was just saying what I wanted to hear. And he definitely didn't want to use a sperm donor. I think those two years of trying with Shaz killed any desire he had for kids. And I really want children. He was so angry when I told him I was pregnant. Not at me, but at the situation. I think for him, it was all over as soon as I told him. He said, 'I hope you'll be very happy,' and hung up."

"I'm so sorry."

I sigh. "Ever since the trivia night I've been torn between the two of them, but that choice has gone now. Unless…" I sip my coffee. "I've been thinking about terminating the pregnancy."

She stares at me, and we study each other for a long moment.

"So you can be with Henry?" she asks eventually.

I lean on the table and put my face in my hands. "Don't say it like that. It sounds so fucking callous. But if it's the only way I can be with him… Ah jeez…"

"You can't do it for Henry," she says. "You'll never forgive yourself if you do it for that reason, and even if he doesn't want the baby, it'll always be between you."

"I know." I blink away tears and lower my hands. "You think I should keep it?"

"Ah… Juliette…" She takes my hands in hers. "You shouldn't ask me."

"I am asking you, though. I want to know what you think."

"Well, Tyson and I are trying to have a baby, and we're not sure if he can have kids yet, so I'm the wrong person to ask. A baby seems like a beautiful gift to me, no matter who the father is. But our situations are very different. I'm married, with a loving husband. And I think it's a bad idea to stay with Cam for the baby."

I nod slowly. "I agree. But the only other alternative is to have it on my own, and…" I pause, not sure how to voice my frustration. "I know it sounds pathetic—there are loads of single mums out there who bring up kids on their own without any problems at all. But I'm scared."

"Of what?"

"Being pregnant, to start with. I don't know anything about pregnancy, or childbirth. And of having to bring up the child on my own. I'm terrified."

"Aw, you'd have me, and Missie, and Aroha, and your mum to help."

"Yes, that's true. But…" I swallow hard. "Having Cam's baby is going to tie me to him, even if we don't live together. And I keep thinking about how hard it'll be. He's not a bad guy, and I'm sure he'll be a good dad, but he's such a narcissist. Everything is about him, and I can just foresee so many issues, trying to get him to pull his weight financially and with his time. It's going to be a constant battle, and I don't know if I've got the strength for it. In many ways, it would be easier to stay together, you know?"

"I can see what you mean."

"I know that's wrong though. Of course it is. So the only other option is to have an abortion. And then I feel bad because it's not the baby's fault, and I think about you and women like you who struggle to get pregnant, and then I feel terrible."

"Oh God, don't think like that."

"It's impossible not to." I press my fingers to my lips, trying not to cry. "It's such a fucked-up situation. We came so close to making it. Henry wanted me to leave Cam, and I think if I'd done it earlier, and we'd spent some time together, he might have been open to the idea of bringing up the baby as his own. But now he's actually said he wouldn't want to bring up another guy's child. I think I've sort of been spoiled for him."

And then I do cry, silent tears that Gaby tries to mop up with serviettes, and she can't think of anything to say to comfort me, because what is there to say? I don't want to be with Cam, and I'm too scared to have the baby on my own, and the only way to be with Henry is to terminate the pregnancy, and Gaby's right—I can't do that just to get him, because I'll never forgive myself. I'm just going around and around the maze, trying to find my way out, and I can't, because all the exits are blocked.

What the hell am I going to do?

Chapter Twenty-Six

Henry

Despite the way my personal life is collapsing around my ears, as usual I have no problems with my professional life, and on Saturday the conference goes swimmingly. Tyson and I make a good double act, providing just enough humor to warm the audience, while being knowledgeable enough to convince them we know what we're talking about. Tyson gives a moving talk about his own experience, and I keep them captivated as I show footage of MAX and THOR, our exoskeletons, and show interviews with those whose lives we've changed.

After our presentation, during lunch, we talk to health professionals and industry experts, and we exchange business cards and come away with lots of exciting contacts.

When we're done, we head to the airport feeling as if we've conquered the world.

"Alex is going to be pleased," Tyson says.

"Yeah, I'm glad we did okay," I reply. "I was worried you'd miss James and I'd ruin everything."

"Hardly," he scoffs. "James might be Mr. Smoothie, but you're still Head of HR. Your people skills are pretty hot."

"Not where girls are concerned," I say somewhat gloomily.

"Chin up," he says. "Gaby was going to see Juliette this morning. I'll call her when we're at the gate and see what she found out."

I glare at him. "I didn't know you were going to tell Gaby."

"I tell Gaby everything. I thought you knew that. We have no secrets from each other."

I think about that as we check in and drop off our bags. I tried opening up to Juliette, but it didn't get me anywhere. God, I miss her. I've texted her several times, but she still hasn't come back, and when I rang, it went to voicemail again. I didn't leave a message the second time.

Sure enough, once we've got to the flight lounge and ordered some dinner, Tyson heads off to call his wife. He's gone for a while. I sit and pretend to read on my phone, but I'm surprisingly nervous to discover what he's found out, and I end up flicking through TikTok and Insta, doom scrolling and not really reading anything.

When Tyson eventually comes back, his face is serious, and he doesn't smile as he sits.

"Everything all right?" I ask.

He leans back as the waitress delivers our pasta, and he picks up his fork, then puts it down again as she goes off.

"Did Gaby meet Juliette?" I prompt.

He nods. "Juliette's staying at a hotel."

My eyebrows rise. "Why?"

"She didn't want to stay at the apartment because she thought Cam would call in to see her. She said she wants some time alone."

My heart slams to a stop. "Really?"

"She's trying to make her mind up what to do." He puts pepper on his pasta, then puts the grinder down and leans on the table. "I'm sorry to tell you this, but Gaby's really concerned about her. She said that Juliette cried, and she seemed quite panicky and upset. Apparently…" He hesitates and meets my eyes.

"What?" I snap.

"She's thinking about terminating the pregnancy."

My jaw drops. "Really?"

"Gaby doesn't think she will. But she said Juliette doesn't want to be with Cam. She doesn't want to go to Australia. But she doesn't want to bring the baby up alone either. And she told Gaby that you apparently said to her that you wouldn't want to bring up another man's child."

I lean back and look up at the ceiling for a moment.

"Did you tell her that?" Tyson asks.

I nod slowly. "We'd been talking about the fact that she wants children and I can't have them. I said I'd go through IVF if she wanted to, but I think she realized that I don't really want to do that. And I told her I wouldn't want her to have a sperm donor. That's when I said I wouldn't want to bring up another man's child. I'm not proud of that, but I said it would feel too weird."

"And she's extrapolated that to mean you're not interested in being with her now she's pregnant with Cam's baby."

"Yeah. It doesn't help that I reacted badly when she told me." Jesus, I feel so ashamed.

"So the only way she can think of to be with you is to terminate the pregnancy," Tyson says. "But she said she'd feel too guilty to do it for that reason. She's really confused, and genuinely doesn't know what to do."

I'm shocked, but I can also see why she's considering it. The poor girl. On the surface, it's such an easy decision. Remove the whole quandary with one easy pill, and we'd be able to start again. She's not a practicing Hindu, or a Christian. She's not bound by religious dogma, and she needn't tell her parents.

But I know her well enough to understand that faith is different from religion, and this is going to evoke all kinds of moral questions that won't be easy to answer.

I cover my face with my hands, then run them through my hair. "I'm such a fucking idiot."

He tips his head to the side. "So you would consider being with her now, if she wanted to be with you?"

I look away, out at a plane that has just landed and is taxiing to the gate. "It's not the perfect situation. She'll never be free of Cam if she's pregnant with his baby, and he'll continue to be a fucking thorn in my side. But it's done. And if I want her, I guess I need to accept his baby, too."

"Maybe the best way to think about it is that it's her baby," Tyson suggests.

I look back at him. "Yeah, maybe." It's not the baby's fault that this is happening. The child is innocent, free of sin, and deserves the best start in life it can possibly have.

Is that with me? Is that really the best option for it? Or would growing up with Cam be better? I think of James, who's adopting Leia, because he insists she deserves better than her birth father. I happen to agree with him, but is it really his decision to make? To take the choice away from Leia's birth father?

"Having one daddy is great," Tyson says. "So having two must be double great, right?"

"I don't know how Cam would feel about the baby calling me Daddy."

"True. Maybe you'll just be Henry. Either way, you'd be the one who got to live with Juliette, and who'd be there looking after the kid day in, day out. Cam would be in Australia. It'd be hard for him to be too much of a pain in the arse if he was over there."

Privately, I think he could still manage to cause trouble even if he moved to Venus, but I don't say so. If I want this to work, I'd have to find a way to work with him, and for us to at least be civil toward one another.

He'd obviously play a major part in the baby's life. Juliette would have to consult with him about all the major decisions like health and education. And what if his opinion was different from mine? I can foresee all kinds of pitfalls, with Cam doing his best to make it as difficult as possible. He's that kind of guy—jealous and vindictive—and it would be impossible for it not to turn into a war.

Do I have the stomach for that?

These are the questions that Juliette must be asking herself. We all like to think that love conquers all, but there's so much more to this than who loves whom the most. For her there's the added weight of duty and responsibility. For Cam there's revenge and control. And all I feel is a kind of hopeless impotence, because once again everything seems to be out of my hands.

I wish she were pregnant with my child. I wish I could do that for her. But I can't. And at least this takes away the problem of sperm donors and adoption. The baby is half hers. That's the best I'm going to get.

I look outside, to where it's starting to rain, pattering on the windows.

Juliette. She might not even have me now. I fucked up by reacting badly, and she might decide she's better off alone.

I need to get back and talk to her. Until then, I'll just have to be patient, and hope that she's strong enough to cope on her own, without going back to him.

*

Because you have to be at the airport three hours before an international flight, and we didn't want to leave the conference until after lunch, our plane leaves at seven p.m. It would have been easier to fly out on Sunday, but both of us wanted to get home as soon as possible, so we had to put up with the late time. The flight is three hours, but Sydney is two hours behind Wellington, so it's midnight before it lands, and nearly one a.m. before I actually get home.

There's still no message from Juliette. I do have one missed call from Rangi, but it's too late to call him back now. I'm tired from the trip and the energy I had to summon for the presentation, and I go straight to bed and crash out.

Next morning, I text Alex, who's away with James, witnessing his marriage to Aroha, and let him know that it went well, then I try to call Juliette again. It goes to voicemail. Frustrated, I'm considering calling Gaby to demand to know which hotel she's at when my phone goes. Expecting to see Juliette's name, I experience a leap of the heart, which plummets again when I realize it's my brother, Philip.

"Hello?" I say.

"It's me," he replies.

"Hey, what's up?"

"What are you doing right now?" he asks. "Can you come over?"

I frown. "Why, what's the matter?"

"It's Rangi."

I get to my feet and go over to the window, my pulse picking up. "What's happened?"

"He took an overdose last night."

"Jesus." I run a hand through my hair, remembering the call I missed. Ah, fuck. "How is he?"

"The hospital took him in and pumped his stomach, but they let me bring him home this morning. He has to go in for some kind of psych evaluation this afternoon. He's…" He pauses. "He's just lying on his bed, crying. I don't know what to do. He won't talk to me. Look, I know we haven't always seen eye to eye. But he trusts you. And… he's my boy. I didn't think he'd do something like this. Will you come and talk to him?"

"Of course," I say immediately. "I'll be right over."

"Thanks, bro."

"See you soon."

I dress quickly, grab my keys and wallet, and head out. Soon I'm flying along the state highway, heading to Philip's house.

On the way, I call Greenfield Residential School and ask to speak to Atticus Bell. I'm not sure if he'll be there as he often goes out into the mountains on camp, but after thirty seconds or so there's a click, and he says, "Atticus speaking."

Atticus is in his mid-fifties, tall and slender, with thick gray hair and a gray beard and mustache. He's the closest thing I have to a father figure, and he was instrumental in helping me become the man I am today, so I have a lot to thank him for.

"Atticus, it's Henry West."

"Henry! It's good to hear from you. How are you doing?"

"Yeah, not bad. Sorry for the sound quality—I'm in the car."

"No worries, you're pretty clear. What's up? Have you been thinking about what I said?" As I mentioned to Alex, he's asked me to consider leading some of the adventure therapy sessions.

"I have, but that's not why I'm calling."

"Oh, what's up?"

I tell him about Rangi, about the fact that he got his girl pregnant, that she terminated it, and that he's so upset by it, he tried to take his own life. I know he won't be judgmental. He deals with young men and women on a daily basis who get themselves into far worse scrapes than this, and he's all about solving the problem rather than apportioning blame.

"Aw," Atticus says when I'm done. "The poor lad."

"Yeah. My brother's asked me to go over, which shows how bad things are. Look, I've mentioned to him about sending Rangi to Greenfield before and he's always said no, but I think maybe he'll be open to the suggestion now. So I wanted to ask, do you have any room there this year?"

"We'll make room, Henry. You've given enough to the place to warrant something in return."

I send regular donations to the school, and recently gave an additional sum toward the building of a swimming pool for the students.

"I don't do it for this reason," I say awkwardly, conscious that I sound like one of those people who donates to hospitals then expects to jump the queue when they need treatment.

"Of course you don't. But even so, it's the least we can do. How old is he?"

"Sixteen."

"So year twelve? Yeah we've still got a couple of places."

"I'll talk to them this morning and get back to you."

"Sure, no worries."

"How are things going with you anyway?" I ask, coming off the State Highway and heading into the city. "How's Clem?" I'm very fond of his wife, who bakes the best blueberry muffins in the country.

"She's good thank you, in fine form."

"And Joel and Fraser?" I spent a lot of time with his boys during my stay at Greenfield, and keep in touch with them. I sometimes wondered whether Atticus was worried that the troubled adolescents would corrupt his children, but with their good manners, hardworking attitude, and sense of humor, all three of his kids were a positive influence on the residents, rather than the other way around.

"Yeah, both working hard." Atticus has a passion for history and archaeology that he handed down to his children, as well as many of the kids who passed through his care. Fraser now runs a museum in Wellington, and Joel is an underwater archaeologist.

"And Elora?" I ask softly. "How's she doing?" His daughter, Elora-Rose Bell, is four years younger than me. When I first arrived at Greenfield, she was only ten, but she had blonde plaits and big, innocent blue eyes, and from the start I adored her as if she was my own baby sister. I haven't seen her for a while, though, and Joel hinted that she'd been in some trouble a few years ago, but he wouldn't elaborate, so I don't know what happened.

"She finished her degree last year," Atticus says, "and she's doing a Masters in Archaeology now. She's smarter than both the boys put together."

I chuckle. "Yeah, I know." I indicate to turn toward Philip's road. "So... uh... did you hear about Linc?"

Lincoln Green started at the school with me, and the first time we met—when I joked that he was named after the color of Robin Hood's tights—he hit me, but it was just the start of a beautiful friendship. Like me, at the time he'd been an angry and resentful young guy, born into poverty, and with no positive role models or opportunities to improve himself. After Linc's father beat him so badly that he ended up in hospital, a teacher put Linc's name forward to Atticus, who took him in hoping he could turn things around for him.

Linc spent four years at Greenfield and was doing just fine until Atticus caught him kissing Elora. Linc was eighteen and she was only fourteen, and Atticus went supernova on his arse and told him he had to leave the school. Linc had caught the archaeology bug from the family and had developed his obsession with Egypt by that point, and Atticus had just found him a place on a youth volunteer group in Cairo, so within a week, Linc was sent packing, and as far as I know, he hasn't been back. Elora cried for days after he left, but Atticus remained unmovable and announced that if he found Linc within a mile of her, he'd call the police and have Linc put behind bars for being a pedophile.

I was gutted for Linc at the time, and shocked at Atticus's reaction. It was just a kiss, after all; it wasn't as if Atticus had caught them having sex. But Elora is his baby girl, and he perceived Linc's actions as an abuse of his generosity, his kind nature, and his investment in the lad. Privately, I think Atticus saw Linc as a third son, which is why Linc's behavior shocked him maybe more than it ordinarily would have.

Last week, though, Joel texted me to say he'd heard that Linc's father had died, and he was returning to New Zealand for the funeral.

"I heard," Atticus says. "I told him nine years ago that if I caught him within a mile of my daughter, I'd wring his neck, and nothing has changed in that regard."

I give a sad sigh. Now I'm older, I understand his protectiveness toward his daughter, but I'm sure that Linc would like to see him again, as Linc thought of him like a father, the same way I did. Still, it's none of my business.

"Well, I'd better go," I say awkwardly. "I'll call you when I've spoken to Philip."

"Yes, we'll speak soon."

I end the call. I feel a little more hopeful now, although of course it doesn't mean that Philip will let Rangi go.

My heart aches at the thought of what the kid's been through. It feels ironic to be in a similar situation with Juliette, and to be as powerless as Rangi to affect the outcome.

I navigate the maze of roads into the suburb where Philip lives. It's one of the poorer areas of the city, where the houses are smaller and close together, the crime rates are high, there are burnt-out and abandoned cars, and someone was even murdered last year in a house in a nearby street. I wish he'd let me buy him somewhere nicer, but that's never going to happen.

Still, hopefully he'll now let me help his son.

I pull up outside his house, only then wishing I'd brought the Range Rover rather than the BMW, but it's too late now. Glaring at a couple of youths who are hanging about further down the street, I lock the car and head up the path to the front door.

Philip opens it and gives me the upward nod of the head that's a silent welcome. I return it, walk by him into the hallway, and go through to the living room.

Everyone's there—Mum, Teariki, Philip's current wife Hine, their young daughter Kaia, Philip's other two children, our sister, Liza, and her husband and kids, and also Philip's first wife and Rangi's mum, Ngaire.

Jesus. Poor Rangi.

Everyone says hello, and I bend to hug Kaia as she runs up to me. "Are you here to help Rangi?" she asks. There are tears in her eyes.

"Yeah," I say, rubbing her back. "Come on, he'll be all right."

"Kaia found him yesterday," Ngaire says.

Ah, man. I kiss Kaia on the top of her head. "I'm so sorry," I murmur as she hugs me tightly. "But we'll do our best to help him, eh?"

She nods and releases me as her mum pulls her away.

"Come on," Philip says roughly.

I follow him out into the hallway, then catch his arm as he goes to walk upstairs. "Can I talk to you first?"

He nods, and we go out into the kitchen. It's a mess out here, with dirty pots and pans in the sink and plates covered in half-eaten food stacked up on the draining board. I try not to look at it and focus on his face.

"I want to talk to you about Greenfield," I say.

He leans against the sink and folds his arms. "I thought you might."

I fix him with a firm gaze. "Come on, he needs help—more than a stern talking to about being a man. He's lonely and lost, and this—losing Ellie and the baby—has crushed him. He needs something to hang onto, or it's just going to happen again."

"I know." He's stiff with resentment and dislike, but then he brushes a hand over his face. "Okay. If he wants to go, I won't stop him."

I feel a flood of relief. "It's a good place, and hopefully it'll give him a new purpose. Turn things around for him."

Philip nods. Then he looks away out of the window. "Do you ever think of Dad?"

I blink. I made the decision not to tell him what I discovered about our father from Rawiri because I didn't think he'd be able to handle the news that Dad was still alive. It was bad enough to think that he died in an accident; it would destroy Philip to learn that the abandonment was purposeful.

"Sometimes," I reply.

"I've always wished he hadn't died. But I know if he hadn't, things wouldn't have been much better." His gaze came back to me. "Do you remember what he was like? The arguments? The beatings?"

"Yeah. I know it was worse for you."

He shrugs. Then he says, "I don't want to be like him." He meets my eyes, then drops his gaze guiltily. He knows he's already walked in our father's shoes for far too long. Anger flares inside me at the thought of what his kids have had to go through.

But I clamp down on it. This isn't the time to berate or condemn him. Recognizing the problem is half the battle, right?

"That's good," I say roughly. "And this is the first step, right? To do the best you can for your boy."

He nods and swallows.

"All right." I clap him on the shoulder. "I'm going to go up and see him."

I make my way up the stairs, go along the landing to Rangi's door, and knock on it. He doesn't reply. I wait for a bit, knock again, then turn the handle and go in.

He's lying on his bed, on his back, his headphones on, staring up at the ceiling. He's not crying, but he looks so miserable it breaks my heart. He glances over, though, and when he sees me he takes off his headphones and sits up.

"Hey, bro," I say softly.

"Henry," he says, and his bottom lip trembles.

"Hey." I sit on the bed next to him. To my surprise, he moves over to hug me and starts crying.

"Ah, it's okay." I hold him tightly and rub his back. "Everything's going to be all right."

We sit there like that for a while. It rains for a bit, hammering against the window, and then the sun comes out—four seasons in one day, typical Kiwi weather. Eventually he stops crying, and I pick up the toilet roll someone's conveniently left on the bedside table and peel off a bit for him to blow his nose.

While he's composing himself, I look around. It still looks like the room of an eleven-year-old, with LEGO models, old posters on the walls, and a box of toys against the wall that are far too young for him. It reminds me of the boy who used to love skateboarding, and who used to watch Shrek with me.

But he's not eleven anymore. He's sixteen, old enough to have consenting sex and get married, to hold a learner driver license, to leave school, and to be paid the minimum wage.

"I'm sorry you've been going through a difficult time," I tell him.

He moves back against the pillows. "They won't let me see Ellie anymore."

"I know."

"I love her," he says. "They think we don't know what love is because we're young, but we do."

I nod. "I know. I can see how you feel about her. And I'm sorry you can't be with her right now. Maybe in the future, after she turns sixteen, you might be able to start dating her again."

"I don't think her parents will let her," he says doubtfully.

No doubt Philip and her folks will kill me for saying this, but I reply, "There's not much they can do about it when you're both sixteen and old enough to leave home."

He heaves a big sigh. "I wish I was older. I'd buy her a house so we can be together. But I've got no job, nowhere to go. Nothing to give her."

"You've got lots to give her. You're a decent guy, and you're loving and affectionate. That's more than a lot of men have to offer." I lean forward, elbows on my knees. "Look, what you need is a way to break the cycle. You need an education, a job, money, and prospects. And that's where I think I can help. I've spoken to your dad, and he's agreed that if you want, you can go to Greenfield."

He stares at me, his jaw dropping. "Seriously?"

"Yes. I'd pay for all your fees. You'd go and stay there during term time, and come home for the holidays. The thing is, your future is up to you. If you work hard, they'll help you get qualified in something that interests you, and help you get a job. I was thinking maybe as a mechanic?"

He blinks. "Do you think I could do it?"

"Of course." He's not an academic, but he's smart, and he's always enjoyed tinkering with cars and bikes. "Greenfield runs an apprenticeship program, and they teach automotive in Year Twelve, so it's not as if you're behind—you'd be going straight in. It'll take time to get qualified, but if you can prove to Ellie's parents that you're working hard and that you want to get a job and provide for her, maybe they'll change their opinion and let you see her."

It's a long shot, but it's possible. The thing is, while he's away he'll meet lots of other people and probably find a new girl. And if he doesn't—if he does continue to harbor feelings for Ellie—it will help him to prove that he's willing to change for her.

He gets up and throws his arms around me again. "Thank you," he whispers. "Thank you for understanding, and for everything."

"It's okay," I say gruffly. "I'm so sorry I missed your call last night—I was on the plane back from Sydney, and when I got home it was one a.m. and I thought it was too late to call you back. I should have, and I'm sorry."

"It's okay."

"I'm always here for you. Remember that." My throat tightens even more at the thought that I might have been too late. "Come and find me if you ever feel bad again. Don't do anything without speaking to me first. I couldn't bear it if I lost you."

His arms tighten, and we sit like that for a long time, while the rainclouds clear, and the summer sun shines once again.

Chapter Twenty-Seven

Juliette

"Pregnant?" My father stares at me, joy lighting his eyes. "*Meri pyaari beti*, that is wonderful news!" It means 'my lovely daughter' in Hindi. He comes forward to give me a hug.

Over his shoulder, I catch my mother's eye. "Is it Cam's?" she mouths. I blush and nod, and her brow furrows. "Krish," she says to my father. "Tone it down. We have to talk."

Dad steps back and looks at her, then at me. "What's going on?" He still has an Indian accent, although his speech contains many Kiwi and Māori phrases now.

"Sit down, Dad," I say, and we take our seats again.

We're in their home, in the affluent suburb of Merivale, overlooking the Avon river. I grew up in this house, and my bedroom here still bears some of my childhood things—several stuffed bears, a lamp with Cinderella dancing with the prince around the base, even some drawings I did as a girl. The tug of the past is comfortably familiar, but also a reminder of the principles instilled in me as a girl that are giving me such grief now.

I don't know why I came here. I wasn't planning on telling them about the baby. But I spent all yesterday afternoon and all morning walking and thinking, and I still haven't come to any conclusion, and I just need to talk to someone.

Sure enough, when Mum says, "She's not happy with Cam," my father's expression darkens.

"What do you mean, not happy?"

"We've been growing apart for a while," I tell him. "I was on the verge of breaking up with him, and then it was Christmas, so I thought I'd wait until the New Year, and then his brother had a heart attack, and his mother was sick, and I couldn't bring myself to do it to him."

"Sounds like excuses to me," he says. "If you wanted to leave him, you should have been honest with him and got it over with."

"It's not as easy as that," I say, blushing again, because I know he's right, and I'm ashamed of myself for dragging it out.

"She's fallen in love with someone else," Mum tells him.

His eyes widen. "Who?"

I close my eyes. I didn't know Mum was going to mention him. "Henry."

"Henry West?" he says, astonished.

"Yes."

There's a brief silence. "Have you been unfaithful to Cam?" he whispers. I put my face in my hands, and it's answer enough, because he gives a big sigh. "Juliette," he says sadly.

I begin to cry. There's nothing like a dressing down from your parents when you're an adult to make you feel two inches tall.

"Krish," Mum scolds, "come on, give her a break. It wasn't quite like that. She thought it was over with Cam." She gets up, comes to sit next to me on the sofa, and gives me a hug. "*Taku aroha*, come on, everything's going to be okay."

"It's not." I wipe the tears from my face, but fresh ones take their place. "Henry told me he doesn't want to bring up another man's child. I don't want to stay with Cam. And if I keep the baby, I lose Henry."

Her hand stops in the process of rubbing my back. "What are you saying? Are you thinking about an abortion?"

I look at my father. His expression is heavy with disapproval and sadness. "You would really consider terminating this pregnancy?" he says stiffly.

I study my hands. I like to think I'm a modern, independent woman, but the truth is that I was brought up to respect my elders, and even now I find it difficult to stand up to him.

"I'm ashamed of you," he says. "Whatever was going on between you and Cam, you owe it to this baby to make it work between you."

I knew he was going to say that, and I think perhaps I wanted to be challenged because I thought it would force me to realize it's not what I want. But instead all I feel is guilt and shame, and it just makes more tears flow.

"He wants us to move to Australia," I say, trying not to sob. "To be with his family. He doesn't care about me being with mine."

That makes him blanch.

"I don't love him anymore, Dad. He makes me unhappy. Is that really what you want for me?"

He stares at me helplessly.

"Krish," Mum says softly. "Give us a few minutes, okay?"

He gets to his feet and, without another word, leaves the room.

"There, there," Mum says, giving me a hug. "Come on, you knew what he'd say. He's very traditional, but he loves you and only wants the best for you."

"I don't know what to do," I say, with little hiccups in between the words. "Gaby said if I terminate the pregnancy for Henry, I'm going to regret it, and I think she's right. But I don't know what else to do. I don't want to be a single mum. I don't think I'm strong enough."

"Well that's rubbish," Mum says briskly. "If you were to choose to have the baby on your own, we'd manage together. But have you spoken to Henry about it? He's definitely said he's not interested in being with you?"

I wipe the tears away again. "We haven't really spoken at length. The thing is, he was married, and they were trying to have a baby for years, and eventually he found out he's infertile. So we were talking about alternatives, and he said he wouldn't want a sperm donor because he wouldn't want to bring up another man's child."

"That's a slightly different thing," Mum says.

"But when I called him to tell him I was pregnant, and that Cam told me we should stay together for the baby's sake, Henry got really upset and hung up on me."

She frowns. "Well, that's not really a surprise. If he knows you well, he would understand how you have strong principles. He would assume you wouldn't leave Cam."

I stare at her. I hadn't thought of that. "That's true." The more I think about it, the more I question my understanding of the situation. Henry was shocked, but she's right, he wouldn't abandon me just because I was pregnant. It's my fault for telling him the way I did, and I misinterpreted his reaction. Oh shit.

"We've brought you up to have a sense of duty and responsibility toward your family," Mum says. "It was important to both of us. But we also want you to be happy."

I rub my nose. "I know Dad likes Cam."

"He made sure to like him because he's your partner. But the truth is, he's very disappointed that Cam hasn't asked you to marry him."

"Really?" I didn't know that. "Cam says he doesn't believe in it."

"I know."

I look at her with a weak smile. "Henry told me that Cam has no claim on me because he never asked me to marry him. And he said he wants to put a ring on my finger so everyone knows I'm his."

Mum's lips curve up a little. "And you really think he's going to turn his back on you because you're pregnant?"

I frown. "I don't know. God, I'm in such a muddle. I keep telling myself that I need to concentrate on what's best for the baby. And isn't that staying with Cam?"

"What's best for you is what's best for the baby. Yes, of course, in an ideal world you'd stay with Cam and play happy families, but if being with him is only going to make you miserable, what's the point in doing that? Surely it would be better for the baby if you're with someone you love and trust?" She tips her head to the side. "You never answered my question."

"Sorry?"

"Which man smudges your lipstick, and which smudges your mascara?"

I wipe beneath both eyes, then give a short laugh. "Henry definitely smudges my lipstick."

"Well, there you are, then." She kisses my temple.

"But Dad—"

"Don't worry about him. I'll talk him around."

I inhale, then blow out a long breath. "What if you're wrong, and Henry says he can't bring up another man's child?"

"Well if that's the case, he's not the man for you. I don't think you should stay with Cam out of duty. If neither man is right for you, you should bring the child up yourself. You're stronger than you think, *tōku tamāhine ataahua*." It means 'my beautiful daughter.'

She rubs my arm, then says, "I'll go and make us a cup of fruit tea. It's probably best if you don't drink too much coffee now." She walks off into the kitchen.

I rest my hand on my tummy, trying to calm my shaky breaths. I hadn't thought about cutting my caffeine content. I know so little about pregnancy and babies, only what I learned at school. I haven't been around anyone who's been pregnant, and I've never been particularly interested in babies, so I haven't had the inclination to read about it all. I think there are certain foods you're not supposed to eat, like mayonnaise and cheese for some reason. I have no idea why. I'm going to have to do some research to make sure I don't do anything stupid.

I'm so scared at the thought of doing this on my own. I think of Dad, no doubt walking up and down in his office, which he always does when he's stressed or anxious. I feel so sad that I've made him ashamed of me. I want him to be proud of me. But do I want that enough to stay with a man I don't love anymore?

All these thoughts and emotions are like butterflies fluttering in my brain, going around in circles. And I'm tired and confused.

I think about Henry, and the smell of his cologne, and the way his blue eyes stare right into mine while he's making love to me, and that makes the tears come, because I don't know if he wants me anymore, and what if I never get to experience that again?

*

I know I should think about my situation. Draw up the advantages and disadvantages of various options. Talk to my friends, to Cam, to Henry, and make a rational decision. But I can't bring myself to do any of that. Instead I spend the rest of the day in the hotel. Cam continues to text and call, so I keep my phone switched off so I don't have to hear from him. I know Kathy is sure to be in a state after finding out I've left, and I don't want to have to deal with him or his family right now.

Tomorrow is Monday. I need to go to work because I've had a week off and it's the first day for the main staff. Hopefully I can catch up with Henry at lunchtime or something, and we can have a conversation.

But for now, I put my brain in standby and watch *The Fellowship of the Ring* for the umpteenth time while I eat popcorn, which seems to be one thing that doesn't make me feel queasy. Then, exhausted from all the emotion, I crash out and sleep soundly all night.

I brought one of my suits to the hotel so I'm okay to dress for work the next morning, but I have to check out, so I'll need to go back to the apartment after work. That means I'm probably going to have to talk to Cam. Today's the day, I guess. One way or another, I'll make myself come to a decision.

I drive to work, park outside the building, then sit there for a moment. Oh fuck, I feel sick again. I've already thrown up once this morning. I get out and go inside, head straight for the bathroom, relieved to find it empty, and vomit into the toilet, hoping nobody else comes in.

When I'm done, I go out on shaky legs. I want to go to my office and bolt myself in, but it's nearly eight thirty, which is when our morning meeting usually starts, and I know I have to go.

The place is busy, everyone talking about what they got up to over Christmas, and I stop a few times on the way to talk to people, answering their questions as best as I can, even though my mind is buzzing. Ahead of me, I can see the boardroom through the glass walls. Alex, Tyson, and Henry are already there. James is off this week. Alex and Tyson are sitting at the table. Henry's making himself a coffee. My heart rate immediately doubles. He's wearing my favorite suit of his—navy with a thin pinstripe. He looks so handsome.

I don't know what I'm going to say. I should have rehearsed this, planned our first conversation, but I can't think as my feet move automatically toward the door. I watch him turn from the table and stop to look out of the sliding doors at the view of the Avon as he sips his coffee. Alex glances up and sees me, and he says something, and then as the automatic doors open, Henry turns around.

"Juliette." He whispers the word, and I remember him saying *Your name feels like a spell*.

I don't know what I expected. Maybe that he'd still be angry. Or ignore me. Or tell me quietly that we'll talk later.

Instead, he puts down his coffee cup and walks straight up to me. "Sweetheart, I'm so sorry," he says immediately.

The apology whips the rug out from under me, and I bury my face in his shirt.

"I'm such a fucking idiot," he says, putting his arms around me.

"Many a true word is spoken in jest," Tyson says from behind us.

I turn my head to look at the table and find both him and Alex smiling.

Henry rolls his eyes, takes my hand, and leads me out onto the terrace. It's still a little cool, but the bright sun promises it's going to be a beautiful summer day. Down by the river, a group of ducks paddle slowly past the willow that drapes its arms across the water gracefully like a ballet dancer. I can smell the muffins made in the nearby café, and it makes my empty stomach rumble.

He takes my face in his hands and looks into my eyes. "Are you okay?"

I nod.

"Baby girl," he says. "I've been going out of my mind." He brushes my cheeks with his thumbs. "Ah, sweetheart. I've made such a mess of everything."

I give a short laugh. "*You've* made a mess? It's me who's screwed everything up."

"No you haven't. You haven't done a single thing wrong. You're the sweetest, kindest, most loyal girl I know, and you've just made the best of a difficult situation while you've tried to help people." His eyes search mine. "Listen, I reacted badly when you called me, and I'm so sorry about that. I thought you were saying you want to stay with Cam and go to Australia with him. I assumed you'd feel you had to do that. But when I heard you weren't with him this weekend, it gave me hope."

I look up at him, my heart lifting. "Henry, I—"

I stop, and we both look through to the boardroom at the sound of raised voices. I inhale sharply. "Oh fuck."

It's Cam, followed closely by the receptionist, who's objecting loudly.

"I'm so sorry," she tells us as we walk back into the boardroom. "He wouldn't stop." She glares at Cam.

"It's all right." Alex holds up a hand to her. "Don't worry."

Giving Cam one last glare, she backs away, and the doors close.

"I'm her fucking partner," Cam says to Alex, gesturing at me. "I don't appreciate being treated like I'm invading the premises."

"Amy's a temp," Alex states, "and she doesn't know you. We don't let just anyone walk in here." Somehow, even though his tone is mild, he manages to make it sound as if Cam isn't wanted.

"What are you doing here?" I ask Cam, my heart hammering.

"I need to talk to you," he snaps. "And you won't return my calls. I had no idea where you were, but I knew you'd be here this morning. You wouldn't miss the chance to see him." He nods angrily at Henry.

"We work together," Henry points out.

"Not if I have anything to do with it," Cam says. He looks at me. "Let's go to your office. We need to talk."

I bristle, embarrassed at his demanding tone. "I'm busy."

"We're in the middle of a meeting," Henry says.

Cam glares at him. "I'm not fucking talking to you. I'm talking to my girlfriend."

"Not if I have anything to do with it," Henry replies.

Cam glowers. "Keep out of it, West. You're just something she amused herself with in passing. She's my girl."

Oh, now he's decided he wants me. Talk about dog in the manger.

Henry moves closer to him. "Or maybe she needed a real man because the one she had wasn't up to the job."

"A real man would be able to get his woman pregnant," Cam states. "Too bad you're shooting blanks."

Henry's eyes blaze. "At least I can shoot without needing someone else to guide the rifle."

His words reveal that I've told him about Cam's issues, and it tips Cam over the edge. Furious now, he snaps, "We're leaving." He grabs my hand and pulls me toward the exit. I stumble, and the other guys exclaim with indignation.

Alex and Tyson jump to their feet, but Henry's already onto it. "Get the fuck away from her," he snarls. He marches up, grabs Cam by the throat and pushes him up against the glass wall. There's a huge clang, and everyone in the surrounding offices looks around and stares.

"Pistols at dawn it is, then," Tyson says.

Cam tries to give Henry a right hook, but he moves back just in time, and Cam's fist sails through the air. Henry then punches him full in the face, and blood sprays over them both.

I squeal, and Alex barks, "Henry!" He grabs Henry and hauls him off Cam.

Cam grabs a serviette from the table, and tries to staunch his nose. He looks visibly shaken, his hand trembling as he mops up the blood.

"That's it," I say. Without looking at Henry, I tell Cam, "Come on."

I stride out of the office, not waiting to see if Cam's following. My face burning, I walk past the people who are watching and talking behind their hands, go into the lobby, and cross it to the exit. Only when I go through the sliding doors do I stop and turn.

Cam is six feet behind me, and he follows me outside. He looks at the tissues in his hand, which are covered with blood.

"Fucking animal," he says. "That's the last straw. I don't want you seeing him anymore."

I study his face, which I know so well. "Cam," I say slowly, "you've been through so much, and I know you've done your best to make things work between us. But it's just not enough. Not for me, anyway. I've tried. God knows, I've tried so hard. I know that relationships are about more than sex and excitement. They're about loyalty and trust and duty and responsibility. But they should be about sex and excitement too. Or, at least, about love and physical affection. If sex was our only problem, I might be able to work through it. But you don't show me any physical affection. You keep saying you'll change, but you don't, and I can't live without it. A friend told me that I deserve to be happy, and I think she's right. And Henry makes me happy."

He lowers the tissue. He looks absolutely destroyed. "But… the baby…"

"The baby's yours, and you'll always be its father."

"I'm not staying," he says stubbornly. "I'm going to move to Australia."

"If you want to, that's your choice."

His expression turns pleading. "Lettie, come on… don't leave me, not now. I need you. Mum needs you. We all need you."

I move back from his hand. "No."

"Please… I can't live without you. I don't want to live without you."

That final sentence kills any affection I still have for him. I turn and walk back inside, and I don't look back.

Chapter Twenty-Eight

Henry

I stand over by the windows, looking down at the Avon. I feel as if someone's reached into my chest and ripped out my heart with their bare hands.

She's gone with Cam. I went too far, and she obviously couldn't bear the thought of Cam being hurt. It's made her realize she wants to stay with him.

Hands on my hips, I rest my forehead against the glass and close my eyes. I can hear Alex and Tyson murmuring behind me, moving around as they clean up the blood that had sprayed across the room. It's all over my shirt and my hand. I'll need to go home, shower, and change. At the moment, though, I can't even move away from the window. I think I might crumble into tiny broken pieces if I do.

I can't believe I've lost her. I'm such a stupid, fucking idiot. Why can't I keep my temper checked? Why do I—

"Henry," Alex says.

I don't reply, needing every ounce of control just to breathe.

"Henry," he says again.

"Just… just give me a minute."

"All isn't lost, my friend."

"Alex, I really can't deal with your positive reassurances right now."

"Bro," he says. "Turn around."

I open my eyes and blink a few times. Then I push off the glass and look over my shoulder.

Juliette is standing in the doorway. The automatic doors slide closed, and she steps back to avoid them, then curses and moves forward again to make them open. This time, she walks into the boardroom. Behind her, people are watching, wide-eyed, but she's clearly oblivious of anything but me.

"It's over," she says.

I turn slowly.

She swallows hard. "It's done. I've told him it's over. I don't want to be with him anymore. He doesn't make me happy. You're the only one who makes me happy. But… I know I've put you through it. I'm not expecting you to bring up another man's child. I'm not expecting anything. But maybe we can go get a coffee or something, and then… we can…"

Her eyes widen as I stride across the room, and then she laughs as I sweep her up into my arms.

"Baby," I say, "ah my God, I don't believe it, *e te tau, ka nui taku aroha ki a koe…*" It means 'my darling, I love you so much.'

She puts her arms around my neck and hugs me tightly. "*Main tumse pyar karthee hoon…* I love you, I love you, I love you."

I wrap my arms around her waist, turning in a circle. Delight pours through me like sunshine, beaming from the end of my fingers and the tips of my hair.

"Aw," Tyson says from behind us. "Are you trying to make us cry?"

I put her down and glance over at them. Alex has sat down, and he stretches his legs out and gives me a look that says, *I told you so.*

"Permission to have the day off with my girl, boss," I say to him.

He laughs. "Granted."

"Alex," she says, "I know it's my first day back, and I've got loads to do…"

"It'll wait," he says. "Some things are more important. Go on. Get a room, the two of you."

Grinning, I grab Juliette's hand and lead her out of the boardroom. All around us, members of staff are smiling, and they cheer as we walk out, making us laugh.

"Jesus, look at the state of you," Juliette says, looking at my shirt.

"I know. I need to go home and change."

We go out through the front doors and stand outside in the sun. She looks around, then blows out a relieved breath. "He's gone. For a minute I thought he might still be here."

She lifts her gaze to mine, and we study each other for a moment, then both smile.

"I'm free," she says. "Oh my God, I feel light as a feather."

My heart lifts. She doesn't belong to someone else anymore. I mean, I know she doesn't belong to anyone—women aren't possessions. But she's free, and I never thought that word would make me feel so ecstatic.

We study each other. Suddenly there's so much to say that I don't know where to start. I want to kiss her, but for some reason I'm as tongue-tied as a schoolboy about to ask a girl out for the first time.

"You want to come to my place?" I ask. "We need to talk."

She nods, face flushing. "Okay. I might drive over, if that's all right, so I have my car."

"Of course." I take out my phone and text her. "You can follow me, but there's the address in case you need it."

She checks she's got it, then nods. We walk out to the cars and pause by her Toyota.

"I'll see you in a bit," she says, somewhat shyly.

I nod. "Okay."

We part, get in our respective cars, and soon we're on the state highway, heading over to Sumner Beach.

As we drive, I glance frequently in my rearview mirror to make sure she's still following. I half expect her to change her mind, turn the car around, and head back the way she came, but she doesn't. All the way home, she's there behind me, and when I finally arrive and enter the gates to the drive up to the house, she follows me slowly.

I park behind the house, she slides the Toyota in beside my BMW, and together we get out.

"Oh…" she says. "Henry, the view."

"Come in," I tell her. "It's even better from the deck."

I unlock the door and hold it open for her, and she walks inside. I follow her in and lead her through the lobby, then into the main living room. It's strange having someone else in the house with me. I'm so glad the first person to come here is her.

She inhales as she walks past the black leather sofa and recliners, past the dining area and the huge kitchen, and over to the far wall, which is all glass, overlooking the ocean.

I undo the sliding doors and pull them all the way back, and she goes out onto the deck. The view is absolutely magnificent. The breeze tugs strands of hair from her bun, but the air is warm, and the smell of the ocean mixes with the jasmine growing in my garden, the amazing scent of summer.

I love this view, but I can't take my eyes off her. I've pictured bringing her here so often, but I never thought it would actually happen.

Her gaze comes back to me, and she smiles. Then her brows draw together, and she reaches out and strokes my cheek. "You're covered in blood."

"I'll go and clean myself up," I say. "Give me a minute." She nods, and I walk back into the living room. "Make yourself a drink if you want," I call out. "Or I'll make us one… whatever." I stride toward my bedroom, cursing under my breath. *Pull yourself together, dude.*

I go straight through to the bathroom and stare at myself in the mirror. Christ, it's a good job the police didn't stop me on the way home—I look as if I've committed murder. I switch on the shower, strip off, and take thirty seconds to scrub myself clean, then come out, dry myself, and put on clean track pants and a tee, all in the space of about five minutes.

When I walk out, barefoot, hair still wet, she's just boiled the kettle, and she's pouring hot water into two cups.

"You have fruit tea," she says. "I didn't expect that."

"I'm civilized," I protest.

She laughs, squeezes both the bags, and takes them out. "Where's the rubbish bin?"

"Over there."

She disposes of the bags and stirs the teas. "Mum said I should limit my coffee intake, and I've already had one cup this morning." She pushes one mug over to me. I take it, not caring what's in it. She made it for me, and I love it already.

We sip our tea, leaning against the kitchen counter, watching each other. Then we both start laughing.

"I didn't expect this," she says. "I thought you'd have carried me off to bed over your shoulder like a firefighter."

I smile. "It's only nine thirty. We've got all day."

She gives a delightful giggle. Then she says, "Will you show me around?"

"Sure."

"This kitchen is gorgeous."

"The chef loves it," I say, and grin when she laughs.

"Do you never cook?" she scolds.

"Nope. Far better things to do than that."

She opens a few cupboards, looks in the fridge, murmurs approvingly at the sight of champagne, then sighs as she obviously realizes she's going to have to limit her alcohol intake, too.

She follows me into the living room. "A PlayStation and an Xbox."

"All the mod cons."

"I like the dining suite. Did you have an interior designer?"

"No, it's all my choice. I quite like furniture shopping."

She smiles, and we slowly walk across the room, sipping our tea.

We go into the corridor leading to the rest of the house, and I show her the gym, the laundry room, the spare bedrooms, and the main bathroom, with its amazing sunken bath that overlooks the ocean.

"I can see that getting some use," she teases.

"Definitely."

Her face flushes, and I smile. This is so strange. I feel excited and nervous. We need to talk, but I don't know where to start.

There's no rush, though. We're feeling our way around this, and I'm kind of enjoying the anticipation.

We stop by the master bedroom, and she goes in and walks around it quietly. I'm glad it's tidy, apart from the clothes I ripped off and tossed on the bed before showering. While she looks at the books on my bedside table, I pick the clothes up and put them in the laundry bin in the walk-in wardrobe.

She follows me in and walks slowly around, brushing my clothes with her fingers. My shirts and suits, the racks of ties, the shelves of tees. She runs her fingers over the table by the window, across the box of watches and cufflinks and tie pins. It's odd—we've been as physically close as two people can be, but this feels intimate in a different way. I like the way she's touching everything. It's as if she's taking possession of me. Claiming me.

"I like the duvet cover," she says, going back into the bedroom. It's black and white, with geometric shapes. "It's very you."

I just smile.

"It's a nice room," she says.

"I'm hoping we'll spend a lot of time here." I smirk and she gives a shy smile.

Steady, Henry. Nice and slow.

I indicate with my head for her to follow me out and along to the next bedroom. We walk in. It's simply decorated, with just a few items of furniture—a bed, a table, a chair.

I watch her walk over to the window and look out. "Such a beautiful view," she whispers.

"I thought this would be a good choice," I tell her.

She turns to face me. "For what?"

"For the nursery."

She stares at me, and we study each other for a long moment.

Her mouth opens, but no words come out. She looks around as if picturing it full of all the paraphernalia a baby brings with it. Then finally her hand strays subconsciously to her belly, "But... um..."

I walk forward to stand in front of her, put her mug with mine on the table, and take her hands. "What I said, about not wanting to bring up another man's child... I was talking about if we were together, that I'd prefer not to have a sperm donor. I didn't envisage this situation, and I'm so very sorry for reacting badly when you told me."

Her bottom lip trembles. "That's okay."

"It's not, and I'm going to spend the rest of my life making it up to you."

Tears tip over her lashes. "Oh, Henry..."

I look into her eyes. "I love you. And I wish I could give you a baby, but I can't. But even so, it turns out that you're pregnant." I look down at her belly and run the back of my fingers over it. "You're growing a little person inside you. And I think that's amazing."

"But, it's Cam's..."

"It's yours. And if you'll have me, I'd love to bring the baby up with you."

She laughs then and wipes her fingers under her eyes to brush away the tears. "I don't know what to say." She inhales, then exhales slowly. Her light-brown skin has taken on a pale tinge.

I frown. "Are you okay?"

She breathes in and out again. Then, suddenly, she says, "I'm so sorry. Excuse me."

I watch her run away, and follow her back into my bedroom. She's gone into the bathroom, and as I open the door I hear the distinct sound of her vomiting into the toilet. Oh jeez, it must be morning sickness.

I go in, take a clean face cloth out of the cupboard, wet it with cold water under the tap, then fold it and place it on the back of her neck as she vomits again. "It's all right, sweetheart." I smooth the strands of hair back from her face.

She stops, waits, then flushes the toilet. I pass her some paper to wipe her mouth, then run her a glass of water from the tap. She takes it and has a mouthful, swirls and spits, then turns and sits on the floor, her back to the wall.

I sit beside her and wipe her face with the cloth. She watches me, her eyes wide.

"Okay?" I ask.

She nods. "I'm so sorry. It's hardly the most romantic way to kick off our relationship."

I give her a big smile.

"What?" she asks, her lips curving up.

"You said relationship."

She gives a short laugh.

"I'm so sorry you have to go through this," I tell her.

She moistens her lips. "I need a drink."

"Of course. What would you like?"

"I don't suppose you have any Sprite?"

"Sure. Come on." I get up and pull her to her feet, then lead her out into the living room. "Go and sit outside in the fresh air," I tell her, "and I'll bring you a Sprite out."

She hesitates, so I say, "Go on." She nods and goes out onto the deck, and sits on the rattan outdoor daybed that I love so much, putting her feet up and closing her eyes.

I take a can out of the fridge and pour it into a glass with some ice. Then, quickly, I Google 'snacks for morning sickness.' It recommends toast, crackers, and protein-rich foods. I look through the cupboards and find some crackers, spread a couple with peanut butter, because I know she likes it, and take the plate with the glass outside.

"This is nice," she says, brushing the daybed. It's large and circular with a hood and cushions.

"I know. I love it. I read out here in the evenings." I put the glass and plate beside her on the table. "I've just read that small, regular meals might help morning sickness, so I thought you might like something like this. No worries if you don't."

She looks at the plate, then back at me. "You just read about it for me?"

I climb onto the daybed beside her and lean back on the pillows. "I did."

She looks back at the plate. Then she picks up a cracker, sniffs it cautiously, and takes a bite. "Mm," she says. "That's okay."

I smile, leaning an elbow on the back and my head on a hand.

She eats quietly for a while, looking out to sea, thinking, while I watch her taking small bites of the cracker and picking up crumbs from her lips. When she's done, she has a few sips of the Sprite, then finally looks back at me. "Thank you."

"You're welcome."

She turns a little to face me, curling up. She nibbles her bottom lip. "Henry, look. This is such a crazy situation. It's kind of you to say that you'd like to bring the baby up with me, but it's a huge ask of you. I don't expect you to jump straight in like that. If you want to date for a while, get to know one another first, and make sure we're, you know, suitable, I'll understand."

"Well, I've known you for six years, so I've been in love with you for about… ah… two thousand, one hundred and ninety days. I think that's enough to get to know someone, don't you?"

She gives me a wry look. "You know what I mean."

I give a patient sigh. "Juliette, I've worked beside you for years. I've seen you happy, sad, tired, irritable, lonely, unhappy, every emotion I can think of. I know that your favorite foods are peanut butter and sushi and curry as long as it's not too spicy, and your favorite chocolate bar is a Twix. That you love champagne and hate Tequila. I know that you love netball and you became a physio because you broke your ankle when you were fourteen, which put paid to your plans to play it professionally."

I reach out and take her hand in mine. "I know you get grumpy when you haven't had enough sleep, and that you're at your most passionate when you're talking about making children better. You're sweet and fiery and determined and a little bit outspoken, and I love that. I think I know eighty-five percent of you, and I desperately want to get to know the other fifteen."

"That's wonderful," she says, "but what if that turns out to be the fifteen percent you don't like about me? Wouldn't you rather live apart for a while until you're sure?"

"It'd be pretty odd for two married people to live apart."

Her jaw drops, and she gives a short laugh. "Henry!"

"Look. I told you at Damon's wedding that I'm going to marry you, and I haven't changed my mind. It's going to happen—it's just a matter of when. I'd do it tomorrow. I'm sure of what I want. I've been sure for years. But if you want to wait, I understand. If you want to live apart for a while, I understand. I won't like it, though, and I'm going to ask you to move in with me every day."

Her lips curve up. Then her smile fades again, and she looks away. "I just feel so bad putting all this on you so early in the relationship. Normally people have months or years getting to know one another, having lots of sex, and being free before they settle down and have kids. I mean, I'd hope there'd still be sex, but I have no idea whether it's safe when pregnant, and obviously there's the birth, and I don't know—"

I pick up my phone and hold up a hand. "Just a sec."

"—whether... oh..." She stops and frowns.

I type something in. Read a bit. Then I say, "All right, so I Googled whether it's okay to have sex during pregnancy. It says the baby is protected by the amniotic fluid and the strong muscles of the uterus, and that sexual activity won't affect the baby as long as you don't have complications." I put the phone down. "So that's one problem solved."

That makes her laugh. "Hurrah for Google."

I reach out and tuck a strand of her hair behind her ear. "So neither of us knows anything about pregnancy... So what? It'll be fun to read about it. We'll research together. Find out how big the fetus is week by week. We'll read about morning sickness and shop for maternity clothes and cots and breast pads and fuck knows whatever else you and the baby need. Aroha will help, and I'm sure Saxon's Catie would love to talk about her experiences. You have people around you, Juliette, you don't have to do this alone."

She swallows hard. "There's one more thing... Cam."

"Yeah, I know."

"I don't know what he's going to be like. If he goes to Australia, he might actually want nothing to do with the baby. But I have a feeling he's going to go the other way and make it really difficult for us."

"It wouldn't surprise me. Look, he's the baby's father, so he has every right to be involved. I don't have to like the man to accept that. He can be involved with the baby as much as you want him to be. We're grown ups, so we'll sort something out—visitation rights, involving him in decisions, that kind of thing. Equally, if he's a pain in the arse, we'll sort it. We'll get a lawyer if we have to. It'll be about what's best for the baby."

I give her a firm look. "But where you're concerned, he has no rights at all. Zero, you hear me? If he comes within three feet of you without prior arrangement, I want to know about it. You're mine now. And the sooner he realizes that, the better."

SERENITY WOODS

Chapter Twenty-Nine

Juliette

My lips curve up at his possessive tone. He's doing his absolute best to be calm and understanding, bless him, but I can see that deep down he's furious over what happened with Cam today.

"I knew it would annoy you when he called me his girl," I tease.

"Annoy is too mild a word."

"Infuriate?"

"That's more like it."

I giggle, and his lips curve up.

A seagull flies low in front of the deck, drawing my gaze away, out to sea. It's such a beautiful day. This house is absolutely stunning. I can't believe that Henry is asking me to share it with him. I know his privacy and his peace are important to him. Does he understand how me being here, especially once the baby arrives, is going to tear that peace apart? I suppose he does. He's an intelligent guy. But I do worry that he hasn't thought it through.

It's been such a strange morning. I've fantasized about this moment, leaving Cam and telling Henry I want to be with him, and in my mind we went straight to bed and made mad passionate love for days. I hadn't anticipated this quiet, thoughtful discussion. But I'm glad of it. I needed it, even though I didn't realize it, and I'm so thankful he's taking it slow.

I look back at him. "There is one thing I want to talk about."

"Okay."

"I'm only seven weeks pregnant. First, miscarriage is very common, so we have to be aware of that."

"Yeah. Hopefully you'll be fine."

"But… I want to say… it's not too late."

"For…"

"To terminate it."

We study each other quietly. I don't know what his views on abortion are. I just feel that it's something we should talk about.

His expression has gone carefully blank. "Gaby told Tyson that you'd thought about it."

"If I keep the baby, Cam's always going to be around, and part of me wishes that wasn't the case. Terminating would be one way to cut myself off from him completely. We would never have to deal with him again."

He looks away. He's so handsome. His hair is still wet from his shower. He's missed one small speck of blood that's still on his temple. I want to reach up and wipe it away, but I hold back. He hasn't touched me yet, apart from tucking my hair behind my ear. He hasn't kissed me. I long for him to take me in his arms, but I understand that we need to settle everything first.

He's still silent. Eventually I say, "What are you thinking?"

His gaze comes back to mine. "That it's your decision, not mine."

"Henry... come on. I know you better than that. Don't give me the pro-choice argument. I want to know what you think."

Still, he hesitates, and it's only then that I remember what's been happening with his nephew. "Oh, what happened with Rangi?" I ask.

He exhales with a deep sigh. "His girlfriend had the abortion. On Saturday evening, he took an overdose."

I gasp. "Oh no!"

"He's okay," he adds hastily. "They took him to hospital, but he's back home now."

"Oh, you should have told me." But of course I'd turned off my phone, so even if he wanted to, he wouldn't have been able to call me.

"I was on my way back from Sydney," he reminds me. "I didn't get in until one a.m. I saw that Rangi had called around eleven but I was too tired to call him. It was only the next morning that Philip rang to tell me."

"How was he?"

"Philip said Rangi wouldn't stop crying or come out of his room, and he asked me to come over and talk to him."

My eyebrows rise—I know Henry doesn't get on with his brother, and it must have taken a lot for Philip to call him.

"I'm going to send Rangi to Greenfield," he says. "I'm hoping it'll turn things around for him. He'll either forget about Ellie, or he'll have the opportunity to qualify in a trade or something and find himself a job, and then he'll be able to prove he's a better prospect for a boyfriend to her parents."

"And Philip agreed?"

"Yeah, so it shows how desperate he is. I'm glad he's letting me help."

I nod. "That's good. And was Rangi pleased?"

"Yeah, I think so. He was just so sad about the baby. I felt bad about it."

"Because you weren't there to take the call?"

"Yeah. And because when he told me Ellie was pregnant, I said he had to keep his opinions to himself." He picks at a piece of fluff on his track pants. "Maybe if Rangi had told her parents that he wanted the baby, they'd have let him stay with Ellie and bring the baby up together. They probably wouldn't, but I took that option away from him."

"You didn't, Henry. Society did. It's tough for guys to just sit back and do nothing."

"I know it was the right thing to do. But I feel bad, that's all."

I catch his eye. "That's why I want you to be honest with me. I want to know what you really think about me having this baby. I'm not saying the decision is up to you. But I do want to know."

He drops his gaze to my tummy for a long moment. I can see him fighting with himself, debating whether to do as I ask, or keep his opinions to himself. He said that Shaz accused him of not being open with her. I'm sure that's going to affect his decision.

Sure enough, he looks back at me and says, "I want to be with you. But… I don't want you to terminate it for me."

I inhale, then let out a long, relieved breath as I smile. "All right."

His eyebrows rise. "You're okay with me saying that?"

"Yes. I wondered whether you were secretly hoping I'd get rid of it so we could start afresh, that's all. I'm glad that's not the case."

"We're two healthy adults, with no real problems and plenty of money. And I can't have kids, so I need to accept that another man will be the father of your child." He huffs a breath. "And although it pains me to admit it, Cam's not a bad guy. He's honest and hardworking. Decent enough. He won't be a bad father."

I'm not so sure, but I don't want to spoil the moment. I'm just so relieved he wants me to keep it.

I look into his eyes, which are filled with love and affection. Then I drop my gaze to his mouth. "Are you going to kiss me?" I whisper.

His lips curve up. "I thought you'd never ask." He slides his arm down around me and pulls me close.

"You were waiting for me to ask? You have grown."

He chuckles. "I didn't want to rush you."

I lift a hand to his face. He shaved this morning, and his jaw is smooth. "I've been starved of physical affection. I want you to kiss me and hold me and touch me and make love to me as much as you possibly can."

His eyes light up. "Yes, ma'am," he says. And then he crushes his lips to mine.

Mmm... at last... I lift an arm around his neck and slide my hand into his short hair as he presses kisses across my lips. My fingers slip through the wet strands, then move down to touch the warm skin on the back of his neck. He's so strong; everything about him is big and solid. He feels like my rock, a man I can anchor to when the world wants to sweep me away.

He slides his other arm beneath my knees, and before I can say anything he lifts me up onto his lap, then lies back on the cushions so I'm half lying on him. His body is taut and muscular, his arms like steel bars around me. He tugs at my bun, and so I push myself up, take out the pins, then let the locks unravel. He takes them in his fingers and unfurls them, smiling as they fall to my waist like brown ribbons.

"So soft," he murmurs, tangling his fingers in them.

Then he slips a hand to the back of my head and brings me down for another kiss, brooking no refusal.

I don't want to stop him, though. I don't ever want to stop him kissing me. His kisses are addictive, and they're like chili or a spicy curry, almost too hot to bear, searing into me, heating my blood as it speeds around my body.

He kisses me for ages, his tongue teasing mine, his teeth nipping my lips, and then he progresses to my jaw, my ears, my neck, my throat, as if he wants to reclaim every inch of my skin.

I give a long, heartfelt sigh, and he moves back then to look at me. "All right, baby?" he asks. "You feel okay?"

I nod. "I'm happy," I whisper back. "So, so happy."

He grins and, before I can catch my breath, sits up, bringing me with him. "I want you," he says firmly. "Right here."

I blink and look around. We're halfway up a cliff and miles from anywhere, but even so, I'm not used to having sex outdoors. "What if someone has a pair of binoculars?"

He barks a laugh. "Then I hope they enjoy the show." He takes my top by the hem and says, "Lift."

Obediently, I raise my arms, and he peels the top up my body, watching the way my hair goes with it then floats down as he drops the top onto the deck. Next, his eyes lighting up, he undoes my bra and peels the straps down my arms.

Bashfully, I let him take it off and toss that away, too. I never did anything like this with Cam. He wasn't a spur-of-the-moment kind of guy at the best of times, and certainly not in the latter part of our relationship.

But Henry is a whole new ball game, and I have a feeling I'm going to have to get used to some very different experiences.

He turns me and lowers me onto my back, then undoes my trousers and slides them down my legs.

"What about you?" I protest, flustered, as he slips his fingers into the elastic of my knickers and removes them as well.

"All in good time." He moves up over me and, a hand on either side of my waist, looks at me. Slowly, he slides his gaze down my body, drinking his fill.

I look up at the sky, trying not to squirm, and just enjoy being admired. I've longed for this all my life, and I can't believe I've finally got my wish. Is this really happening, or am I going to wake up at any moment?

He lowers on top of me then, and kisses me again. "*Taku kuru pounamu,*" he murmurs as he kisses down my neck. 'My precious one.' "*E te apa tārewa kei raro au i tō ātahu.*" I don't speak Māori quite as well as he does. I think it means something like 'enchanted one, I am under your spell.'

He kisses my breasts, then trails the tip of his tongue around each nipple before covering them with his mouth and gently sucking. I groan and arch my back, need already burning inside me, and he growls and does it harder, until I cry out, "Oh God!"

Heat flares between us, and he moves down between my legs and pushes them up before saying, "I want to taste you."

"Mmm…" I lift my arms above me onto the cushions, and close my eyes.

He nuzzles me down there and inhales, then licks me all the way up. "*Me te wai korari,*" he murmurs, 'as sweet as honey.' "Ahhh…" He circles the tip of his tongue around my clit and begins to tease it with slow licks and quick flicks.

I bathe in the warm sunshine, feeling like a part of summer, ascending into the sky with the seagulls and the clouds as he arouses me. He strokes the outside of my thigh with a hand while he teases my entrance with the fingers of the other, and he's so gentle, it brings tears to my eyes.

Unsurprisingly, it doesn't take long before I feel the approach of an orgasm. "I'm going to come," I whisper, just in case he wants to stop and slide inside me. But he doesn't; he murmurs his approval, then sucks my clit carefully, and I relax into my climax and clench around his fingers, feeling pleasure flow over me, sweet and warm as the summer breeze.

When the pulses stop, he lifts up, tears off his tee, and rids himself of his track pants and boxers. Then he stretches out beside me on the daybed and pulls me into his arms.

"You want me to wear a condom?" he asks.

I shake my head. "I got tested after Cam… you know."

"And I had to be tested at the clinic."

"And there's no worry about getting me pregnant." My lips twist.

He tightens his arms around me so our bodies are flush from chest to thigh. I thought he would be inside me immediately, but he takes his time to arouse me again, skating his fingers over my skin while he kisses me. It's heavenly, lying there in the shade of the daybed while the summer breeze brushes over us, just taking our time. And there's no rush. No reason to feel guilty. I'm not cheating. I'm with the man I love. He wants to marry me. There's nothing wrong with what we're doing. The realization hits me, and it's only then I understand how the weight of guilt and regret has been weighing me down up until now. I'd thought my time with him was wonderful, but this is so, so much better. Finally I understand the power and the beauty of freedom, and everything it entails.

When I'm sighing again, my body feeling as if it's humming with pleasure, he finally lifts my leg over his hips, positions the tip of his erection at my entrance, and slowly slides inside me. He takes his time, easing in gently, then withdrawing, until he's coated in my moisture, and I'm relaxed enough to allow him to slide all the way in.

Mmm… I tip back my head, feeling full and stretched, and give a long, satisfied moan of contentment.

"*Ko Hine-tītama koe matawai ana te whatu i te tirohanga*," he murmurs, kissing me in between the words. Something about being like Hine-tītama, the dawn maid, and a vision that makes his eyes glisten.

Oh this man... I kiss him, delving my tongue into his mouth, enjoying his answering deep groan. I want to give him pleasure, to watch that fierce frown on his face, and to feel him come inside me. I begin to thrust my hips to match his, and our bodies move together in a slow, glorious dance, gradually speeding up as our desire grows.

Ahhh... I want to do this every day for the rest of our lives. I've already wasted so much time. Sorrow mixes with the pleasure in a kind of painful bliss, and tears prick my eyes as he holds me so tightly, as if he wants us to become one person, so we'll never be apart.

"*E taku kōmata*," he says, which is the highest point of the sun, and I know he's saying I'm perfect, I'm everything he wants, and I watch as he can't hold back any longer and comes, his whole body stiffening as he twitches and spills inside me.

Even before he finishes, he rolls me onto my back and continues to thrust, grinding against me, and it takes less than a minute before I come too, shuddering and squeezing him so hard that he groans.

When we're sated, he withdraws and lowers down beside me, then gathers me up in his arms. We lie there together, legs tangled, skin glistening, and listen to the cries of the seagulls as our bodies slowly drift back down to earth.

*

We stay there for ages, letting the summer breeze cool our hot skin, talking and laughing, while he strokes my back and gives me occasional kisses. Eventually, though, he asks if I'm hungry, and when I tell him I could probably manage a snack, we dress and go into his kitchen.

We go through the cupboards and fridge, and I cut thick slices of homemade bread spread with butter and put it on a plate with cheddar cheese, pickled onions, and cold chicken while he makes us another cup of fruit tea, and we take it outside again, and curl back up on the daybed.

He puts some music on his phone, and we listen and talk while we eat. Henry asks what I want to do about our living arrangements, and we talk about options. I don't want to go back to the apartment I shared with Cam, even if he isn't there. I could go to a hotel temporarily. Then rent a place of my own.

But in the end, I think what's the point? I want to be with Henry, and he wants to be with me. I know myself well enough to understand there's a small percentage of fear hidden inside that desire, because I don't want to be alone, and he's an easy option. In the end, I tell him that's what's bothering me, and he just looks puzzled.

"I don't care," he says. "At root, we're just animals. You're pregnant, and it's natural to want a man to look after you and protect you. I don't find that an insult. It's a compliment, if anything, that you've chosen me."

That makes me laugh, because it's a very Henry answer. It's old-fashioned, and I'm sure it would make some women inhale with indignation. But I know him well enough to understand that he doesn't mean it like that. I've watched him talk to many women over the years, and he's never anything but respectful and kind. He believes in equality and that women can do and achieve anything that a man can. But at heart he's a caveman who wants to protect his woman. And why should I be indignant about that when it warms my heart so much?

"I love you," I tell him. "And if you definitely want me to, I'd be thrilled to come and live with you."

He's so speechless at that, it brings tears to my eyes again. It must be the baby hormones; I've never cried so much in my life. He holds me and lets me sniffle, then suggests we go back to my apartment and collect as many of my things as we can fit in his Range Rover.

"I might call Cam and suggest he goes out," I tell him.

"Not a bad idea."

I hesitate. "I'm worried he's going to be nasty."

He tips his head at me. "You want me to stay? You don't have to do this alone. We're a team now."

I nod, and so we sit together while I call, and I put it on speaker phone so Henry can hear what Cam says.

The conversation is brief. "It's me," I say when Cam answers. "You're on speaker phone, and Henry's with me."

"What do you want?" he says gruffly.

"I wanted to let you know that I'm moving in with Henry. And I want to come back to the apartment and pick up some things." I wait, heart racing.

Cam's silent for a moment. Then he says, "Whatever."

"Are you at the apartment?"

"No, I'm at Mum and Dad's. We've had to call the doctor out. She freaked when I told her we'd broken up. She's had a complete meltdown."

I press my fingers to my lips, hating the thought of Kathy being upset. But it's not my responsibility now. Henry strokes my back, and that gives me the courage to go on.

"Okay. I'll pick up what I can," I whisper. "Then later we'll have to talk about you taking over the rent."

"Fine." He speaks curtly, maybe upset that I didn't say I'd come over and help.

"Bye." I end the call, shaking like a leaf, but relieved it's done.

Henry pulls me back into his arms. "It's all right, sweetheart. Well done."

I bury my face in his shoulder. "Why's it so hard? I just want him out of my life."

"I know. But we can take something positive from that call."

I move back a little, trying not to cry. "What?"

"He told his parents that you've broken up." Henry lifts my chin and looks into my eyes. "He's accepted it's over. That's a big step for him."

Tears tip over my lashes. "I want to be happy," I say, sniffling, "I don't want the shadow of my past hanging over me."

"I know. But it's a fresh wound at the moment, that's all. It'll heal. *He rā ki tua.*" It means better times are coming.

I let him hug me, trying to believe him. Cam is my past. Henry and the baby are my future. He's right; I just have to be patient, and let time heal me.

Chapter Thirty

Juliette

Our first week together isn't quite the blissfully happy time I'd hoped for.

I wish I could say that the two of us sailed off into the sunset with no other problems. But I swing between ecstasy and... well, not despair, but some kind of misery that takes the shine off my happiness with Henry. It makes me angry and resentful, but Henry remains calm and cheerful, insisting it's not a problem. He has me, he says, and that's all that matters. Everything else we can deal with.

I'm not so sure. I don't know whether it's the new baby hormones raging through my system, or my incredibly strong sense of duty that I'm starting to hate, but I feel wracked with guilt, and I'm conscious it's like acid, eating away into my new life.

The source of my heartache is, of course, my ex. Because that's what Cam is now, despite his unwillingness to accept the title. He said that he told his parents we'd broken up, but he seems to think it's a temporary state of affairs. He calls me every day and texts me frequently, telling me how Alan and his wife are struggling, how his mother is descending into the deepest depression he's seen, how his father is on the verge of walking out, and how he himself misses me. I tell him he doesn't love me, and he only wants me because I'd sort out a lot of his problems for him, but he insists that isn't the case, even though his behavior isn't loving by any means.

Henry is surprisingly patient with him. "He had you and he lost you," he tells me. "Of course the guy's unhappy." Worried that he's thinks Cam's going to influence me, I always put him on speaker and stay in the room so Henry can listen to the conversation, but he remains quiet and lets me deal with Cam as best as I can.

Things come to a head when, on Thursday evening, Cam calls me while we're having dinner.

After a stressful week, I don't want to talk to him. Henry surveys me, though, and to my surprise he says, "Go on, talk to him."

I answer it and put it on speaker. Cam starts speaking immediately, hysterical and upset as he tells me that Kathy is out of control, that his father has walked out, that he doesn't know what to do, and that I have to help. I start crying, and for the first time, Henry intervenes.

He picks up the phone, takes it off speaker, puts it to his ear, and walks out of the living room and onto the deck.

"Cam," he says, "you've got to stop. She's pregnant and you're upsetting her, and I won't have it."

I press my fingers to my lips. I suppose I should be insulted that he's taken it upon himself to sort my life out for me, but I'm not. I'm relieved and thankful. He's been so good to me this week. At work, he comes to see me during the day, delivering his usual treats, but also checking that I feel okay, and asking if there's anything he can do for me. He comes with me to see my parents, and he calls my dad 'sir', and tells him he's going to look after me, and I can see he's won my father over.

At home, he treats me the way he promised he would—like a queen. He fetches me cushions and drinks and snacks and anything else I want. He listens to me talk, holds me when I cry, and tells me not to worry when I apologize. And he makes love to me for hours, trying to prove with his body how much he loves me, as well as lavishing me with endearments in English and Māori.

I watch him on the phone to my ex, listening to him being firm but patient and kind, and I wipe my cheeks as the tears refuse to be held back. "I know," he says to Cam, "I understand why you're upset. Of course. She knows that. Yeah. No, that's not going to happen. Bro, listen to me. She's a lovely girl, and she'll help anyone in need, but I'm not going to let her do that. Yeah, yeah, I don't care, blame me all you like, she needs taking care of now, and I'm the one she's with, and you have to let her go."

He listens for a bit, and I think about the way Cam must be pleading with him, trying all the tricks he knew might work on me, using emotional blackmail to try to twist my feelings for him into making me help him. But they're not going to work with Henry.

"Cam," he says eventually, his voice turning harder, "I'm going to make things very clear for you. You and she are over, and I don't want you to call her again about anything to do with your family or your personal situation. If you need to talk to anyone, you can talk to me. You're the father of her child, and that gives you rights where the baby's concerned, but not with Juliette. Do you understand?"

He pauses, listening. He has one hand on his hip, and he's looking out over the ocean. He looks so big and strong, like a statue overlooking and guarding entry to the harbor. He's like Tangaroa, the

Māori *atua* or god of the ocean, the son of Ranginui and Papatūānuku, Sky and Earth, the magnificent painting of whom hangs in Kia Kaha. Tangaroa made laws to protect the ocean and all the sea creatures that lived within: *Tiaki mai i ahau, maku ano koe e tiaki.* If you look after me, then I will look after you. Just like Henry.

"How is she now?" he asks in a gentler voice, and I realize they're talking about Kathy. "Yeah, I understand. It's tough when someone you love is suffering like that. It's a lot on your shoulders, especially if your father's had enough. Look, I'm going to make a suggestion. I know a private treatment facility that deals with people who are suffering with problems like this. They provide home care and support for family members, and they also take people in for days or weeks to give their family a break. Will you let me call them and send someone around to you?"

He listens for a bit. I can imagine Cam stressing about paying for it. He's an accountant, so he's always earned relatively well, but the rent on our apartment is high and he knows he's going to have to take it over now I've left. Add to that the fact that he's left his job, and I know he's going to be anxious about paying for private treatment.

To my shock, Henry tells him, "Bro, I'm saying I'll pay for it." Cam obviously then asks him why he'd do that, as Henry answers, "Because I love Juliette, and she cares for Kathy, and I don't want her to worry. No, you don't have to pay me back. Cam—we're not enemies. We're going to have to learn to get on for the baby's sake, aren't we? I work in the health industry, trying to improve people's lives. It's what I do. I want to help."

He pauses again. Then he says, "Fair enough. If you'd rather, you can wait until tomorrow and sort something yourself through the public system, it's up to you." He glances over his shoulder, sees me watching, and winks at me. "Yeah," he says, looking back out to sea. "They'll come around and assess how she is. I can ask them to take her in for a few nights to sort out her meds and give you and your dad a break. Then you can come up with some kind of plan. Actually I know a good therapist who might be able to help. Yeah, she's an expert with depression, especially with women."

He chats away to Cam, reassuring him he'll take care of it. At the end of the call, he says, "Remember, call me, not Juliette, please. I'm going to tell her not to answer if you ring over the next few days. If you persist, I'll tell her to block you. She needs rest, so I'm going to take her away for the weekend. Yep, I'll call them now. Okay, bye."

He hangs up, but stays on the deck, and I watch him pull up a contact and call them. He asks to speak to a Dr. Crest, but says, "Hi Rob," when the guy answers, so he obviously knows him well. He explains the situation—that a friend's mother is unwell and needs assessment, and then asks if they have any space at the moment to take her in for a few days. "The guy's at his wits' end," he says, "and his father's walked out. The two of them need a break so they can decide what they're going to do. You can bill me for it all, whatever you end up doing for her, for the next few weeks, anyway. Yeah, yeah. He's my girlfriend's ex, and she's upset about it all, and I want to put her mind at ease. Thanks, Rob." He gives him Cam's number, then hangs up and comes back in.

"Hopefully that'll help," he says, sitting back at the dining table.

"I don't know what to say," I whisper. "You're such a good man."

"No I'm not. I couldn't give a fuck about him," he mumbles. "You're the only one I'm worried about."

But I know he's lying. He doesn't like hearing about other men suffering, or about someone else being in pain, physically or mentally.

"Life's hard enough," he says, picking up his fork. "Everyone needs a helping hand every now and again."

I get up and bend over him from behind, wrapping my arms around his neck. "I love you," I whisper.

He laughs, turns in his chair, and pulls me onto his lap. Then he kisses me, long and lingering, and for the first time, I really feel as if maybe I can begin to heal.

"So, we're going away?" I say when I eventually lift my head.

"Thought it might be fun," he replies. "We deserve a break. It's been a hellish few weeks."

I smile. "What did you have in mind?"

"Just a few nights away. I know you're feeling sick a lot of the time, so nothing stressful. I thought maybe we could fly to Wellington and call in and see Saxon and Catie—he said she's got some pregnancy books for us. Then afterward, we could hire a car and take a drive up the coast. I found a great place to stay online, a lighthouse miles from anywhere. There's a viewing room upstairs, and I thought we could sit there and watch the sun go down."

"It sounds amazing," I say, sniffing.

"I'll organize it, then." He kisses me. Then he strokes my cheek. "Everything's going to be okay, *taku aroha*. You'll see."

And for the first time, I think it actually might.

*

On Saturday morning, we take Kia Kaha's private plane, The Orion, to Wellington, hire ourselves a car, and then drive to Island Bay to see Saxon and Catie.

I know Saxon pretty well, as I've seen him many times since I first met Damon at university. I don't know Catie quite as well, but Damon told us about her story—that after her parents died, she was abused by her stepmother and stepsisters, and she came to Wellington virtually penniless, hoping to start a new life. She'd met Saxon back in Auckland, though, and fell pregnant after a one-night stand, only to discover he was the boss of the company she was temping for in Wellington.

Damon explained that when she first met Saxon she was completely clueless about pregnancy, so I'm somewhat surprised to discover that she has a huge pile of books for me.

"Saxon bought them for me," she explains when I go with her into what she calls her library in their house. It's a large room with two walls filled with books, and there's also an office desk on one side that's filled with papers, more books, and a laptop. "He knew a lot about fertility and conception," she continues, "but not so much about what happens during pregnancy, so we learned together."

I know that Saxon is a computer engineer who's been developing an IVF program using Artificial Intelligence to try to predict which embryos will lead to live births.

"I guess he knows a lot about the technical side," I say.

"Yeah, but not so much about the practical." She smiles as she stacks half a dozen books into a pile. "These are the best ones. Take whatever you want."

"Thank you." I glance at the papers and notes on the desk, which are covered with neat handwriting that's obviously computer code and diagrams. "I'm guessing this is Saxon's?"

"Actually, no. It's mine."

"Oh, of course, I forgot you were a computer programmer."

"Yeah, I'm taking a degree now. But in my spare time I've been working on a pregnancy app."

My eyebrows rise. "Oh, really?"

"Yeah. Saxon knows so much about conception and fertility, and he was happy to explain a lot of the terminology, and once I started reading about it, I found it fascinating. He's always trying to gather more information, and I had this idea of an app that pregnant women could use. They input things like the date of their last period and the length of their cycle, and it predicts when they're going to ovulate, which, along with monitoring basal body temperature, can help them when trying to get pregnant. And then it predicts the due date. The idea is that, if they agree, this data would be shared with Saxon's company to help him improve his work with IVF."

"That's amazing," I say, genuinely impressed. "How on earth do you get time to do all this with twins?!" Her twin boys, who are about ten months old, are currently in the living room, being entertained by Saxon and Henry.

"It's a struggle," she says, laughing. Then she says, a twinkle in her eye, "and it's not going to get any easier now I'm pregnant again."

"Oh!" I laugh too and we exchange a big hug. "I'm so pleased for you," I tell her. "How far along are you?"

"Actually only nine weeks. We haven't announced it yet, they tell you not to before you're three months, but I figured that we can compare notes and it'll make it more fun."

I get the feeling that's a polite way of her saying she wants to help, because I'm sure that Henry has told Saxon how I'm anxious because I know so little.

"That'll be great," I tell her, genuinely thrilled. "Have you had a scan yet? Is it twins again?"

"God, I hope not!" But she laughs. "No, you get your first scan between eleven and fourteen weeks."

"Oh. See, I didn't even know that!"

"Well, we're not born knowing. If you're anything like me, and you didn't know anybody who was pregnant, there's no need to read about it until it happens." She tips her head at me. "How far gone are you, exactly?"

"Exactly? Um… about eight weeks, I think, although I'm not a hundred percent sure."

She brightens. "Maybe we should try out the app on you!"

I smile. "Sure."

"All right." She pulls up a couple of chairs, and we take out our phones. "First of all, download the app," she says, and she shows me where to get it. I wait for it to download, then bring it up. There's a picture of a stork on the opening page, and it's all in bright colors.

"Okay." She opens the app on her phone. "We'll go through it together, and that way we can compare notes. So put in your name and age there, and your hometown. Click that button if you don't mind sharing your data with Kingpinz." That's Saxon's company. I click the button, then press Go.

"Right," she says. "The first thing is to select the first day of your last period. Do you know it?"

"Yes—I keep a note of my cycle on my phone."

"Excellent, that makes things much easier." She watches me input the fourth of December. "Okay, now press the green Go button." We watch a flying stork come up while the program runs through the calculations, and then the results pop up. It shows a calendar, the actual days of the month in blue, and then the days of my cycle in green.

"There you go," she says. "So your next period—highlighted in red—would have been due on December 31st. Which means you would have ovulated on day fourteen of your cycle—highlighted in yellow—which in this case was December 17th. The days before it are also highlighted because you can get pregnant up to five days before you ovulate, because sperm can live for five days inside you."

"Oh, I didn't realize that." I study the dates. "This isn't quite right—my period was due on the fourth of January."

"Oh shit." She laughs. "I forgot to ask how long your cycle is. The average is twenty-eight days, but of course every woman is different."

"Mine's long—usually thirty-two or even thirty-three days."

"Right, so go back, and in that box type thirty-two. Yep, and press Go again." We wait for the results and look at the new calendar. "Yeah, there you go," she says.

"It's changed the date of ovulation."

"Yes, because you ovulate fourteen days before your next period begins. So for you, the twenty-first of December. Which puts your fertile window from the sixteenth. Your due date is estimated as September the thirteenth because your cycle is a little longer than average. It'll be great to have a spring baby!"

I study the calendar. "Yeah." Then I frown. "It's not quite right, though."

"Oh?" She peers at the screen. "That's good in a way. I'm still trying to iron out any issues. So what's wrong?"

I tell her. She asks a few questions.

"Huh," she says. She chews her bottom lip and meets my eyes. "I think we need to speak to Saxon," she says softly.

Chapter Thirty-One

Henry

"So," Saxon says, "you're gonna be a dad! That's great news."

We're lying on the floor on each side of the twins, who are both on a mat, playing with the objects dangling from the arch he placed over them.

"Well, sort of," I say. I glance over my shoulder to make sure the girls are still in the library, then look back at him. "I wanted to talk to you about that, actually."

"Oh?"

"Yeah, about IVF. The chances of getting pregnant after the first cycle are around fifty percent, right?"

"Yeah, although we're working on improving the selection of embryos, so between you and me, I think we can get that figure up a little higher."

I nod, holding out a finger for the twin nearest to me. They both have Catie's red hair, and Saxon's mother's bright blue eyes. "Which one's this?" I ask as the baby grabs my finger.

"No idea," Saxon says, and I laugh. He grins. "It's Aidan. We try to dress him in something with blue in it, and Liam in red. But they also have different shaped birthmarks on the back of their necks."

"Thank God for that. I bet there are stories of where twins have been mixed up for years."

"Oh fuck yeah, we heard all kinds of horror stories while Catie was pregnant, so we were determined to find something to distinguish them when they were born." He helps Liam sit up, and the baby plays with the teething ring he's holding.

Then he looks at me. "Why did you ask about IVF? Are you thinking about doing it after this one's born?"

"Maybe. I'd like to be able to give her a baby. But I went through so much with Shaz. Trying to get pregnant is a horrific process when it doesn't work out."

"Yeah, I see a lot of couples who are close to throwing in the towel."

"Oh, of course, yeah, you must do."

"It'll be at least a year down the line, though," he says, "so maybe you'll feel differently by then."

"I hope so. I thought that—" I stop as the girls come back into the room and smile. "Hey you two. Find some good books?"

"Mm." Catie sits on the sofa, and Juliette perches next to her. They both look anxious.

I sit up. "Is everything all right?"

"Yeah," Catie says. "We've just been going through Juliette's dates." She looks at Saxon. "Can I go through them with you?"

He obviously picks up their tenseness and frowns. "Why, what's up?"

"Nothing bad… I just want to double check something. Can we sit up at the table?"

Leaving the twins to play with their toys, the four of us go up to the table. I sit next to Juliette and opposite Saxon, with Catie next to him. Juliette still won't look at me. My heart rate picks up. What's this about?

Catie is holding a printout, and she puts it on the table. "This is from the new pregnancy app I've been working on," she explains to me. She turns it to show me and Saxon. The page shows the calendar months of December and January, one above the other. The days of the month are in blue, and then there's a scattering of other highlighted days and numbers in different colors.

"Okay," Catie says, "so we start here. This is the first day of Juliette's last period." She taps the fourth of December, which has a big red number one next to it. Then she follows the days forward. "An average cycle is twenty-eight days," she says. "But Juliette's is thirty-two. This means her next period should have been due on the fourth of January. To work out when she ovulated, we count back fourteen days from that day." She counts back with her pen, and lands on day eighteen of the cycle, highlighted in yellow.

"And this is the fertile window," I say, gesturing at the five days before, all highlighted in yellow. "I know about this from when Shaz used to calculate ovulation."

Catie nods. "Because sperm can survive five days in the womb, right?"

"Yeah." I glance at her, then at Juliette, who's staring at the piece of paper. "So what's the problem?"

Catie taps the page. "The problem is… I'm sorry to mention it, Henry, but the last day that Juliette had sex with Cam was the tenth of December." She taps on the day. It's day seven of her cycle.

I look at Juliette. "Your birthday."

She nods. On the trivia night, she told me that was when they had last had sex, and they argued because he came inside her without a condom.

Catie's waiting for the penny to drop. She looks at me, then at Saxon. "She slept with Henry here," she says, and taps the twenty-first of December. Day eighteen of Juliette's cycle. The day she would have ovulated.

Saxon stares at the calendar, then leans back.

I frown at him. "I don't get it."

"The chance of getting pregnant if you have sex six or more days before you ovulate is virtually zero," he says softly.

I look at Juliette. "I didn't realize," she says. She looks bemused. "I assumed a woman ovulated fourteen days *after* her period, not fourteen days *before* her next one. I didn't know my longer cycle would screw up the dates."

I look back at Saxon. "So what's the problem?"

"They had sex three days before her fertile window started," he says.

"So?"

He just looks at me.

"Saxon," I say carefully, "I can't be the father. I'm infertile."

He tips his head to the side. "I don't like the word infertile. Men with low sperm counts can still father children. What was your sperm count?"

I stare at him. "Uh… fifteen million per milliliter, I think."

"Okay, twenty to forty million is average, so that's below, but not severe."

"No," I say, "I tried for two years to get pregnant with Shaz. It didn't happen, not even once."

He doesn't reply, but he continues to study me thoughtfully.

"Henry's right," Juliette says. "It's a lovely thought, but it can't be the case. We used a condom."

"Well, I know from personal experience that doesn't matter," Catie says sarcastically, and Saxon gives her an 'eek' look.

"Condoms are only eighty-seven percent effective," he says.

"Ah…" My brain feels as if it's working slower than usual. "We didn't use a condom."

Juliette stares at me. "Yes, we did. I remember."

"We did in the morning. But we didn't the first time, after the trivia quiz."

She stares at me.

"We got carried away," I say lamely.

Her jaw drops, and I can see her trying to think back. "But..." She trails off. "Oh..."

"But it doesn't matter," I say. For some reason I'm getting angry, and I stand up. "I'm not the father."

"All I can say is that it's very unlikely that Cam is the father if those dates are right," Saxon says.

"But not impossible."

He tips his head from side to side.

"Come on," I say, "we're told at school that you can get pregnant at any time of the month, even when a woman's on her period."

"That can happen if the girl has a very short cycle," Saxon says. "In that case, she would ovulate much earlier, so if she ovulated on day ten, and she had sex toward the end of her period, the sperm could survive long enough for her to conceive. But Juliette's cycle is longer than average, not shorter."

"Okay, but surely it makes more sense that her having unprotected sex with Cam on the tenth resulted in pregnancy than if she had sex with me, with my sperm count?"

"On the day she would have ovulated? You want my professional opinion?"

"No," I snap. "It doesn't make sense."

He holds up a hand and looks at Juliette. "I'm guessing you haven't had a paternity test done?"

She shakes her head. "I didn't think I needed one," she whispers.

"Okay. Well then, let's go and sort this out now." He gets to his feet.

"Wait," I say, "is it dangerous?"

"Nope. A blood test for Juliette. A cheek swab from you. And it can be done from the seventh week of pregnancy."

"How long does it take to get the results?" Juliette asks faintly.

"Usually a few weeks," he says, "but luckily you know someone in the business." He smiles. "I'll pull some strings, and we should hear today."

I look at Juliette, whose eyes have lit up. "Don't get your hopes up," I say sharply. "It's not going to turn out to be mine."

Her smile fades a little, and she nods. Saxon looks at us, but doesn't say anything. "Come on," he says, "I'll drive us to the hospital."

Catie gives Juliette a hug, then stays behind with the boys, and Saxon drives us there. Sure enough, he takes us straight through to have her blood sample taken, and the nurse also takes a cheek swab from me. He gets on the phone to the lab and talks to someone there and tells us we should hear in a few hours.

"Let's go home," he says. "Jack will call me when he gets the results. I'll make us some lunch."

On the way back, Saxon chats to Juliette about pregnancy stuff, but I look out of the window, not speaking. I feel stiff with resentment, angry that he's dangling the idea of this like a carrot under Juliette's nose. She's going to be gutted when she finds out I was right, and somehow the baby is still Cam's. I can't have gone through two years of trying with Shaz—who had her fertility checked, and she was fine—only to knock Juliette up literally the first time I slept with her. I'm not that lucky. I got the girl, and that was my luck used up for the next twenty years.

When we get back to Island Bay, Saxon talks to Catie in a low voice, presumably telling her what's going on, and she gives us a bright smile and says we'll have some lunch, then go for a walk. Saxon cooks us all a steak sandwich, which we eat sitting out on the deck, and then afterward she piles the boys into a dual stroller, and we walk slowly along the beach, looking out at Taputeranga Island in the distance, surrounded by choppy blue waves.

Juliette holds my hand, and when Saxon and Catie draw ahead a little, she murmurs, "Are you okay?"

I nod stiffly. "I just don't want to see you disappointed, that's all."

"I know," she says. "We've got nothing to lose, right? We both know it's likely to be Cam's. At least this way we can put our minds at rest."

I nod, then put my arm around her and pull her toward me. "It was supposed to be a relaxing weekend," I tell her, kissing her temple. "I didn't want you stressed out."

"I'm okay, honey, really. I'm not getting my hopes up."

But they're just words, and she wouldn't be human if she didn't harbor a small amount of hope.

I do my best to fight it, though. I'm not going to give myself a second of hope that the baby could be mine. Even one second will mean feeling devastated when I find out it's not, because I'd like so much for it to be the case.

It's not, it's not, it's not, I tell myself like a mantra, all the way along the beach, and then all the way back. It's not, it's not, it's not…

We've just settled down with a cup of tea in the living room when Saxon's phone finally rings.

We all exchange a glance, and then he gets up and answers the phone as walks over to the window. "Hello?" he says. He listens for a bit. His back is to us, so I can't see his face. "Yeah," he says. "Right. Yep. Okay, thanks, see you Monday." He hangs up. He waits a few seconds, then he turns to face us.

His expression is sad. "That was Jack," he says softly. "Look, I have to point out that there is a very, very slim, 0.01 chance that it might be wrong…"

"Saxon," I say gently, "it's okay. I knew what the result was going to be."

"…but there's a 99.99 percent probability that you're the father." His eyes gleam. Then he gives me a mischievous smile.

"Saxon," Catie scolds, and he grins.

Silence falls. I stare at him. Then I look at Catie. She gives me a happy smile.

Finally, I look at Juliette. She stares back at me, her eyes filling with tears.

I get to my feet. "No," I say. "Nope. No. You've got it wrong."

Saxon shakes his head. "It's right, man. You're going to be a daddy."

"No." Anger sweeps over me, hot and fierce. How dare he give me hope like this! "I tried for two years, and it never happened, not once!"

He shrugs. "I guess you were waiting for Juliette."

"Don't fucking make fun of me."

Juliette stands and reaches out for my arm, but I rip it away from her.

"I'm not," Saxon says, unperturbed. "I was serious. There's more to conception than science, Henry. That's definitely something I've learned from all this time working on IVF. I've seen couples who've given up get pregnant a month or two later. It happens more than you'd think. Stress is a huge factor in fertility. You weren't trying to conceive with Juliette. You've loved her for a long time. And when you slept together, subconsciously you knew you were with the woman you've always wanted. And it just happened."

I'm trembling now. "That's all just New Age bullshit, and I don't appreciate being patronized."

He walks toward me and fixes me with a firm glare. "And I'd appreciate it if you didn't talk to me as if I'm the fucking post boy. I happen to be a fertility expert. You're not." He claps me on the shoulder. "Come and have a whisky. You look like you need it."

But I can't stay there and look at him and Catie and Juliette all smiling as if this is some kind of miracle, as if Jack whatever-his-name-is isn't going to call in five minutes and say he looked at the wrong results, or that he got his test tubes mixed up.

I turn and walk through the sliding doors, then stride away, across the road and down toward the beach. It's not mine, I tell myself fiercely, my eyes burning. The tiny embryo growing inside her, the baby, it's not mine. It's not, it's not, it's not…

I stop on the edge of the sand. I can't breathe. My eyes have blurred. Ah jeez… I sit down heavily and put my face in my hands.

It's not mine… it can't be…

I sob, years and years of pain and heartache finally pouring out of me. All those months of disappointment, of feeling like a failure, of feeling less than a man.

You're going to be a daddy… Ahhh… it can't be true…

Behind me, I feel a hand on my shoulder, and then Juliette falls to her knees behind me and loops her arms around my neck.

"*E ipo*," she says, which means 'darling,' "*ngakau reka*," 'sweetheart,' "it's okay."

"I'm sorry," I say while I bawl my eyes out. "I'm sorry."

"It's all right." She kisses my neck and hugs me tightly. "It's a huge shock."

"It's not that I don't want it…"

"I know!"

"I just can't believe it."

"I know, me either. When Catie first pointed it out, I was adamant she was wrong. I didn't want to hope. But it's nearly a hundred percent accurate." She moves to my side, pulls my hands away from my face, then holds my chin to force me to look at her. "We're having a baby," she says, smiling, as she looks into my eyes.

I continue to cry, unable to hold back the tears.

She moves to sit on my lap and puts her arms around me. "Hey, come on, why are you so upset?"

I brush my hand over my face. "I was thinking about Shaz."

"Ahhh…"

"I was unfair to her."

"Why, sweetheart?"

"Because I lied to her. I said I didn't have feelings for you, but I did. Right from the start."

She rests her head against mine.

"Do you think Saxon was right?" I ask. "That there's more to it than science? I wonder if a part of me didn't want children with Shaz, and so my body refused to comply. I let her down, because it wasn't her fault, and forced her to endure all those months of unhappiness when she discovered it hadn't worked."

"Aw, Henry. Come on, you didn't do it on purpose."

"No, but I think maybe I did it subconsciously."

"Love, I think you have great discipline, but I don't think even you could convince your own sperm not to swim upstream."

That makes me laugh, and she grins.

"It's really true?" I ask.

"It seems so! We made a baby. Oh my God, I don't believe it." She kisses my cheeks, brushing away the tears. "You clever, clever man."

I give a short laugh and wipe my face. "I worked really hard at it."

She giggles and throws her arms around me, and we have a big hug.

"You know what this means," she whispers. "I can say goodbye to Cam properly."

I bury my face in her neck, thinking of her ex, and feeling some pity for him. "Do you think he'll be upset?"

"Honestly? Maybe a little. And maybe not. I think he'll probably feel relieved once the shock wears off. It would have meant a whole lot of hassle for him and not much fun. He needs to meet someone else more suitable for him. He understands his issues more now, and he can look for a partner who'll be able to help him."

She moves back and kisses me. "And we can start together properly. With our baby."

The warm summer breeze whips at our hair and blows sand across us, but we don't care. I kiss her, and then we just hold each other, letting the realization sink in that, corny as it is, this is the first day of the rest of our lives.

*

When we get back to Saxon and Catie's house, Saxon says, "I think you should stay the night and we should get drunk," and I laugh and agree. So he pours us both a big whisky, and while the girls sip their lemonade and talk about babies, the two of us discuss being a dad, and our hopes and dreams for fatherhood.

Juliette and I sleep in their spare room, and then next morning we say goodbye with big hugs and promises to see more of them, and head up the coast to the lighthouse where we've booked to stay that night.

Later that day finds us sitting together on the sofa in the viewing room, watching the setting sun flood the sky and the ocean with blues and purples and oranges.

I'd already talked to the baby in Juliette's tummy before we found out it was mine. I'd been determined to love it and treat it as my own. But knowing it's mine makes it extra special.

I sit in the corner of the sofa, and she sits with her back to me, and I rest my hands on her belly as I kiss her.

"I can't wait until you have a bump," I murmur.

"And stretch marks," she says. "Yeah, terrific."

"I'll kiss every one."

She rolls her eyes. "You're full of shit."

"I mean it!" I brush up to her breasts. "And I look forward to seeing what happens to these, too."

"Yeah, Catie gave me a few warnings about that." She laughs.

I chuckle and kiss her cheek. "I'm glad we've got them to call on."

"Yeah, me too. For the first time, I don't feel scared about it. I mean, I know you would have been supportive and everything, even if it wasn't yours, but I did feel kind of alone. Now, I don't. I feel as if we're in it together."

"Definitely." I slide a hand beneath her chin and lift it so I can kiss her lips. "*Ka nui taku aroha ki a koe.*"

"I love you too." And she kisses me back, while the sun bathes us both in its caramel-colored light.

Epilogue

September 12th

Henry

"It won't be long now," Alex says.

I'm lying on a row of chairs in the hospital waiting room, looking up at the ceiling as I talk to him on my phone. It's just gone eleven p.m., and I've been up since three a.m., which is when Juliette's contractions started, so I'm pretty exhausted.

"The midwife says it might still be a few hours," I point out.

"Eh," he says, "I have a feeling it's going to happen this side of midnight. It wants to be born on my birthday."

I chuckle, glad I gave him his present of a framed photo of him and his family yesterday. "Maybe."

"I'm guessing you're tired," he says.

"I'm considering taping my eyelids to my forehead to keep them open."

"Couldn't you get a few hours' kip now?"

"I'll sleep when she does," I tell him.

"You old softie."

"Yeah, I know." I sigh. "Anyway, you said on your text you wanted to talk to me about something?"

"It could have waited, bro."

"Yeah, but Juliette sent me out while the midwife does an internal, so I'm at a loose end. What's going on?"

He hesitates. Then he says, "Oh, I guess I might as well tell you now. Missie's pregnant."

My eyebrows lift in surprise, and my lips curve up in a big smile. "Alex! That's wonderful news." He and Missie had a double marriage with me and Juliette back in April. It was a lot of fun, and the girls have grown to be good friends and are a great support for one another.

"Thanks, yeah, we're pretty stoked."

"How far along is she?"

"Only three months. I've been itching to tell the world, but she made me wait."

I grin. "Luckily I didn't have that problem." Because we were so thrilled that I ended up being the father of Juliette's baby, we blurted it out to everyone as soon we got back from Wellington. "How's Finn taking it?"

"Ah, he's a good lad, he's thrilled."

I'm not surprised—Finn idolizes Alex and calls him Dad.

"Mr. West?"

I sit up as someone says my name and see the midwife standing in the doorway. She smiles. "Juliette's ready to push now. Baby's coming soon!"

"Thank you, I'll be right there." I get to my feet. "I've got to go," I tell Alex, "she's ready to push."

"Good luck," he says, "let us know as soon as it's over!"

"Will do. Thanks." I end the call and jog down the corridor.

The rest of the hospital is relatively quiet, the main lights all dimmed as it's so late, but when I go into the delivery room, I find it bright and bustling. Two midwives are moving around, bringing over trolleys full of alarming instruments, while another nurse brings Juliette a cup of ice chips and makes her comfortable.

"Hey, babe," I say to my wife as I walk over to her. "How's it going?"

"I feel like I'm sitting on its head," she says. "I think it wants to come out now." She smiles, but her eyes hold a glint of fear, and her forehead glistens with sweat. "I'm not sure I can do this." She trembles, reaching out for my hand.

"She's in transition," Pam, one of the midwives, says, "it's normal to feel overwhelmed at this point." She gives Juliette a reassuring smile. "Deep breaths, love. You're doing great."

I grip Juliette's hand and sit on the stool by her side. "I'm not going anywhere," I tell her firmly. "We'll do this together, okay?"

She nods and swallows hard, then winces as another contraction starts.

The next half an hour is the most difficult of my life. I told her we'll do it together, but of course that's ridiculous, because I'm completely useless and have no way of helping her through it. I wish with all my being I could take her pain onto myself, but I can't, and even if I could, I doubt I could bear it the way she does. She breathes through her contractions, even though they're powerful enough to make her groan, and she even gives me brief, reassuring smiles in between them, which makes me want to cry. Once again, I'm impotent, unable to do anything other than kiss her fingers and repeatedly tell her she's so strong, so incredibly amazing, and I love her more than anything in the world.

And then the midwife says she can see the top of the baby's head, and I move to watch my baby being born, which is the most magnificent, messy, miraculous thing I've ever seen. Through all the blood and pain, a tiny person emerges from Juliette, and tears pour down my face as the midwife gathers the baby up and gives it a quick check. Its wail cuts through the air, and she picks it up and places it straight onto Juliette's tummy.

Juliette's eyes fill with tears. "It's a boy," she squeaks.

I stare at the baby boy, unable to speak, completely overwhelmed, as Pam dries him, then wraps him and Juliette in warm blankets.

"You have a son, Henry," the midwife says with a smile.

I blink at her. I have a son?

I watch Juliette examine his fingers and toes, then check out his face, his button nose and screwed-up eyes. He squirms in her arms, and that shocks me—for some reason I'd pictured the baby like a doll, and it's a surprise to watch him moving, breathing, and crying. He's a real, live person, with his whole life stretching out in front of him. Completely innocent and free of sin, full of hope and potential.

"Let's latch him on," Pam says, and she helps Juliette to put him to the breast, where he immediately starts sucking. "That'll help deliver the placenta," Pam explains.

I wipe my face and bend over Juliette to kiss her. "You were absolutely amazing," I tell her. "I can't believe you did it. I wish I could have helped you."

"You did," Pam reassures me. "You encouraged her and comforted her. That means a lot, doesn't it?"

Juliette nods. "I couldn't have done it without you."

I know that's not true, but it's nice to be told, anyway.

I look at my phone—it's two minutes to twelve. Alex was right! The baby was born on his birthday. I send him a quick text to tell him, smiling as I type the words for the first time: *It's a boy!*

After a while, Pam cuts the cord, then picks the baby up and leaves Juliette in the hands of the other midwife to deliver the placenta. I follow Pam over to the table where she weighs the baby—a healthy seven pounds two ounces—announces his Apgar score is nine, carries out a few checks, gives him a Vitamin K injection, puts a hospital band around his ankle, and cleans him up a little.

Then she wraps him in another blanket and smiles at me. "Ready to hold your son?"

I nod wordlessly, and she hands him to me, showing me how to hold him and support his head. "There you go," she says. "I can see he's going to be a Daddy's boy." She grins and begins to tidy up the table.

I glance over at Juliette. She's sitting up in bed, and the nurse is bringing her a cup of tea and a biscuit. She looks tired but oh, so happy, and she gives me a big smile as I walk over to her.

"I've got a boy," I say, and she laughs.

"Have you decided on a name?" the nurse asks, drawing a blanket over Juliette to keep her warm.

I look at Juliette, who nods. "Nikau," she says. Although the last two vowels are supposed to be pronounced separately as 'ah' and 'oo', most people run them together, so it sounds like nik-oh.

"That's a gorgeous name," the nurse says, and she comes up to stroke my son's head. "Hello, little Nikau!" She smiles and leaves us to help tidy up.

Juliette sinks back into the pillow and yawns. "Wow, I can't believe it's all over."

"You are the most amazing woman who ever lived," I tell her, and she laughs. I look down at the baby boy in my arms. "My boy," I whisper.

"He's all yours," she says. "For better or for worse." She yawns again.

Nikau opens his eyes and looks up at me, and I have to catch my breath. They're the same color as mine—a bright blue—and he seems to stare right into my soul.

"He's beautiful," I say, my voice little more than a squeak. "Thank you so much." I bend over and kiss her, then turn the baby and put him into her arms.

"He looks like you," she whispers before kissing his forehead.

I stroke his cheek. "My life's been a struggle at times, especially when I was young. But hopefully his won't be."

"It won't," she assures me. "He'll be surrounded by people who support him, and we'll do our best to give him all the love, care, and opportunities in the world so he can grow up big and strong and happy. And so he can be a good man. Just like his father."

I swallow hard. It's the nicest thing she could ever have said to me.

She looks up at me. "I love you."

"I love you, too." And I kiss my wife, then my baby boy, feeling happier than any man has the right to be.

SERENITY WOODS

Newsletter

If you'd like to be informed when my next book is available, you can sign up for my mailing list on my website, http://www.serenitywoodsromance.com

About the Author

USA Today bestselling author Serenity Woods writes sexy contemporary romances, most of which are set in the sub-tropical Northland of New Zealand, where she lives with her wonderful husband.

Website: http://www.serenitywoodsromance.com
Facebook: http://www.facebook.com/serenitywoodsromance